Blood Vengeance

Douglas Jackson is the author of twenty historical novels and mystery thrillers, including the critically acclaimed nine-book Hero of Rome series. He was born in Jedburgh in the Scottish Borders and now lives in Stirling. Originally a journalist by profession he rose to become Assistant Editor of the *Scotsman* before leaving to be a full-time writer in 2009.

Also by Douglas Jackson

The Warsaw Quartet

Blood Roses
Blood Sacrifice
Blood Vengeance

DOUGLAS JACKSON
Blood Vengeance

CANELO

DK | Penguin
Random
House

First published in the United Kingdom in 2025 by

Canelo, an imprint of
Canelo Digital Publishing Limited,
20 Vauxhall Bridge Road,
London SW1V 2SA
United Kingdom

A Penguin Random House Company
The authorised representative in the EEA is Dorling Kindersley Verlag GmbH. Arnulfstr. 124, 80636 Munich, Germany

A CIP catalogue record for this book is available from the British Library.

Print ISBN 978 1 83598 368 3
Ebook ISBN 978 1 80436 619 6

Cover design by Black Sheep

Cover images © Alamy, Shutterstock

Printed and bound in Great Britain by Clays Ltd, Elcograf S.p.A.

Look for more great books at
www.canelo.co | www.dk.com

I

For my mum, June Jackson 1934–2025

The life that I have
Is all that I have
And the life that I have is yours.

'The Life That I Have', Leo Marks, SOE cryptographer: a poem issued to agent Violette Szabo as a base text for coding and decoding

GLOSSARY

German

Begleitkommando – Hitler's personal bodyguard of SS troops

Führersonderzug – Hitler's personal train

Funkabwehr – German radio counter-intelligence organisation

Gestapo – *Geheim Staatspolizei*, German secret state police

Hauptsturmführer – SS rank equivalent to captain

Kriminalassistent – Gestapo rank equivalent to sergeant

Kriminalkommissar – Gestapo rank equivalent to captain

Kriminalsekretar – Gestapo rank equivalent to sergeant major

Obersturmführer – SS rank equivalent to lieutenant

SD – *Sicherheitsdienst*, the Reich Security Service

Unterscharführer – SS rank equivalent to corporal

Polish

Armia Krajowa – 'Home Army.' Poland's principal Resistance movement

Cichociemni – 'Dark and silent ones.' Polish SOE operatives

Do ciebie również – 'To you also.'

Dwór – a Polish manor house

Gdybym mógł zamienić słowo – 'If I could have a word.'

Pierdol się – Polish expletive

Powodzenia – 'Good luck.'

Tutaj jest – 'Here she is.'

Wigilia – the traditional Polish Christmas Eve supper

Wszystkiego najlepszego w nowym roku – 'Happy New Year.'

Zabawa w chowanego – hide-and-seek

ZWZ – *Związek Walki Zbrojne* – 'Union of Armed Struggle' – Polish resistance organisation set up in 1939. Precursor to the *Armia Krajowa*

Miscellaneous

Gazogene truck – vehicle which runs on self-generated wood gas

Milice – Fascist French militia active in Vichy France 1943 to 1945

Mossie – The de Havilland Mosquito, British twin-engined multi-role aircraft in World War Two

Petites Polognes – Polish communities in France, lit. 'Little Polands'

SOE – Special Operations Executive

Srbosjek – a Croatian knife

WAAF – member of the Women's Auxiliary Air Force

PROLOGUE

Arisaig, Scotland

24 December 1943

Stillness came naturally to her. In the darkness, the deeper shadow of the tall pine trees swallowed her up entirely. Streaks of black camouflage paste broke up her features and disguised the paleness of her flesh. The voluminous Commando smock over the coarse battledress of her uniform kept out the worst of the cold, but in truth she no longer felt it anyway. A light flicked on in the big house and a shadow drifted across the window. He was working late. He always worked late, but then they all did. How much did he know, or think he knew? She'd seen him watching her. That wasn't unusual in this place, where a woman was such a relative rarity. But it was the *way* he watched her. She knew that look.

She'd seen enough. She turned away and walked through the trees down towards the sea, placing her feet carefully, as she'd been taught, to avoid roots and rabbit holes. Somewhere a hunting owl cried out and she shivered. At finishing school in France, in that other lifetime, she'd read Shakespeare's *Macbeth. It was the owl that shriek'd, the fatal bellman.* A portent of death. But not here. She was safe here.

The night was her friend, sleep her enemy. Sleep brought memories – nightmares. It opened doors in her head that must remain closed if she was to retain her sanity. She only slept when she took the pills, but it was not a true sleep, more of a blessed unconsciousness.

She checked her watch. The luminous hands showed it was just before midnight. This was the hour they had come for her, when she had been huddled, shivering, on the damp concrete floor of the prison cell, nose filled with the rank scent of her own filth, still suffering the agonies of the previous night's interrogation. She shuddered at the memory, so clear and terrifying that it took her breath away for a moment. The dreaded stamp of hobnailed jackboots in the corridor. Praying that for once they'd come for someone else. That she would hear someone else screaming tonight. Rattle of the keys and rasp of the bolt being withdrawn. Door opening and four of them bursting in, all boots and fists, targeting the stomach and the ribs, but never the face. No malice here, just a calculated reminder of what was to come.

At first, it was the pliers she'd dreaded most. Her feet shackled to the table and the cold metal grips fixing on the nails. *Give us a name.* The searing rip and the scream so loud it couldn't have come from her, heart thundering fit to burst and her toe on fire. That soft, seductive voice. *Just one name and it can all be over.* Another toe, and she was pleading with them not to hurt her any more. *We know who you are and why you are here.* The pliers dangled in front of her face, a bloody scrap hanging from their tip. *Why should you suffer any more? Just one name. He will be long gone by now. What harm can it do?* She bit her lip until she could feel the blood running down her chin. Then one night it had been different. Wires and clips, a pain like no one could ever have endured. Still she'd held out. Then they'd put the thing inside her. That awful moment of being violated before they flicked the switch. Searing agony in every nerve end from the heart of her to her very eyeballs, before blessed oblivion. They'd brought her round with a bucket of ice water, just so she could see that look in his eyes. The look that said: when next we bring you down here, you will be screaming everything you know even before I lay a hand on you. And he'd been right.

When Raoul's people got her out, she'd asked them to shoot her for fear of being recaptured and returned to the Gestapo. On the Lysander that flew her back to Britain, she'd vowed never to put herself in that position again.

And now those dangerous fools in the Vienne had asked for her to be sent back. To face it all again. Only Raven would do. They trusted no other agent to lead them because she'd been so successful in those few short months. Didn't they understand she wasn't the person she had been two years earlier? She wasn't brave, or confident. She was broken.

The instructors here knew it. They could sense the tremble in her fingers when she handled the detonators, and see the pistol shots that landed an inch away when a year before they would have struck the heart. Once, they wouldn't have hesitated to send her back to a desk among the London Poles, or in the French section. But not now. Raven was too important.

So she would go back. Because they needed her. Because those bridges must be blown. Because even a broken Raven might make a tiny difference.

When they'd ordered her to Arisaig for the basic skills refresher course, she thought she'd left it all behind for a while, but it didn't take long to discover it had been waiting for her all along. Jealousy, anger and deceit, all just biding their time, along with that lust for vengeance that would never leave her.

A rustle among the bushes startled her and she froze. Was that lovesick fool Jean-Marc stalking her like a puppy again? God, men were such fools. They saw a pretty face and a bulging shirt and their brains turned to mush. No, she decided, it was nothing to concern her. Perhaps a rabbit or a mouse? She smiled. *Lucky little mouse, that I'm not that owl.*

The wind was rising, just a soft rustle through the trees, but experience told her there was more to come. There would be a storm tonight, and the thought produced a moment of exhilaration. In a way, the storm was her element, the mirror of her tortured soul, and nature's way of projecting her unquenchable anger. She could hear the waves breaking on the rocks now, and the salt scent of the sea mingled with the sweetness of the pine sap. The soft rhythm helped calm her, but what she really needed was for all this to be over, and to be back in the High Tatras with soft powder under her skis and a fifty-degree slope over the next rise. To escape a life that had become as much a prison as the cell in Lyons.

Escape? She was deluding herself. There was no escape from duty, just these small escapes into the night, or among the mountains, where she could be free of it all for a short time. It was on one of her small escapes that she'd discovered the Tenth House. What would people think if they knew what went on there?

She felt the familiar heat rise within her at the memory and had to stop for a moment, breathing hard. She closed her eyes, trying to use the calm of the forest and the whisper of the rising breeze to fight the surge of raw emotion.

A single soft step behind her. One arm wrapped around her throat; the other fumbled for the correct grip. She understood perfectly where

3

this would lead. The old Raven would have thrown her attacker and killed him in any number of ways. Instead, she let it happen. The grip tightened, hardened muscles putting the pressure just where they should.

Perhaps there was an escape after all.

CHAPTER 1

London

28 December 1943

The big Humber staff car sped through the deserted, blacked-out streets, driven by an army sergeant thankfully well accustomed to both the route and the faint glow provided by the hooded headlamps. In the rear of the car, Jan Kalisz sat back on the polished leather seats and tried to stem the unease that made his heart pound and his throat constrict. Something was missing; what was it?

It took a moment before he understood.

Death.

Every day for the past four years he'd woken with the shadow of death hanging over him, certain that each dawn would be his last. Suddenly, he had to adjust to an entirely different existence. His mind demanded to know what had happened to the barbed wire check-points and the dangling rows of corpses that had become his daily Warsaw reality, the Gestapo snatch squads that stalked the night, and the machine gun emplacements with their cold-eyed, trigger-happy defenders.

The immaculately turned-out British captain to his left must have sensed his unease, because he shifted a little to give himself more space. Kalisz didn't blame him. Two days and nights on the move had steeped him in a heady aroma of unwashed body, mildew and gasoline fumes.

He closed his eyes and tried to quiet his exhausted, reeling mind. There'd been plenty of time to ponder his situation during the long, almost unendurable journey since he'd left Warsaw with the words 'mission of national importance' ringing in his ears. Not that he'd come up with any answers. All Kalisz knew was that someone important in London had wanted him and someone important in Warsaw had

5

made sure they got him. After that, Jan Kalisz was just a package to be delivered.

Despite all the uncertainty, he couldn't help being impressed by the ruthless efficiency that had brought him here. As a Pole, he'd been part of an army that had lurched from one misfortune to the next. They'd lost battles, then the war, and finally their country. This was all very different.

First, there'd been the jerky, stop-start five-hour journey hidden beneath a mouldering, tick-infested pile of ancient sheepskins in the back of a lorry to a peasant farm somewhere in the south of Poland. Then the long wait for the cover of darkness, until he stood, shivering uncontrollably, in a pitch-dark field while shadowy figures stared at the stars until the distant drone of an aircraft could be heard. *Theirs or ours?* No matter; the signal fires were lit and, after a couple of circuits, an enormous thundering shape descended from the night sky and bumped to a halt perilously close to the trees at the edge of the field. Kalisz was half carried, half dragged to the doorway as four or five more shadows emerged from the plane to join the group on the frosty grass. Gloved hands reached down and hauled him inside what smelled like a giant petrol tank. The same hands pushed him into a metal seat and strapped him in, pushing a coarse blanket into his lap. By now they'd turned and, with a roar of engines, the straining propellers clawed the big transport plane back into her natural element.

Daylight brought a featureless airstrip he later gathered was some-where in southern Italy. At first nobody knew who he was, or what to do with him, then – what was that expression they'd used? – 'A Pole, one of the funnies.' – which seemed to explain everything. From somewhere, they'd eventually rustled up a new plane – a Mossie, his Polish pilot proudly informed him, twin-engined and agile, and fitted with long-range fuel tanks. They'd crossed the Alps two hours later at an astonishing height, traversed the breadth of France and the English Channel unhindered, before landing at an airfield to the north of London.

They'd taken him first to Portland Place, the temporary home of the Polish government-in-exile. There, a short, bespectacled man in a sharp suit – some kind of secretary – thanked him for his co-operation, measured him for a uniform – was he a tailor in his spare time? – and finally explained, more or less, why they'd gone to so much trouble to bring Investigator Jan Kalisz of the Warsaw Kripo, reviled collaborator, Resistance double agent, and not long for this world Polish patriot, to England.

'A distinguished Polish soldier has been found dead in suspicious circumstances,' his host informed Kalisz gravely. 'For the honour of Poland, her relationship with her allies, and the peace of mind of the soldier's family, it is crucial that the precise circumstances should be established by an experienced, and respected –' he rewarded Kalisz with a tight smile – 'detective from the Motherland. You have been brought here to investigate whether a crime has, indeed, been committed, to identify any perpetrator or perpetrators, and, if necessary, bring them to justice.'

Kalisz waited, but apparently no more detail was to be provided. Was the man mad? A stranger in a strange country was supposed to achieve all this in the perilously short window he'd engineered to disguise his absence from Warsaw?

'You will lodge overnight in the Euston Station Hotel,' the secretary continued. 'Your uniform, necessary documentation and funds suffi-cient for the duration of your, er… assignment will be delivered to your room. Your train departs from platform thirteen at ten a.m. precisely. I would advise being punctual.'

The secretary pressed a button on his desk. 'A car is waiting to take you to the hotel, but first a representative of the British government has requested an interview. Your English is up to the task, I suppose?'

'With the greatest respect, Mr Secretary –' Kalisz was too tired to hide his anger – 'my English is perfectly adequate. And I must remind you that, when I was first recruited by the ZWZ, it was on condition my identity was known only to a single individual in the Resistance movement. Now I find that not only are members of the *Armia Krajowa* high command aware of who I am and what I have done, but that some nosy English *pen-pusher* also thinks he can demand my time. This not only places my own life at significantly greater risk when I return to Warsaw, but also those of my family and friends. It is not correct, sir.'

The secretary's only reaction was a slight twitch of the lips. 'I am sorry, Investigator Kalisz, this is out of my hands. If it is any consolation, I believe you will benefit from this encounter. The gentleman you are meeting is much better acquainted with the details of the case than I am.'

At last the car slowed and the driver stopped outside a pair of broad metal gates, part hidden by layers of sandbags that left a gap in the centre just wide enough for a vehicle to enter. Two soldiers appeared from the darkness and opened the gates to allow the Humber to slip through and down a broad driveway that brought them into the courtyard of a large building. A shadowy figure appeared to open Kalisz's door, and he was surprised to discover it was in the shape of what the English called – for some obscure, but no doubt fitting, reason – a London 'bobby'.

'Good evening, sir,' the policeman greeted him cheerfully. 'Or is it morning?'

'I'll take it from here, Stubbs,' Kalisz's companion said.

'As you wish, Captain Oliver,' the policeman agreed, taking no offence.

Oliver led Kalisz up a set of worn stone stairs to a broad terrace and a singularly unimpressive doorway that sent the unmistakeable message 'servant's entrance'. A gloomy corridor ran directly ahead, but the captain turned immediately right and up two sets of carpeted stairs dominated by large landscape paintings in ornate frames.

At the top of the stairs, another corridor, as gloomy as the first; the house was bigger than Kalisz had thought, because it stretched far into the distance. For the first time, he began to wonder about the identity of his 'English pen-pusher'.

'If you'll just wait here, sir.' Captain Oliver stopped outside a wood-panelled door and slipped through. Kalisz heard the murmur of voices, but not what was said. The soldier reappeared within a minute. 'He'll see you now.' He held the door for Kalisz and closed it behind him as he stepped inside.

At first, the Pole was forced to squint against the glare of two bright table lamps. The room was smaller than he'd expected, but it was only as his eyes adjusted that he was able to properly identify the two men who already occupied it. One, older and balding, more heavily built, wearing a dark suit almost as crumpled as Kalisz's own, a black bow tie askew beneath his heavy jowls, sat at a large desk. The younger – tall, slim and narrow-eyed – stood slightly behind him, with the nervous air of a mother hen guarding her chick.

The older man stood, and for a brief moment Kalisz had the impression the piercing, ice-blue eyes were searching his soul.

'You know who I am, Investigator Kalisz?'

'Of course, sir.'

'Then let us waste no time,' said Winston Churchill. 'We do not have much of it.'

CHAPTER 2

'You must be famished.' The British prime minister pointed towards a polished wood sideboard where a platter of meat, cheese and bread had been laid out beside three or four plates. 'I have a few things to say, so you may as well eat while I'm talking.' Churchill's voice had a gravelly quality and his words emerged in staccato bursts, like a misfiring machine gun. Kalisz recognised the stern, jowly features from the Nazi propaganda posters that depicted him so unflatteringly. 'Jock,' Churchill said to the younger man, 'a drink for Investigator Kalisz.' He turned back to Kalish. 'Jock is my private secretary.' The secretary poured a hefty slug of tawny liquor from a decanter into a glass and laid it beside Kalisz, automatically charging Churchill's drink in the process. 'Your health, sir.'

Kalisz raised the glass to his lips and drank, sending a ribbon of liquid fire down his throat that made him erupt into an uncontrollable fit of coughing. Eventually, he managed to choke out an apology.

'Nonsense,' his host snorted. 'Don't stand on ceremony, man. Eat. At least the food won't kill you.' Churchill took a seat in an armchair and waved Kalisz towards a matching sofa opposite.

For a long moment, Churchill only stared at him, as if he couldn't quite believe what he was seeing. 'How...?' The question fluttered on his lips before he thought better of it, and he shook his head.

Without prompting, Jock picked up a dun-coloured file from the desk and offered it to Kalisz, who put his food aside to accept the folder. He opened it to reveal a slightly blurred photograph of a young woman in some kind of neat service uniform and cap. Dark hair fell in folds from beneath the cap to frame features set in a serious frown. His first thought was that she was quite beautiful and, in that moment at least, terribly proud; his second, that he recognised her from somewhere. It must have been taken at some sort of ceremony because a medal hung on a ribbon over her left breast.

'I'm grieved to say that this is your victim, Investigator,' Churchill continued. 'Krystina Kowolska, aged just twenty-seven, daughter of a Polish father and a French mother, dual nationality and multilingual, and at the time of her demise, serving with the British armed forces. She was found dead on Christmas Day during a refresher and evaluation course at one of our special training facilities in Scotland.'

Kalisz continued to study the photo, but the Krystina in the picture had nothing to tell him for now. He felt an odd kinship with another mongrel – the only difference being that Kalisz's mother had been German, which had kept him alive while so many others were being butchered in the basement of Aleja Szucha and the forests around Warsaw. 'How did she die?'

Jock took up the story. 'She was found hanging from a tree.'

'Yes?' Kalisz persisted testily. He had a distinct sense of being patronised. *Our little Polish guest.* Thirty-six now, at least for another few months, though the war and his years of playing *zabawa w chowanego* – hide-and-seek – with the Nazis had added a few more wrinkles. And taken a toll on his patience.

'The doctor who examined her believes she was dead before she was hanged.'

'"Believes"? He must be certain, surely?' Kalisz corrected him. 'Otherwise I wouldn't be here.'

'That is correct, Investigator Kalisz,' Churchill resumed. 'And I have no doubt you are wondering just *why* you are here. I'm afraid if anyone is to blame for that, it is I. You see, Krystina Kowolska is – was – no ordinary servicewoman. She was an undercover agent, a quite successful undercover agent as these things go, a member of an organisation known as the Special Operations Executive. For that reason alone, her death is of great concern.'

'But not, itself,' Kalisz countered, 'of enough concern to bring me from Warsaw to investigate when one of your British detectives could do it equally well, and at much less cost.'

'Indeed,' the prime minister conceded. 'As I have said, Krystina was a brilliant woman and a heroine, but that is not all. Her parents were aristocrats who moved among the highest levels of Polish society. Sadly, her father made some poor investments in the early thirties and lost his family's entire fortune. Ancient history, you may say, Investigator, but bear with me. As a result, he and his wife took their own lives, leaving

Krystina an orphan at the age of fifteen. Fortunately, close friends of her parents took her in and raised her discreetly as part of their own family. That family was called Leśniowski. Is the name familiar to you?'

Kalisz shook his head. 'I don't believe so, sir.'

'Then perhaps it would help if I told you that she was a bridesmaid at the wedding in 1936 of Stanisław Leśniowski, the man she regarded as a brother, and a rather lovely Polish girl by the name of Zofia Sikorska.'

Kalisz noticed the slight catch in Churchill's voice when he uttered the name, and he began to understand the true extent of the political tentacles in which he found himself entangled. Zofia Leśniowska was the daughter of General Władysław Sikorski, former prime minister of the Polish government-in-exile. She had died with her father nine months earlier in a mysterious plane crash in the Mediterranean Sea off Gibraltar. In Warsaw, the Nazi propagandists had let it be known that the 'accident' was arranged on the orders of the Soviet leader Josef Stalin, but, depending on who you listened to, the blame might be apportioned to Sikorski's government rivals, or even – Kalisz stared at the man opposite – Winston Churchill himself.

Churchill nodded. 'I see you understand. There has been certain – ' a throaty harrumph punctuated the words – 'unfounded speculation about General Sikorski's death. For my part, I lost a staunch ally and some very good friends. Zofia, in particular, treated me with great kindness. An alliance such as ours, Investigator Kalisz, containing so many different nations, with so many competing priorities, and often with different end points in mind, requires careful nurturing. In essence, it is held together by three different elements – necessity, trust and faith. If any one of those elements is weakened, it can place the entire structure in jeopardy. Am I making myself clear?'

'I believe so, Prime Minister.'

'Following General Sikorski's death, trust between Poland and its allies was in short supply.' Churchill held out his glass to be refilled. 'I pride myself that we had largely restored it. But now this. The unnatural death of someone so closely linked to the family. And at this time.' The pale eyes gleamed, his voice took on a new force and, to Kalisz, Churchill seemed to grow in stature, to become something like the Churchill of his imagination: the man behind the myth, whom his enemies feared. 'Very soon, the armies of freedom will cross the Channel to create a Second Front that will leave the Nazis between the hammer of our Allied forces and the anvil of the Red Army. Herr Hitler knows we are coming, but he does not know where. He will do everything in his power to stop us, and wherever it is, we will need every man of every nation in this bastard coalition of ours, including your Polish comrades in arms, straining every sinew to defeat the enemy. That is why, when your prime minister, Mr Mikołajczyk, came to me with his concerns about the death of Krystina, I was moved to suggest that the case should be investigated by a Polish detective with experience of murder inquiries.' A bitter laugh escaped the compressed lips. 'What I did not bargain for – and for which you have my sincere apologies – was that the only suitable candidate they could agree upon would have to be flown one thousand miles from Occupied Europe to do the job.'

Kalisz could feel their eyes on him. In a way, it all made perfect sense. The war created strange undercurrents, and this wasn't the first time during its course he'd found himself drawn into an inescapable maelstrom of murder and politics. All a man could do was keep swimming until he either found somewhere to crawl ashore – or went under.

'Then there is nothing more to say, Prime Minister.' He looked up to meet Churchill's gaze. 'You have my assurance that I will investigate Krystina Kowolska's death using whatever talents and experience I possess. For me, this is not about politics or international statecraft, but providing a brave young countrywoman with the justice to which she is entitled.'

'That is all I can ask, Investigator. Now, is there anything else I can tell you?'

Kalisz stifled a humourless laugh. He had so many questions, but his first priority was to reach the crime scene. It would already be tainted, of course – there was no helping that – but the quicker he reached there, the more likely it would be to reveal its secrets. 'Perhaps I could be told where I am going, unless that is a state secret? And you mentioned a refresher course. May I ask, a refresher course in which subjects?'

Jock leaned forward and whispered something in Churchill's ear.

'Of course... How could I have forgotten? But first to your questions, Investigator Kalisz. As to the refresher course, Krystina would have been brushing up on the finer points of unarmed combat, silent killing, demolition, radio telegraphy, and, quite possibly, breaking and entering and forgery, for all I know. She had already shown great aptitude for all of these disciplines during her previous missions. Which brings me to the point that should not have escaped me earlier. Krystina Kowolska was, apart from her other deadly talents, also regarded as a leader and a talisman by those she had previously worked with in France. For that reason, when the *reseau* – that is, the Resistance network – she had fought beside and helped lead on her original mission, were tasked with carrying out a very difficult operation central to the overall strategy of the Second Front, they asked for her.'

'In fact,' Jock intervened, 'they *demanded* Krystina. Specifically, they said that if they were being asked to commit suicide, they would only do it with a fair chance of a successful outcome, and under the guidance of someone they knew and trusted.'

'And, despite the emotional and physical trauma of her most recent, rather less successful mission, Krystina did not hesitate to volunteer,' Churchill said. 'She was quite a remarkable woman.' He leaned forward in his chair and looked directly into Kalisz's eyes. 'It is absolutely crucial that we know whether her death had anything to do with her upcoming mission. When we invade Europe our most vital commodity will be time. Time to put men ashore in their thousands and tens of thousands, supported by plentiful supplies and the machinery of war. Time to create an impregnable defensive bridgehead from which we can break out at the opportune moment and smash the enemy. Krystina Kowolska was to parachute into France months ahead of the invasion, and buy that time at the crucial moment by delaying an entire SS Panzer division for at least three days. If her operation has been compromised, we have a choice of putting off the invasion for weeks, perhaps months, or risking slaughter and the possibility of complete failure. We *must* know one way or the other, Investigator.'

Kalisz frowned. 'Are you saying that should be my priority, Prime Minister?'

Churchill exchanged a glance with his private secretary, who shrugged.

'Discover the identity of the murderer and his motive, and you will provide the answer,' the prime minister said. 'Though I do not delude myself that it will be a simple matter. I have given orders that you should receive every co-operation, but your destination is a place of secrets, Investigator Kalisz, populated by men – and women – whose very survival depends on their ability to conceal their true selves. On which note… a word of warning. No doubt as you carry out your investigation you will hear hints of these secrets – perhaps even be tempted to seek them out. If that is the case, I beg you to close your ears and deny temptation, for your own sake. Arisaig, in the north-west of Scotland, is an area of majestic, rugged beauty, but a very dangerous place indeed. Probably the most dangerous place in Britain, I dare say, but you must find out why for yourself.'

If Kalisz had ever had any doubts that his was a mission of war, Winston Churchill's solemn warning dismissed them. He felt something grow inside him: a glow that might have been anger, but was actually a furious determination to survive whatever Britain threw at him and return to his wife and son before the Nazis discovered he was missing.

'Do make sure you take plenty of warm clothing when you travel north. It's very cold in Scotland at this time of the year. You've sorted that out, Jock? Good.' Churchill held out his right hand and Kalisz shook it; the old man's grip was stronger than he'd expected. 'Thank you for coming, Investigator. I look forward to reading your findings soon.'

When Kalisz was gone, Churchill returned to his place at his desk. 'So, what did you think, Jock?'

'Of Kalisz? He's not much to look at, but he's no fool. As for the whole thing, you know my opinion, Prime Minister. A waste of time and resources that is unlikely to do any good and may well backfire badly on us.'

'In the circumstances…' Churchill frowned. 'I had to give the Poles something, and it may just make a difference. Mr Mikołajczyk is no General Sikorski. There are some very strong feelings against us among the London Poles and their counterparts in Warsaw. He needs all the help he can get to keep them on side. Now, to the pressing matter of security. You say Kalisz insists on returning to Poland?'

'In three weeks, or less. Some ruse involving a hospital isolation ward. If it's discovered, his family would be in real peril. He demanded guarantees as part of his agreement to come here.'

Churchill sighed. 'That is unfortunate. It may be in the best interests of the war effort, and of Investigator Kalisz's well-being, that he does not return to Warsaw at all.'

CHAPTER 3

The Children's Hospital on Kopernika, Warsaw

Maria Kalisz tried to concentrate on the weekly roster for the orthopaedic ward, but it was difficult to focus on the list of names after a long, restless night in a lonely bed. She raised her head at the soft tap on the door and called to whoever it was to enter. Maria thought she knew everyone on the staff of the Children's Hospital, but she was certain she'd never encountered the nurse who slipped quietly into the office. Tall, and perhaps in her early forties, with a sharp, hawklike profile and narrow, deep-set eyes, she was dressed appropriately enough, but something told Maria her visitor didn't belong in the familiar uniform with the red cross on the starched white bib. Yet there was an authority about the woman's bearing and expression that dared anyone to question her right to wear it. Maria felt a momentary unease beneath the scrutiny of those pale eyes, until she remembered this was her hospital and her office.

'Can I help you?' The question was polite enough, but there was no mistaking her tone: *What are you doing here?*

The woman closed the door at her back, but her eyes never left Maria. Now Maria felt as if she was being weighed and measured – perhaps, even, being judged.

'I certainly hope so.' The newcomer's voice had a harsh, almost ragged quality and every word seemed to contain a challenge.

Now, unease was replaced by a flutter of panic. Did this have something to do with Jan? Her husband had rushed from their apartment more than thirty-six hours earlier after a secretive late-night phone call. She'd watched him pack, each item of clothing rammed into the small valise with a fury that conveyed more eloquently than any words his reluctance to abandon her. He'd held her for a moment as a car idled in the street outside, and whispered that he might be gone for several days and that 'arrangements' would be made. They'd faced many challenges as a family in four years of war, but somehow for Maria this unheralded departure was the most frightening. She'd barely been able to conceal the shock she'd felt from their son, Stefan, and the sense of helplessness and confusion of that moment was still with her. Thankfully Jan was on Christmas leave, so there was no reason for his superiors in the Warsaw Kripo to ask any awkward questions – yet – but she'd still spent every moment since waiting in terror for the telephone to ring. Now this.

'I'm sure you're wondering why I'm here.' The woman might have read her mind. 'Would it surprise you to know that your husband sent me?'

A surge of relief was swiftly replaced by the wariness instilled by four years of life in the shadows. 'And I'm just meant to trust you. Is that correct? The only thing I know for certain about you is that you're not a ward nurse. You're too old, for a start. And no nurse would wear her cap for long at that jaunty angle before the ward sister knocked it off.'

'How very perceptive of you.' The visitor's hands automatically went to her headwear to straighten the offending item, but the imperious tone didn't waver. 'And you're right to be suspicious. I could be anyone. Perhaps it would help if I told you that I'm aware that you are a member of the *Armia Krajowa*, and that your superior officer is a man you know as Tadeusz.'

Maria's fingers tightened so powerfully on the pencil she held that she feared it might snap in two, but she managed to retain her composure. 'Whether that is true or not, is it not just the kind of thing the Nazis would say to win my confidence before they dragged me off to Szucha Avenue?'

'Very well… if you insist I unnecessarily prolong this conversation.' The woman didn't hide her irritation. 'Your husband left home hurriedly after he received a phone call that lasted less than ninety seconds around midnight on Saint Stephen's Day. Did he tell you he had been specifically chosen for a mission of national importance? No, I doubt he would. He is a careful man. Which is why he is still alive. For the last four years, Jan Kalisz has been working for the *Armia Krajowa* under the guise of his collaboration with the occupiers as an investigator with the Warsaw *Kriminalpolizei*. Of course, part of our protocol is to pretend that you don't know this, and I certainly shouldn't be telling you, but neither of us are fools.' Her manner softened for a heartbeat and the voice lost its ragged edge. 'It is my sense that Investigator Kalisz could not have survived for this long without the support and active co-operation of his family. I certainly hope that is the case, because I am here to ask you for help, Mrs Kalisz.'

By now Maria had already made her decision, but she still needed time to think. 'You know my name, but I don't believe you mentioned yours?'

'You may call me Katya. It is the name by which your husband knows me.'

'Well, *Katya*, I am a mother as well as a wife, and I will need a little more convincing before putting my own head and my son's into the lion's mouth. That is what you want me to do, isn't it?'

'Yes, you certainly deserve that.' Katya nodded. 'The mission on which your husband has embarked will take an unspecified, but necessarily finite period of time. For that reason, it has been deemed appropriate to create a cover story to justify his absence from his desk for an extended period. Jan Kalisz's superiors have been told that he contracted an infectious skin disease as a result of his time trapped inside the ghetto earlier this year. This has necessitated treatment at a specialist facility on the Baltic coast, where a combination of physicians with expertise in this area, and the sea air, offer the best possibility of a speedy recovery. As a nurse, am I making sense?'

'I think so.'

'Of course, there is also the question of identification. The deception could not succeed if, for instance, one of Jan's colleagues were to appear at the hospital with the intention of visiting him. To that end, the doctors at the Medical and Tropical Hygiene Centre in Gdynia have decided that the best form of treatment for this particular disease is to swathe the patient entirely in bandages soaked in a suitable soothing balm—'

'I've seen similar measures used in the treatment of burn victims.' Maria nodded.

'Exactly. So there is no question of our volunteer being exposed as a substitute for your husband.'

At last, Maria saw what was coming. 'But…'

'Yes —' a thin smile — 'there is always a "but". In the natural course of things, the sick man's family would visit him, recognisable or otherwise, even despite the distances involved. That is what I would ask you to do,

Mrs Kalisz. Go to the bedside and sit for an hour or so talking nonsense to a man whose identity you will never know. If you are willing to make this sacrifice, it is also possible that you could do your country a great service.'

CHAPTER 4

Euston Station, London

29 December 1943

Platform 13, with minutes to spare, but Kalisz felt entirely lost in the great throng of servicemen and women in their bewildering array of different uniforms. Officers and men alike barely acknowledged his existence in their rush to board, not just the Glasgow train, but at least three others on the neighbouring platforms. He looked vainly at his ticket: First Class Carriage J, compartment three. But the train seemed to stretch forever in a series of identical grimy, red-brown carriages. He struggled up the platform, pristine new army boots clattering on the wooden boards, hefting the suitcase that now contained everything he owned. As well as the suitcase, he carried an officer's greatcoat of heavy cloth over one arm and the briefcase containing the details of the investigation in his left hand.

With relief, he spotted a tall, grey-moustached figure in what he took to be a railwayman's uniform standing like a rock amid the flow of passengers. 'Excuse me, please.' He thrust his ticket towards the man. 'Can you direct me to Carriage J?'

'I'm sorry, sir, there's no Carriage Y on this train.' The railwayman frowned and looked Kalisz up and down. Churchill's people had supplied him with a British officer's battledress uniform, and some clever soul had promoted him to major, to give him a level of authority Lieutenant Jan Kalisz would never have had. If the man wasn't impressed by his accent, he knew enough about military ranks to respect the crowns on his shoulder straps and the decorative medal ribbons on his chest.

'Not Y – *sczh.*' Kalisz's lips twisted as his tongue struggled to find the right consonant. 'See?' He raised the ticket so the man could read it, and in his anxiety the correct combination of English words eluded him. 'Is vital for war, yes?'

'Isn't everything, sir?' The railwayman shook his head. 'Rush, rush, rush. They rushed my lad off to Malaya and the Japs nabbed every last one of them as soon as they got off the ship. Proper waste. The Lord only knows when we'll see him again.' Kalisz darted a glance at the station clock, but the railwayman smiled. 'You don't have to worry about the old *Royal Scot* leaving without you. She's not going anywhere till I blow this.' He raised a silver whistle on a chain. 'Now, Carriage J, is it? If you'll just follow me. I'll take your case.' He peered at Kalisz's red shoulder patches. 'Polish, eh? We get quite a few of your lads coming through here. Bomber boys, mostly.' He stopped outside one of a pair of carriages slightly less grimy than the rest, opened the door and manoeuvred the heavy case inside with practised ease. 'Third compartment on your right. Now, sir, if I can take a look at your travel warrant, just to keep the office wallahs happy?'

Kalisz reached into the breast pocket of his battledress jacket and produced a sheet of paper he'd been given. 'Is this it?'

The railwayman studied the warrant. 'Final destination Fort William.' The location inspired a raised eyebrow. 'That means you'll have to find somewhere to stay in Glasgow tonight, if you haven't already. This train won't arrive at Central Station till after seven at the earliest, and the last train to Fort William leaves Queen Street – the other station across the city – at about the same time.'

He returned the warrant and Kalisz thanked him. 'Fort William.' He tested the words, trying unsuccessfully to form the *W* he found such a trial in English. 'One of your great northern defensive positions, no doubt?'

The man gave him a wry smile. 'In a manner of speaking, sir. In a manner of speaking. Safe journey.'

Kalisz carried his baggage to the compartment, which was empty for the moment. A few minutes later, he heard a piercing whistle. The carriage gave a lurch and he felt a surge of anticipation as the train jolted into motion, seeming to strain desperately as it attempted to pick up speed. Outside the compartment soldiers filed past through the corridor, but no one joined him. He put the greatcoat on the seat to his left and opened the strap on the briefcase to remove the folder of documents they'd given him at the hotel.

Naturally, Jan Kalisz could not be in England, so his identity card was in the name of a Major Jan Zamoyski, which made him smile. The Zamoyskis were aristocrats and landowners, and Kalisz was the son of a Silesian coal miner. A photographer had been waiting for him at the hotel, and Kalisz's face stared back at him from the left of the card, grim and unsmiling, dark eyes buried deep, but you could sense the anger in them. God, he looked old. He'd been wearing his civilian suit at the time the picture was taken, but by some miracle of the forger's art the man in the picture was in uniform.

According to the card, he was a member of the Allied Land Contingent – Polish Forces. Surname: Zamoyski. Christian name: Jan. Rank: Major. He was five feet six inches tall; his eyes were brown, as was his hair, though Kalisz would have said black. No distinguishing marks. Date of birth: an accurate 25.7.1907. A washed-out magenta crown had been stamped in the centre of the card, so it took in the lower quadrant of the photograph. The same photo and some of the details were recorded in his paybook, but in both English and Polish. Unusually, it also contained a slip of paper that explained the medal ribbons on his chest. These turned out to be not quite as decorative as he'd assumed. One of them was the Cross of Valour, an award for courage on the battlefield. If Kalisz remembered the date correctly, he'd received it for an action at Sochaczew during the defence of Warsaw, in which he'd been one of a very few men to survive. It was the first he'd heard of it.

From a train carriage, London appeared a drab place that seemed to go on forever and consisted of rows of smoke-blackened terraced houses. Kalisz glanced at his watch. Twenty minutes now, and he'd never seen a blade of grass.

The watch was a Patek Philippe Genève Chronograph, and much too expensive for him. It rightly belonged to another man, but it was a good watch. Maria, Kalisz's wife, had forced it into his hand as he left home with the suggestion that it might, if needed, help buy his way out of trouble.

'How...?' Kalisz knew what Churchill had wanted to ask: *How did you survive? How have you survived this long?* The truth was, because he was good. Not a good spy – he still shivered at the number of times his ineptitude could have got him killed – but a good detective. Kalisz had been recruited by a fledgling Resistance outfit while he was in hospital just before Warsaw's capitulation. They'd asked him to return to the detective's room at Department V and co-operate with the Nazis. He'd done as he was ordered, kept his nose clean, first as a clerk, then as a translator. Gradually, the Germans realised they couldn't operate efficiently without the support of a few compliant Poles. With the help of an SS doctor called Mengele, he'd helped hunt down a serial killer known as The Artist, a Nazi official with a taste for eviscerating young girls. The result had pleased everyone, apart from the killer, who died with Kalisz's bullet in his head, but no one more than SS-*Hauptsturmführer* Hoth, Kalisz's boss, who had restored him to investigator status.

There'd been more, of course. A murder victim who seemed to live three separate lives: as a legitimate German businessman, a crooked SS officer, and a Ghetto Jew who'd huckstered his way to a fortune but never had a chance to enjoy it. Could it be a coincidence that the Axel Weiss case had also involved a hanging? Kalisz doubted it. More likely, someone had seen it as the qualification that placed him at the top of a list. The list that had brought him here.

And now Winston Churchill was sending him to 'probably the most dangerous place in Britain' – whatever that meant – on a mission the result of which might, or might not, affect the course of the war. Did they genuinely want him to find the truth? The Polish secretary's 'if necessary' in regard to whether Kalisz should bring the perpetrator to justice injected a certain ambiguity. Why would it not be necessary? Yet, if Krystina's mission was so vital to the Second Front, was it not also possible that her killer, potentially a fellow agent, might be equally indispensable?

Not that any of it mattered, because Kalisz intended to do his job and *do diabła z nimi* – to hell with them. He pulled the dun-coloured folder from the briefcase and opened it. All it contained was the photograph of Krystina Kowolska and a single sheet of paper with a frustratingly brief biography – name, age, length of service in the Women's Auxiliary Air Force – that told him nothing more than he already knew. He studied the features in the photograph, and as he met her eyes a vow swam unheralded into his head. *I will find your killer if it is humanly possible, so help me God.* He remembered her from a ski competition, at Zakopane, a resort in the Tatra mountains, about a year before the Nazis invaded Poland. They hadn't met, but he'd noticed her. Who wouldn't? A slim figure in navy ski pants and a light blue jacket, sun goggles tangled in her dark hair, laughing with the throng of male admirers who were never far away. He particularly remembered the way that her skis had seemed part of her. She'd attacked the most difficult runs with a natural rhythm and grace that might have taken her to the Olympics, had it not been for the war. A few months later, a sketch likeness of the same face had appeared on a poster promoting winter sports in Poland.

Kalisz placed the photograph aside, face down, and picked up a short note that had been hiding beneath the biography. It suggested that he would have access to Krystina's full service record when he reached his destination. Only now did he notice that someone had stamped the back of the picture with purple ink. The stamp said OPERATION BISHOP.

CHAPTER 5

OPERATION BISHOP

Monts du Lyonnais, France

April 1943

Krystina Kowolska hung in the still air beneath the parachute as the sound of the big plane faded into the distance. The silence and tranquillity came as a blessed relief after being assailed by the roar of the Halifax's four massive engines for the past three hours. This was their third attempt to get her here, after two missions were cancelled as a result of poor weather, and they'd dropped her at a relatively high altitude because of the mountainous terrain. Away to the south, far beyond the horizon, a series of flashes lit the sky where the bombers that had covered the Halifax's approach were dropping their deadly cargo. The ground a thousand feet below was just a dark shadow, but in the moonlight Krystina could see the pale discs of the six container parachutes that had preceded her.

She felt a sudden surge of exhilaration. She was back in the war.

Krystina had been staying with her mother's family in Paris when the Nazis invaded Poland almost four years earlier. She'd immediately volunteered for the PSK, the Polish Women's Service, but Poland had fallen before she could return to her homeland. Stranded and frustrated, she'd thrown all her energy into helping relief organisations process the flood of soldiers who fled Poland through Hungary and Romania to continue the fight. Their efforts were in vain, as it turned out, because when France surrendered in 1940 they were forced to flee again – to Britain. Krystina could have gone with them, but some instinct made her stay. For the first time, she entered the clandestine world of secrets and spies.

For Poland was far from done with the fight. During the Great Depression of the early 1930s, more than a million and a half Poles had migrated to France to work in the coalfields. They formed their own communities, with Polish shops, churches and schools, filled with taciturn, tight-lipped men and hard-faced women. When the Wehrmacht marched into the Nord-Pas-de-Calais, the Poles just turned their backs on the enemy and clustered even closer together. But nobody was forgetting or forgiving what had happened in their homeland: an entire society dedicated to resistance. All they needed was organisation.

And who better to maintain contact with the various groups than someone who could travel with relative ease and shed her French socialite skin to become an authentic Polish patriot in a heartbeat?

They did a little damage, though never quite achieved the potential they might, but it was eventually to lead her to Northumberland Hotel in London – and the Special Operations Executive.

By now, Krystina could make out a monochrome patchwork of fields and woods, and she pulled on the left riser to slip towards the dull glow where they'd extinguished the signal fire. A big landing zone, but her welcome party would have sentries out on all sides watching for German patrols. They wouldn't have any trouble finding her.

She counted down the seconds in her head and, when she reached tree level, went through the sequence: legs together, knees bent; the ground smacked the soles of her boots and she felt a twinge in her right ankle; forward roll and hit the quick-release mechanism to free the chute. A perfect landing, apart from that ill-placed stone, but she would soon walk off the sprain. She got to her feet and started to drag in the parachute silk by its cords, only to freeze at the sound of running feet. Almost without conscious thought a silenced Welrod pistol appeared in her fist from the pocket on her left thigh. It was an assassin's weapon, more or less noiseless, but it was also experimental and she'd never fired it in anger, which wasn't ideal.

A slight figure appeared out of the darkness and, barely giving her a glance, began bundling up her parachute. A bigger man ran up, carrying a short spade. 'I am Henri.' He began to dig a hole in the stony ground to bury the chute, cursing the rocks under his breath.

Krystina kept the pistol in her hand. 'Plate.' Under the circumstances, the identifying protocol seemed not just superfluous, but silly, but the procedure had saved lives in the past, so...

Henri looked up at her, at the pistol in her hand, shook his head. 'Knife.'

He said it in French – the quite distinctive, heavily accented French of the Lyonnais she'd practised incessantly for six weeks – and she waited.

'*Putain de bêtises,*' he muttered. 'All right… Knife.'

This time it was in English. She put the pistol on the ground and unzipped her jumpsuit, throwing it to Henri so he could bury it in the same hole as the parachute, which the boy had brought to him. The Frenchman checked the pockets, removing anything of value, before pushing it into the pit and shovelling earth on top of it. Krystina retrieved the pistol and put it in the leather satchel that had been beneath the overalls.

'You're a girl.'

Krystina saw that the boy was staring at her. He must have been fifteen or sixteen and was as thin as a skinned rabbit, with narrow, feral features, and untidy dark hair that flopped over his wary eyes. His clothes were a mixture of over- and under-sized, but universally patched and ragged. The most distinctive things about him were the sawn-off double-barrelled shotgun he carried and the bandolier of cartridges slung across his shoulder.

'It's a long time since I've been called a girl.' She smiled.

She was conscious of his gaze and aware how exotic she must have seemed to him, even in the dowdy, home-knitted, dirt-brown jumper she wore beneath a mildewed overcoat designed for a woman ten years older. Her sensible skirt came to well below knees that were already hidden by thick winter stockings, and the ensemble – naturally, all locally made or provided – was completed by a pair of sturdy worker's shoes.

'You're laughing at me.' The pale brow furrowed in a frown.

'No,' she said. 'I would never do that. You're a soldier, like me. A warrior. I can see it in your eyes. I will be proud to fight at your side.'

He took time to process whether he was still being mocked, and she recognised the moment of decision. 'I am André.' He held out his hand and she shook it.

'And I am Odile.' The name was plucked from the memory of her previous mission to the Vienne, and not the one she would use as part of the circuit.

'Stop gawking at her like a love-struck bull calf.' Henri replaced the turf on top of the pit where he'd buried her equipment. 'We need to get to the farm at Le Mailliard by dawn.'

André led the way into the darkness and they followed. After about five minutes Krystina sensed activity around her. 'This is the gathering point for the equipment,' Henri said quietly. 'Six canisters they dropped and six canisters we must have. So now we wait. But we have been waiting a long time, Odile. That is the way of the Maquis du Mont. At least from tonight, thanks to you, we will have a means of fighting back.'

'There is a small suitcase in one of the containers.'

'Of course.' Henri slipped away, and after a whispered conversation returned with the valise they'd packed for her back at Tempsford, in that other world.

They marched through the night, across fields and along trackways through otherwise impenetrable woods, skirting farms and small settlements. This was mountain country, and Krystina blessed the muscle-aching twenty-mile route marches she'd endured in the Scottish hills that made the trek little more than a stroll. A soft drizzle fell, but the coat kept her relatively dry.

They never stopped apart from the occasional tense, restless halt while André, who seemed to be the unit's scout, assessed some perceived threat or danger. 'He is a good boy,' Henri whispered. 'Careful.'

Three times, small parties separated from the column of *maquisards* and she guessed they were burying the containers for later recovery.

They seemed to be making good progress when the column froze at the sound of a sudden shout from ahead and to the left. The Welrod was in Krystina's hand, but Henri touched her arm. 'Wait here,' he hissed.

Without warning, the crack of a rifle split the night like a hammer blow, quickly answered by the unmistakeable metallic clatter of a Sten gun. Now, a proper volley of rifle fire from perhaps a dozen weapons and the firefly sparkle of muzzle flashes beyond the trees. Whoever they'd stumbled into were here in numbers. A different sound, and a patch of the wood lit up like distant lightning, accompanied by the twin *boom, boom* of a shotgun being discharged. It wasn't a killing weapon in this kind of fight – with the barrels sawn down, the birdshot would scatter far and wide – but it certainly annoyed somebody. The rifle fire intensified and concentrated on one patch of the forest. A few seconds passed before another double blast from the shotgun, but this time from a different place. André was shifting position to confuse the enemy like a good little soldier.

'Come.' Henri was back. 'He is leading them away. Do not waste the time he buys for us.'

–

Much later, she laid her head on the rough wood of a table in a rustic farmhouse. The last image in her mind before sleep enveloped her was the joy in André's eyes when she'd told him she'd be proud to fight beside him.

–

She woke to the sound of the door opening and closing. Lucienne, a slim blonde who managed to look like a fashion model even in men's clothes, brought her a bowl of stew and a hunk of bread on a tin plate and sat down beside her. Henri stood by the door with two young boys vying for his attention, but he shooed them away. One of the other *maquisards* approached him for a whispered conversation.

'He would not let them take him alive,' Lucienne whispered. 'Jacques was close by and saw it all. Do not grieve for him, Odile. André was a refugee. We were all the family he had, and he sacrificed himself for us. In these times, what more could one ask?'

CHAPTER 6

England

Kalisz laid the file aside and his eye was drawn to the curtain-framed window. The train was well out into the countryside now, amid flat, mostly featureless, farmland, dotted with small nameless villages and towns and patches of dark forest. And camps. They were well camouflaged, but his soldier's eye couldn't be mistaken: row after row of tents; great parks of lorries, tracked vehicles and tanks. The sight, and the knowledge it would be replicated all across the country, made his heart glow, until he remembered that all this great gathering of firepower would never be used to free Poland from the Nazis. That would be left to the Red Army, which, after the revelations the previous year about the massacre by the Soviets of tens of thousands of Polish soldiers at Katyn, was the equivalent of trading a plate of arsenic for cyanide.

By now, the corridor outside his compartment was filled with men in uniform. Soldiers in side-caps and flat bonnets, wearing the same dirt-brown serge in which he was clad, some with rank stripes and divisional patches. Sailors in dark greatcoats with pristine white flat hats, and airmen in neat blue jackets and trousers. They lounged against the carriage walls talking together, sitting on cases or kitbags, or leaning out of the windows, smoking.

Kalisz returned his papers to the briefcase and withdrew a brown paper parcel tied with string he'd been told contained his rations for the day. When he opened it, he prodded the coarse, dry bread and lifted the top slice to reveal a pink rubbery substance smeared with some kind of relish. Better, probably, to eat it later. He closed his eyes and slept.

A restless sleep, unconscious mind haunted by memories of the past. Kalisz's eyes snapped open and he found himself sitting opposite a young officer: a captain, if he identified the insignia correctly. The soldier was staring at him with undisguised interest. Kalisz's first thought was for his briefcase, but it was safe beneath his left hand. His fellow occupant wore a flat bonnet, similar to a French beret, with a badge that combined a cross, a unicorn and a wreath of thistles, and his tunic had a shoulder flash bearing the word 'Canada'.

'Polish, huh, sir?' The young man smiled and shook his head ruefully, as if being Polish was a matter of some regret. 'I guess that would account for the nightmares. I'm Canadian, so I reckon that makes us both foreigners. Say, I have a couple of Polish guys in my outfit. One of them comes from Kraków – you know it?'

Kalisz returned his smile. 'My English...' He shrugged. 'Only for ordering pint of bitter, yes?'

The captain tried again two or three times more, offering a drink from a silver flask, but gave up when Kalisz closed his eyes again. When he opened them the train was approaching a station and he was alone. He wasn't certain, but he had a feeling he'd just gone through some kind of test.

Something must have gone wrong with the carriage heating, because Kalisz was forced to huddle for warmth beneath his greatcoat as sleet and hail swept out of the darkness to hammer the windows. Dark, mysterious shadows flashed past, and he guessed they were in the suburbs of a city, though the only other evidence was an occasional glint of light from a poorly fitted blackout curtain. Thankfully, a young officer, accompanied by a burly military policeman, was waiting on the platform to drive him across Glasgow, to where he was to catch his connection for Fort William.

'If you follow the corporal, sir, he'll show you to your train. Good luck, sir.'

Kalisz returned his salute and hurried after the MP corporal as he disappeared inside a cavernous hall beneath a roof of girders and glass. At a platform to Kalisz's left, a small train of four soot-stained carriages waited behind an ancient green locomotive with LNER painted in large letters on the tender. The corporal marched the length of the train, swinging his free arm as if he was on parade, and Kalisz became aware that his little party had become the focus of hostile glares from every man on this side of the carriages. When they reached the front of the train, Kalisz's escort placed his suitcase in the carriage, turned, saluted and strode off without a word. Kalisz climbed gratefully aboard.

Every eye in the coach turned to stare at him through a haze of cigarette smoke so thick it caught in his throat. Like the previous train, this one was packed with soldiers, but soldiers of a very different nature. These were men who reminded Kalisz of the wolves he sometimes encountered in the High Tatras. Lean and hungry, they wore normal British army battledress, but with green berets either on their heads or tucked in their shoulder straps. Shoulder patches proclaimed them as Royal Marine Commandos, along with a badge that seemed to combine an eagle, a rifle and an anchor.

The carriage lurched into motion and Kalisz would have fallen over his suitcase if his neighbour – a tall Commando wearing sergeant's stripes – hadn't gripped his arm. 'I think this must be yours, sir.' He nodded to a vacant seat to the right of the aisle. Kalisz saw that it had a piece of cardboard with the word 'Reserved' placed on it. He muttered his thanks and reached for his case. Before he could pick it up, another Commando took it and placed it in the luggage rack above his seat. As they left the station the lights flicked off, and Kalisz sat in the darkness with men all around him, wondering why he'd never felt so alone.

'He's a cop, I can tell them a mile away.' The words in an unfamiliar language and with a strong regional accent took time to filter into Kalisz's brain. 'Why else would he have a Redcap for an escort?'

'Shut up, Briggsy.' Another voice. 'He's a major and he'll hear you.'

'Think I care?' said Briggsy. 'He's a Polack. A Polack pinched my girl. Those fookers are worse than the Yanks. Why's he here, if not to spy on us? We should chuck him out of the door when we get up north. No one will ever find him.'

'You're just worried he's after those dodgy watches you keep trying to sell us.' Someone laughed.

'Save your breath, the lot of you.' Kalisz recognised the voice of the sergeant who'd helped him. 'From what I hear, we're going to need it. And, Briggs? He's not just a major. They kept the train back a whole hour for him. That means he's important, which is more than you are. The next time you open your mouth, it'll be you who's going out of the door.'

Kalisz relaxed and closed his eyes. Maybe he wasn't so alone after all.

Fort William. Midnight. No sign of a fortress – just a small station in a small town, beside a vast expanse of water that shimmered and glittered in the moonlight. Outside the station a convoy of lorries waited, and the Commando NCOs herded their men aboard. They rumbled off into the night, leaving Kalisz, his suitcase, and four other men on the tarmac. The others huddled together, smoking and muttering, arms hunched to try to keep the icy wind from piercing the battledress blouses that were their sole protection. Kalisz picked up a few words: not English, certainly; southern European, perhaps Italian or Slovenian.

Eventually another canvas-covered truck appeared and drew up beside them. 'Major?' The driver saluted and picked up Kalisz's suitcase. 'You're in the front with me. You lot,' he roared. 'In the back. The back.' He pushed the suitcase inside and rapped the tailgate of the lorry to emphasise the order. 'God only knows where they get them from.'

They drove north out of the village before turning left at a junction. Almost immediately the driver stopped in the centre of the road. Kalisz looked on, bewildered, as he jumped out of the truck, returning moments later with a pair of basket-shaped metal grilles, which he put under his seat. 'We'll take our chances with the Luftwaffe, if that's all right with you, sir. If I drive this road with blacked-out headlights, they'll be having their breakfast before we get to Arisaig, if we get there at all. More likely, we'd end up in a loch.'

Kalisz saw what he meant as they progressed along the narrow potholed road that wound its way along the lake shore, making frequent stomach-churning detours into the hills or lurching across crumbling stone humpback bridges. At one point they were forced to halt by an enormous red deer stag that stood in the centre of the road for a full minute, daring them to try to pass, before becoming bored and ambling into the trees.

About an hour into the journey, the driver noticeably slowed.

'Is there a problem, Private?' Kalisz asked.

'You'll see, sir,' the driver muttered. 'Or maybe not.'

A mile further on, they rounded a sharp bend to find a fallen pine tree blocking the road.

' 'Ere we go again.' The driver shook his head and Kalisz froze as four or five men with blackened faces, dressed in dark overalls, appeared in the headlights, rifles aimed at the cab. 'Nothing to worry about, sir,' the driver assured him. 'It happens all the time up here. The place is a madhouse.'

Something metallic tapped on the driver's side window. The soldier wound down the glass to reveal a shadowy figure dressed identically to the men in the headlights, pointing a not so shadowy revolver at the occupants of the cab.

'If you'll just sign this piece of paper confirming that the passengers in this Bedford are all dead, please,' the ambusher said with an easy drawl, 'and that it's been destroyed by Mills bombs, we'll forget about your flouting of the blackout regulations.'

'Of course, sir.' The driver pulled a pencil from behind his ear and signed with a flourish. 'My pleasure.' Meanwhile, the men in front had already dragged the fallen tree to one side. When the road was completely clear they drove on as if nothing had happened.

Kalisz waited until his heartbeat slowed. 'Just out of interest, Private, how did you know he was an officer.'

'That accent, sir,' the driver said with a grin. 'It's unmistakeable.' He chuckled. 'He's going to have fun tomorrow explaining to his CO how he came to ambush Charlie Chaplin.'

It must have been close to two in the morning when they turned off the road and down a narrow track. A hundred yards on, the driver parked the truck in a moonlit courtyard in front of what appeared to be a very grand house. 'This is us, sir. I'm sure somebody will be out to welcome you soon.'

Kalisz got down from the cab and stretched his legs. One of the young men emerged from the rear with his suitcase and laid it on the gravel at his feet with a shy smile, before joining his friends. They stood around waiting and smoking, and in the silence Kalisz could hear the soft murmur of waves crashing on a shore somewhere in the darkness.

Without warning, an object sailed through the air to drop not far away. There was an enormous explosion like a clap of thunder, accompanied by a flash of incredibly bright light. Blinded and deafened, Kalisz was under the lorry before he even realised he'd moved, his hand reaching for a non-existent pistol beneath his left armpit and his mind trying to work out what calibre of artillery was targeting them. The others stood around, bewildered, crouching in a protective huddle as another two explosions echoed from the building's walls and lit up the impressive frontage.

As the ringing in his ears faded, a pair of bedroom slippers appeared in front of Kalisz, followed soon after by a moustached face, as the owner, wearing a worn greatcoat over striped pyjamas, bent to study him.

'You must be Zamoyski,' the man said. 'Major Frank Dempsey.' He offered his left hand to help Kalisz out from under the truck. Kalisz noticed that he'd lost his right just above the wrist, leaving the sleeve empty. 'Welcome to Arisaig House.'

'What...?' When Kalisz straightened, he discovered that his knees were shaking.

'Oh, this...' Dempsey laughed. 'A traditional greeting for the new chaps. Just our little reminder that here at STS 21 you must always expect the unexpected. I must say, Major, you're the fastest man I've ever seen in an emergency, and I've seen a few. That will certainly stand you in good stead during your time here.'

'I suppose I must take that as a compliment.' Kalisz brushed damp leaves from his coat and picked up his briefcase from the gravel.

'Very much so. Hodges?' Dempsey called to the truck driver. 'Get these chaps to the pier and let Grundy know they're to be settled in up at Meoble Lodge.' He turned to Kalisz again. 'I'll look after you, Major. We've put you in the main house as it's more convenient for the... er, bodies. The colonel will see you at zero nine hundred hours – that would be nine a.m. – so I'd advise an early breakfast. He's very keen for you to do your job and be on your way.'

'Bodies?' Kalisz blinked. 'I was only told of one body. Krystina Kowolska.'

'Goodness.' Dempsey chewed his lip. 'That is unfortunate. A breakdown in communications, no doubt. Still, all will be explained in the morning.'

CHAPTER 7

30 December 1943

Nine a.m.

'His name was Jean-Marc Fontaine, a French-Canadian officer training for his first mission. He was known to be infatuated with Krystina. I'm surprised they didn't tell you this in London, Major Zamoyski. I fear you may have wasted your time entirely.'

The speaker sat at the far side of a polished wooden desk. Lieutenant Colonel Baldwin wore thick spectacles that gave him the goggle-eyed look of a startled frog, and he had the air of a disciplinarian school-master. He didn't hide his distaste either for the proceedings or the man opposite. A slim woman in uniform sat by the tall window in the corner of the office, with her legs crossed and a notebook and pencil in her hands. Kalisz couldn't help noticing that she didn't take any notes.

He'd spent the night in a small but comfortable room at the rear of the house, and been woken at seven by a knock on the door. When he'd washed and shaved, he'd enjoyed a surprisingly good breakfast of smoked fish, eggs and the dusty bread that seemed the British army's staple diet.

'May I ask how the gentleman died?' Kalisz asked.

'A bullet wound to the right side of the head.' Baldwin sniffed. 'He was found with a pistol in his right hand. It seems clear to me, Major Zamoyski, that the two casualties were involved in some kind of lovers' tiff, in which Warrant Officer Kowolska sadly died. Her lover then tried to cover up her death by making it look like a suicide, before being taken by a fit of remorse and shooting himself.'

'That seems a perfectly reasonable explanation under the circum-stances,' Kalisz acknowledged.

'I'm glad we're in agreement,' Baldwin said. 'MacDonald, the local constable, would have been perfectly capable of carrying out the investigation without any interference from London. I expect you to complete your inquiries and submit a final report in a day or two at most. An open-and-shut case.'

'You have my assurance that I will conduct my inquiries with all the thoroughness the case merits.' Kalisz could feel the woman's eyes on him. He'd barely glanced at her when he'd entered the room and taken his seat. Just a fleeting impression of studied indifference, wrapped in a uniform and topped by a mane of mahogany-brown that fell to her shoulders in waves. Yet there was something almost interrogative in her silence. A feeling of every word being measured, and perhaps doubted.

Baldwin removed his glasses and rubbed them with a cloth whisked from his tunic pocket. 'You must understand, Major Zamoyski, that I am responsible for ten facilities – Special Training Schools – at Arisaig and in the surrounding area. Each of them makes a considerable input into the war effort, and several house men –' a covert glance at the figure in the corner – 'and women, preparing for missions that could affect the entire course of the war. Thanks to this nonsense... do not think me callous, Major, but like any military unit, we have our share of losses. Accidents happen and people die, more frequently than I would like. Now, thanks to this business, I have orders to lock down the entire process. Those men you arrived with last night are destined for a remote lodge which was empty at the time of the deaths, but otherwise no one will arrive and no one will leave until I have your report. Missions – vital missions – will be delayed or cancelled entirely. That is why I hope you will expedite your investigation with the utmost celerity.'

Kalisz nodded his understanding of the need for a swift outcome. 'Then I should get started.' He picked up his briefcase and rose from his chair. 'Perhaps if I could be shown the murder scene and the bodies of the deceased?'

'Of course,' Baldwin said. 'Flight Officer Devereux will show you the way. Like the victim, she is a member of our Women's Auxiliary Air Force, and the liaison officer sent by the War Department to ensure you receive all the help you require. She'll introduce you to our medical officer, who examined the bodies.'

Flight Officer Devereux stood and brushed down her skirt. She wore a close-fitting tunic in what Kalisz now thought of as RAF blue, and something about the quality and fit made him suspect it had been tailored for her, rather than being standard issue. It had four large pockets, a broad belt at the waist and polished brass buttons. Two pale blue stripes at her wrist presumably announced her rank.

'Major Zamoyski.' She held out her hand and he took it. A very feminine hand, warm and delicately boned, but with calluses on the palm that spoke of regular labour of one sort or another. He had a feeling she half expected him to bend and kiss it.

'Flight Officer. I'm very grateful for your assistance.'

'If you'll follow me, sir.'

Baldwin stood to see them out, and Kalisz saluted. He saw the colonel grimace.

'Did I do something wrong, Flight Officer?' he asked as the WAAF led the way down a broad wooden staircase to the hallway.

She looked back over her shoulder. 'You used the Polish two-fingered salute – *Honor I Ojczyzna* – which is rather frowned upon by the British army. The Poles in Britain have been using the open-handed salute since 1942.'

Kalisz's greatcoat hung on a stand in the hall, and he struggled into it while Devereux retrieved an overcoat, her uniform cap and a leather satchel from a cloakroom.

'You speak Polish?' he asked.

'Of course, Major Zamoyski,' she said. They walked from the entrance hall into the courtyard, and she turned right onto a path round the side of the house. 'That's why they assigned me to you. My mother was Polish. How did you want to proceed?'

Kalisz considered for a moment. He liked the fact that they were of a similar height and he could look directly into her eyes. 'For a start, you can stop calling me "Major Zamoyski". I suspect you already know I'm not really a major, and my name isn't Zamoyski. While we're working together you can call me Jan, which is my actual name. If you feel that's too casual, "Investigator" will do fine.'

Devereux studied him with her head slightly tilted, almost as if she was considering some kind of alien species. 'You're very... shall we say forthright? – considering we just met five minutes ago, Major Zamoyski. I'm not sure that our ranks or our short period of acquaintance quite warrant that level of informality.'

'Look, *Flight Officer*.' Kalisz heard his tone harden, but he didn't really care. 'I am a Pole, and for the last four years my country has been eviscerated by the Nazis, my people tortured and murdered. If I am abrupt, it is because I don't particularly want to be here. The quicker I get this done and go home, the better it will suit me. Now, you can be of great help – there are things, like that salute, that I don't know about and other things I don't understand – but we need to be entirely candid with each other if this is going to work. I'm a simple policeman. I don't have time for the niceties of military etiquette and playing silly games with made-up names. Is that clear enough?'

'Yes, sir!' Devereux straightened to attention, but there was a glint in her eye that made it a jest. 'By the way, what was it you didn't understand?'

'What is a "fooker"?'

She blinked. 'A "fooker"?'

'Yes. A soldier on the train said, "Those fookers are worse than the Yanks."'

'It is not a compliment,' she said carefully.

'Yes, I had gathered that.'

She hesitated. 'I believe in Polish you would use the word *skurwiel*.' Her cheeks reddened slightly.

'*Skurwiel*.' He smiled. 'Yes, that would make sense. Now I understand.'

'Do you really think you can wrap this inquiry up in a few days, Jan?' Kalisz noted the use of his given name with satisfaction. 'A great deal depends on the outcome.'

'If I am to be Jan, I can't keep calling you Flight Officer,' he said.

'Lucy Devereux.' She held out her hand again. 'Very pleased to meet you, Jan.'

'Likewise… Isn't that what you say in England, Lucy? A good name.' He nodded. 'If the case is as straightforward as the colonel describes it, then perhaps it can be done within his time frame. But whether this is a case of lovers falling out or not, we have a murder here. In my experience, murders are like weeds – they grow and grow until they engulf everything around them. Find a piece of evidence that solves one mystery, and it creates two more. How would I like to proceed? First, I need to know where the bodies are being kept.'

They rounded the corner of the building into beautiful winter sunshine, but the west wind had teeth and its icy bite made Kalisz's eyes water. His room had been at the rear of the house, and he hadn't appreciated its position or its grandeur until this moment. In Poland it would be called a *dwór* – a manor house, and a very grand one at that. Constructed of grey stone with a slate roof, it stood three storeys high and was built around three sides of the courtyard where he'd arrived the previous night. It sat on a raised shelf of land surrounded mostly by forest, but with views over walled gardens and grassland to the shore about five hundred metres away. Seldom had Kalisz experienced air so clear and sharp. The sea shimmered somewhere between grey and blue and green, sometimes encompassing combinations of all three. In the distance, great snow-capped mountains loomed like shadowy, slumbering giants over the ocean, their flanks occasionally turning brown or gold as the sun caught them. For a moment it entirely took his breath away.

'We're fortunate that many of these big estates were built with ice houses for keeping food supplies cool and meat fresh.' Lucy pointed to a patch of trees between the house and the sea. 'And that it's been a particularly cold winter here. That's where they're being kept.'

'And the crime scene?'

'Over there, in those trees to the left of the pasture.'

'Then the bodies can wait. Whatever they have to tell us will keep, but the evidence from the scene will be affected by the elements and by nature. That is where we will start.'

They walked down a set of steep steps to the walled gardens and trudged across the meadow towards a pair of stout brick huts in front of the trees. Kalisz was glad of his new army boots in the wet grass and muddy soil. His companion wore formal, heeled black shoes, and the hesitant way she placed her feet on the springy turf told him she wished she'd chosen footwear more appropriate for the terrain and the weather. He wondered what she'd expected when she'd been assigned to him, and what she'd been told. Was her job to ensure the Polish investigator received the co-operation he needed, or was she here 'to keep an eye on him', as the English said? In any case, he'd be glad of an assistant, and she seemed intelligent enough and eager to help, which was all he asked for in a partner.

'Have you visited the scene?' Kalisz asked.

'You're the detective, Investigator.' For some reason the question appeared to have annoyed her. 'I'm just your dogsbody.'

The unfamiliar word stopped him in his tracks. 'Dogsbody?'

Lucy turned to snap at him, before it occurred to her just how ludicrous the expression must sound to a foreigner. 'Your servant,' she explained. 'The person who does your fetching and carrying.'

'This is good to know.' He smiled.

They reached the trees and Lucy stopped to find her bearings. 'It must be this way,' she said.

A faint path led up a slope into the shadows beneath the pines. From a distance the wood had appeared dense, but the individual trees were well spaced and the ground was relatively clear around them, apart from occasional patches of impenetrable rhododendron bushes. They walked on for perhaps another thirty paces before they emerged into a clearing with a large skeletal tree at the centre. A wooden ladder lay propped against the trunk, and from a branch perhaps four metres above the ground hung a length of rope with a loop at the end.

At the sight of the makeshift gallows, Kalisz's steps faltered and he fought a nausea that made his head spin. For a moment he was back in Warsaw, where such nooses, with their dangling crop of fresh corpses, hung from trees in the parks, from makeshift gallows on street corners, from lamp posts, and from balconies overlooking the boulevards. Mostly the victims were anonymous, but all too often he would see someone he knew staring back at him with vacant, unseeing eyes.

'Are you all right, Jan?'

'Memories,' he said. 'Just memories of home.'

CHAPTER 8

Nowy Sjazd 1, Warsaw

The previous day

'Thank you for seeing me at such short notice, *Hauptsturmführer* Hoth.' A large portrait of a uniformed Adolf Hitler hung on the wall behind Hoth's shoulder and Maria suppressed a shudder of unease. The Nazi leader appeared to be staring directly into her eyes, and she had a horrible feeling he could read her mind.

The head of Department V, and her husband's commander, rose from his desk and extended his hand. After a momentary hesitation, Maria managed to take it without showing the distaste she felt. It was a surprisingly soft hand, and almost femininely delicate for such a large man.

'Please, Mrs Kalisz, take a seat.' Hoth ushered her to the chair on the opposite side of the desk. 'Be assured no thanks are necessary. Everyone here at Nowy Sjazd 1 was shocked to hear that your husband had been struck down by this dreadful disease he contracted in the line of duty. If there is anything we can do – anything at all… Do you have any news?'

'The doctors at the institute in Gdynia say he is gravely ill, but they are confident he can make a full recovery given the right treatment and conditions. He requires complete rest, and it could take some weeks.'

'Of course.' Hoth frowned. 'It must be very difficult for you.'

'That is why I am here, Herr *Hauptsturmführer*.' Maria seized her opening. 'It would be an enormous comfort to me if Stefan and I could visit his father. Even to sit by his bed for an hour would give us some solace.' She put a hand to her mouth to allow herself to gather her thoughts; was she overdoing it? A jug of water sat to one side of the desk, and Hoth filled a glass and handed it to her. She took a sip and swallowed. 'I've been told it could take days, perhaps weeks, if I applied for a travel warrant to Gdynia through the normal channels. I hoped—'

'Of course,' Hoth said briskly. He reached down to open a drawer and placed a form on the leather pad on his desk. He took a gold fountain pen from its holder and began to fill in the details. 'But wait. Surely we can do better than this? I will allocate you a car and an officer to drive you to Gdynia in half the time.'

Maria's heart stuttered. Katya had never anticipated this. Should she accept? A few hours in an official car with no chance of the mysterious 'package' that had arrived at the house from Katya being searched. It was so tempting. But what if the driver insisted on accompanying her to the hospital where the handover was due to take place? Worse, he could be one of Jan's colleagues, who'd want to see his comrade in person and take some kind of report back to Hoth.

She hesitated for a moment, aware that she needed to find just the right tone for what she said next. 'I appreciate your most kind offer, Herr *Hauptsturmführer*, but you must remember that although my husband is a German –' she couldn't bring herself to utter the word 'loyal', though the situation may have warranted it – 'I am a Pole, and, I hope, a patriotic one. Given the circumstances we find ourselves in, I would prefer not to be witnessed taking advantage of an official car provided by the Occupation authorities. This is no reflection on you or your colleagues, of course,' she hurried on. 'I hope you accept my decision in the spirit in which it is given.' This was dangerous territory for a Pole, even one ostensibly married to a German, but Maria felt she knew her man. According to Jan, Hoth – though both a strict disciplinarian and a Nazi – was first and foremost a policeman, and at heart, despite the uniform he wore, a decent man.

Thankfully, his next words confirmed that view.

'I, too, would wish the circumstances were different, Mrs Kalisz.' He picked up the pen and completed the document. 'And were the situation reversed, I have no doubt I would feel the same.' He moved the form aside and replaced it with a piece of headed notepaper. 'With your permission, I will add a short note which will hopefully facilitate your uninhibited passage. One never knows what one will encounter on a journey of this nature.'

Stefan was waiting outside the building, where she'd left him with their luggage under the gaze of the *Ordnungspolizei* guards. They wore great-coats buttoned to the neck against the bitter cold and their ears shone red beneath the rims of their polished steel helmets. She recognised the look on Stefan's face, but knew to wait until they were out of earshot to ask what had caused it.

'They were laughing at me,' he hissed. 'Trying to get me to say stupid things in German. Then, when they were sure I couldn't understand what they were saying, one of them told me I'd soon be going up the chimney like the Jews.'

Maria winced. After the liquidation and levelling of the ghetto, no one in Warsaw had any doubt what 'going up the chimney' meant. 'They were just making fun,' she tried to reassure him.

'No they weren't, Mama.' Stefan's words contained a chill certainty. 'But it doesn't matter. Hating them will make it all the easier when the time comes.'

–

They reached the station with ten minutes to spare, and Stefan carried their suitcase as they manoeuvred their way through a maze of ladders and scaffolding where builders were still repairing the damage caused by Luftwaffe bombs four years earlier. The combination of Hoth's letter and the travel warrant eased their way past the security checkpoints, and Maria breathed a sigh of relief when they took their seats.

Their train was decorated in the livery of the Deutsche Reichsbahn company, but the interior signage confirmed this was a Polish carriage, and being under German control didn't make it move any faster. They crossed the Vistula eastwards and made a circuit of the Praga stations before turning north for Targówek and Toruńska. The first challenge came at Pomiechówek, thirty kilometres into the journey and where they left the authority of the General Government. While they were replenishing water and coal for the engine, police and security officials boarded the carriage to check their papers. Others had their luggage searched, but a cursory glance at Hoth's letter earned Maria and Stefan a nod and a salute. It was very different a few hours later at Iława, where they entered West Prussia and came under the control of Reich District Danzig.

The pretty little lakeside town with its fine buildings was Prussian territory by inclination and tradition, where the locals had voted to become German in the plebiscite of 1920 and celebrated the arrival of the Panzers during the Nazi invasion of 1939. This time, two men in civilian clothes accompanied the railway police and everything about them reeked of Gestapo. The older of the pair was tall and thin, and wore his homburg hat set well back above a broad forehead. Maria held her breath as they approached up the aisle, making no allowances for the time they took or the inconvenience to the passengers. The meticulous way they checked both papers and baggage made her think they were looking for something – or, perhaps, someone – specific. She could feel the tension in Stefan, who sat beside her with the small suitcase Katya had supplied them at his feet. He still believed they were travelling to visit his father, but Maria had felt bound to make him aware of her mission for the Underground. She laid a hand on his, meaning to reassure him, but all it earned her was a grimace of irritation. Despite the chill in the poorly heated carriage, she felt a tiny drop of sweat run down the flesh of her back and she had to suppress a shiver.

'Your papers, please.' The request was made in heavily accented Polish.

Maria handed over their identity cards, travel warrant and the letter from Hoth. The Gestapo man checked the cards, made a point of studying the photographs and their faces, and handed them back. 'Open your case, please.'

'Sir, this letter from *Hauptsturmführer* Hoth of the Warsaw Kripo...' Stefan appealed in German. 'My father is—'

'The Warsaw Kripo has no jurisdiction here, young man,' the Gestapo agent snapped. 'And I don't care who wrote your letter. Open the case. I will not repeat myself again, is that clear?'

Maria took the case from her son and opened it on her knees. The agent grimaced when he saw that it mostly contained her underwear, but he made a show of searching through it. He frowned as his hands touched something solid and drew out a small bottle. He studied it for a moment. 'French perfume?'

'A gift from my husband before he became ill,' Maria said in Polish. 'I believe it came from the head of the *Werterfassung* in appreciation for his work during the liquidation of the ghetto.' She reached into the case. 'This jewellery also.' She opened an ornate jewellery box and showed him the contents. 'Though art deco is not really to my taste.' She held up a gaudy necklace of oddly shaped gold charms.

The German had been about to open the perfume bottle, but he dropped it hastily back into the case and rubbed his hands together. The *Werterfassung* had been set up to exploit Jewish property and possessions looted from the Warsaw Ghetto, and he clearly found any contact with their wares distasteful.

'Very well.' He gave Stefan a hard stare. 'But keep your son under control. Otherwise that mouth of his will get him in trouble, no matter how good his German is.'

'Of course, sir.' Maria lowered her head and made to tidy the contents of the case as the Gestapo and their followers moved on. They waited, hardly daring to breathe, until the train shuddered into motion.

'That nonsense about the *Werterfassung* was a master stroke, Mama.' Stefan grinned. 'He looked as if the bottle had burned his hand.'

Maria flexed her spine, so the papers fixed to the small of her back with surgical tape were a little less uncomfortable. Her heart was pounding so hard it felt as if it was about to burst out of her chest. The perfume bottle and the jewellery had come from Katya, along with the case. Maria had no idea what the contents were – only that they were as important as the papers she carried. If the agent had opened the bottle... She looked at her watch. Three hours until they reached Gdansk and the likelihood of another inspection. She closed her eyes and tried to fight the nausea that threatened to overwhelm her.

'Stefan, there is something you should know about your father.'

CHAPTER 9

Arisaig

9:30 a.m.

Kalisz placed his briefcase on its side among the grass and carefully folded his greatcoat and laid it on top, along with his peaked cap. He ran a hand through his hair and stood for a while, trying to understand precisely what he was seeing. The tree lay directly to his front, twenty paces distant, with some form of yellow cloth tape sealing off everything within a radius of fifteen paces of the trunk. He walked up to the tape, focusing for the moment on the ground beneath the noose. It was disappointing, but just as he'd suspected. The compacted red leaf mould had been disturbed by several pairs of feet. He looked with more hope to the foot of the ladder, where whoever had hung the body from the tree must have stood for at least a moment, but that, too, was unreadable. Naturally, the first instinct of those who'd discovered Krystina's body would have been to check for signs of life, and then to get her down. At that point, presumably, there had been no suggestion of murder, and therefore no reason to assume this was a crime scene. Still, Kalisz dropped to a crouch and studied the tree again, rubbing the leaf mould through his fingers as though the texture of it might open his mind to hitherto unconsidered possibilities.

'What kind of tree is this?' he called to Lucy.

'I don't know. Does it matter?'

'Perhaps.'

'Then I'll find out,' she said.

Kalisz moved to his right, studying the tree and its surroundings from a different angle. There had been a lot of movement to and from the area beneath the branch, but almost all of it from the side closest to the house. Yet as he moved round the taped perimeter, he could just make out a faint trace in the leaves leading up a slight slope to the north-east that could warrant closer investigation. Of course, it might be the tracks of a deer, or a fox – predators would have been attracted by the scent of the body – but it was the first hint of a clue: a single piece of the jigsaw that might eventually make the whole.

'What do you see?' Lucy called.

'The same as you. What I can't see is any suggestion of a second body. Where was it found?'

'I don't know,' she admitted. 'The medical officer was supposed to meet us here, but he hasn't turned up.'

'Then we—' An enormous explosion shattered the silence and echoed through the hills to the north.

'Silly buggers will have used too much dynamite again. They enjoy blowing things up, you know. Especially when it's government property.' The speaker was a short, portly officer who'd appeared on the path behind them. His English had an unusual accent that was melodic to Kalisz's ear, and he carried a brown leather bag in his right hand and a large envelope in his left. 'Major Llewellyn, Royal Army Medical Corps, formerly Royal Welch Fusiliers, but currently seconded to STS 21, for my sins. I'm sorry I'm late, but I thought you'd probably like to see these.'

Llewellyn handed over the envelope and Kalisz, his senses heightened by four years of alcohol deprivation, caught the slightest hint of whisky on the doctor's breath. He pulled the first of several photographic prints from the envelope.

'They've just arrived from the studio in Glasgow,' the major said.

The first photograph showed the tree with a female body in dark clothing hanging by the neck below the branch. Her face was hidden by a curtain of dark hair, and the head was tilted to one side at an angle that would have been impossible had she been alive.

'This was taken before the scene was disturbed?' Kalisz asked.

Llewellyn winced. 'I'm afraid not, laddie. By the time I arrived they'd already managed to get poor Krystina down. When I examined her and discovered she couldn't have died in the manner that was being suggested, I insisted they recreate the scene exactly as they found it. I hope I did right?'

'Of course.' Kalisz managed a wintry smile, reflecting that the contamination of the scene could now be multiplied by two. 'I will need the name of every man who was present.' He went through the photographs one by one. They showed the same scene taken from different angles that might tell him something later. Then the image changed.

'Where was this taken?' He showed the major a photograph of a male lying face down among a clump of bushes. His left arm was sprawled to one side, and the right angled towards his head. He held some kind of pistol in his hand.

'A little to the north of the tree. That would be this way.' Llewellyn pointed up the slope and set off at an amble, with Kalisz and Lucy in his wake. 'We only found him by accident. Almost as if he'd been so ashamed of what he'd done, he'd hidden himself away.'

They walked what seemed a surprising distance through the trees before the major found what he was looking for. 'Here it is.' He pointed to a bush surrounded by the same yellow cloth tape. 'This photograph was taken before the body was moved in any way, of course,' he said, with just a touch of acid.

Kalisz considered the bush and its proximity – or lack of it – to the tree, and the nearby Arisaig House. 'I forgot to ask...' He directed his question to Lucy. 'Did Krystina have a room in the main house?'

'No, she shared a cottage in the grounds with her... with another student.'

'And Jean-Marc Fontaine?'

Llewellyn frowned. 'His group was based at Borrodale, another large house up towards the road. Why do you ask?'

Kalisz ignored the question. 'How far?'

'Two hundred yards or so up the hill, through the trees.'

'I see.' Kalisz nodded thoughtfully. 'Perhaps we may look at the bodies now?' They walked downhill past the cordoned-off tree and Kalisz picked up his briefcase, coat and cap. 'One more thing, Major Llewellyn... Where did the ladder come from? Judging by your photographs, it must have been used by the killer to suspend Krystina Kowolska from the tree, as well as to take her down. I assume it has been checked for fingerprints?'

'Yes, MacDonald, the local constable, examined it. It turns out that bare timber is not the most conducive surface to facilitate the forensic art, as it were. In short, he detected nothing of interest. As to the ladder's

49

previous whereabouts... I suppose the most likely place is the shed in the walled garden.'

'Then perhaps we should check,' Kalisz said to Lucy. 'And I think we can move the rope now.'

The 'ice house' was actually a small man-made cavern hacked from the rock and reached by a set of narrow steps that led to a wooden door. Even Kalisz had to crouch down to enter. Inside, the gloom, the musty dampness and the smell of death reminded him of the sewers beneath the Warsaw Ghetto, where he might have been still, but for the sacrifice of a few brave men and women. A sudden light filled the vaulted chamber and banished the memory. Two clothed bodies lay side by side in the centre of the floor, illuminated by the small torch Lucy had taken from her shoulder bag, with blocks of melting ice arranged around them.

'It's the best we could do,' Llewellyn apologised. 'There's no shortage of customers around here, but our masters decided proper mortuary facilities were not part of the requirement for this type of establishment.'

There was plenty of height in the centre of the chamber, but Kalisz had to push past the bulky medical officer and step over the corpse of Jean-Marc Fontaine to reach the lifeless vessel that was all that remained of Krystina Kowolska. It always struck him as a waste when a young person died, but he found it even more so in a case where the victim had been so vibrant and full of potential. Oddly, much that was superficially beautiful about her remained in the serene features. Her eyes were closed and she might have been asleep, but for the grey-green pallor of early decomposition that had settled on her flesh. She wore some kind of camouflage smock over a soldier's serge battledress jacket and trousers, and her feet were encased in scuffed army boots.

'She—'

'Please.' Kalisz cut the medical officer off. 'I must see for myself. Is this normal dress for your trainees?' He pulled back the smock to reveal the dead woman's neck.

'The Denison smock would only be worn if it was particularly cold or wet, but otherwise, yes.'

Kalisz studied the angled furrow where the rope had bitten into Krystina's flesh, and the abrasions it had caused. As he had expected, it didn't run the full circumference of the slim neck. Instead, the nape was unmarked where the knot had been pulled up and away from the body by the suspending rope. There were none of the signs of asphyxia you would expect from a suicide, and when he moved his fingers over the back of the neck he could feel a complete break of the third vertebra.

'Does your examination agree with my conclusions?'

Llewellyn couldn't hide his anxiety.

'If you mean that she was already dead when the body was suspended, yes,' Kalisz said. 'Her neck was broken there –' he touched his finger to the cold flesh of the nape – 'in a manner I would describe as quite deliberate in its methodology, perhaps even clinical. That should give us an initial avenue of investigation.'

'I wish you luck with that.' Llewellyn puffed out his cheeks. 'One of the first things every soldier who trains in Lochaber is taught to do is how to kill a sentry quickly by breaking his neck. That would make every man within about ten miles of here a suspect.'

'Nevertheless, an autopsy will tell us more.' Kalisz hid his frustration. 'What did you make of these streaks of dark grease beneath her chin?'

'Good God,' the medical officer exploded. 'How could I not have noticed? When she was found she had black camo paint on her face. Some fool must have wiped it off.'

'Camo paint?' Kalisz turned to where Lucy was making notes by the light of her torch.

'Camouflage paint,' she explained. 'The Commandos use it to blacken their faces and break up their features for night exercises or operations.'

'And was Krystina on a night exercise on the evening she died?'

'I don't believe so,' Llewellyn said. 'But a look at the training log will tell us for certain.'

Kalisz moved to the second corpse: a young man in his twenties with swarthy, handsome features and dark hair, matted with blood at the right temple. He took the head and gently turned it so he could see the entry wound in the skull. 'So...' He frowned and considered for a moment. His companions watched in puzzlement as he immediately abandoned the head for the corpse's feet.

'Is something wrong?' Lucy asked.

Kalisz looked up. 'Only that this man was never near the tree where Krystina was discovered, he did not shoot himself, and he was not killed by the pistol in the photograph. We are now looking at two murders.'

CHAPTER 10

'That's impossible,' Llewellyn spluttered. 'How can you tell all that within thirty seconds and without making a proper examination?'

'It's simple enough if you know what you're looking for,' Kalisz assured him. 'The pistol in his hand in the photograph is a Browning 9mm, a comparatively powerful handgun. In fact, the muzzle velocity is such that if he'd used it to kill himself in this fashion, he'd probably have blown half his head off. Then there's the wound itself. It's from a smaller calibre weapon, probably a 7.65mm round.'

'How can you be so certain, Jan?' Lucy asked. 'The difference must be minimal.'

Kalisz rose from the body with a grunt and rubbed his back. 'After the surrender in Warsaw –' he ignored her warning look – 'when it became clear what was happening to the Jews, we had a large number of suicides, quite often entire families. Many of the city's garrison handed over their sidearms to friends and acquaintances before they became prisoners of war, so there was no shortage of handguns. If you're going to kill your family, better you use a pistol than a kitchen knife, yes? The Nazis, of course, didn't require these deaths to be investigated, but the Germans are a meticulous race, and they did want them recorded. So I must have seen a hundred and more people with holes like this in their heads. In a torso wound, it would be much more difficult to tell, but there is little or no elasticity in bone. A 7.65mm hole is a 7.65mm hole. Believe me, this was not made by a Browning 9mm. There is also the fact that a determined suicide will always place the muzzle directly against the skull. Here we have no sign of a powder burn from the muzzle blast, not even singeing of the hair, so our friend was shot from a distance.'

He moved back to Krystina and raised her right hand to examine it, followed by the left. 'No sign of defensive wounds,' he said, almost to himself.

'You mentioned the tree,' Llewellyn said.

'Yes,' Kalisz nodded. 'You remember we talked about the tree?' he said to Lucy. 'I'd never seen a tree like it. Unless I'm mistaken, it is quite exotic. The fallen leaves are a very distinctive red colour and they've decayed into a thick layer that covers the entire area beneath the branches.' He moved to Krystina's feet and removed her right boot. 'You can see definite traces at the heel and among the metal studs, where her body has been dragged across to the tree. Doctor, take a look at the male victim's boots, please, and tell me what you see.'

'There's only mud. No sign of any red leaf mould at all.'

'Precisely. So he was never near the tree where Krystina Kowolska was found hanging.'

'Christ,' Lucy hissed.

Kalisz had removed the dead woman's army sock to reveal her foot. Every toenail was missing, replaced by puckered and twisted flesh. He looked up at Lucy. 'We're going to have to take off their clothes – I assume they've been searched? – to check for any other injuries. You don't have to be here.'

'I originally trained as a nurse, Major.' The storm-grey eyes flashed a challenge. 'I've seen plenty of dead bodies. There were enough and more to spare on the Jarama.'

The snapped rebuff provided Kalisz with not just the information she imparted – he knew that the battle of Jarama had been a particularly bloody episode of the civil war in Spain – but an insight into the qualities and character of his new assistant. He found himself both pleased and surprised. 'Very well.' He nodded. 'Doctor, if you'll look after our male victim, we will deal with the lady.' He moved to the upper part of the dead woman's torso. 'I'll have to cut the smock, tunic and blouse off her. Do you have scissors or a scalpel?'

'I came prepared.' Llewellyn delved in his bag and handed over a large pair of scissors. 'We thought it best to leave their clothes on until you'd had a chance to inspect the bodies.'

'You were right.' Kalisz crouched over the body and, with some difficulty, cut his way through the thick fabric of the smock. 'Did you find anything unusual in their pockets?'

'The students here are encouraged to cultivate anonymity wherever possible, and to only carry what they need. Lieutenant Fontaine had a pack of gum, to which he was habituated, in his top left pocket.

Krystina had the stub of a pencil in her tunic and a small pocket knife in her trousers.'

'Her other foot is the same,' Lucy announced. 'God, the agony the poor woman must have suffered.'

'Every student who passes through the doors of Arisaig and the other training houses knows it could be their fate to fall into the hands of the Gestapo,' the doctor said solemnly. 'It is a testament to Krystina's character that she went through such pain, but was prepared to go back. I doubt I could have done it.'

Lucy wrestled with the dead woman's trousers. 'Look at these pink spots on her lower legs.'

'It's called lividity,' the doctor said without looking up. 'Where the blood pooled in her legs after she was hanged.'

'And which tells us she was hanging for some time,' Kalisz said.

'You must remember, Major, that this was Christmas morning.' Llewellyn's voice took on a defensive note. 'Even though this is a military establishment, there weren't many people about. Most of the staff had been celebrating at the hotel in Morar and were late abed. I was one of them. It must have been after nine when the body was discovered.'

'"Most"?' Kalisz repeated.

'The colonel didn't go, or Bill Sykes –' Llewellyn worked methodically to strip the dead Fontaine of his clothing – 'which, frankly, was unusual, because Bill likes a pint.'

'Didn't anybody notice she was missing?' Kalisz asked. 'She must have shared lodgings with someone.'

'She did, but Krystina's nocturnal wanderings were part of Arisaig legend. She was never where you thought she would be and, sometimes, if she turned up on time, or even at all, you'd be surprised.'

'What are those?' Lucy interrupted.

Kalisz had cut away the dead woman's brassiere to reveal her breasts, which were pockmarked by dark brown spots, each the size of a thumbprint.

Kalisz studied the scars. 'They are cigar burns, Flight Officer Devereux.' He saw her wince, and it took an effort to keep his voice steady. There must have been six or seven marks on each breast, one of them directly on the nipple itself. 'A favoured Gestapo technique. The cigar is drawn upon until the tip is a glowing red and then applied to the flesh. As effective as a red-hot poker, but much more manageable.'

'May I borrow your torch, Flight Officer?' Llewellyn left the dead man to crouch over Krystina's body. He ran the torchlight over the dead flesh, experimenting at various angles. 'I thought so,' he said. 'You can only see it in a certain light because of the decomposition, but there are definite hints of bruising on her stomach and forearms… the thighs, too.'

Kalisz frowned. 'Yes, so faint I would have missed it if you hadn't pointed it out.' He peered at the marks. 'But these bruises didn't happen in the last few days, and she was in Gestapo custody in July. A bruise isn't a cigar burn. It would have faded entirely in five months.'

'So she must have suffered a beating more recently?' Lucy said. 'This isn't the first time she'd been attacked.'

'No, but the question is,' Kalisz mused aloud, 'whether the perpetrator was the person who killed her, or someone else entirely? It occurs to me that Krystina Kowolska, for all her beauty and talent, was a most unfortunate and unlucky young woman. Attack or accident, this must have caused her intense pain at the time. Doctor, could it be that she consulted you?'

Llewellyn considered for a moment. 'The people who come here to train are broadly of two types – either introverts, in the reticent sense, or extremely self-disciplined. In either case, they must be mentally and physically strong, or they would not survive the course. They are not the type to show weakness, and Krystina was no different—'

'So what's our next step?' Lucy interrupted.

'First we'll need a proper autopsy, to establish the precise details of the deaths.' Kalisz looked to Llewellyn.

'We call them post-mortems in Scotland, old chap, and they're not my strong point. In any case, we have no facilities here. It's possible that the military hospital at Onich has a surgeon capable of doing the job, but Glasgow is the nearest place with the proper facilities and the expertise.'

'Glasgow, then,' Kalisz agreed. 'There's little doubt about the cause of death and we already have a fairly rigid time frame. Make sure to let them know Mr Churchill wants it to be a priority, and they are to inform us immediately if they discover anything surprising.'

'Churchill,' Llewellyn muttered. 'That explains a lot.'

'We'll go over the scene properly later,' Kalisz said to Lucy. 'Shall we say after lunch? I'll need a long tape measure, and surgical gloves and bags for removing any potential pieces of evidence. I'll also need help. It would be good if you could gather all those involved in the recovery of Krystina's body for the working party. That way, we roast two pieces of meat over one fire.'

'I beg your pardon?'

'You don't have this saying in England? To do two jobs at the same time.'

Lucy laughed, which seemed odd while sharing a makeshift crypt with two corpses. 'We say "to kill two birds with one stone".'

'Yes?' Kalisz shrugged. 'Just so. Thank you for your help, Major Llewellyn. One further thing occurs to me. The autop— The post-mortem should prioritise the removal of the bullet from Lieutenant Fontaine's skull, and we need to arrange a ballistics report.'

'I'll take care of that,' Lucy said.

'Good. We should now interview the housemates of our two victims, but first I have an unpleasant task to complete.'

'What task?'

'I have to tell Colonel Baldwin that his open-and-shut case is twice as open as he expected, and is unlikely to be closed for quite some time.'

CHAPTER 11

OPERATION BISHOP

Monts du Lyonnais

The stuttering gazogene truck pulled off the road to allow a long line of Wehrmacht lorries, packed with soldiers in grey-green uniforms, to squeeze by on the winding, potholed road. 'Boche bastards,' Krystina's driver, Franco, spat from between teeth still clenched on the stinking pipe he'd puffed all the way from Saint-Pierre-de-Palud. 'They'll be off to search for that drop the other night. Bad news for the folks up where you came from.'

When she'd been briefed back in England, they'd told Krystina that Saint-Pierre had a large Polish community, composed of miners recruited to work the town's pyrite deposits. Even so, she'd been surprised when Franco and his wife had spoken to each other in Polish when Henri had dropped her off at their house in the town. It had taken all her willpower not to interrupt in the same language. She'd had no idea what pyrite was until Franco explained it to her. It amused her to think she was travelling in a lorry filled with fool's gold.

A few minutes later they were approaching the outskirts of Vaugneray, a small town midway between the mountains and Lyons, and therefore an ideal link in the chain of resistance that managed to survive here despite the depredations of the Gestapo and their local informers. They turned a sharp bend and Franco cursed.

'Milice.' Four or five young men in dark uniforms, wearing black berets and with shouldered rifles, emerged from a makeshift wooden hut on the verge. One of them stepped into the road and raised a hand for them to halt. Heart thundering, Krystina removed her pistol from the satchel and placed it under her seat out of the way, but still within reach.

Franco eased the truck to a halt. 'Just try to relax.' He pulled back the window. 'Good morning, sirs,' he called cheerfully.

'Your papers.' The young man ignored the greeting.

Franco reached under the dashboard for a tattered *Carte d'identité*, and Krystina rummaged in her satchel and passed him her own. This was the first test of its authenticity, but she had good reason to have faith in the SOE's forgers.

'We're just down from Saint-Pierre with a load of pyrites for the sulphuric acid plant on the other side of the river. Marie, here, is my daughter-in-law. She's taking Fifi to be seen to at the vet's in town.'

'Fifi?'

Krystina lifted the wicker basket in her lap so the militiaman could see what was inside: some kind of cross between a papillon and a Jack Russell, if she was to make a guess. A ball of fluff with a bad temper and sharp teeth that she now bared at the stranger with a vicious snarl.

'She looks healthy enough to me.'

'You'd be surprised.' Franco scowled. 'Shits everywhere. Me, I wanted a truffle hound, but the wife...'

The young man studied the photographs in the identity cards and the occupants of the truck just long enough to know he was making them uncomfortable. Eventually, he handed them back to Franco with an unpleasant smirk. 'On your way.'

Krystina waited until they were round the next bed before she allowed herself to breathe.

'They're worse than the Gestapo,' Franco said, as she returned her pistol to her satchel along with her papers. 'Because they're French and from around here. It's as well you kept your mouth shut, because they can tell which village you come from by your accent.'

When they reached the town, he turned off the street and into a narrow lane, which, in turn, led to a disused stables. Franco parked and helped her unload her suitcase.

'They will be here soon.' He handed her the dog in its wicker basket. '*Bonne chance.*'

'What am I supposed to do with this?'

'Take her to the vet. It's the kind of thing they check.'

When he was gone, Krystina sat on the edge of a decaying wooden horse trough. Franco's wife had given her a piece of ham for the journey, and she fed Fifi small nibbles while they waited. There was a certain comfort in the pistol in her satchel, but she doubted she'd get the chance to use it if they came for her. Even if she did, it would do no good, because the Gestapo would have the place wrapped up as tight as a mummy's shroud. Her only salvation would lie in the L-pill, the rubber-coated cyanide capsule sewn into the collar of her blouse.

Her nose told her she had company before her other senses reacted. The sweet, rich, balsam-heavy scent of someone's eau de cologne. As they closed in she heard soft, barely audible footsteps, each tread placed with the precision of the professional. One was behind her, and the other approaching the door to the front of the stable.

'Eagle.'

The voice was almost in her ear. *Christ, how had he got so close?*

'Raven,' she managed.

'Then you're welcome.' She heard the soft *snick* of a safety catch being placed in the on position.

Krystina turned to face him. Tall and slim with narrow shoulders; a sportsman, was her first thought, perhaps a long-distance runner. Dark hair swept back from a wide brow, and, on his upper lip, a very French pencil moustache. Handsome, in a certain, undefinable way. Not film star handsome, but most definitely so if you were a woman. He was leaning against a pillar in a confident, just short of arrogant, way that stirred something inside her: not quite dislike, but...

'I am Raoul.'

She took his extended hand. 'Marie.'

Fifi produced a little whimper. 'I see you've brought us a new recruit, Marie.' His measured tone suggested things like this happened every day in occupied France.

Krystina told him about being stopped by the Milice. 'Yes.' Raoul nodded thoughtfully. 'Franco was right. It is the sort of thing they would check. As it happens, it suits us perfectly.'

–

'Look happy.' Raoul took Krystina's arm as they walked through the narrow streets towards the town centre. He carried her suitcase and she swung Fifi's basket in her free hand. He wasn't the person with the eau de cologne, but she guessed they weren't far away. 'We're a young couple in love who've just been reunited, and we're looking forward to an afternoon rekindling our passion...' She glanced at him, but he was perfectly serious. 'Chat,' he ordered. 'You must have something to say after such a long journey?'

'Did you know that Saint-Pierre has a pyrite mine?'

'As it happens, I do.'

'The road between Saint-Pierre and Vaugneray is awful, Franco is a crazy driver, and the smoke from his pipe almost suffocated me, but that has its compensations.'

'Yes?'

'Because Fifi suffers from terrible flatulence.'

Raoul laughed. They turned in to the Rue du Dronaud and walked down the hill until they came to a substantial three-storey building. A sign above the main door said 'Vétérinaire'.

She looked at him. 'A coincidence?'

He shook his head. 'Franco is one of the few who know about this place.'

He opened the door and ushered her inside. A young receptionist greeted them in a way Krystina thought appeared awkward or forced. She rose from behind her desk to approach the elderly woman who was the sole occupant of the waiting room. 'Monsieur Doulangard will see Loulou now, madame.'

The woman picked up a small box from the seat beside her, and disappeared through a curtain at the far end of the room.

Krystina stared after her.

'A stick insect,' the receptionist said by way of explanation. She took the basket from Krystina's hand. 'I will see that Fifi gets back to her owner. Franco called from the Gruet house.'

Raoul nodded and led Krystina through a door behind the reception desk, to a set of stairs. She followed him to the top floor.

'I'm told this isn't your first time?'

'I know my way around,' she said.

'You'll be my second in command. Fr— Armand has been doing the job, but he needs to concentrate on his own. You'll meet him soon.'

'I think I already have.' She'd caught the familiar scent of that eau de cologne. Raoul gave her a hard stare, and she vowed not to be too clever in future. Her new organiser was clearly touchy.

They reached the top floor and Raoul opened a door into a quite spacious apartment. A young man lay back on a sofa in the living room with his feet up, reading a newspaper. Krystina knew from the cologne that this must be Armand. Raoul introduced them.

'Call me Freddie,' the young man said cheerfully. 'Everybody else does.' Raoul shook his head at what was clearly an ongoing battle. Freddie got to his feet to shake Krystina's hand. He was as tall as Raoul, with bushy brown hair and an open, guileless face. He had a strong handshake, but a surprisingly delicate grip, his long fingers barely encompassing the top two joints of hers.

'Armand is our WT operator. There are things I need to tell you, but I suppose you need some rest.'

For some reason, Raoul's solicitude lit a little fire in her. It was on the tip of her tongue to say 'because I'm a woman?', but she bit back the retort. 'No thank you, I slept on the journey,' she lied. 'But I haven't eaten properly since the night I landed.'

'I'm sure I can rustle something up,' Freddie said without being asked. 'And I'll take your case through to your room.' He left them alone.

Krystina took a seat on the sofa and Raoul pulled up a chair opposite her.

'What do you think of our little set-up?'

'From what I've seen, it looks pretty secure,' she said briskly. 'People will come and go from the vet's all the time and a few more are unlikely to be noticed. You have a separate exit, a private stairway and the apartment is self-contained. Presumably the middle floor is used as a storeroom, or something of that sort? So you don't have any neighbours to worry about.'

'Exactly.' He looked pleased. 'And there's the added bonus that our landlord can patch up any lightly wounded we have.' He clearly expected more of her approval, but she waited. 'Yes...' The pleased look had frozen on his face. 'Right. Well, our first priority is to gather intelligence and identify targets for future operations.' Raoul went to a sideboard beneath the main window and fumbled at the side until a hidden compartment opened with a sharp click. He returned with a large map in his hands and spread it out on the floor between them. 'Lyons is a strategically important transport link between southern and central France. For our purposes, we assume the Second Front will be launched somewhere on French soil. Whether it's north or south or west, the roads, railways, the Rhône and Saône rivers, and the canals that pass through the city will be vital for the transport of troops, equipment and supplies to combat any invasion.'

Krystina studied the map and one aspect drew her attention. 'So we're looking at the railway lines themselves.' She ran a finger from the city centre to the northern edge of the map. 'Bridges, tunnels, convenient sites for ambushes?'

'That's right, and places where the rivers or canals could be easily blocked by a strategically placed sinking.'

'It's going to take an awful lot of people.'

'Yes,' he agreed. 'And that's the problem. People we don't have. The Gestapo rolled up the previous Lyons circuit in a single night. A hundred and sixty people dragged off to the cells at Montluc Prison, including the organiser, radio operator, couriers and almost all the group leaders. It understandably left those who survived more than a little nervous. Most went to ground and are keeping their heads down. A few have been making overtures, but who can we trust?'

'That takes time and patience,' she said.

'Time we don't have, either. But we've been working on it. We've identified someone who, on the face of it, would make a good group leader. We've been watching him, but it's about time we dangled a handkerchief in his direction. That will be your job. We'll let you take a look at him, starting tomorrow.'

CHAPTER 12

Arisaig House

11:15 a.m.

'Perhaps we should bring in the SIB, sir?'

Baldwin tapped the top of his walnut desk with an army-issue pencil. 'Of course I value your opinion, Flight Officer.' Even Kalisz could tell his tone implied just the opposite. 'But I feel the last thing we need is the Special Investigation Branch trampling over Arisaig and its environs with their size eleven flat feet. It's bad enough Constable MacDonald wanting to charge anyone who's so much as mislaid a tin of bully beef.'

Baldwin had reacted with barely suppressed fury to Kalisz's announcement that he was now investigating two murders. However, he clearly realised that, given the political implications, he had no option but to allow the inquiry to run its course. His only stipulation was that it must be carried out with the utmost urgency.

'If time is a priority,' Lucy persisted, 'surely more manpower to help Major Zamoyski—'

'The orders I have been issued suggest that Major Zamoyski is eminently capable of carrying out the investigation on his own – and, indeed, that it's advisable he does so. What is your opinion, Major?'

'I am your guest, sir.' Kalisz bowed his head. 'I am happy to abide by your decision.' He heard Lucy suppress a snort of indignation.

'The Special Investigation Branch is a perfectly laudable and competent organisation,' the colonel continued. 'But their true specialism is theft – the large-scale plunder of army stores from dockyards, bases and depots to supply the black market. Cigarettes, sugar, petrol coupons and army rations are their stock-in-trade. Not murder.'

From his own experience in Warsaw, Kalisz suspected this was not quite true. The people who ran black markets, and those who supplied

63

them – civilian gangsters, rogue officers and soldiers, and deserters – were perfectly capable of murder. He was sure the military investigators would have encountered many such cases. But Baldwin was not finished.

'Look at these complaints.' The colonel pulled a sheaf of letters from his desk drawer. 'Some madman decided it would be a good idea to poach a salmon or two to supplement his rations, and ended up killing a hundred of them in the pool with a hand grenade or dynamite. His lordship's rage at the sight sends a shiver through me yet. The illicit shooting by torchlight and subsequent butchery of red deer – and, God help me, even a Highland cow. Breaking and entering and theft from about half a dozen empty lodges and houses. Theft of vehicles for the purposes of what the Americans call "joyriding". The poaching is one thing, but that grenade or dynamite must have come from army stores. Likewise, the rifle that killed the deer. I would venture that half the men here have an illegal weapon in addition to their officially supplied handgun. That's actually fine with me, because they have to get used to carrying them and keeping them hidden, but the SIB would have a field day. I wouldn't be surprised if they tried to close us down. The prime minister wouldn't allow it, of course, but it could cause us no end of trouble. However, I will concede this... If the culprit is on active service and an arrest is to be carried out, it is only right that it should be made by the British authorities.'

'That would be agreeable to my superiors, I'm sure,' Kalisz said. 'Given the identities of the victims and the method of their deaths, I will need your permission to question every man and woman under your command. For the moment, I intend to concentrate my inquiries on Arisaig House and its environs, but it may be necessary to broaden the search to the outlying schools.'

Baldwin hesitated for a moment, his lips pursed. 'Very well, I'll draw up a letter and a list of houses and their locations, and forward them to Flight Officer Devereux. STS 23 and one other lodge were empty at the time, so I won't waste your time by including them. Some of the others are quite remote or only accessible by boat. I'll leave it up to you to decide if it's worth the effort.'

'We'll also need transport, sir,' Devereux pointed out.

'I'll include a chitty that will give you access to a vehicle from the motor pool and a warrant for a boat from Mallaig to the outlying schools. But I must stress, Major Zamoyski, that it is entirely up to the men you will meet whether they speak to you or not. They have been taught here that their very survival depends on anonymity and silence, and once that becomes ingrained, it becomes a very hard habit to break. Not everyone has been informed of Krystina's death, but most are aware there is a *hitch* that is delaying departures and curtailing training. Your appearance will undoubtedly be associated with that hitch and your presence will be resented. These students have been preparing for their missions over many months, here and elsewhere. In some cases, they have given up everything. They will not take kindly to anyone who stands in their way.' Kalisz and Lucy rose and turned to go, but the colonel wasn't finished. 'One other thing. The prime minister clearly did not intend this to be an open-ended arrangement. I will give you ten days, and inform my superiors that I will expect your report within that time, whether you have succeeded or not. Is that understood?'

'Of course, sir,' Kalisz said. 'I have one more request, and a question. The Krystina Kowolska file handed to me in London was hardly what you would call comprehensive. It contained a note suggesting I would find greater illumination in the service files you keep here at Arisaig House. Also, I know nothing of Lieutenant Fontaine.'

'Of course, I'll arrange for you to have limited, supervised access to the filing room. And your question?'

'May I ask why you did not attend the Christmas Eve gathering at the Morar Hotel?'

Baldwin blinked and his lips set in a hard line. 'All right.' He nodded slowly. 'I suppose you must ask these intrusive questions of everyone, even me. I prefer not to attend these events unless it is really necessary, to avoid any notion of familiarity with my junior officers. This is not a gentleman's club – we are here to do a job. On Christmas Eve I worked late, drank a small glass of whisky and went to bed. I was having breakfast the next day when Major Dempsey approached me discreetly to say that a body had been found. I finished breakfast and called Constable MacDonald, as the area's civilian authority. Does that satisfy you?'

'Of course, sir. I'm told another officer resident in this house also missed the gathering. His rank escapes me, but I believe the name was Sykes.'

'Major Sykes.' Baldwin reached for the telephone on his desk. 'You'll want to speak to him, I assume?'

'If it is convenient, sir.'

'He was due to be teaching pistol shooting to the chaps from Meoble Lodge today at Glasnacardoch, but under the circumstances we thought it advisable to keep them at the house.' He turned away and spoke a few words into the phone. 'Good,' he said. 'Bill will be waiting for you in the drawing room. Don't be fooled by his mild-mannered demeanour, Major Zamoyski. Bill Sykes may look like a retired bank manager, but he's far and away the most dangerous man in Arisaig.'

'Was that a threat?' Kalisz asked as they descended the stairs.

'I'm hoping it was more of an observation.' Lucy smiled. 'And what was all that meek "I am your guest" nonsense? Surely you'd appreciate some help if it gets you back to Warsaw more quickly?'

'To be honest,' Kalisz said, 'I much prefer working alone. And if I need any help, I always have you.'

'I'm beginning to think you're a bit of a charmer, Major Zamoyski.'

Kalisz smiled. 'Then let us go and see if I can charm the most dangerous man at Arisaig.'

More a benign bishop than a bank manager, in Kalisz's eyes, Major Eric 'Bill' Sykes sat in an armchair opposite them and daintily poured tea from a flower-patterned pot into delicate china cups. Of middle height and perhaps already in late middle age, with receding silver hair, he was dressed in British Army battledress at least one size too large, wore wire-framed glasses, and affected what Kalisz felt certain was an entirely concocted air of mild bemusement.

'Earl Grey, though Lord knows where they get it. Help yourself to milk and sugar, or whatever's your poison. The Spam sandwiches are very tasty once you get used to them. You wanted to know about Christmas Eve, the chief said?'

'Yes. The medical officer said you didn't attend the celebration in Morar, despite being a sociable type.'

'Oh, yes, a sociable type, that's me.' Sykes had the sort of smile that belied his expression. Not a challenge exactly, but... 'I've been suffering from heartburn lately and had a particularly bad attack that evening. So bad, in fact, that I went to the doc. He gave me a couple of spoonfuls of liquefied concrete to ease the indigestion and a pill to help me sleep. I woke up next day right as rain.'

Kalisz felt Lucy stir on the chair next to him, but he willed her to stay quiet. Something told him Sykes needed careful handling, and an interruption might change the course of the interview entirely.

'Were you well enough to join the party that recovered the body of Krystina Kowolska?'

'No,' Sykes said evenly. 'The pill must have been quite powerful—'

'That's a pity,' Kalisz said. 'Your insight would have been valuable.'

'But I did see the bodies later, at the invitation of the medical officer.'

'In the ice house?'

'That's right.'

'And...?'

Sykes smiled. 'Look, Major, why don't we get to the point?'

'What point is that, Major Sykes?'

'The point where you ask me if I killed Krystina.'

'Did you?'

'If I'd killed her, the chief would have put it down as accident, illness or suicide, and you wouldn't be here. See this table...?' He waved a hand at the pot and cups, assorted silverware, sugar bowl and milk jug that separated them. 'I could take any item on there and kill you so thoroughly you wouldn't realise you were dead. I wouldn't even have to bother with the butter knife. That frilly doily would do just fine.'

'You haven't answered my question,' Kalisz persisted.

'No, I didn't kill her.' The mask dropped for a moment and Sykes's voice hardened. 'I trained her, you see, Major, and I take it as a personal affront that she allowed herself to be killed. She was better than that. Tough as teak, aggressive, and totally without pity was our Krystina. Fast, too. Lightning fast. Oh, they'll tell you that she'd lost her edge, but I could see it was still there, buried deep.'

'Just what do you teach here, Major Sykes?' Kalisz frowned at Lucy's intervention, but he sensed the moment of crisis had passed.

'Why, I'm the angel of death, ma'am.' Sykes took a sip of his tea. 'The official name is "silent killing", but the reality is that it's just plain killing, or butchery, if you like. People come to me as meek as lambs, and I teach them to kill with their bare hands, their feet and their teeth, or to use anything to hand. Any weapon is better than none – half a brick, a bottle, a piece of wood, that delicate milk jug there smashed against the table edge and the remains jabbed into your eyes or your throat. The key is to be more aggressive than your enemy. To fight and keep fighting until he goes down, and then kill him. Of course, it saves a lot of time if his back is turned in the first place. Don't look so shocked, ma'am.' A grin split his weathered features. 'There's no room for gentlemen or ladies in this game. It's kill or be killed.'

'And yet, Krystina was killed?' Kalisz resumed.

'Yes, and that's the puzzle.' Sykes got up from the table. 'Let me show you something, Major. If you'll just stand up clear of the table with your back to me. Yes, just like that. Now, relax. See, I place my left arm across your throat, thus.' Kalisz felt muscles like iron tighten across his windpipe. 'I take my right hand and place it just offset on the crown of your head, like this. A simple increase of pressure, and a twist.' Sykes was only going through the motions, but Kalisz could feel the lethal potential in his hands. 'And now, Major, you are officially dead. With the angels, so to speak, or the other chap, if you prefer.'

'Very efficient,' Kalisz congratulated him.

'Very deadly.'

'And yet you said "puzzle"?'

Sykes frowned. 'You know that feeling when you get a little worm in your head telling you something's wrong? Well, I've learned to trust that worm. Maybe it's the technique, or the fact she didn't fight back, but something doesn't fit. I can't work it out now, but if it comes to me I'll let you know.'

'That's all we can ask. Is there anything else you can tell us?'

'Lieutenant Fontaine was not killed by anyone I trained.'

'You're certain?' Kalisz said.

'Watch.' Sykes dropped into a crouch; his hand went to his pocket and a gun appeared with the seamless swiftness of a conjuror's trick. 'Bang, bang.' The pistol was aimed at his heart, and Kalisz knew he would have been dead before he'd even blinked. 'Two shots – always two shots – and directed at the largest part of the body. We teach it until it becomes instinct. If Lieutenant Fontaine had been a clear threat to one of my boys or girls, he'd have had two holes in his chest.'

'Instead, he was found with one in the head, which means—'

'He was executed.'

CHAPTER 13

'I think that man would have killed you without a second thought,' Lucy said.

'He was certainly capable of it.' Kalisz swallowed at the memory of the grip around his neck and the firm hand clamping his head in position. He'd been utterly helpless.

'We only have his word that he was asleep,' she pointed out.

'When he said he could have killed Krystina and made it look like an accident, I believed him. Whether the murder was planned or an act of opportunism, the disposal of the body was hurried, over-complicated and bungled. Our meticulous Major Sykes would have made none of these mistakes.'

Lucy looked at her watch. 'We just have time to interview Krystina's housemate before our helpers gather at the murder scene. Major Dempsey is arranging it. I've asked him to do nothing until you are present.' She led the way along a path from the house down among the woods. 'They shared a small cottage not far from here, just the two of them. Her name is Yvette, though whether that's real or an alias, I don't know, and she was to be Krystina's wireless operator.'

They emerged from the woods twenty or thirty paces from a low stone-built cottage with a slate roof, just in time for Kalisz to catch a glimpse of a khaki-clad figure slipping away through the bushes. He knocked on the painted wooden door, and a few moments later it opened to reveal a diminutive figure wearing battledress beneath the all-engulfing folds of an overcoat several sizes too large.

'Yvette?' They'd agreed Lucy should open any conversation in the hope that speaking to another female would put their subject at ease.

'I am Yvette, yes,' the woman said warily. She had dark hair cut unfashionably short and delicate features that might, fairly, have been described as elfin. 'How can I help you?'

'My name is Flight Officer Devereux, and this is Major Zamoyski. We're here to ask you some questions about Krystina Kowolska. Is this a convenient time?'

A snort of bitter laughter escaped Yvette. 'I have been trapped in this house for two days waiting to answer your questions, even though I've already told them everything I know. So, yes, now is a very convenient time. Please come in.'

'We're sorry you've been inconvenienced.' Kalisz removed his cap and followed Lucy into the cottage. A small table and two wooden chairs sat to the left of the doorway, with an internal door beyond, and a primitive kitchen range to the right, with a lit stove. Another door led from the rear of the kitchen. Condensation ran down the window panes, and Kalisz noted that it had been appreciably warmer in the ice house. 'At least you've been able to have visitors.' It was a statement, but the way he said it made it a question, and a sort of blankness fell over Yvette's face.

She waved to the sink, where a loaf and a small bottle of milk sat on an adjacent wooden board. 'A kindly mess room orderly brought me some rations from the big house.' She managed a smile. 'They could not let me starve, after all. Can I offer you a coffee?'

'Coffee?' Kalisz blinked. 'The true coffee?'

'I do not know, but it is good. Like in France before the war. It is not easy to come by, but somehow Krystina always managed.' The name caught in her throat. She turned away, so her face was hidden, to fill a large metal kettle and place it on the stove. 'She managed to make most things work. It's still difficult for me to believe she won't walk through that door again.'

'I'm sorry.' Lucy exchanged a glance with Kalisz. 'We'll make this as quick and as easy for you as we can. Please, can we sit?'

She and Yvette sat at opposite sides of the table. There was no seat for Kalisz, so he leaned against the sink and waited for the kettle to come to the boil. Lucy began. 'Firstly, you mentioned that you'd already told "them" everything. Do you know who they were?'

'Colonel Baldwin, that oaf MacDonald the policeman, and another man – tall, a civilian wearing a suit, but he gave the impression he outranked the colonel. Not the type you would cross in a hurry.'

'Thank you, Yvette,' Lucy said, as if the other woman had presented her with a precious gift. 'Now, please tell us what you told them. Don't leave anything out.'

'They asked about Christmas Eve – I already knew Krystina was dead – and if I'd heard anything unusual that night. All I could tell them was that Krystina was agitated, as she sometimes was, and went for a walk to calm down. That was the way she was. She would walk and walk and sometimes not appear until late the next morning. Sometimes she was away for a day and more. Occasionally –' she met Lucy's eyes – 'she would come back smelling of cigarette smoke.'

'Why was that significant?'

'She didn't smoke.'

'Pardon me for interrupting,' Kalisz said. 'But was this permitted? These prolonged absences.'

'Not for most people, but Krystina was different. This was her third time here. She knew the course inside out and the area well. If there was something she thought she needed to know, she would turn up on time and absorb it in a way others couldn't. She'd also proven herself in the field, multiple times. She'd won a medal, and she'd suffered.'

'We know.'

'There was something else...' The kettle emitted a sharp whistle and Kalisz removed it from the stove, muttering a curse as the handle burned his palm. He found a damp cloth on the sink and used it to protect his fingers. Yvette had put coffee in three tin mugs and he poured the boiling water over it, savouring the acrid scent of the fumes he created. He asked if they took milk, and both nodded. 'The milk is there,' Yvette said. 'There's no sugar, but if you like it sweet there's a can of syrup in the wall cupboard.' She frowned. 'Yes, there was something special about this mission she was to lead. That made her special, so the instructors here gave her a long leash.'

'But not you?'

Yvette gave her a tired smile. 'No, not me. Yvette is not special.'

'That kind of treatment must have made people jealous.' Kalisz put two cups in front of them.

'Not me,' Yvette repeated. 'But you're right. You have to understand that nobody comes to Arisaig to make friends. We're here to learn the skills to survive in the deadliest environment on earth. Living and working under the noses of the Gestapo. Mostly they keep us apart, but for pistol shooting, unarmed combat, silent killing and the like, they pair us with the other students. It is incredibly competitive and, sometimes, people get hurt. Krystina was very good. Aggressive and quick, deadly with her hands and feet. She made enemies because she enjoyed beating the men, and not just beating them – humiliating them. There was a sergeant instructor… Connors, I think his name was. She made him scream out and laughed at him in front of the other students. He said that the next time, he'd kill her.'

'You heard him say that?' Lucy wrote the name down in her notebook.

'Yes, we all did.'

'And you told Colonel Baldwin?'

'Of course. He said he'd look into it.'

'I'm surprised he didn't mention it,' Kalisz said. 'Though perhaps not, given that he'd prefer this investigation didn't exist. We should check with him to see what he discovered. You say nobody comes here to make friends,' he continued. 'Was Krystina your friend?'

Yvette turned to meet his eyes. 'I would have liked to be her friend, yes, but she wouldn't allow it.'

'Why not?'

'Because I was to be her wireless operator, and she knew that, at some point, she would have to give me an order that would probably get me killed.'

Kalisz would have concentrated on Yvette's relationship with the victim, but Lucy chose a different line of approach. 'It must be hard for everyone here, but especially a woman.'

'It's true that the instructors think we are the weaker sex,' Yvette agreed. 'It irritates them when we prove otherwise. That makes them push us harder, to try to break us. But the women here are all volunteers and it is our pride not to be broken. A man, especially an officer, will always be given a second chance. A woman, never. What is worse is that it's the same in the field. This was to be my second mission, so I know. It seems to me that the circuit organisers use women as a shield, sometimes against the enemy, and sometimes against their own inadequacies. A circuit leader will spend most of his time in a remote farmhouse, emerging only for an occasional meeting. A woman courier – and they are almost always women – will carry incriminating material every second or third day, coming face to face with the enemy, never knowing when they're going to be searched, or if their destination has been compromised. We wireless operators are told to change our position every four or five days to avoid detection, but is the next house any safer than the current one? Is it worth the risk of trudging through the streets carrying a suitcase with your wireless, or on the train, where you could be confronted at any moment? They say we must not transmit for more than fifteen minutes at a time, but we can have material from a dozen sources. What to leave out? This might save a hundred lives, or this could destroy an entire Nazi tank regiment. What would you choose?'

They sat in silence for a while. Kalisz knew Resistance couriers in Warsaw rarely lasted longer than a month, and often much less. Yet the girls, some of them no older than sixteen, lined up to volunteer. It broke his heart. He cleared his throat. 'You say they asked whether you'd heard anything unusual that night, but you didn't tell us your answer?'

'I heard nothing.'

'Yet Lieutenant Fontaine was shot in the head not two hundred paces from here.'

'Shots are not uncommon in Arisaig,' she told him. 'It is the nature of what happens here. But if a pistol was fired so close, I would have heard and noticed.'

Kalisz nodded. 'And was Lieutenant Fontaine Krystina's lover?'

'I do not believe so.' Yvette stared at him, not hostile, just letting him know she thought the question intrusive. 'In fact, no. She treated him like a puppy. She put up with his antics, but when he became too... How do you say *frío*?'

'Frisky.' Lucy smiled.

'Yes, frisky. When he became too frisky, she wasn't afraid to slap him down, and not in a pleasant way.'

'Thank you, Yvette.' Kalisz stood. 'I assume Colonel Baldwin and his companions made a search of Krystina's room?'

'Yes, I had the impression they found nothing.'

'Still, I think I must take a look. Which room is it?'

'Through that door –' Yvette pointed towards the rear of the kitchen – 'and next on the left.'

Kalisz left them alone and went out into the hallway. Before he turned the door handle into Krystina's room, he pulled on the pair of gloves he'd used during the search of the murder scene. Not that it would make a difference – the room had already been contaminated – but it gave him a sense of normality. He was Jan Kalisz, he was on a case, and the job would be done properly, whatever the circumstances and despite whoever wanted to stand in his way.

He stepped inside and stood for a moment, taking in his surroundings by the light from a single small window. Dust mites danced in the rays of the low winter sun and the room smelled of damp and mothballs. Whoever had searched the place had been thorough, but not particularly orderly. The cotton sheet and heavy army blanket had been stripped from the thin mattress, which itself was pushed across the bed to reveal the springs and iron frame. In one corner an upright locker that had acted as a wardrobe hung open to reveal metal hangers, an army greatcoat and a suit of functional – but clearly quite expensive – female civilian clothing that, on closer examination, bore the label of a famous French fashion house. The upper drawer of the chipped sideboard held a jumble of underclothes, and a brassiere strap hung out of the lower.

The room's only visible ornaments were two photographs in gilt frames on top of the sideboard. Both showed wedding scenes. One was very formal: a man in a dark suit and a woman in an elaborate white dress perched uncomfortably side by side on matching chairs, staring sullenly at the camera as if they couldn't wait to escape the lens. Kalisz guessed he was looking at Krystina's late parents. A small cross on a silver chain hung from the corner of the frame.

The other picture presented a much more relaxed image: a smiling young woman in a smart suit and a fur stole stooping to accept a bouquet of flowers from a small girl with braided hair, dressed in what Kalisz recognised as traditional Polish costume. Beside her, a handsome young army officer looked on with a proprietary air. Kalisz didn't recognise either of the newly-weds, but a familiar stern face in the background confirmed this was the wedding of Władysław Sikorski's daughter, Zofia Sikorska. The photographs were further evidence of Krystina's disdain for authority. The first thing the people running STS 21 would have done on her arrival was insist she hand over any property of a personal nature.

Kalisz checked the contents of the wardrobe, finding nothing in the pockets of the greatcoat or the suit jacket. The bed seemed barely worth bothering with, but he ran his hands over the mattress with similarly negative results. What was he searching for? He had no idea. A possibility. A whisper in the air. The link that would lead him to the next link. He only knew he would know it when he found it.

Next, the contents of the sideboard. He'd done it many times, but it always made him slightly uncomfortable handling the intimate belongings of a woman. Despite the earlier search, the contents retained a sense of order. Underwear to one side of the drawer. Not the functional cotton pants of the military he'd expected, but exotic wisps of ivory silk that would have made the instructors choke if they'd seen them. Army blouses crumpled in next to the pants, but he guessed they'd have been neatly folded before the search had disturbed them. He was getting a picture of Krystina now – one slightly at odds with her public persona. On the surface, the dedicated, disciplined soldier, tidy and organised, while beneath, she never let go of the young woman she really was. The bottom drawer held brassieres, thick military socks, a make-up set with a round mirror, and a metal teaspoon. He picked up the spoon and studied it. Just an ordinary spoon, probably British Army issue, not an heirloom or a souvenir. Soft, whispered voices drifted on the air from next door. He replaced the spoon and continued his search.

Nothing behind the curtains. He crouched to check the wide skirting board that ran round the base of the walls, but found it solidly fixed. A threadbare rug covered the floor in front of the chest of drawers and stretched beneath the bed frame. Nothing at all out of the ordinary.

He returned to the kitchen. 'They seem to have done a professional job.' He glanced at his watch. 'Time to meet our search party, I think.'

'*Bien sûr.*' Yvette peered at the watch. 'Is that a Patek Philippe? Krystina had one like it, but smaller, a ladies' one.'

'I'm keeping it safe for a friend.' Kalisz smiled. 'Is there anything else you can tell us that might be useful?'

Yvette looked to Lucy, as if seeking her approval. 'Two things,' she said eventually. 'Things that I did not tell the colonel. Firstly, Krystina hated the Jews, hated them with a terrible passion. She blamed them for the loss of her family's fortune.'

'And the second?'

'I had orders that, when we reached France, if I had the slightest doubt about her loyalty, I was to shoot her in the head.'

CHAPTER 14

Warsaw

30 December 1943

After a night in a cheap hotel down by Gdynia's docks, Maria and Stefan made their connection to the Gdansk–Warsaw Express and arrived home at 35 Kopernika in the early afternoon. Stefan crammed a crust of stale bread into his mouth and immediately announced that he was going to see his friend Anka – girl friend or girlfriend, Maria still wasn't certain – and dashed off within minutes. Left alone in the apartment, Maria sat back and closed her eyes, experiencing an unexpected pang of guilt that she'd been told to take as much time as she needed while Jan was recovering from his 'illness'. Dissembling and dishonesty didn't come naturally to her, and she felt terribly tired.

She'd been met at the hospital in Gdynia by a competent young woman who'd led her into a consulting room and relieved her of the contents of the suitcase and the papers she'd been carrying. A triumph, it seemed, and a genuine service to the war effort. The perfume bottle had contained a sample of fuel for some kind of new weapon the Nazis were developing, and the odd jewellery in the box had been made up of tiny engine components. Together with the documents Maria had been carrying, they would give the Allies an insight into what was coming their way in the not too distant future, and hopefully help them to develop the means to counter it.

When the exchange had been made, she and Stefan had spent a surreal ninety minutes sitting at the bedside of the man who wasn't her husband. What the anonymous figure wrapped up like an Egyptian mummy had thought of her inane ramblings about what was happening in Warsaw, and how his colleagues were desperate to have him back, she would never know. Thankfully, Stefan had played his part whenever

76

she began to flag, talking about his schooling and plans for after the war, though she wasn't sure she entirely approved of his ambition to become a racing driver.

The journey, and the particular perils that accompanied it, must have exhausted Maria more than she realised, because she was asleep when the telephone rang.

Her hand shook as she picked up the receiver. Was this the call she'd dreaded receiving for all these years? 'Yes?'.

'May I speak with Investigator Kalisz?'

'I'm sorry, my husband is... indisposed.'

Her words elicited a soft grunt of disappointment. 'Is he likely to be available any time soon?'

'No, I think I can say that with some certainty.' A long pause, and she sensed the man was thinking of hanging up. 'But perhaps *I* can help you?'

A simple question, but evidently one without a simple answer, because the caller took time to consider it. 'Before you decide that – and it must be your decision, Mrs Kalisz – perhaps it would be best if you know with whom you are speaking.'

Maria noted that her caller spoke with careful precision, and had a slight accent that suggested Polish was not his first language. There had been hints over the years that Jan's perilous double life meant exposure to – and contact with – some of Warsaw's less savoury elements. She had a feeling she was speaking to one of them. 'Please continue,' she said warily, 'but I'm sure I don't have to remind you that sometimes it is unwise to be too candid with someone to whom you haven't been introduced.'

Her suggestion triggered a full-blooded laugh. 'Now I understand why you and your husband are such a fine match.' This was showing more familiarity than her hint warranted, but Maria chose to ignore it. 'I can assure you that we would not be using this method of communication if there had been the slightest suspicion we might be overheard. So you may trust me that we can be entirely "candid". My name would be of little interest or use, because it changes often, but your husband would know me as "the Bulgarian". You should be aware that, despite your husband and I belonging to opposite ends of the spectrum of our particular – shall we say, interest? – we have become close associates over the past few dangerous years. He did me a great service at the beginning of the Occupation, but I believe I have been able to repay it in kind. Now, I like to think we are in a form of partnership that brings solace and comfort to those who need it most and the opposite to those who do not. I realise I am being cryptic here, but I am walking a tightrope of those details your husband would be happy for me to reveal and those he would not.'

'I am aware that he works for the… For the benefit of Poland.'

'Oh yes, but there are things your husband has done for the benefit of Poland not even his true masters in the *Armia Krajowa* are aware of.' Now he *had* surprised her. 'Things known, until this moment, at least, only by we two. I am telling you this, Mrs Kalisz, because I find myself in the rather embarrassing and unusual position of being more or less helpless. Helpless in a matter of life and death.'

'In that case, you have said enough, Mr Bulgarian. How may I assist you?'

'May I come to see you in person?'

Maria thought of her German neighbours across the landing. 'It would be best if you could be discreet.'

A hoarse chuckle greeted her words. 'You may be assured, Mrs Kalisz, that discretion is my middle name.'

CHAPTER 15

Arisaig

'Does nothing surprise you, Investigator?' Lucy asked as they ate a snatched lunch of bread and soup in the mess.

'I've learned that life is never simple.' Kalisz shrugged. 'Why?'

'You acted as if it was the most natural thing in the world for Yvette to be ordered to kill her comrade.'

'In a way, in their world – the world of the underground, of resistance, of life in the shadows – it is. Krystina's escape from the Gestapo raises certain questions. But it's of no immediate consequence, apart from being another piece of the jigsaw. Yvette didn't kill Krystina or Fontaine.'

'No,' Lucy agreed.

'What Yvette said about Krystina's hatred of the Jews, however, may be significant. Do you think you can get a list of people of the Jewish faith here at Arisaig and in the other training centres?'

'Including the officers and instructors?' Kalisz nodded. 'If I use Churchill's authority, I don't see why not.'

'And one of us should check through Major Llewellyn's list of possessions. I don't remember anyone mentioning an expensive watch. Right –' he checked his own – 'time to meet our search party.'

They walked across the pasture below the walled garden towards the murder scene. A squad of about a dozen men huddled in the shelter of the nearest trees for protection against the chill breeze, smoking and talking among themselves. As Kalisz and Lucy approached, Major Dempsey broke away from the group to meet them.

'I heard you wanted to talk to anyone involved in recovering the bodies,' the major said. 'Since I was there, I thought it made sense to take command of the search party. You know Constable MacDonald already went over the ground?'

'No whizz-bangs today, Major?' Kalisz ignored the implication he was wasting their time. 'We're very grateful for your help. As for the original search... The prime minister had not taken a personal interest at that point. Perhaps that will make all our eyes a little sharper, yes?'

'You're in charge, Major Zamoyski,' Dempsey said graciously. 'Just tell us how we can assist you.'

'First I'd like to speak to all the men who helped recover the dead woman. Then we will search the ground.'

Dempsey nodded and walked off, shouting a string of names. Six men formed up in a line in the open, and Lucy stood back to allow Kalisz to approach them alone.

Kalisz studied the row of men. They were arranged from left to right by height, with a very tall man on the left and a soldier an inch or two shorter than Kalisz on the right. None of them looked at home in uniform, and they all stared past him into the distance, as if he didn't exist.

'First of all, I must thank you for your co-operation. And for volunteering to come out on this cold afternoon.' That raised a few ironic smiles, as he'd hoped. The concept of volunteering was singularly flexible in any army. 'May I ask who initially found the body, and how?'

'I did, sir.' The tall man took a step forward. 'Private Greaves. The mess room corporal decided at the last minute that he wanted a centrepiece for the officers' Christmas dinner table. I was sent out to look for fir cones.' His lips twitched. 'He's a bit of an artist, sir. There are quite a few fir trees in this part of the wood, so I thought I'd start here. That's when I saw the woman hanging from the tree. I was able to reach up and check the pulse on her wrist, so I knew she was dead. I immediately ran back to the house, where I encountered Major Dempsey and informed him of my discovery.'

'And I arranged for a party to come down and recover the body,' Dempsey said.

'So you are a mess room orderly, Private Greaves? How many are you?'

'Three, sir. Me, Davis –' Greaves nodded to a man in the middle of the line – 'and Titch Collins there, on the end.'

'And what happened then?'

Dempsey took up the story. 'I ordered the men to untie the rope and lower the dead woman to the ground.'

'The ladder was against the tree?'

'Yes, we couldn't have managed without it.'

'It did not occur to you that it would have been impossible for Krystina Kowolska to hang herself and then place it where it is in this photograph?' Kalisz pulled a picture from the envelope Llewellyn had given him and showed it to the major.

'No, it did not.' Dempsey stiffened. 'I'd asked Colonel Baldwin to send for the medical officer, and when Llewellyn arrived he confirmed that Warrant Officer Kowolska was dead. It was only when he examined her properly that he became suspicious about the cause.'

'I meant no criticism, Major,' Kalisz assured him. 'In the circumstances it is not surprising you didn't notice the ladder's position. It must have been quite shocking to see one of your students dead. May I ask who discovered the second body?'

'That would be me, sir,' Collins called out. 'The medical officer ordered me to go back to the house to fetch a blanket to cover the dead lady until the authorities arrived. Purely by chance, I noticed the poor bugger's boot sticking out from under a bush.'

'Thank you, Private. Major? Your men will form a circle approximately forty paces from the tree – that is, beyond the point where Lieutenant Fontaine was found – and work their way in towards where the body was suspended. You've brought gloves and bags? Good. Your first priority is to find exactly where the lieutenant was killed. It was certainly not where his body was discovered. It is asking a lot after all this time, but the spot may be marked by an outpouring of blood, or perhaps a bullet casing. If you see anything of that nature, or anything you believe is significant, call me immediately. Anything remotely out of place should be regarded as evidence.'

Dempsey marched the men off, calling orders, leaving Kalisz staring thoughtfully after them. Lucy joined him.

'Was that helpful?' she asked.

'It was.' He replaced the envelope in his briefcase. 'But perhaps not in the way you might think. None of those men was the "kindly mess room orderly" I saw leaving Yvette's cottage. If she lied about his identity, what else was she lying to us about?'

Kalisz watched the men form a loose circle around the tree in a reasonable approximation to the distance he'd asked for. The circumference meant there were quite wide gaps at the moment, but that didn't concern him. They would fill as the searchers closed on the murder scene proper. He and Lucy took their places among those closest to where Lieutenant Fontaine had been found.

'All right,' he called. 'Begin.'

They moved forward slowly at a crouch, eyes on the ground ahead of them. Each man wore a pair of heavy gloves, probably from the engineering stores, and carried a brown paper bag Kalisz suspected had been liberated from a local grocery shop. He had little hope of success in the case of Fontaine's murder site. There wouldn't be any brain matter from such a small wound, and blood spots would be difficult to discern against the winter foliage. So he was surprised when a voice sang out from his left. 'Sir, I think you should see this.'

He left the circle and ran around the ring of men to where Private Greaves stood beside the low hanging branch of a sturdy oak tree. 'Here, sir. I would never have noticed it if it hadn't been for this bare patch of bark.'

Kalisz looked at the patch where some kind of animal, probably a deer, had chewed the bark away to leave the bare wood. A splash of dark material stood out against the white of the timber, and when he looked closely he could see tiny spots of the same element. 'Good job, Private,' he said. 'You have excellent eyes.'

'How do you know it's blood?' Major Dempsey had crossed from the far side of the circle. 'Could be anything at all from what I can see.'

'True,' Kalisz said, but his eyes were searching the ground along the course of the splash. There it was again on the grass: a broken line, now dried and near invisible. 'But please have this area cordoned off. Hopefully, Major Llewellyn will be able to tell us for certain.' There was no elation in his voice. They already knew Fontaine was dead and how he'd been killed. But it made sense. Kalisz studied his surroundings and their relationship to the nearby SOE properties. 'I think the killer was standing behind this tree when our victim came down from Borrodale House. Perhaps Fontaine had seen Krystina in the moonlight, or he knew her haunts. He passes the tree, and our man steps out and shoots him from close range. The dying lieutenant spins, blood spurting from the wound to mark the tree, and ends up with his head approximately here.' He indicated a slight indentation in the foliage close to the spots of dried blood.

'But we're only two hundred yards from the quarters he shared at Borrodale, and a hundred and fifty from Arisaig House,' Dempsey pointed out. 'And nobody reported hearing the sound of a shot.'

'Yes,' Kalisz agreed. 'But a shot there most certainly was. Perhaps we may continue, but please ensure no one disturbs this area.'

–

They searched for another hour. Kalisz insisted the men drop to their knees and cover the ground by the inch as they drew closer to the tree, but they discovered nothing more.

When they'd completed their task, Kalisz turned to Lucy. 'Flight Officer Devereux, may I ask you to check with the sergeant clerk that Colonel Baldwin has authorised our access to the filing room. Given his impatience, I'd have thought he would have been keener to help. After all, the answer to this puzzle is as likely to lie there as anywhere else.'

'All right,' she agreed. 'But don't go anywhere without me.'

As Lucy left for the house, Kalisz turned to Dempsey. 'I wonder if I may borrow Private Greaves for an hour?'

'Of course,' Dempsey said. 'Greaves?' he called. 'Major Zamoyski has appointed you his factotum. Be back at the mess by five.'

'Sir!' Greaves saluted.

'Factotum?' Kalisz frowned.

'I'm to do your fetching and carrying, sir. Major Dempsey is a veritable walking dictionary.'

'Not "dogsbody", then?'

'Oh, I'm sure I can manage that as well, sir,' Greaves said cheerfully. 'Man of many talents, that's me. Now, sir, what can I do for you?'

'You have straw men here, for bayonet practice?'

'Straw men, sir? Oh, I see. Old Bill – that is, Major Sykes – might have something in that line for his silent killers to chop up. If not, I'm sure we can rustle up something similar. Anything else?'

'House bricks… seven or eight of them. And a length of rope, as close to the type she was hanging from as you can find.'

Greaves pondered for a moment. 'The gardener's hut in the walled garden would be the most likely place for bricks. Maybe the rope, too.'

'No joy, I'm afraid,' Lucy called as she approached across the meadow below Arisaig House an hour later as the light began to fade in the western sky. 'It appears the colonel has other things on his mind.'

She watched as Kalisz struggled at the top of the ladder with what appeared to be a crude life-sized dummy of a person, manufactured from hessian potato sacks and straw. As she watched, he tried to manoeuvre it into position on the branch from which the rope had hung. A similar coil of rope lay on the ground below. Something fell from the dummy's torso and landed with a thud on the packed earth, and she recognised a house brick. Kalisz muttered a Polish curse and said, 'Enough.'

'May I ask what you're doing?' she said.

'It is an experiment,' Kalisz explained as he worked his way cautiously back down the ladder with the dummy under one arm. 'It occurred to me that it would have been difficult, if not near impossible, for even a strong person to carry the body up the ladder and hold it in position long enough to place the noose around her neck. A newly dead body is not co-operative. It is literally a dead weight, and until rigor mortis sets in the limbs flail about in the most unwieldy manner. I used the bricks to partially compensate for her weight.'

'Couldn't he just have carried her halfway and then put the noose on her?'

Kalisz shook his head and dropped the dummy at her feet. Despite the cold, he was sweating. 'No, there had to be a drop for it to look as if the hanging had broken her neck. Krystina's skin had abrasions where the rope rode up as she fell. See where the thin branch just above you has been broken as her corpse was wrestled into place? That shows how awkward it must have been.'

'What does it mean?'

'If I'm correct, Flight Officer Devereux, it means that not only do we have two bodies, but we may also be looking for more than one murderer.'

CHAPTER 16

Multiple murderers. Suddenly everything became much more complic-ated, but Kalisz was certain he was right. It would have been impossible for a single person to manhandle Krystina's body into position without inflicting further scrapes and scratches on her exposed flesh. More than one murderer meant it would be doubly difficult to break down any alibi they concocted, because each would vouch for the other. But what motive could the killers have had to conspire to murder Krystina Kowolska? Or did he have it back to front, and Jean-Marc Fontaine was the intended target in the first place? No, that didn't make sense. Krystina's hanging had been intended to look like a suicide. If Jean-Marc had been killed first, it would have been much simpler just to shoot Krystina as well. The result would have been the same – a murder–suicide – but without the complications.

That was the problem with Krystina's death. Everything about it was too complicated. He could hear the sound of the waves in the distance. Wouldn't it have been much easier to take her body down to the sea and let time and tide dispose of it? Even if it was discovered quickly, the broken neck could have been passed off as an accident. He'd no doubt Colonel Baldwin would have used the opportunity to ensure there was no scandal and no interruption to his mission. *Accidents happen and people die, more often than I'd like.*

He realised Lucy was staring at him. 'Sorry.' He smiled. 'I was lost for a moment. What's in the box?'

'Hershey Bars. Major Llewellyn says they might help smooth the way with the locals. Apparently, they'd sell their souls for a chocolate bar. An American former student sends him a regular supply as a thanks for saving his leg. "I use them to reward my patients for being good boys and girls."' She laughed.

Kalisz frowned. 'You don't think that's odd?'

'What is odd?'

'"Good boys and girls" obviously refers to the "students" here. Yet he gave the impression when we were examining Krystina's body that they seldom consulted him.'

'Is that significant?'

'I don't know,' he admitted. 'But it bears thinking about.' Kalisz looked up towards the big house where a careless chink of light escaped from behind the blackout curtains in one of the upper windows. He hadn't realised how dark it had become. 'We should just have time to speak to the men who shared Lieutenant Fontaine's quarters at Borrodale House.'

She looked doubtful. 'They dine early at Arisaig. We don't want to miss dinner.'

'You don't need to come,' Kalisz said. 'Just remind me of the name of the victim's room-mate.'

'His name is Pierre Renan,' Lucy said, 'but you don't get rid of me so easily, Investigator. I've been told to stick to you like glue.'

Kalisz smiled. 'I hope you aren't going to take the order too literally. Are you here to spy on me, Lucy Devereux?'

'You may be assured that I have your best interests at heart, Investigator.'

'Then we should proceed. If we do miss dinner, we can always share a Hershey Bar.'

–

By the time they reached Borrodale, the house was only vaguely discernible in the gloom. It had a broad stucco frontage studded with small windows that was topped by a slate roof, from which four further roofed windows protruded. It might have been quite elegant, but for the elongated porch above the entrance that made it look as if it had a cowshed attached, and the large barn-like building that loomed from the shadows beyond.

Lucy took a key from her satchel, but before she could use it Kalisz tried the door handle and found it was open. The door led into a cramped hallway with inner doors to left and right and a set of stairs to the upper storey. From beyond the left-hand door Kalisz heard the murmur of voices, interrupted by a sharp thud and followed in quick succession by two more. He opened it and stepped inside a lounge area lined with bookshelves, where a wood fire blazed in an enormous fireplace.

'No.' Lucy cried a warning as one of the two men in the room spun, with the blade of a long knife held in his fingers at shoulder height and with muscles tensed, ready to throw. Kalisz froze, knowing that in the other man's eyes he was already dead. In a moment of supreme clarity, he registered a dartboard hanging on the wall over the fireplace, with three identical knives embedded around the bullseye. For an instant they were frozen like a marble tableau in a museum, before the lethal intent in the knifeman's eyes faded and he lowered the dagger. Kalisz breathed again.

'It is not a good idea to surprise people around here,' the man said in heavily accented English. With one smooth movement, he turned, and his arm whipped forward to send the knife thudding into the centre of the board fifteen feet away.

'I will be sure to remember in future,' Kalisz assured him. He picked up one of a pair of boots drying by the fire and studied the sole.

'What are you doing?'

'These aren't military boots?'

'Army boots are shit.' The man shrugged. 'Fall apart in snow and mud. The ghillies wear these.'

'Hunting guides,' Lucy said, before Kalisz could ask.

'You're not here to clean our boots.'

'We're looking for Pierre Renan.'

'He went out.' This from the second occupant of the room. They could have been brothers: tall and spare, with broad shoulders, spiky black hair and the type of facial stubble that needed shaving twice a day. The first man was older, perhaps in his early thirties, the second five or six years his junior. They shared a sullen demeanour and a grudging way with words that reminded Kalisz of his days on the beat in Mokotów, when the cop was every man's enemy. It wasn't that they didn't like him personally; they didn't like anybody, and they didn't care who knew it.

'Then perhaps we can talk to you?' Kalisz took a seat in an armchair to the left of the fire. 'You've heard about Krystina and Jean-Marc, of course?'

'Sure.' The older man shrugged. 'Poor Krysia. He couldn't stay away from her. She didn't like it very much, and... *boom.*'

'*Jesteś Polakiem?*'

A shadow fell over the dark eyes. '*Pewny. A ty?*'

'It's just that I couldn't place your accent,' Kalisz continued in Polish. Lucy had been standing next to him, but she moved to a wooden seat in the corner and Kalisz noticed the younger man shift, almost imperceptibly, to cover his partner's flank.

'That's because we're Bosnian Poles. The old folks settled by the Sava river in Bosanska, but that doesn't make us any less Polish.'

'An interesting knife.' Kalisz rose and plucked the dagger from the dartboard, and studied it. It had a narrow, double-edged blade about the length from his wrist to his fingertip, a needle point, and the grip was protected by a slight cross-guard. He tested it for balance and liked what he felt. 'May I?' he said.

'Help yourself.'

Kalisz turned and, with a flick of his wrist, whipped the knife point-first into the exact spot he'd taken it from. 'Not bad,' he said.

The throw earned him a cold smile. 'It was designed by Major Sykes. He says you can kill a man with it in any one of a dozen ways, but Witold and me reckon someone with an imagination could think of a few more.'

'A hard war, where you come from?' Kalisz resumed his seat.

'There's no such thing as a soft war.'

'So how do you come to be here? Mr...?'

The other man went very still, the way a forest animal does when it scents danger. 'You don't want to know about Jean-Marc and Krysia?'

'If you had anything important to tell me, you'd have done it by now.'

'You're a cop, right?' He pulled a packet of cigarettes from his tunic pocket and lit one. 'You can call me Jerzy.' He grinned. 'For all the good it will do you.'

'So...?' Kalisz persisted.

'We're from a place called Gradiška. Not much of a town, and being Poles, we didn't fit in too well. Better than the Jews, though. The war was somebody else's problem at first, but then the bodies started coming down the river. Ones and twos at the beginning – men, women and children – then a steady flow. Heads bashed in and throats cut, mainly, but some had suffered worse. Couples and whole families tied together with wire.' There was no anger or sorrow in his voice; the delivery was almost mechanical. 'Well, whoever was doing that was the enemy, and they turned out to be Croats from up at Jasenovac, which they'd made into a slaughterhouse for the Serbs and the Jews. We tried to join Mihailović and the Chetniks, but they weren't too fond of Bosniaks, Polish or otherwise, so we ended up with Tito. With our decent English, the partisans reckoned we'd be of the most use guarding the leader of a British mission that had just parachuted in. We went through a lot of scrapes together, yes? Became good pals – brothers, even. When Tito decided every partisan gotta be a Communist, that didn't suit us. So we told the boss we'd volunteer to fight Nazis in the Motherland – we had certain skills, see...' He plucked out one of the knives from the dartboard and ran his thumb along the edge. 'And when the mission came out, they brought us with them.'

Kalisz heard the sound of the front door opening. 'Can you excuse me for a moment, gentlemen?' Lucy made to rise from her chair, but he gave her a look and she stayed where she was as he hurried to the door. In the hallway, a man in battledress was climbing the stairs.

'Pierre Renan?'

The man stopped and turned. 'Who wants to know?'

'My name is Major Zamoyski. I'm investigating the deaths of Krystina Kowolska and Jean-Marc Fontaine.'

Renan was of middle height, with sandy brown hair that formed a distinctive widow's peak on his forehead. A neat moustache adorned his upper lip. The shape of his face and his build brought the word 'plump' to mind, but Kalisz guessed that was an illusion in an environment where fitness and survival was so central to the curriculum. There was something unthreatening and benign about him that would probably serve him well in the field.

'It would be better to talk in my room.'

'Give me a couple of minutes. I have a few more questions for your friends downstairs.'

Renan shook his head. 'No friends of mine. My room is the first on the right.'

In the lounge, Jerzy eyed Lucy suspiciously.

'*Zrobiłbyś niezłe pieprzenie.*'

She reacted to the obscene suggestion with a bland, uncomprehending smile.

'*Nie podoba mi się to,*' Witold said quietly.

'*To nie ma z nami nic wspólnego.*'

'*Może to zagrozić misji,*' the younger man persisted.

'*Jeśli wścibski gliniarz stanie na drodze misji, zabijemy go.*'

Kalisz reappeared in the doorway. 'Just one more question. How did you spend Christmas Eve and night?'

The two men looked at each other. 'On the twenty-third and twenty-fourth of December, that bastard Dempsey had us on an escape and evasion exercise in the mountains,' Jerzy said. 'On *Wigilia*, for fuck's sake. We were dropped off at the south end of Loch Shiel and spent two days being chased all over Lochaber by hairy-arsed Commandos. We got back here, wet, freezing and exhausted, well after midnight, and crawled into our beds. We didn't stir until about noon on Christmas Day.'

'That's right,' Witold confirmed.

'And you heard nothing during the night?'

'I told you,' Jerzy said. 'We never stirred.'

'In that case, thank you for your time, gentlemen. Flight Officer Devereux.' Lucy rose and brushed down her skirt. As they left, she smiled her thanks.

'Did anything happen when I was away?' Kalisz said quietly as they headed upstairs.

'Only that I discovered they don't like the police – they didn't know I can speak Polish, but that's what you intended, wasn't it? – and that if you get in the way of their mission, they're quite prepared to kill you.'

CHAPTER 17

'You were asked to wait at the house until I had the opportunity to interview you as a potential witness, Sergeant Renan.' The room was small but functional, with two single beds and a pair of green metal army-issue wardrobes. A bathroom on the landing served the entire floor. 'May I ask why you decided to go out, against the colonel's express order?'

'I'm not a child, Major,' the Frenchman replied sulkily. 'I've been cooped up here all day waiting for you, listening to those maniacs playing their crazy game of darts. I needed to get out for some fresh air and a little piece of quiet.'

'Going for walks in the woods seems to be the established recreation around here.' Kalisz had decided to take a more direct interview approach with Pierre Renan. 'I would have thought that unlikely, given the amount of physical exertion this course asks of you.'

'It's true they work us hard.' Renan managed a smile. 'Most of the time we're too tired to do anything. But when you're not so tired, a walk along the shore or through the forest keeps you sane.'

'It got Krystina Kowolska killed,' Lucy pointed out.

Renan glared at her. 'That had nothing to do with me,' he snapped. 'And if you ask me, Jean-Marc had nothing to do with it either. He thought he was in love with her. Maybe he found the body and shot himself out of grief.'

'Why do you think he wouldn't kill her?' Kalisz resumed.

'I told you. He was in love with her. He would never have harmed her. In fact, I would say that Jean-Marc would have died for Krystina, fool that he was.'

'Why do you say that?'

'Because she treated him like dirt on her shoe. The way she treated everybody.'

'You didn't like her?' Lucy asked.

'*Non*,' Renan said through gritted teeth. 'I thought she was a rich bitch playing at soldiers, if you really wish to know.'

'Was it because she'd rejected you?'

The Frenchman laughed, but there was no humour in it. 'You think she would ever look at the likes of me? Well, I knew that, and I knew better than to even consider it.'

'What were you doing on the night she was killed?' Kalisz asked.

'Sleeping. Jean-Marc and I played cards until ten thirty, and then we went to bed.'

'Jean-Marc didn't leave the house until later?'

Renan shrugged. 'Of course, but I don't know what time.'

'The Poles say they arrived back here after an exercise early on Christmas morning. Did you hear them?'

'Naturally. They are like elephants, those two, and they don't care how much noise they make. Polish pigs.'

'So did he go out before, or after, they came back?'

'I... It must have been after,' Renan said. 'I would have been asleep for a while.'

'But you did hear him go?' Kalisz persisted.

'Yes.'

'What then?'

'I don't understand.'

'Did you hear anything? A shot, perhaps? Your window faces down towards where the bodies were found. Maybe you looked out and saw something unusual?'

'No. No shots.'

'Did the colonel show you the gun that was found in Jean-Marc's hand?'

'Yes, he did. It was a Browning High Power 9mm manufactured at the Herstal factory in Belgium under the German occupation.'

'You know a lot about guns. Was it Jean-Marc's pistol?'

'Yes, it was his personal weapon, carried at all times. I was to be his armourer. When they're short-handed at Glasnacardoch I sometimes double as the armourer there. We were due to join an established circuit in southern France. It's my job to be familiar with every type of weapon we might encounter. The Browning is a good pistol for the likes of us, because the Germans use a lot of 9mm ammunition. Our Sten is chambered for the same round as the MP40 for that very reason. If you ambush an ammunition convoy, it's like Christmas and your birthday all at once.'

'You and Jean-Marc must have been close,' Lucy suggested.

'He led and I followed.' A regretful smile. 'But, yes, we were friends. He was a man who inspired loyalty. Jean-Marc had a good heart, but she liked to twist it in her hands.'

'Were they ever here together?'

'Not while I was at home, but who knows?'

'If you think of anything that might help, please let us know,' Kalisz said as he headed for the door.

'Of course.'

On the way downstairs, Lucy touched Kalisz's arm. 'There's something not right about him, Jan. I can't explain it, but there is.'

'You have good instincts, Lucy Devereux.' Kalisz smiled. 'Pierre Renan is the man I saw sneaking away from Yvette's house earlier.'

'Why didn't you confront him about it?'

'Because I believe it would be more productive to approach the problem from a different direction. I think we will pay Miss Yvette another visit tomorrow.'

Lucy gave a hiss of frustration. 'Is this usual, this infuriating lack of progress?'

'Oh, I wouldn't say we haven't made any progress.' He smiled. 'But nothing is simple about a murder investigation. It would be nice, though, if tomorrow we spoke to just one person who didn't lie to us.'

–

Back at Arisaig House, Kalisz asked the sergeant clerk if he could see the training log for the night of the murder. It confirmed that the two Poles at Borrodale were marked as being on exercise with a company of Commandos based at the Achnacarry estate, which a glance at the map on the office wall confirmed must be at least forty miles away.

'While you're here, sir, Colonel Baldwin says I've to get the files out for you first thing tomorrow. Just give me a shout after breakfast and I'll let you into the cellar.'

Kalisz thanked him and went to the mess, where he sat at a table with pen and notebook, putting together an account of the day's investigation. He could see why Lucy found their failure to make headway frustrating, but a murder inquiry wasn't a sprint. It was more like a fifteen-hundred-metre race: the start could seem glacially slow; you had to stay in the hunt through the mid-part; but the important thing was to be on your quarry's shoulder when the finishing line approached.

'May I ask how things have gone today, Major?'

Kalisz looked up to find Major Dempsey standing in the doorway. A big man, taller than the impression he'd given in the open at the murder scene, and almost excessively soldierly in his bearing. What did they say? Yes, that was it. A ramrod for a spine. The same languid drawl that seemed to identify a certain class of English officer. 'That bastard', Jerzy had called him. Kalisz had known proper bastards in the army and the Kripo, and nothing he could see here said 'bastard' on any level. Then again, some bastards hid it well.

'We have a saying in Polish that for every two steps forward, one takes another step back,' Kalisz said evenly. 'I believe I am building a picture of the events, but it is a murky one at the moment. Hopefully, tomorrow will bring more clarity. Flight Officer Devereux has arranged a meeting with Constable MacDonald. In my experience, a local policeman knows as much about what is happening beneath the skin of his community as the doctor, or even the priest.'

'Ah, MacDonald.' Dempsey clicked his tongue against his teeth. 'A good chap, and no doubt a fine country policeman, but... er, shall we say, a product of his environment.'

'What do you mean?'

'Arisaig is an ideal location for the kind of work we do here, and the way of life in this strip between the coast and the mountains contributes to that. We require complete privacy, which is why the lodges and houses are so far apart and most of them quite difficult to access. You may have noticed that the roads around here are not what they might be. The people of the west coast of Scotland are hardy and self-sufficient, but they also have a tradition, that dates back for several hundred years, of keeping their secrets to themselves. They don't tittle-tattle...' Dempsey smiled. 'That means they do not tell tales, Major Zamoyski. In many ways, this is a backward place. There is no electricity here, apart from that produced by our generators, or central water supply. But that is not my main point. It is about a state of mind, evidenced by the fact that I have heard numerous people here raise a toast to the "King over the Water" before they drink, and not in an ironic way. They are very different from the English. When you speak to Constable MacDonald tomorrow, please bear that in mind. You will be talking to a man who is living in a past to which you will find it difficult to relate. Goodnight.'

–

The substance of the dream was always the same. This time, an exhausted Maria was clutching a slippery, moss-covered rock on one side of a raging torrent, with certain death waiting at the precipitous falls just beyond, while his son Stefan clung to an identical rock on the other side. Both were calling desperately for Kalisz's help, but he was caught in the centre of the current a little upstream, the rushing water tearing at his legs and the gravel shifting beneath his feet. Each of them believed he could be their saviour. Launch himself to his right, and he might save Stefan. To the left, and it could be Maria's life he preserved. He *must* choose one or the other, but how did a husband and a father make that choice? And with each passing moment his own situation became ever more precarious. If he didn't decide now, all three of them would be swept to their deaths. Yet he could only stand rigid with terror and indecision as their strength – and his – faded. In the end, he would do nothing for any of them – not even himself.

He cried out as first Maria, and then Stefan were swept away, and the current dragged his feet from beneath him…

CHAPTER 18

31 December 1943

Nine a.m.

It took Kalisz a moment to recognise the Lucy Devereux who was waiting for him at the bottom of the stairs the next morning. She'd exchanged her blue tunic and skirt for plain khaki battledress unadorned by badges of rank, and her feet were encased in a shiny pair of army boots, though she'd retained her WAAF peaked cap.

'You look as if you mean business, Flight Officer,' he said, meaning it as a compliment.

'I ruined a perfectly good pair of shoes yesterday.' She smiled. 'So it seemed sensible to dress more appropriately for the weather and the terrain. Fortunately, the stores here had a uniform to fit.'

The sergeant clerk appeared from one of the offices. 'If you'll follow me, sir, ma'am. The file room is in the cellar. I've looked out the ones they said you'd be interested in.'

'Thank you, Sergeant.'

They followed him to a narrow doorway, which he unlocked with a brass key, and down a set of stairs to a large room lit by a single naked bulb. The bulb illuminated a table in the centre of the room, which held two dun folders. Shelves of files lined the walls, apart from one, which had a rack of dusty bottles. Some kind of small window, or perhaps a delivery hatch, was set high in one wall. 'As you'll see, sir, the room also doubles as a wine cellar. Major Dempsey expressly told me to tell you to keep your mitts off it.'

Kalisz smiled. 'So the major has a sense of humour?'

'So it appears, sir. Now, I've been told to stay with you as long as you're down here. Please just act as if I don't exist.'

'You hold the files here for all the students who have attended Arisaig's training schools?'

'Just those currently in residence, sir, plus the management, the training staff and all us other odds and sods.'

Lucy opened her mouth to translate, but Kalisz smiled. 'It is all right, Flight Officer, we have a very similar expression in Poland. Now, let us see what we have. We'll start with Lieutenant Fontaine's file first, I think. I don't expect to learn much from it, but one never knows.'

Lucy picked up the folder with Fontaine's name on it. 'Born Quebec, Canada, in 1919, to a French father and Canadian mother. Fluent in English and French. Top of his class at school. Athletics champion and captain of the ice hockey team.'

Kalisz studied the photograph she showed him. 'And handsome with it. A young man with everything to live for.'

'Also a patriot. He joined a Canadian unit called the Fusiliers Mont-Royal at the outbreak of the war. They spent a year on garrison duty in Iceland before they came over to England in 1940. But, if he was looking for action, he would have got all the excitement he wanted, and more, in August 1942, when the regiment took part in Operation Jubilee, the bungled raid on Dieppe.' Kalisz nodded. The name was familiar to him because of a Nazi propaganda film of scores of bodies washed up on a shingle beach like a shoal of stranded fish. 'Jean-Marc was mentioned in dispatches, which means he was probably recommended for a medal. He was spotted by an SOE recruiter when he applied for a transfer to the Commandos in early 1943.'

'And here we are.' Kalisz sighed. 'Nothing in his background that would account for his murder, which means we must continue to assume it was his pursuit of Krystina Kowolska which led to his untimely death.'

The Kowolska file confirmed what Churchill had told him about her personal details. She'd been in Paris when the war started, immediately volunteered to serve with the PSK in Poland, but had never had the chance to return. When the Nazis overran France she had opportunities to flee to Britain, but didn't take them up. Why was never explained. Somehow she'd carved a role for herself as a liaison officer for a fledgling Polish intelligence network called Operation Monika, travelling between the small communities of the northern coal regions called *Petites Polognes* – Little Polands. It was her first brush with the secret life, and Krystina had thrived, helping create escape lines that allowed thousands of Polish soldiers stranded in France to reach Britain and rejoin the fight.

That wouldn't have been so difficult at first, while the Wehrmacht acted as if they were just military tourists passing through on their way to London, Madrid and Lisbon. Yet Kalisz knew the task would still have had the usual perils of underground work: betrayal, blunder and sheer bad luck.

Somehow Krystina had survived even as the Nazis tightened their grip on the Occupied zone.

And became noticed.

It appeared she'd been exfiltrated from France in much the same way Kalisz had been brought out of Poland, because the next entry took place in London: a record of an interview at the Northumberland Hotel, with a Captain Jepson. He wrote:

> *This lady is of excellent character and has already shown a remarkable coolness in the face of the enemy and an aptitude for a life undercover. She is fluent in Polish, English, French and German, with a reasonable command of Spanish. I would recommend that she proceed to further training at the special operations centre in Lochaber. She has expressed a wish to be put to work in Poland, but I believe circumstances and the war effort would be better served by her employment in Occupied France.*

Kalisz doubted Krystina had ever been allowed to lay eyes on her personnel file, but he could imagine her reaction if she'd seen it. She was clearly used to having her own way, and everything he'd read had proved her determination to serve the Motherland in whatever way she could. On the other hand, he could only applaud the anonymous Captain Jepson's decision. The report was dated July 1941, a period when the Nazis had increased their stranglehold throughout Poland in the wake of Operation Barbarossa. Krystina would have been fortunate to last a week.

Attached to the form were various evaluations from Krystina's instructors at Arisaig and another training school, presumably somewhere in England. She had excelled at unarmed combat, pistol shooting, and in the various simulations and exercises included in the course. Only her wireless telegraphy skills had caused any real concern, but her instructor believed the reason was lack of interest, rather than of ability.

Another trainer was more relaxed:

> *This student's temperament is perhaps a little too energetic and active to make her an ideal WT Operator. On the other hand, she has the skills to make a good courier, and the intelligence and initiative to take on more responsible roles.*

Others were less impressed: *She is tough and self-reliant, but also vain and arrogant. Her vanity could prove costly in the field.* The terse comment was accompanied by a pencilled note – *Dislikes women!* – but whether it referred to instructor or student wasn't made clear.

Eventually, she'd been sent on her first mission.

Krystina – code name Raven – had been parachuted into the Vienne region of France, near Poitiers, in early 1942, to join an established SOE operation – the file described it as a *circuit* – named ATHLETE, to replace a courier arrested by the Gestapo. From what Kalisz could gather, the ATHLETE circuit had responsibility for co-ordinating the activities of all Resistance organisations in the area. Not long after her arrival, Krystina's organiser, the officer in charge of the circuit, had become ill, and she'd volunteered to take on his responsibilities. The report talked glowingly of the parachute drops of weapons and equipment she'd organised, the intelligence gathered, the expansion of Resistance manpower under her leadership, and all while continuing her perilous task of carrying messages and funds under the noses of the German security police. When her organiser recovered sufficiently to resume his duties, the SOE high command decided Krystina would be of more use elsewhere, and she'd been pulled out of the Vienne and flown back to London.

Of course, they hadn't given Kalisz everything. The files provided him with an insight into Krystina's character and the type of work she'd been doing. Her associates were identified only by letters of the alphabet. Monsieur A was the head of the *reseau* based in Chatellerault. Radio Operator B had recently moved from a farm near Chauvigny because of German activity in the locality. There would have been debriefings and further training, but none of this was mentioned.

The next report began on a similar note. In April of 1943 Krystina parachuted back into France to replace a courier who'd died during his insertion with a new organiser and a radio operator. Their job had been to set up an entirely new circuit, BISHOP – Kalisz recalled the name from the stamp on the back of Krystina's portrait – in the Rhône Valley, south-west of Lyons, to replace another recently broken up by the Gestapo. Kalisz could only imagine what it must have been like to organise a Resistance movement from the bottom up in an area where the Nazis had just achieved a major success: hundreds arrested; the bravest of the brave tortured and killed; every new contact risking immediate betrayal. No one could entirely be trusted, but the mission could only succeed if they recruited enough people they believed worthy of their trust. Krystina would have been unable to relax for a single moment, with capture and death lurking around every corner. Kalisz knew that feeling very well, and he understood how clandestine work sapped the energy and shredded the nerves. At first, all had gone well, but a report by the circuit leader – a man called Raoul – dated September 1943 and dictated in London, revealed what had happened next.

Krystina had been captured by the Nazi security services and taken to a prison in Lyons. Here she'd been questioned by the Gestapo, which explained the injuries Kalisz had seen on her body. It seemed she was destined to be shot, but somehow she'd escaped – the organiser described the breakout as 'audacious and risky' – and been flown back to England.

At the end of the report, another note had been added to the margin:

The manner of this agent's escape from Gestapo custody has raised questions in the minds of some senior members of the executive, and these have been exacerbated by whispers emanating from the operational area of BISHOP. Department X has investigated the matter, and it has been decided there is no reason why she cannot continue in a non-operational role. However, this should be borne in mind if she is ever considered for a return to front line duty. CH

Kalisz showed Lucy the page. 'Do you know whose initials these are?'

'"CH" is Sir Charles Hambro.' She frowned. 'He was the head of SOE up until September last year. The official word is that he resigned, but there's a rumour that Churchill sacked him.'

'So, the very top?'

'I would say so.'

'At least this explains why Yvette was ordered to shoot her if there was any sign she was a traitor. Someone was taking no chances.'

All very interesting, but what did it tell him? Krystina had been a woman of genuine character, and of great bravery. She'd risked her life time and time again, suffered agony at the hands of the Gestapo, and still she had agreed to put her head in the lion's mouth once more. Then someone had snapped her neck. That made Kalisz very angry indeed.

CHAPTER 19

OPERATION BISHOP

Place des Terraux, Lyons

They'd been watching him for three days. He made it simple for them, because he was a creature of habit and unvaried routine. Every lunchtime he came to the same cafe in the square and ate a meal of ham, bread and cheese, accompanied by a single glass of good white wine, which the proprietor kept for him in his personal bottle. After lunch he would read his newspaper and return without fail to his office when the town clock struck two.

Raoul and Krystina had relocated to another apartment, this time in Lyons. It was one of several made available to them off the books by a *résistant* who ran a property rental company. Today, Krystina was accompanied by Freddie as they sat in the other cafe on the far side of the square. She'd dressed smartly for the occasion and, to all intents and purposes, they were just another couple enjoying the spring sunshine.

'Lord, he's as dull as dishwater, this one,' Freddie murmured. 'Do you think his wife winds him up in the morning before she sends him on his way?'

'Not everyone can be like you, Freddie.' Krystina smiled. She'd come to appreciate the Londoner's cheerful personality, that seemed to energise all who came into contact with him. 'Sometimes, in our business, dullness is an asset. Better to be the grey man against the grey background when the Gestapo raid a bar or a restaurant, than someone who stands out.'

'I'll bear that in mind, love.' Freddie's perfectly arched eyebrow suggested that he took no offence.

Guy Moreau had been identified as a potential recruit by Elise, the veterinary receptionist. She remembered him as a peripheral figure in the previous circuit – not an active participant, but someone who could be called on to help in time of need. His brother had been killed in 1940, defending the Maginot Line, which meant he had no reason to love the Germans. Of course, the fact that he hadn't been rounded up with the other *résistants* raised certain questions. That was why they were here.

Could he be trusted? Krystina was to make the approach; only she could decide that, and she knew her life depended on it.

Raoul believed it was worth the risk. Moreau's family ran a successful cheese-making business, and he was in charge of production in the Rhône Valley and surrounding area.

'They have a processing plant and a warehouse in the southern outskirts of the city,' he'd explained when he'd briefed her. 'The firm supplies the local Wehrmacht headquarters, which gives Moreau a certain privileged position. His tankers travel to the remotest mountain farms to collect ewe's milk, and his delivery vans transport the cheese he makes to German supply depots and certain select shops. These vans are part of the scenery and go largely unhindered. If you can recruit him, we can use that familiarity to smuggle weapons and people across the city, and from the city to the country. It could be invaluable.'

'Boche,' Freddie whispered as a group of off-duty German soldiers strolled across the square between the SOE agents and the man they were studying. 'Did you see that?'

'Yes.' She'd been watching for it. Hidden behind his newspaper, Moreau had given the Nazi soldiers a look of pure hatred and mouthed something after them. 'I think he called them pigs.' It wasn't the first time they'd witnessed this. Krystina made her decision. She waited till the Germans were gone before she rose from the table and brushed down her skirt. 'Now is as good a time as any, I suppose. It might be better if you make yourself scarce in case something goes wrong.'

'You must be thinking of somebody else, love.' Freddie made no effort to move. 'I'll be right here in case you need me.'

As Krystina walked across the square she felt as if every eye was on her, but she'd done this before and she had her escape route worked out, if one was needed. A woman stood outside a *boulangerie* on the north side of the square and their eyes met for a moment. A glance to her right told Krystina the hands on the clock in the tower of the Hôtel de Ville indicated five to two. She approached Moreau's table from an oblique angle. Everything depended on his initial reaction.

She was almost past him before she turned with a gape of surprise. 'Guy? Can it really be you? It's Odile. We were at school together.' Before he had the chance to reply, she took the seat opposite him and graced him with her brightest smile. 'It must be fifteen years, but you haven't changed a bit.'

To his credit, and to her relief, he took the lie – clearly he knew it was a lie – at face value. He stared at Krystina for a moment, before folding his newspaper and placing it on the table between them. A neat, tidy movement from a neat and tidy man; the striped business suit he wore had seen good use, but was clearly of some quality. Monsieur Guy Moreau was of average height and slight build, but there was something imposing – an authority – about the way he sat, his head cocked slightly to one side, contemplating her as if she were a culture in a laboratory jar.

Krystina broke the silence by calling to the waiter to bring her a glass of white wine.

'From my bottle, Pierre.' Moreau spoke for the first time. 'In the meantime, perhaps you could tell me what brought you to my table. By the way, I may not have changed much, but you certainly must have, because I attended an all-boys school.'

As humour went, it was as dry as a Sardinian summer, but humour it was, and it gave Krystina encouragement. 'I was hoping to meet a patriot,' she said.

The waiter returned with a glass and placed it in front of her. Moreau waited until he'd left before he replied. 'What is a patriot these days?' He shrugged. 'Some would say patriotism is defined by loyalty to one's government. Should they not be able to depend on our support in these difficult times?'

Krystina pretended to consider for a moment. 'I would say that patriotism, in this case, is a question of one's loyalty to France. A France that is currently under occupation by a foreign power. And it is every French patriot's duty to oppose those occupiers, wouldn't you agree, Monsieur Moreau?'

Moreau took a deep breath, and for a moment she thought she'd gone too far. She might even have impugned his honour, and, in her experience, French males could be overly sensitive about such things. But when he spoke again his voice was devoid of emotion.

'And if I did agree, what assurance do I have that you are who you purport to be? A pretty face is no guarantee of integrity or fidelity. Did not Jezebel bewitch Naboth, to his eternal regret?'

'If we're going to trade mythical characters, I prefer to think of myself as Nemesis rather than Jezebel. To answer your question...' She raised her hand, as if to summon the waiter again. 'If you look over my left shoulder, you will see a lady with whom you're acquainted leaving the *boulangerie*. She will wave to you. If you believe I am who I say I am, it would be polite to return the gesture.'

Now was the moment of decision. If he didn't respond, she would get up from the table and walk away. But Moreau didn't hesitate. He returned Elise's greeting with an extravagant wave.

'So what now?'

'Now you return to work, having been slightly delayed by an old friend. Do you have a telephone number where I can reach you direct?'

He took out a small notebook with a propelling pencil attached and wrote down a number.

'This approach is not entirely unexpected.' He chose his words with care. 'And I have some idea of what value I can be to you. I am not the only *patriot* at the plant, and I know who can be trusted and who cannot. Do you understand what I am saying?'

She nodded. He already had a network in place. It would save a lot of time.

He hesitated for a moment before continuing. 'There is also a friend of mine, a former soldier.' He wrote something else on the paper, before tearing out the page and slipping it across the table. 'He can know nothing about what happens in the factory, but I know he is desperate to get back in the fight. This is his address. His name is Émile Berard.'

CHAPTER 20

Arisaig House

9:45 a.m.

'This is the list of training schools Colonel Baldwin provided.' Lucy handed over a piece of paper as they walked out into the courtyard of the house.

Kalisz took it and frowned. 'STS 21, STS 22, STS 22a... But this tells me nothing?'

'Security here is very tight, as you would expect,' she said. 'It's forbidden to mention the names or locations of the houses in official signals traffic. The colonel felt it would be wrong to give the information to an outsider, even one as well connected as you.'

'It is preposterous,' Kalisz choked. 'I will protest.'

'However,' Lucy continued patiently, 'he has given *me* a list of the locations. The one you have is grouped so those training schools most accessible – those between Arisaig village and Mallaig – are at the beginning, with the least easy to access at the end. The final two, STS 24a and 24b, are only reachable by boat. Each school is run by what they call a "conducting officer", who is responsible for all aspects of the students' welfare. Whether or not we can talk to the students will be the decision of those individual officers. All you have to do is let me know which schools you want to visit and I'll take you there.'

'I still think it's ridiculous.' Kalisz knew there was little point in further argument.

A battered and dirty civilian motor car was parked in front of the house, and Lucy inspected it with a look of consternation. 'I think this must be our transport.'

'You think they are trying to tell us something?' Kalisz kicked one of the rear tyres.

'There's one other thing, Maj— Jan.'

'Yes?'

'I don't think I'd feel safe driving this rusting excuse for a car in these boots.'

'In that case, I will drive.' After a moment's hesitation, he got behind the wheel and Lucy joined him in the passenger's seat. 'Everything is on the wrong side,' he whispered to himself.

'Just be sure you drive on the left side of the road.'

'On the left, yes.' He tentatively moved the gearstick and prodded the fuel pump lever.

'I think it's some kind of ancient Austin,' Lucy offered. 'The transport people must have brought it here from somewhere, so it should be warmed up. You shouldn't need to use the pump. Try starting it with the key first.'

Fortunately, the motor fired after two attempts. Kalisz put the car into gear with a metallic crunch and they lurched into movement. A roar of the engine and another grinding gear change, and they accelerated out of the courtyard, bucketing over the potholes and with Kalisz wrestling the steering wheel as if it were a living organism.

Lucy clutched the door handle and gritted her teeth. 'I think this is going to be a long day.'

When they reached the road, Kalisz turned left up a steep hill. He resisted the temptation to change down to a lower gear, and kept his foot on the accelerator as the underpowered Austin laboured up the slope. It didn't sound as if it was doing the engine much good, but at least he felt in control now.

'Tell me...' He kept his eyes on the road ahead. 'Who is "the King over the Water"?'

Lucy frowned. 'Why would you ask that?'

'Major Dempsey mentioned him last night. I was just curious.'

'Have you heard of Bonnie Prince Charlie, Jan?'

'I don't believe so,' Kalisz admitted. 'My English history is a little rusty.'

'His father, James Stuart, was king of Great Britain about two hundred and fifty years ago, but was deposed by his son-in-law with a Dutch army. The king fled to the continent, but many people, particularly in Scotland, continued to support him. Prince Charles returned to Scotland from France, landing not far from here at Glenfinnan, and raised an army to win back the crown – an event known as the Jacobite Rebellion. He almost succeeded, but was driven back north and eventually defeated at a place called Culloden. Many of his followers were slaughtered, but he managed to escape with the help of a few loyalists. He eventually fled to Rome, where he spent the rest of his life and eventually died in relative poverty. One of the places he hid was said to be Borrodale House, where we were yesterday.'

'You sound as if you almost regret his failure?'

'I'm a romantic,' she said lightly. 'And it's a romantic story. What did Dempsey say about him?'

'He said the locals still drink a toast to the King over the Water.'

'That would mean they still believe in the Jacobite cause.'

'Yes…' He nodded. 'It makes sense now. People living in the past.'

The hill seemed to last forever, but eventually the Austin wheezed its way over the rise and they were greeted by a spectacular vista of mountains and sea. Kalisz managed to change gear and allowed the car to coast down the next slope. Driving on the left was less of a problem than he'd anticipated, because most of the winding road was little more than a car's width across and so far they hadn't met another vehicle.

'The prime minister is very pleased with your progress.'

'You spoke to him?' Kalisz wasn't sure whether to be surprised or not. 'I thought we hadn't made any progress?'

'Thanks to you, we know Jean-Marc didn't kill Krystina, and that whoever did had at least one accomplice.'

'Not for certain,' he corrected her. 'Until we prove there was an accomplice or accomplices, it's only a theory.'

'In any case, he is pleased. But he said to tell you that the clock is ticking.'

'Of course.' Kalisz grimaced.

They drove on for a time, mountains to the right, the glittering sea visible through the trees to their left. 'You never say much about Krystina, Jan. That surprises me. A fellow countryman, a beautiful Polish heroine, yet it seems to have barely touched you.'

He resisted the temptation to look towards Lucy. 'An investigator can never be influenced by his emotions. Krystina is what she is – a victim. My job is to find out who turned her into a victim. My feelings are irrelevant, but for what it's worth, I think she was brave and resolute and passionate, but she could be cruel, vindictive and spiteful. In short, she was a perfectly normal, flawed human being. Part of me regrets that her killer deprived her of her final mission, but another part is relieved she did not have to endure it. I do not think it would have ended well. Christ!'

As they approached a sharp bend, an enormous army lorry turned the corner on two wheels and rushed towards them, entirely filling the road ahead. Kalisz instinctively hauled the wheel to the left and the car bumped across the verge onto the heather, perilously close to a steep drop, as the truck shaved by within inches. He braked to a halt, but left the engine running and willed his thundering heart to still. Lucy Devereux sat with her eyes screwed shut, muttering an admirable assortment of English curses, some of which were entirely novel to him.

'You can look now.'

She opened one eye first, and took a deep breath. 'Well, that almost brought the investigation to a premature conclusion.'

Kalisz eased the car into gear, and they bounced over the rough ground back onto the road. 'I suppose we shouldn't be surprised. As the prickly Colonel Baldwin kindly warned us, accidents happen all the time at Arisaig.'

Arisaig itself was less a village than a scattering of houses just off the main road, overlooking a wide bay. A large square church tower on the hillside above provided a reminder to any of the faithful tempted to allow their morals to stray. Behind the church, jagged saw-toothed mountains rose in layer after layer to meet the ash-grey sky. An odd place to base a clandestine training centre, Kalisz thought, until you remembered Major Dempsey's homily about secrets and secrecy. A road led down towards the sea, where most of the low, slate-roofed houses had conglomerated, and the view opened up to reveal the two arms of the bay cloaked in scrubby trees, tormented, twisted and shaped by wind and weather. Away to the north-west, in the far distance, he had a faint impression of an island, where a great wall of sea cliffs soared from the ocean, topped by a mountain shaped like a shark's fin.

It didn't take a detective to identify the police station, which had a black car parked outside with a sign on the roof that said 'Police'. The building was low and squat and constructed of dark stone, and only differentiated from the other houses by a blue door and a board that announced its function. As they walked to the door, Kalisz noticed a motorcycle leaning against the outer wall.

Inside the entrance, they were met by a wooden counter with a door to one side. Beyond the counter, a large man dressed in a pale blue shirt and a black tie sat hunched over a desk covered in papers, peering through wire-rimmed spectacles at a single-page document. He must have been in his late fifties, and his bald head was partly camouflaged by strands of silver hair grown long and combed over the pink scalp.

'Constable MacDonald?'

The policeman looked up from his papers. 'Aye, that'll be me.'

'Major Zamoyski, and this is Flight Officer Devereux. We're here about the deaths at Arisaig House?'

MacDonald looked up at a clock on a wall blanketed with yellowing posters warning against giving information to spies, advice on how to identify enemy uniforms, and advertising local dances at the village hall.

'Och, is that the time?' He swept a meaty hand to encompass the documents on the desk. 'I've been drowning in paperwork. A form for everything and a new regulation every second day.' The policeman spoke slowly and deliberately, which suited Kalisz, because he also had a strong accent. 'I even had to arrest the minister last week for holding a dance that turned out to contravene the War Charity Act. Come away in.' MacDonald rose from the desk and opened the door to let them into the main office. Kalisz waved Lucy to an empty chair on the opposite side of the desk and perched himself on a stool by the counter. 'I can make you a cup of tea, if you'd like?' He waved to a large tin mug on the top of the desk, that appeared to be filled with brown sludge.

'That won't be necessary,' Kalisz said hurriedly.

'Suit yourselves.' MacDonald shrugged and picked up a teaspoon, with which he delicately added five heaped spoonfuls from a sugar bowl to the concoction. He tapped the spoon against the mug's lip to dislodge the last grains and took a long, noisy slurp that made Lucy wince.

'Why would...?' No, that could wait, but Kalisz filed the thought that had occurred to him away for further consideration. 'Constable, I'm sure you must be aware that we are now treating Lieutenant Fontaine's death as murder?'

'Not through any official channels.' MacDonald shook his head. 'But, yes, I'd heard. I thought there was something funny about it at the time, but the colonel was most adamant. I had the feeling he just wanted it to go away.'

'Was there anything else about the crime scene you thought was *funny*?'

The constable considered for a moment. 'Aye, it struck me as odd that our killer went to all that trouble to fetch the ladder and rope from the gardener's hut when he could just as easily have carried the body down to the rocks and thrown it into the sea. Another corpse washing up on the shore would barely have been noticed around here.'

'Why is that?'

'Because it's an all too common occurrence in this part of the world, sir. Sailors from sunk ships, airmen from crashed planes, soldiers lost on exercises, and the odd local who takes his lobster boat out after one dram too many. I must have picked up at least seven or eight poor souls from the beach in the last two or three years. Everything washes up in the bay sooner or later – bodies, torpedoes, bits of boats and planes. If the lassie had gone in the water, I believe that would have been the end of it. It would have been near impossible to tell exactly what killed her, and in any case, Colonel Baldwin would have had her in the ground before anybody could get a look.'

CHAPTER 21

'Would it be correct to characterise your relationship with the military authorities as strained?' Lucy asked.

'"Strained"?' MacDonald considered the word with a wisp of a smile on his lips. 'Aye, "strained" would describe it very well.' He stood up and pulled a blue logbook from its place on a shelf. 'What you have to understand is that this wee village of ours could very rightly be described as the crime capital of Scotland at the moment. Between the army, and the students, and the Gorbals evacuee lads and lassies, I probably investigate about twice as many crimes in a month as a Glasgow policeman.'

'What kind of crimes?' Kalisz decided a professional interest would help keep MacDonald talking.

'Take a look for yourself.' The constable handed over the logbook. 'Soldiers will steal anything that's not screwed down or that will provide them with a meal. We've had cows shot, hens and ducks regularly go missing or turn up as piles of feathers behind the mess kitchen. No sheep around here is safe. One of my jobs is to issue firearms certificates to civilians, but at the same time, military weapons are being stolen or "borrowed" from the armouries. Pistols, mainly, but someone pinched a .303 rifle and a hundred rounds of ammunition from the range at Glasnacardoch. You'd think one war would be enough for them.'

Kalisz noted the name and flicked through the book with particular interest. 'You mentioned students? There's a reference here to four of them suspected –' he faltered as three sharp cracks interrupted his question, but the policeman didn't even blink – 'of breaking into a lodge house two weeks ago.'

'That'll be the mad major "encouraging" some of his trainees.' MacDonald gave a wry shake of the head. 'You learn to tell the difference between his thunder flashes and a three-inch mortar round at

Camusdarach, or the plastic explosive and dynamite they use up at the big house. The break-in? Aye, just one of many. But this time they left evidence behind. When I traced them to the house up the loch, I was told by their conducting officer, who stays in a cottage nearby, that he wouldn't divulge their identities, despite being asked several times. I was forced to go to Colonel Baldwin at Arisaig House to ask him to use his authority to get the names. Instead, he told me he accepted full responsibility for the thefts and he could not allow me to see the students – his very words, sir. Now I know they're doing important work here, and I try to take that into account in my dealings with them. But the law's the law. I noted down his full name and particulars, and cautioned and charged him with obstructing the police in the execution of their duty.' He smiled at the memory. 'Mind you, that was just me howling at the moon, as it were. We both know nothing will ever come of it.'

Kalisz met Lucy's eyes, and he could tell she was trying not to laugh at the thought of the look on Baldwin's face as he was charged.

'One last thing, Constable,' Kalisz said. 'Did any of your contacts with Arisaig House involve the victims?'

'Only the once.' MacDonald frowned. 'It was a week or ten days before she was killed. There's something of a tradition around here of what Colonel Baldwin would call "high jinks", which means his students and the Commandos up at Inverailort testing their "skills" against one another. In this case, Gardener's Cottage, where Krystina Kowolska was staying, was the target of a break-in. Some items of clothing were stolen, and a watch. Miss Kowolska said she didn't want to make a fuss and would never have reported it but for the watch, which had sentimental value. All she wanted was it back.'

'Do you think it could have had anything to do with her death?'

'You can't rule anything out,' the policeman said. 'I was going to talk to Major Gunn about it before Baldwin warned me off.'

'We'll take care of that,' Kalisz assured him. 'But first we need to have another word with Miss Yvette about why she didn't mention the burglary. You searched Krystina's room?'

'Not me personally. A civilian accompanied Colonel Baldwin and me when we interviewed Yvette Messier, and he insisted it was his job.' MacDonald's expression implied he didn't approve.

'Then it won't do any harm to have another look.' Kalisz ignored Lucy's puzzled look. 'Thank you, Constable.'

'I thought you'd already searched the room?' Lucy said as they got back into the car.

'I have, but a little bell inside my head is suggesting that I do so again. The first rule of Polish police work – never ignore the little bell.'

Kalisz put the Austin into gear, only to be greeted by a metallic rattling that seemed to follow them up the road. What now? He stopped and got out, jeered by four or five boys in ragged jumpers and shorts who'd gathered on the tussocky strand by the shore. Someone, presumably the spectators, had tied tin cans to the rear bumper with string. He untied them and kicked them to the side of the road.

'I think we've just been introduced to Constable MacDonald's "Gorbals lads and lassies".' Lucy laughed.

'By the way, Flight Officer...' Kalisz switched on the engine. 'Thanks to the constable's logbook, I now know that STS 25b is a place called Camusdarach Lodge, STS 22 is Rhubana Lodge, and both are relatively nearby, and had confirmation that Glasnacardoch is some kind of weapons facility, so perhaps we can dispense with this secrecy nonsense now. It seems Constable MacDonald did not get the memorandum.'

Lucy's cheeks reddened. 'Very well, Major.'

–

Yvette didn't appear surprised when Kalisz knocked at her door. In fact, she looked as if she'd been expecting them. She invited them inside.

'We're here principally to talk about the missing watch,' Kalisz said.

'Yes?' She took a seat at the table. Kalisz noticed she had her hands clasped tightly together, as if to stop them shaking.

'Constable MacDonald tells me someone broke into this cottage shortly before Krystina died?'

'That's correct.' Yvette nodded. 'But I can't believe it had anything to do with her death. It was just the Commandos at Inverailort House playing their stupid games again.'

'Again?'

'We'd both been burgled on previous visits to Arisaig. They pick the lock, or get in through the window, choose a couple of trophies and then leave again. You don't even know they've been in the house until you find something missing. A few days later there'll be a parcel on the doorstep, with the stolen goods and a bottle of whisky.'

'What kind of trophies?'

Yvette snorted. 'What kind do you think? Underwear, Major. Brassieres and pants, if you wish me to be specific.'

'But this time they took a watch?'

'Yes. Krystina said it had been a gift she received for acting as a bridesmaid for a Polish friend. It was the same make as yours, and quite expensive, I think, but she wanted it back principally because of the memories it had for her.'

'And nothing has been returned this time?'

'No, but the Commandos have been on exercise the past few days.' She shrugged. 'Then Krystina was killed.'

'Did she go to this... Inverailort –' his tongue struggled with the word – 'and ask about it?'

Yvette shook her head. 'There was an officer there she did not like.' She looked from Kalisz to Lucy. 'Perhaps you should know about him, but there are things I would not be comfortable saying in front of a man.'

Kalisz considered this new information. 'Then please talk with Lucy,' he said. 'In the meantime, if you'll excuse me, I would like to take another look at Warrant Officer Kowolska's room.'

'Then you are fortunate,' Yvette said. 'I had word from the big house that someone was coming to clear out her belongings this morning, but nobody appeared.'

Kalisz went through to the room and stood for a moment, re-engaging with his surroundings. It was the chink of MacDonald's spoon against the tin mug that had set off the alarm bell, but for the life of him he didn't know why. He ignored the wardrobe and sideboard and repeated the rest of the search as he'd first carried it out. He pulled back the curtains, then knelt to inspect the skirting board. Only now, from this low vantage point, did he notice a slight mark on the floorboards where the bed had been moved. A threadbare rug covered the floor between the front of the chest of drawers and the bed frame. The positioning struck him as odd.

Kalisz pushed the heavy bed frame aside and lifted the carpet. The floorboards were old and warped, but they'd been put in place by a professional, because the joins were tight and there were few gaps –

apart from in one small place. A tiny slot on one side of a plank, close to where the rusty nail head was just visible in the dark, varnished wood. The slot only drew attention because it was a fraction lighter in colour than the surrounding area. He tried to lift the board using his fingers, but couldn't get any purchase. Then he remembered the spoon in the bottom drawer.

The handle just fitted into the small slot and gave him enough leverage to raise the plank. It came away surprisingly easily, and when he looked at the underside he realised why. Someone had used a file or a saw to cut the point of the fixing nails off level with the wood. Below the board was a dark void, and he reached tentatively inside. His searching fingers froze as they chanced upon a familiar object, and he lifted a small revolver from the recess by its barrel and placed it on the mattress. Next he retrieved two slim boxes about the size of a cigarette packet, and finally a small green notebook.

Glancing at the labels, he placed the boxes beside the revolver and opened the notebook.

CHAPTER 22

Kalisz walked back into the room where the two women were waiting, noting an atmosphere of tension that hadn't existed previously. Lucy Devereux glanced at the object he was carrying, but she knew better than to show any curiosity.

'From what Yvette has told me,' she said, 'I believe we should speak to Major Gunn at Inverailort House sooner rather than later.'

'You think he's a suspect?'

'He has a history with the victim. One that could give him a motive for doing her harm, so yes, I would say so.'

'Then we'll go to see the Commandos next, but first —' he locked eyes with Yvette — 'I have a few more questions to ask this lady.'

He'd packaged the objects from under the floorboards in one of Krystina's blouses, and now he placed it on the table and pulled back the cloth to reveal them. The sight of the revolver brought a hiss from Lucy and a groan of what might have been anguish from Yvette.

'Krystina Kowolska went to great lengths to conceal these items. More so than she did the watch, which meant so much to her. Have you seen them before?'

'Not the gun or the book —' Yvette shook her head — 'but I have seen the pills. She used to say that she took one of them when she wanted to be alive and the other when she wanted to be dead.'

'What do you mean?'

'There were things she needed to forget. You must have seen the scars. But there are worse things than scars.' Yvette looked to Lucy. 'You understand?'

Lucy bit her lip and nodded.

'But when the pills she took to forget stopped working, there had to be more pills to bring back the old Krystina.'

'Do you know what these things are?' Kalisz asked Lucy.

'The ones in the brown box are Benzedrine. It's a stimulant they give to pilots to keep them alert. The others, I don't know. Some kind of sleeping pill?'

'The gun,' Yvette said. 'Why did she have the gun?'

'For protection?' Lucy looked to Kalisz. 'She must have known she was in danger.'

Kalisz picked up the revolver and flicked out the cylinder. 'Not for protection,' he said. 'There's only a single round in the chamber. To me, that means only one thing.'

Lucy flinched as if she'd been slapped.

'No,' Yvette choked. 'Not Krystina.'

'Perhaps we would know more if we could read her journal, but she must have wanted to keep it hidden from the world, because the entries appear to be in some kind of code.' He handed Yvette the notebook and she flicked through the pages.

'From the world, perhaps, but not from Yvette. This will be a code we have practised together.' She frowned in concentration. 'It could be Playfair with a double transposition, but more likely using a one-time pad. We have a book of them that we used. I would encode a message from the sender's sheet, and Krystina would decode it using the receiver's. All I have to do is go through the book and find the single sheet that is missing.' She frowned. 'Although she may have torn out more than one, which would mean it would take me longer.'

'It sounds very complicated,' Lucy said.

'Not if you know what you're doing. It helps if you know specific words or phrases the sender is likely to use.' She locked eyes with Kalisz. 'For instance, there will no doubt be a reference to "sleeping with Yvette".' She shrugged. 'It was the way she lived. Taking her pleasure where she could. It meant nothing to either of us.'

'But you were not always with Krystina?' Kalisz suggested.

'No,' she said. 'Which is why there will also be a reference in the journal to "the dirty Jew".'

'We are talking about Pierre Renan?'

'It was our secret.' She gaped. 'How did you know?'

'That doesn't matter. What does is that you told us you were here alone the night Krystina was killed. Is that true?'

Yvette shook her head. 'I was with Pierre.'

'With him here?'

118

'No. We could never risk Krystina finding us.'

Kalisz considered for a moment. 'But not at Borrodale House, either, I would guess? It would be very hard to keep a secret there.'

'We had – have – our own special place. Pierre found it and made it… comfortable. A cave down towards the shore.'

'You will show us it.'

—

'What did you think?' Kalisz asked later, as he and Lucy walked up the path towards Arisaig House.

'Of their love nest? A mattress and some blankets in a damp hole in the ground.' She smiled. 'It could have been sordid and grubby, but Yvette made it seem almost romantic. They didn't have any choice, really. From what she said, Krystina's reaction to having a Jew in the cottage could have been violent. Is that sort of hatred of the Jews common in Poland?'

'Is it common in England?'

'Of course not.'

'Yet, from what I understand, Mr Churchill seems to regard them as a nuisance, and their persecution and murder by the Nazis as a sideshow to the war.'

'You haven't answered my question.'

'No, I haven't, because it's not an easy question to answer,' he admitted. He'd come across plenty of anti-Semitism in the police, and not just in the lower ranks. Poland hadn't always been kind to the Jews who made up a sizeable proportion of its population – something like three million out of thirty, including more than three hundred thousand in Warsaw. Nominally, the rights of the country's minorities were protected under Polish law. The reality was different. When Marshal Piłsudski had died, right-wing parties in the *Sejm*, the Polish parliament, had introduced new anti-Semitic laws. They'd limited the production of kosher food, restricted the number of Jewish students in Polish universities, and cut the numbers allowed to practise in professions like the law, medicine, finance, and even journalism 'There's been a large Jewish community in Poland for five hundred years. Some, mainly in the large cities, integrated happily into society. They look and act and talk like every other Pole.' He shook his head. 'I didn't realise how many they were in Warsaw until they were forced to wear stars. A majority, though, mainly Orthodox Jews in the countryside, stuck to their old ways and language, and formed their own communities. Jews in the city sometimes became rich and successful, and riches and success create jealousy, so yes, some Poles came to resent, even hate them. Likewise, being different generates suspicion, with the same result.'

'So your answer is yes.'

Something welled up inside Kalisz, and he turned to Lucy and touched her arm, so she stopped to meet his eyes. 'Not so very long ago, some very brave Jews sacrificed their lives to save mine. In Warsaw today there are many hundreds of gentile families sheltering Jews in the knowledge that discovery means certain death. At any moment, they could be betrayed to the Gestapo, dragged into the street, where the Jews would be shot and the Poles hanged, to be left as examples of the price of helping a Jew. At least five families in my own street have been hiding Jews in their apartments since the liquidation of the ghetto in May. How do I know this? Because my wife shares our food with them, though she thinks I can't see what is very obvious in our bare cupboards. This watch —' he showed her the Patek Philippe on his wrist — 'rightly belongs to a Jew, a neighbour who gave it to me for safekeeping when he was forced to take his family into the ghetto. They are all long dead now. Do I feel guilty that I didn't do more to help them? Of course. But we did not know then what would come. There was hardship, but there was hardship for everybody in Warsaw. Nobody knew about the camps then.'

'You wouldn't be here now if you'd helped them, would you?'

'No,' he said. 'So my answer to your question is that there is no answer. Back there...' He nodded in the direction of the cottage. 'The sight of that revolver with the single bullet touched something in you.'

'You're very observant, Investigator.'

'You could say that.' A smile touched his lips, and for a moment Lucy thought he looked much younger. 'May I ask what it was?'

'A memory, as you would say. When I was in Spain with the International Brigade, what seems like a lifetime ago, we nurses were always advised to keep the last bullet for ourselves in case the Moors were about to capture us. It's not something I'm likely to forget. You haven't asked me what Yvette and I discussed.'

A pause, as his mind digested her revelation. 'I knew you'd tell me in your own time.'

'Krystina Kowolska used her unarmed combat skills on Major Gunn during an exercise in the hills. She broke his leg and then abandoned him to find his way home alone. The experience left him with a limp that ended his career as a fighting soldier.'

'Why would she do that – leave him, I mean?'

'Because Major Gunn attempted to rape her.'

CHAPTER 23

Warsaw

31 December 1943

The plumber who appeared at Maria's door was a big man in voluminous, filth-stained workman's overalls, wearing a flat cap low over his eyes and carrying a large toolbox. A length of rubber hose hung over one shoulder. He removed his scuffed boots at the door and loudly asked where the bathroom was.

When they were safely inside, Dimitar Petrov laid his toolbox aside and they contemplated each other for a moment.

'I take it you are here on behalf of my mysterious caller?' Maria said.

'My dear lady, I am your mysterious caller.' The Bulgarian's cultured tones were entirely at odds with his face, which had a fierce quality that suggested a long-forgotten liaison between one of his female forebears and a warrior of one of Europe's many eastern invaders. 'I must thank you for receiving me. These are difficult times, and it is not everyone who would welcome a stranger into their home.'

Maria nodded gravely to show she appreciated the compliment. 'You said you were an "associate" of my husband and I believed you. May I offer you a cup of what passes for coffee these days?'

The offer brought a regretful shake of the head. 'We do not have much time. We must complete our business and I will be gone. Naturally, I will rattle a few pipes before I leave. It is the least your neighbours will expect.' His voice lost its levity, and Maria understood that the *business* had begun. 'I am in charge of a large organisation, some of which is legitimate, but some of it is not. I am being quite candid again. I hope you appreciate that?'

Maria nodded. What her visitor meant was that nothing he said should go beyond these four walls.

'It is, by necessity, a very secret organisation, but recent events suggest that it has been penetrated by someone who does not have my interests at heart. A betrayal, of sorts, that must never be repeated. My various enterprises are quite strictly compartmentalised, so it's unlikely my personal security has been compromised, but until I discover the identity of the betrayer I can trust no one.'

'You mentioned events?'

'Yes. To the heart of the matter. A good friend and his family found themselves in difficulties at the beginning of the Occupation. You understand how these things work, Mrs Kalisz. Registration, a blue star, assets under threat. Well, his assets became my assets – a matter of trust between us – and I managed to find a form of sanctuary for them. He would work in one of my enterprises, and that enterprise would provide a new identity and the possibility of a new life. Quite recently, someone betrayed his identity and his location. He and his eldest son were shot by the Gestapo, but his wife and the other two children managed to escape and found a way to contact me.'

'And now?'

'Now I need to find a new sanctuary for them, but until I discover the identity of the betrayer and the extent of his knowledge, I cannot make use of my extensive and quite powerful organisation to keep them safe. Who can I turn to?'

'We cannot keep them here,' Maria said. Her visitor nodded, and she knew he was satisfied that this was not a refusal, but merely a statement of fact. She must consider other avenues. 'There is the possibility of finding places for the children at the hospital where I work – the staff are already harbouring a number of homeless Jewish children – but not the mother, I think.'

'I doubt she would wish to be separated from her family.'

Maria considered for a moment. 'If my husband—'

They turned at the sound of the door opening, and the plumber's fist went to his armpit with astonishing speed. Maria laid a hand on his arm as a tall figure entered the room.

'My son. Anything you say to me, you can say to him.' She frowned. 'Stefan, where have you been?' The boy's face and hands were covered in black grease.

'Mr Roziki has been teaching us about engines.' Stefan grinned. 'Welcome to our home, sir.' He bowed to the stranger.

Roziki… of course.

'Stefan, I want you to go back to Mr Roziki and tell him to expect a visitor.' She turned to Petrov. 'Did you come in a vehicle?'

'A gazogene truck, parked in the next street.'

'All the better. Mr Roziki will open his workshop for an emergency repair, Stefan.'

–

Antoni Roziki had turned to mechanical engineering late in life, and entirely by chance. He'd begun the war as Doctor Tomasz Novak, an eminent surgeon at one of Warsaw's foremost hospitals, and a respected member of his community. All that had changed when the Nazis discovered a hitherto unknown Jewish grandmother. This instantly turned Novak from a nominal and sceptical Catholic into a person subject to the Nuremberg Laws, which, among many other restrictions, prevented Jewish doctors from treating Aryan patients. Novak had been destined for the ghetto and the gas chamber when Jan Kalisz provided him with a new identity, which declared him an engineer. He'd embraced his new career with enthusiasm: 'After all, the human body is just another machine, it's just a matter of knowing which part goes where.' The Wehrmacht provided a substantial part of his customer base by day, while he treated injured Underground fighters by night. He had premises in the rotunda building on Oboźna, at the top of the Vistula escarpment, once one of Warsaw's most iconic art galleries but now converted into garages and workshops.

'To what do I owe this pleasant surprise, Mrs Kalisz?' Roziki wiped oil from his hands and sized up the man who'd just stepped from the gazogene truck. There could hardly have been a greater contrast than the little mechanic with the cherub's plump features and twinkling eyes, and the massive, dangerous figure in the plumber's overalls.

'This gentleman is a friend of my husband's, Mr Roziki. A trusted friend. He has a problem, and, as another trusted friend of my husband's, I hoped you might be able to help us solve it.'

Petrov explained about the Jewish family. 'It would only be for a short time, until I get my… shall we say… arrangements… sorted out.'

'Three people?' Roziki looked pensive.

'A woman and two children of eight and ten years. I would be in your debt.'

'Between us there will be no debts,' Roziki insisted. 'It is enough that three more Jewish lives are protected for a while. I could organise such a thing with other *trusted* friends, but it would take time. But, as it happens, I may be in a position to help personally. Feeding them might be the greatest difficulty.'

'I will provide food.'

'Very well.' Roziki's eyes roved over their surroundings. 'A garage is full of nooks and crannies, storerooms and workshops, and this one is no different. In truth, this building is too large for my needs, but I feel comfortable here. Come with me.' They followed him to the back of the workshop, which led to a central storage area. An enclosed stairway provided access to the upper level. 'My living quarters,' he said. But instead of taking the stairs, he led them to a large cupboard and opened the doors. Coats and overalls hung from hooks, but he reached past them and fumbled around for something on the rear wall. 'Damn, I can never find it.' Eventually, they heard a quiet *snick* and the mechanic smiled. He pulled the coats aside to reveal a black void. 'The cellar has been here since the rotunda was built. Somewhere cool and dry for the gallery to keep the paintings they weren't able to display. It was only after Jan told me about what happened in the ghetto that I decided to make proper use of it. A friend who is a carpenter put in the cupboard and concealed the door. They'd never find it unless they tore the place apart.' He exchanged a glance with Petrov. 'Of course, that's what they do, but if it's only for a short time...? There is water, an electric stove and a toilet connected to the sewers.'

'I believe it will do very nicely, Mr Roziki,' the big man said.

–

That night, having safely delivered the refugees to Roziki, Petrov drove back to the modest estate on the outskirts of Warsaw where he had decided to base himself until the danger was past, or a more permanent solution became necessary. It was owned under another name and could never be connected to him.

When he'd parked the gazogene truck out of the way among the trees, he walked up the gravel path towards the house. A young man was waiting for him at the door. Without a word, he handed over a piece of paper. Two words. A name. The fruits of a source inside Gestapo headquarters at Aleja Szucha. Germans were as venal as any other race; all it took was a little money in the right place. He read the name with a pang of regret. So young and so full of potential.

He sighed and retraced his steps to the truck. It was going to be a long night.

CHAPTER 24

Arisaig

One p.m.

They'd been told Major Richard Gunn was on exercise with a section of trainees in the hills north of Inverailort House. Kalisz drove up a track until he found the Commandos' transport – a three-ton lorry – and the driver directed them to a small group of men gathered at the top of a steep drop, where an old, now disused, quarry had been cut into the hillside. As they approached, several other soldiers swarmed up the quarry sides on ropes with impressive speed and agility to join their comrades.

Gunn wore the same rough khaki uniform as his soldiers, but Kalisz recognised him immediately by the stout shepherd's crook he leaned on for balance. The major would certainly have seen them coming, but he ignored the two newcomers and continued with his exercise. He formed the men in a line and told them to number off, one to twelve.

'I need six volunteers,' he called.

Without hesitation, every man stepped forward, and he smiled. 'All right, I'll take the odd sods – one, three, five, seven, nine and eleven. Come and line up here.' He indicated a line in the heather perhaps twenty paces from the cliff. 'Sergeant, issue the blindfolds.'

A sergeant handed out strips of dark cloth to the remaining men.

'Now, I want you to blindfold your oppo. Good and tight now. No peeping. Excellent.' The sergeant placed a rifle with bayonet attached at each of the blindfolded men's feet. 'Now, gentlemen,' Gunn continued, 'at your feet you will find a rifle. I want you to pick it up. This exercise is not just about courage and discipline, it is a lesson in trust. I want you to trust me not to kill you. Ahead of you is the edge of a cliff. On the order, you will charge directly to your front and you will not stop until you hear my command.' A rustle of unease ran through the blindfolded men. 'Anyone who does not obey my order or does not put his heart into the charge will be returned to his unit immediately.'

Gunn allowed the tension to stretch out like a taut bowstring. The sergeant had gone to stand at the cliff edge outside the line of attack, and Kalisz saw him give a slight nod.

'Charge!'

Not a man hesitated.

With a great roar, the blindfolded Commandos raced across the heather and tufted grass towards the edge. Kalisz felt as if his heart had stopped beating, and Lucy whispered 'My God' as they raced nearer and nearer the cliff. Ten paces... five. When would the order to halt come? There was no order, and the line of charging men went over the edge to plummet into the quarry and onto the jagged rocks below.

Silence, until after a long pause, a voice announced, 'I think I've shit meself.' Followed by a roar of laughter. Kalisz walked forward to where he could see the net two instructors had put in place while Gunn was going through his theatrics, and into which the charging soldiers had fallen. The Commandos, pale to a man, tore off their blindfolds and grasped the ropes that were thrown to them and pulled themselves up to level ground.

'Gather round, lads,' Gunn called. And when he was surrounded, 'Men, that was an exemplary exercise. The beers are on me tonight. Today's lesson is that your officers will never kill you for no reason. They may sacrifice you, but that's different. In either case, you must never hesitate. If it's your duty to die, you die, because that's what being a Royal Marine Commando is all about. Now gather up the gear.'

Gunn limped across to where Kalisz and Lucy stood, using his stick for support. He was a tall, handsome man with a thin, sandy moustache and an air of mocking authority. 'What can I do for you, Major?'

'Just out of interest,' Kalisz said, 'what would you have done if one of those men missed the net?'

The other man shrugged. 'We would have called it a training accident and given the dead hero a suitable send-off. We lost a man only the other night. This is not a place for the faint of heart, Major...?'

'Zamoyski. I am here about a theft from the female students' accommodation at Arisaig House.'

'Polish, eh?' The thin lips twisted in what might have been derision. 'I served as a liaison officer with the First Polish Infantry Corps after the Dunkirk nonsense. Poorly trained, ill-disciplined mercenaries to a man. I even learned a bit of the language. Does *nie marnuj mojego czasu* ring any bells?'

Kalisz chose to ignore the insult to his comrades. 'I'm not here to waste your valuable time, Major, and things would move along much more quickly if you would treat my visit with the significance it warrants.'

'A last-minute training exercise designed to practise certain skills.' Gunn shrugged. 'The ladies will get their scanties back tomorrow, with a little something to take the edge off their temporary loss. Good of you to come, though, and to bring your secretary.' He looked Lucy up and down and pointed the crook in her direction. 'Very scenic, very scenic indeed. Bucked the lads up no end – isn't that right, lads?'

The men cheered, except for the sergeant – bull-chested, compact and humourless – who sniffed and glared.

Lucy studied Gunn for a moment, before walking towards the men who were gathering up their equipment.

'Sergeant?' she called. 'Pick up that rifle and try to kill me.'

The sergeant exchanged a glance with Gunn, who shrugged.

'If you insist, ma'am,' the NCO said.

'Flight Officer—'

But Kalisz was too late. The sergeant swept up the rifle with the efficiency of long use and in the same movement darted at Lucy Devereux, lunging with the bayonet towards her midriff. At the moment it seemed she must be skewered, she pirouetted in a spin that took her inside the point and, in a whirl of limbs, the rifle tumbled one way and the sergeant the other. Before he could move, Lucy was on him with her forearm across his windpipe.

'You were an instructor at Beaulieu, Sergeant,' she said quietly.

'That's right, ma'am… Perkins.' He smiled. 'And I'm pleased to see you haven't lost your edge. A pity about…'

Lucy pulled herself up. 'Thank you, Sergeant,' she said.

'Ma'am.' He nodded, and walked off to join the wide-eyed trainees.

'As I was saying, Major,' Kalisz said, 'we are investigating a break-in at the residences at Arisaig House. I am afraid it concerns more than…

what did you call them? Scanties?' He dropped his voice. 'I am here on the highest of authority.'

'Who says so?' Gunn demanded.

'You will have to ask my secretary.' Kalisz allowed himself a thin smile. 'Shall we say back at your headquarters in thirty minutes?'

—

'You are a woman of many talents, Flight Officer Devereux,' Kalisz said when they were back in the car. 'What was all that about?'

Lucy kept her eyes on the road. 'I'd rather not talk about it now.'

'Later, then.'

—

'I believe that a number of soldiers under your command broke into the women's quarters at Arisaig House and stole certain items.' Kalisz spoke with the confidence of a man who already had his culprits in the dock.

'What evidence do you have of that?' Gunn fumed. They were in his wood-panelled office at Inverailort House, a sprawling Victorian mansion tucked in the lee of the mountains that made Arisaig look like a small cottage. 'It could have been anyone.'

'Actually,' Lucy intervened, 'you confirmed it yourself, Major, when you assured us the ladies would get their... er, underwear back, with a suitable present.' She smiled sweetly. 'As a secretary, I have a very good memory for conversations.'

'We need to conduct a search of your men's personal belongings,' Kalisz persisted. 'Mr Churchill would appreciate your co-operation.'

Gunn snorted at the mention of Churchill's name, but he pushed himself to his feet with the aid of his stick. 'If you will follow me, Major. But I assure you there will be no need for a search.'

Kalisz stood. 'I think you will find that is my decision, *Major*.'

Gunn led the way to what appeared to be a grand ballroom that had been turned into a dormitory or barracks. The twelve soldiers who'd been involved in the exercise stood at the end of their beds in the long room, under the eye of the sergeant whom Lucy had thrown.

'Attenshun,' the sergeant growled, and the men straightened.

'I will need every man to empty the contents of his neighbour's locker onto his bunk,' Kalisz said.

'As I told you, Major,' Gunn insisted, 'that will not be necessary.' He turned to the assembled Commandos. 'Two of you recently tested their skills in clandestine intrusion against the female quarters at Arisaig House,' he called. 'Step forward, those men.'

One Commando stepped forward immediately, followed a fraction of a second later by the man at the next bed. 'Sir!'

'Very well… Fitch, Stevens, let's see your haul.'

The men went to their lockers and returned carrying two brassieres, blushing at the catcalls from their mates.

'Does that satisfy you, *Major*?' Gunn asked.

'I fear there is also the question of a rather expensive watch.'

Fitch looked at his neighbour in horror. 'You bloody fool, Stevens,' Gunn rasped. 'Bring me the watch from wherever you've hidden it and get your kit together. You're on the first train out of Arisaig, and you can bloody well walk there.' Gunn shook his head in exasperation. 'My apologies. Is that all?'

'There is also the question of the murder of Krystina Kowolska,' Lucy said. 'But perhaps you'd prefer to discuss that subject somewhere more private?'

CHAPTER 25

'You knew Krystina Kowolska?'

Gunn looked across his desk to where Lucy sat with her pencil poised over her notebook. 'Must we?' he appealed to Kalisz.

'It is for your own benefit, Major Gunn, that we have a proper record of our conversation. We will, of course, send you a copy. You knew her?'

Gunn frowned. 'I heard that two of the students at Arisaig had died on Christmas Eve, some kind of lovers' tiff. But we had our own problems. As I said, we lost a man.'

'What was your relationship with Warrant Officer Kowolska?'

Gunn looked up sharply, eyes startled. 'I didn't say we had a relationship.'

'But you knew her?'

'I'd *met* her. "Knew" is probably the wrong word.'

'Where did you meet?'

'Here.' Gunn waved towards the window, with its view of the gardens and the sea beyond. 'At Inverailort, in '41. I was a lieutenant in No. 40 Commando back then. At the time, the Commandos shared the house and the training facilities with the cloak-and-dagger bods – that is, SOE – and Warrant Officer Kowolska was one of their trainees.'

'You were an instructor here?'

'No.' Gunn reached for a packet of cigarettes on his desk and lit one, blowing the smoke in Lucy's direction. 'The unit was here training for a special mission, a clandestine landing somewhere with similar terrain to the kind we have around Inverailort and Ardnamurchan.'

'So how did you meet? Cloak-and-dagger implies secret, as I understand it, but perhaps I'm wrong. Did you socialise?'

'No,' Gunn admitted. 'They always kept us apart.'

'Then how?'

'We met completely by chance in the hills behind the house. We talked for a while and then there was a… a misunderstanding.'

Kalisz laughed, short and bitter. 'It must have been quite the misunderstanding if it left you with a broken leg.'

'Krystina told a friend that you tried to rape her,' Lucy said without looking up from her notebook.

'No,' Gunn rasped. 'I didn't… Krystina was a very beautiful woman and I was attracted to her, yes. But rape? Never. She was foreign, perhaps she misunderstood me? I didn't make my intentions clear enough.'

'She certainly made hers clear,' Kalisz said. 'She left you on the hill to live or die as fate decided.'

'It took me three hours to get back to the road.' Gunn forced the words through gritted teeth.

'And you carry the limp to this day,' Lucy pointed out. 'That medal ribbon on your chest. It's the Military Cross, isn't it? You must have done something very brave. Where did you earn it?'

Gunn's eyes dropped to his desk. 'A place outside Dunkirk. I was a subaltern with the Royal Engineers. We didn't really have any choice but to be brave.'

'A young officer,' Kalisz resumed. 'A war hero, with a long and glorious career ahead of you, and Krystina Kowolska ended it with a single throw. You must have been very angry.'

'It was years ago.' Gunn shrugged. 'One gets over things, even things like that. Forget and forgive, what?'

'But you didn't forget, did you?' Lucy said. 'Not judging by your reaction when she walked into the bar of the Arisaig Hotel while you were there. We have a witness who says you told her you hated her.'

'I was drunk. Not thinking straight.'

'And what was Krystina's reaction?' Kalisz said. 'She laughed in your face. You see, Major Gunn, I don't think you have forgotten or forgiven anything, and I don't believe you met by chance, so far into the hills that it took you three hours to get back to the road. I think you followed Krystina and stalked her with the intention of gaining her sexual favours, one way or the other. Her reaction surprised you, and left you with a career-ending injury and an abiding hatred. A hatred that gave you a reason to kill her.'

Gunn shook his head slowly, but the pale eyes that pinned Kalisz didn't contain denial – instead, something that might have been a challenge.

'But I didn't kill her, Major Zamoyski. I couldn't have, because I was on exercise on Christmas Eve with my men. We were together all the time and didn't get back here until early on Christmas Day. Would you like me to prove it?'

'That will not be necessary.'

'But I insist.' Gunn got up from his seat and went to the door, opened it and shouted into the corridor, 'Simmons, get in here.'

A small, harassed-looking soldier appeared. 'Where were we on Christmas Eve, Simmons?' Gunn demanded.

'On exercise, sir. Small boats. Up to our neck in freezing water all night. You said we should think of it as your Christmas present, sir.'

'Does that satisfy you?'

Kalisz rose, and Lucy closed her notebook and put it into her satchel. 'For the moment, Major,' the Pole said tightly. 'Thank you for your co-operation.'

–

'What did you think of our friend?' Kalisz kept his eyes on the twisting road as they travelled back to Arisaig House.

'I think you were right that he stalked Krystina, intending to rape her. That look when he tried to humiliate me in front of his soldiers... Some men are predators who see all women as prey, and he's one of them. But he couldn't have killed Krystina if he was with his men. It's impossible.'

'And yet I've encountered several killers who somehow made the impossible possible,' Kalisz said. 'So let us not discard Major Gunn entirely as a suspect just yet. If I may change the subject, it seems to me you are not out of place in this environment?'

Lucy stared ahead, but he could almost sense her mind working and the moment she came to a decision. 'I did a course similar to this at Beaulieu, another SOE training centre in the south. They thought I was suitable for the work because of my languages, and at the risk of sounding conceited, I was rather good. I'd probably have been in France now, if I hadn't mentioned the pneumonia I picked up in Spain.

The doctors insisted on checking my lungs using an X-ray machine. They found nothing wrong with them, but while they were doing it they discovered I had an irregular heartbeat, and that was that for my clandestine career.'

'You have a heart, Flight Officer Devereux?'

She laughed. 'Oh, yes, I have a heart, Jan, one that has been broken once or twice. I suppose I'm what might be called unlucky in love.'

'It puzzles me that someone of your class should have volunteered to fight in Spain on behalf of the proletariat. Is that what took you there? Love?'

She considered for a moment. 'His name was John, and he was one of those genuinely good people who are so very rare. We met while I was doing my nursing training, of which my parents already didn't approve, and they disapproved of John even more. They were actually quite relieved when he volunteered to go to Spain, because they thought our relationship would wither and die. A month later he wrote to me that the Republicans were desperately short of nurses, so I went to the poky little office where one volunteered, and a week later I was on a ship to Valencia. It was quite an informal war then, and we were able to spend a fair amount of time together.' Her lips twisted in a sad, almost intangible smile. 'Odd to think that we were at our happiest with Condor Legion bombs falling around us, but that was the reality. Then one day his brigade was involved in an attack at a place called Pajares. We'd set up a first aid station in a farm just behind the front line. They brought John in on a stretcher. He'd been shot through both lungs. There were no touching farewells. I pronounced him dead and closed his eyes and moved on to the next casualty, who happened to be a young Nationalist soldier, perhaps even the one who'd shot John. I fought so hard to save that young man's life, but he died an hour later. Such a waste.'

They drove on in silence and after a while Kalisz heard her say, 'And you, Investigator? Do you also have a heart?'

'Oh, yes, Lucy,' Kalisz replied. 'I have a heart. Only I left it in Warsaw with my wife and son, and you have just reminded me why I must get back to them as soon as possible.'

CHAPTER 26

OPERATION BISHOP

Lyons–Villefranche railway line, south-east of Grand Veissieux

This was their first real test. Raoul had chosen the stretch of track fifteen kilometres north of Lyons because it was the furthest away from any guard huts and relatively easy to access. The sabotage team consisted of Raoul and Krystina, Henri, Lucienne and three other *maquisards* from the Maquis du Mont, and Guy's friend Émile, each with a Sten sub-machine gun slung over their shoulder. Two of the cheese-maker's drivers provided the transport – camouflaged delivery vans – and would return the team to their bases in the mountains and Lyons using the rebranded vans before dawn, when they would be doing their usual rounds. The circuit had received the plastic explosives in an air drop two weeks earlier, and Raoul had decided now was the time to carry the fight to the enemy.

'Firstly, it will give the circuit the opportunity to use the skills we've been teaching them,' he explained to Krystina. 'A mission like this will build their confidence. It's a relatively easy target, the bridges and tunnels will come later, but it will damage the enemy's infrastructure and give us a chance to evaluate their response. We have people in the railway department who will let us know how long the track takes to repair. But most of all, our people will know that they're finally fighting back. And who doesn't enjoy blowing things up?' he concluded with a grin.

This last irritated Krystina, because it was so typical of Raoul's attitude to their mission. They were here to do a difficult and dangerous job, and anybody who didn't take it seriously could be a danger to them all. But she had to admit Raoul's approach to the actual attack had been consummately professional. He, Henri and Émile would lay pairs of half-kilo charges at fifty-metre intervals along the railway line. On this occasion they weren't targeting the actual trains, so rather than using fog signals that would be activated by a passing engine and ignite a length of detonating cord, they would use time-pencils set for an hour. The other saboteurs would provide a defensive screen around the target area.

The vans dropped them on a farm track and Raoul, who'd reconnoitred the area a week earlier, led the way through the fields to the railway line, with Henri carrying the explosives. The circuit leader had deliberately chosen a moonless night for the mission, and the cloud cover made it darker still. Heavy droplets of rain began to fall, driven by a stiff breeze from the south that still carried a taste of winter and made Krystina shiver.

When they reached the embankment, Krystina whispered for Lucienne to follow her.

Their guard position was about two hundred metres away to the right, where a small river ran alongside the embankment. Despite the dark, it was simple enough to follow the track, using the sleepers as steps. The biggest problem was the noise of the wind rustling through the nearby trees and the patter of the rain on the fresh leaf growth, which dulled all other sound. When they reached a point where they could see the river, Krystina wiped the raindrops from her watch face. The luminous hands showed one thirty in the morning. She drew Lucienne down on the side of the embankment and they lay together on their sides, their eyes straining to pierce the darkness to the south. Now they could only wait.

At first she thought she was seeing things. A flicker of light in the distance that disappeared almost as soon as she saw it. But there it was again. Now there could be no doubt. She touched Lucienne on the shoulder. 'They're coming,' she whispered. 'Go back and tell Raoul.'

'How many?'

'I don't know for sure. Certainly more than one. Tell him that, at worst, I'll buy him some time.'

Lucienne slithered down the embankment and disappeared into the darkness, leaving Krystina alone.

The light flickered. A torch. Just the one. On for a few heartbeats, then off again. She guessed it was being carried by a nervous German conscript to illuminate his next few steps as he advanced along the line in her direction. The knowledge gave her confidence, even though she was certain he wouldn't be alone. What happened next depended on how many others there were, and why they were here. It could be just a regular track inspection by a couple of men, but there was always the possibility that someone had reported strangers approaching the line. If that was the case, there'd likely be a full platoon and they'd be on the alert. Well, she had an answer for that. She removed the Sten's 32-round magazine from its socket, checked it was full and replaced it, making sure the safety lock was in the off position. It was risky, but it would take out a few of them, and the noise would give Raoul and the others time to get clear.

When she was satisfied the Sten was ready, Krystina pulled the Welrod pistol from inside her coat and checked it had a round in place. There were five more in the pistol grip, but they had to be loaded manually, so realistically she was limited to a single shot. The Welrod was fitted with a permanent noise suppressor, which made it ideal for murder by stealth, but the sights were rudimentary. If she was to use it, she would have to get close. She laid it on the ground and waited, as always surprised at how little emotion she felt. It had been the same during her training at Arisaig. Faced with a challenge, her mind would go completely cold. Not numb – if anything, it was sharper than ever. She seemed to see everything more clearly, and when the time for action came she was ready to commit herself with deadly speed and precision. Had it been the loss of her mother and father that made her like this? Cold and empty, yet at the same time full of anger. She tried to remember the day the policeman came to the school to tell her that they were dead. Had she been different before she'd listened to the tall man in the dark uniform tell her she was an orphan?

She watched the light come closer. Perhaps fifty or sixty paces away now. Too far to tell anything yet. Her ears strained for the clatter of metal-shod boots on the rails, but the wind defeated her. Thirty paces. Yes, he was certainly nervous. Nervous enough to have his rifle at the ready? No, not when he had to carry the torch as well. Twenty paces, and now she was nearly certain the tracks behind the leading German were not filled with an alert platoon. Two men, maybe three. She made her decision and laid the Sten aside to pick up the Welrod.

Krystina kept her head pressed into the damp earth as the soldier with the torch passed her position, only raising it in time to see a second man stepping warily behind the first. She allowed him, too, to pass, only pushing herself up when he'd taken another four or five steps. 'The Ghost', her instructors had called her, because she had an uncanny aptitude to move silently across the ground. She skipped over the sleepers in her rubber-soled shoes. The Welrod was in her hand, and she placed the muzzle a centimetre from the man's neck. A sharp *phut* and the *snick* of the bolt. His body took time to understand it no longer had a brain, and before he hit the ground she'd tossed the Welrod over the leading soldier's head so it clattered against a rail up ahead. He would have a moment of mind-freezing confusion. He'd definitely heard something in front of him, but had there also been a sound from behind? The wavering torch was in his hand and his rifle slung over his shoulder. She was on him before he could make up his mind what to do with either. Left hand clamped over his mouth, the right fist filled with the razor-edged fighting knife. 'Cut deep,' Sykes had snarled at them, 'don't give him a chance.' She sliced the blade across his throat from left to right, using all her strength and fighting the grip of outraged flesh, muscle and cartilage as it cut through carotid artery, jugular vein and vocal cords. Release, step back, ignore the bubbling, choking gurgle as his heart pumped his lifeblood onto the gravel. It had taken all of twenty seconds from the initial shot.

Someone would come looking for them, but not before the line was blown and the saboteurs had fled the scene. Still, she dragged the man she'd shot to the edge of the embankment and pushed the body so it rolled down into the bushes by the river. The second body followed, but first she cleaned the knife blade on his jacket, and she took care to stay out of the pool of freshly spilled blood.

She heard someone scrabbling up the embankment and went into a fighting crouch, knife at the ready. Émile's eyes widened as he appeared at the top of the bank. Raoul had recruited the former soldier and he'd proven himself a useful addition to the circuit, handy with pistol and knife and with a good eye for ground. He was short and solid, and would be considered handsome by some, but she'd caught him looking at her in a way she didn't much like.

'Lucienne said you had trouble.'

'I dealt with it.'

'But how ma—'

'I said I'd dealt with it, Émile.'

She spoke more harshly than she'd intended, but he'd have to live with that.

'Very well, if you're sure…? Raoul said to get back as soon as you can.' She picked up the Sten and followed him back along the railway line, retrieving the Welrod along the way. Eventually, they made out movement ahead. 'The charges are all laid and the chief wants to get the maquis away, but that fool Henri plans to wait around for the bang.'

'I'll talk to him,' she said.

She went to where Henri, Lucienne and their comrades from the mountains were in an animated discussion. 'You need to get away from here now, Henri, if the driver is to get you back before dawn.'

'I know. Lucienne says I'm an old fool, and maybe she's right. But it would have been good to see something.'

'There will be plenty more explosions, Henri.'

'If only Max could have seen us. He would have been proud.'

'Who's Max?'

The Frenchman tapped his nose and grinned. 'Max is the big boss.'

She went with them back to the transport. Raoul was already there.

'Lucienne said—'

'There were two of them. They won't trouble us any more.'

'And you're all right?'

'What kind of question is that?'

'I just… Let's get going.'

—

When they got back to the Lyons apartment, Raoul sat back in a chair with his eyes closed. Krystina could understand how he felt, and had a certain amount of sympathy for him. Tonight had been Raoul's plan, and his alone – the burden a circuit organiser had to carry. If anything had gone wrong, all of their lives would have been his responsibility. She went to the drinks cabinet and pulled out a bottle of good brandy, poured two large glasses and handed him one. 'Here's to success.'

When she woke up in his bed the next morning, she was as surprised as anyone.

The call came as they were finishing a late breakfast. Raoul answered it and she could tell by his expression that it was bad news.

'The Gestapo took thirty prisoners from Montluc Prison first thing this morning and machine-gunned them where we cut the line.'

CHAPTER 27

Arisaig House

Seven p.m.

Lucy watched as Kalisz devoured two thick slices of venison in a glutinous brown sauce, along with a mound of mashed potatoes. 'You must have been hungry.'

'I'm making up for lost time.' Kalisz smiled, though a little voice in his head told him it couldn't last. Returning to duty looking better fed than when he'd been 'taken ill' would be inviting a Gestapo bullet. 'At home I would be eating stale bread and a small cube of meat that had probably been pulling a cart a week earlier. They feed you well here.' The only other people in the mess were Dempsey and Sykes, who sat at separate tables at opposite ends of the room.

'Well, you have to admit they're special people, and after all, this is a special occasion.'

'Special?'

'Don't you know what day it is?'

'Not really.' He shook his head. 'Since Christmas all the days seem to have run together.'

'It's New Year's Eve. In Scotland they call it Hogmanay.' She gave the word a passable imitation of Constable MacDonald's pronounced accent and they both laughed.

'In Poland it is *Sylwestre* – the feast of Saint Sylvester. So tomorrow is the start of a new year? Then let us pray that it is the last year of this lousy war.'

'I'll gladly drink to that.' Lucy raised her glass of the thin, watery beer they'd been drinking, and he clinked his own against it.

'This is cosy.' Major Sykes approached the table on the way to the door. 'I'm glad you're here. I was a little rough with you the other day, and I thought you might like a little souvenir of your visit. Pop by my office some time.' Kalisz smiled his thanks. 'How goes the quest for truth and justice?'

'The wheels grind slowly, Major.' Kalisz matched his mocking tone. 'But we will get there in the end, I assure you. Do you know if the medical officer is likely to be around tonight?'

'Llewellyn? I doubt it. There's a dance on at the village hall, that's why we have the place to ourselves.'

'And a sociable gentleman like you isn't attending?' Kalisz feigned surprise.

Sykes's amiable smile visibly tightened. 'I just heard that an old chum was killed in Italy,' he said. 'At a place called Salerno. It rather takes the edge off one's appetite for celebration.'

'My apologies, Major,' Kalisz said.

'These things happen in war.' Sykes shrugged. 'That's why we have to end it as soon as possible, and with all means at our disposal. The sooner we get our students into the field, the better. And right now, Major, that's up to you. Goodnight.'

'Llewellyn?' Lucy frowned.

Kalisz lowered his voice. 'Where is the most likely source of the drugs I found hidden in Krystina's room?'

'Of course,' she whispered.

The diminutive mess orderly called Titch approached the table. 'A visitor for you, sir. A young lady.'

Kalisz excused himself and went out into the hall, where he found Yvette clutching a canvas satchel. 'You have decoded the journal already, Sergeant Messier? That is most impressive. I must congratulate you and thank you.'

'It took a little longer than I thought it would, Major,' Yvette explained, 'because the entries are in three languages – English, French, and what I assume is Polish, which threw me for a while. But there aren't all that many of them.' She handed over the notebook. 'Please don't judge her – or me – by what you read here.' For a moment, Kalisz thought Yvette might be going to say something more, but instead she threw a perfect salute and marched from the house.

Kalisz looked down at the book in his hand. The edges of a sheaf of papers protruded from between the pages, but he resisted the temptation to study them immediately.

'Our Yvette appears to have excelled herself. Perhaps we should have an early night and go through her notes in the morning?'

'Are you mad, Jan?' Lucy shook her head. 'We have to look at it now.'

Kalisz looked around, but Dempsey was smoking a cigarette and gave the impression of going nowhere in a hurry. 'If we can find somewhere private, I will show you.'

'Your room or mine?' She laughed at his perplexed reaction. 'No… on second thoughts, mine. I lifted a bottle of single malt from the bar earlier, and you're much too upright and honest to do anything like that.'

–

'I've divided the entries by language.' Kalisz was sitting on the edge of the bed, while Lucy occupied a chair in front of a dressing table in the cramped top floor room. She'd removed her tunic, which was draped over the back of the chair, and her light blue uniform blouse was open at the neck. 'If you take the French pages and I take the Polish, it should save us time. We can go through the English sections together.'

'That sounds sensible.' Lucy took a sip of her whisky and flicked through the sheaf of pages he'd handed her. 'I'll let you know if I find anything that provides us with a breakthrough of some sort.'

They read for several minutes before Lucy shook her head and laid her papers aside. 'This is all very fascinating about her love life, and some of the explicit descriptions make me blush. Yvette was talking guff… nonsense –' she smiled at his bemused expression – 'when she said the relationship meant nothing to either of them. It certainly meant something to Krystina. She felt utterly betrayed when the affair ended, but she doesn't say why. The only other thing of real interest is an entry that seems to have been made a little later. "D thinks he can take up where he left off, but it can never be." It's the only reference to a "D". Most of the rest of the entries are a combination of her contempt for Jean-Marc Fontaine's attention, and the need she seems to have had to encourage, then humiliate him. Not particularly edifying. You?'

Kalisz looked up from his papers and yawned. 'The Polish sections are mainly an internal monologue with her mother and father, but they contain any number of attacks on the Jews. She blames them entirely for the deaths of her parents. Krystina calls Jews "scum" and "vermin", and she applauds Hitler's efforts to wipe them from the face of the earth. She would see them all dead. Even the tiniest baby.'

'Good God,' Lucy whispered.

'On the other hand, the way she expresses her fear of returning to active service, and the even greater fear of failing her comrades, is quite heart-rending. It's perplexing. Taken together, this part of the journal reads like a battle between two different personalities. The monster who is prepared to commit mass murder, and the heroine who is using the shades of her parents in a desperate bid to retain her sanity.' He shook his head. 'I think it would be best for *my* sanity to lay it aside for now.'

'Very well, let's go through the English sections together.' She moved to sit beside him on the bed, and he held the first page of the decoded paper so she could read it, instantly affected by her proximity in a way he found unsettling.

Lucy appeared not to notice his reaction and focused her attention on the first entries. 'No names at all in these entries.' Her face screwed up in a scowl of concentration that made her look quite girlish. 'It also appears to be a series of random observations rather than a journal, as such. But a certain "Doctor L" merits several mentions.' She ran a finger over a section of text and his eyes followed it.

'Yes.' Kalisz saw what she meant. 'Krystina Kowolska brought her skills and experience as an agent to Arisaig, and used them to gather certain information. It must be possible that that knowledge could have led to her death.'

'If we agree that "Doctor L" is Llewellyn, the medical officer, on the face of it, this is utterly damning.'

'Enough to provide him with a motive for killing Krystina if he was aware of what she knew,' Kalisz agreed. 'But we should not jump to conclusions. This notebook poses a lot more questions than it answers.'

Lucy studied the apparently random entries more closely. 'The references to the "dirty J" are obvious enough. We now know Pierre Renan is the only person of Jewish faith at any of the establishments. But on the next page we have "Why does he hate me?", with the "he" underlined twice for emphasis. If she made her contempt for Renan as obvious as he and Yvette suggest, there'd be no question of why, so it's unlikely it refers to him. Llewellyn?'

'It's possible,' Kalisz agreed. 'But in all her other entries she refers to him as "Doctor L". Then here's another passage, the longest single entry, which refers to "D", who is presumably the same person who features in those pages that catalogue what you quaintly refer to as "her love life".' He ignored her answering glare. 'Look here… "Why doesn't D understand? I tried to tell him, but it's as if he's not listening. His carelessness could have killed us all." That sounds as if "D" was part of one of her missions, and suggests a relationship.' He frowned. 'Perhaps the key to this case isn't about the evidence we have, but about links? We already have a link between Gunn and Krystina, and Krystina and Llewellyn…'

'Likewise, Yvette and Renan were connected to her,' Lucy agreed.

'And now we have the mysterious "D". But what if there are others we don't know of? I think our next step has to be to check the files of every person who was at the training schools on the day she died. Can you arrange for us to get access to the file room again?'

The request made Lucy hesitate before she turned back to the notebook. 'What do you make of this final mention? "What would Mother and Father say if they knew about the Tenth House." Could it be significant?'

'I don't know.' Kalisz noticed she hadn't answered his question. 'We know there are ten houses under SOE jurisdiction around Arisaig. Which would be the tenth?'

'Numerically, using the official designations, it would be Traigh House, STS 25c, which is just outside Arisaig village.'

'Then we can check it out tomorrow, after we've re-interviewed Major Llewellyn. What about those files?'

'Yes,' Lucy said slowly. 'I can get them for you if I use the prime minister's authority. That's why he sent me here. But, Jan…' She met his eyes. 'Have you thought this through?'

'What do you mean?'

'Once you've seen these files, you can't unsee them. To get the information you need, you'll have to read everything. That means you'll know the real names and rank of every agent here, from every country, their work names, their most recent operations, their contacts and codewords, whether they're couriers or radio operators or organisers. And every single one of them is here because they have a vital role to play in the Second Front.' Lucy shook her head. 'Do you really believe

Winston Churchill will allow you to return to Occupied Poland with all that information in your head, and potentially walk straight into the hands of Gestapo torturers?'

The answer, of course, was no, Kalisz realised, naive fool that he was. His mind filled with a chilling vision of the last moments of the dream. To solve Krystina Kowolska's murder, he would have to sacrifice the chance to ever again see his wife and son. Oh, he could plead that he'd skim-read the documents, had taken in only the information that he needed, but that wouldn't make any difference to Churchill. And he'd be right. The slightest suggestion that Jan Kalisz had been in contact with SOE and was privy to its secrets would drive the Nazi security services into a frenzy. Kalisz knew in his heart that, no matter how brave he was, he'd break in the end, and then they'd keep him just about alive until they squeezed every last detail from him. Death would be his only escape, and even then he'd die with the knowledge that he'd taken Maria and Stefan with him.

'Jan?' Lucy's voice cut through the haze of his thoughts.

'I'm sorry,' he said. 'You were right. I wasn't thinking. That's not a choice I'm prepared to make.'

'I was saying there may be another way. All of the information from those files will be duplicated in London. We have people who specialise in this kind of thing. It may take a little time, but if any such links exist, we will find them.'

Kalisz released a long breath. The release of the personnel files had always been a possibility, but at the furthest extent of his ambition. This was a new level of co-operation entirely. 'People' meant a team. 'People who specialise in this kind of thing' could only mean counter-intelligence operatives. Spy hunters. That Lucy Devereux was able to conjure up even the possibility of such a rare commodity with more or less a flick of the fingers placed her in a new light altogether.

'Officially, I'm an assistant to the head of the Special Operations Executive.' She answered his unspoken question. 'Unofficially, I act as a link between the SOE, the prime minister's office and the Secret Intelligence Service. A sort of troubleshooter, if you like, to ensure the intelligence services do the prime minister's bidding without treading on one another's toes. A job like that requires strong relationships and gives one a certain level of authority.'

Kalisz bowed his head. 'Then I would be very grateful if you could use that authority.'

Somewhere in the house a clock began striking, and they counted the chimes.

'Lord,' Lucy declared, 'it's midnight.' They stood up together, and she raised her glass, and he touched it with his. 'Happy New Year, Jan.' She leaned forward to kiss him on the cheek and he felt a shiver at the soft touch of her lips. He could smell the malt on her breath, the fragrance of some kind of expensive perfume, and the indefinable scent of a woman. She didn't move away, and when their eyes met he knew she wanted him to stay at least a little longer.

It was a test. Life was full of tests. He passed this one.

'*Wszystkiego najlepszego w nowym roku*, Lucy.' He took a step towards the door. 'And may the coming year bring everything you wish for.'

CHAPTER 28

1 January 1944

Major Michael Llewellyn scowled at his visitors from beneath a furrowed brow, with eyes sunk so deep it was a wonder he could see at all. His face had the complexion and distended quality of an overripe peach, the fumes of last night's whisky hung about him like a peat-scented cloud, and his crumpled battledress tunic gave the distinct impression of having been slept in. For all that, his irritation at the proceedings had an insubstantial quality, as if he didn't quite have the strength or the will to maintain it. Kalisz had left a note in the medical officer's pigeonhole in the hallway requesting the nine a.m. meeting. When he didn't turn up for breakfast, or at the allotted time in his office, Lucy had sent a mess orderly to request his presence.

'This is a bloody odd time for a meeting, Zamoyski, if you don't mind me saying so. Don't you know what day it is?'

'Of course, Major,' Kalisz said. 'But as Mr Churchill said only recently, the clock is ticking, and where I come from, the war doesn't stop for the holidays.'

Llewellyn's nostrils flared, but whatever he was going to say became lodged in his throat and turned into a coughing fit. He took a drink from a glass of pale liquid on his desk.

'As it happens, I'd planned to get in touch later in any case. This arrived by motorcycle courier overnight.' He handed Kalisz a slim file. 'It is the post-mortem report on our victims, though it doesn't tell us much that we didn't know already. There is also this.' He placed a small cardboard box on the desk beside his glass. Kalisz lifted the lid to reveal a slightly deformed, copper-coloured pistol bullet nestling in cotton wool. 'It's the ordnance that was removed from Lieutenant Fontaine's brain tissue. As you surmised, the bullet is a 7.65 calibre round, which entered the skull at the right temple and was fired from a distance of three to four feet, which makes it near impossible the death was suicide.' Kalisz picked up the bullet and held it between his fingers to study it, and Llewellyn continued. 'The only slightly unusual thing about the round is that it is of German manufacture, one of a batch made at the DWM factory in Karlsruhe in 1936. I'm afraid the origin doesn't make it a rarity around here. It's standard practice for our students to train in the use of enemy weapons at STS 22a—'

'That would be Glasnacardoch Lodge?'

Llewellyn frowned. 'It would.'

'We will be giving the staff at Glasnacardoch a visit soon, but there are one or two things I'd like to clear up with you first.'

'I'm always happy to help, laddie –' the medical officer produced a wan smile – 'even when I'm feeling a little under the weather.'

'I spoke to Colonel Baldwin yesterday,' Kalisz said. 'Our conversation was in connection with a sergeant instructor called Connors, who had been heard threatening to kill Krystina Kowolska. He told me that you vouched for the sergeant's innocence.'

'That's correct,' Llewellyn said slowly. 'Sergeant Connors gave me a lift back from the dance on the night she died. It must have been after one a.m. He dropped me off at the top of the drive, and I watched him turn and drive away back towards Arisaig village.'

'He could have stopped a little way up the track,' Lucy pointed out.

'Yes.' Llewellyn's tone belied the word. 'But Krystina was almost certainly dead by then. Connors lost his temper when Krystina humiliated him. She liked to do that to men. He assured me he hadn't seen her since the day of their falling-out. The thing you have to understand about Krystina, Major Zamoyski, is that she was not just affected physically by what happened to her in France, but also psychologically. She suffered from what, these days, we call battle fatigue. It affects different people in different ways, but in Krystina it manifested itself in outbursts of irrational anger, which could dramatically affect her behaviour. What happened with Sergeant Connors was by no means an isolated incident.'

'That is very interesting,' Kalisz resumed, 'but does Colonel Baldwin know about your little arrangement with Connors?'

'Arrangement?' Llewellyn's right hand strayed across the desktop towards his left to combat the shake that had developed in it.

'The one where he bartered army cigarettes and other supplies on the black market to feed your need for drugs. We know Krystina was aware of it. Perhaps she used the information to humiliate *you*, Major Llewellyn. She could have ended not just your army career, but your career as a doctor as well. That alone would have been reason to kill her, wouldn't you say? And surely a man who had already vowed to kill her would have been a willing accomplice?'

'Surely you don't think—'

'All I know —' Kalisz allowed his voice to harden — 'is that two people with a motive and an opportunity to kill her are also the only people who are able to provide each other with an alibi. I don't believe in coincidences, Major. Perhaps you'd like to persuade me otherwise?'

Llewellyn closed his eyes and took a long breath. His hand reached for his desk drawer.

'I wouldn't do that if I were you,' Lucy warned.

A bark of bitter laughter escaped the medical officer. 'You don't know me very well, young lady.' His hand reappeared with a small flat brown bottle and a glass. 'I'm sure you won't mind if I don't offer you one. Happy New Year.' He poured a generous slug of amber liquid and drank with a shudder of appreciation. 'Yes, Krystina knew about my "little arrangement", as you call it, and yes, she let me know that she knew. It amused her to believe she had a hold on me, but the truth was, we had a hold on each other. She struggled with the memories of the foulness perpetrated against her in the cells at Lyons. The pills I prescribed helped her cope.'

'Prescribed?'

'Very well… Let's say *supplied*. Unlike the Americans and some other branches of our own military, the Special Operations Executive expects superhuman behaviour from their people without the benefit of any chemical stimulant. It wasn't possible to get the drugs I required through normal channels, so I went to the people who could supply me. Sergeant Connors is from a rather tough area of Glasgow and had the contacts I needed among the criminal fraternity. After that, it was a simple matter of negotiation.'

'In short, you were dealing on the black market.'

'Don't expect me to feel ashamed, Major,' Llewellyn snapped. 'Krystina wasn't the only one who came to me for aid. Sometimes even the bravest of the brave require help to overcome their fears, particularly if they are about to place their head in the lion's mouth for the second – or even third – time. When a first-class agent comes to me and tells me he's scared he might fall asleep on a night exercise, am I meant to turn him away?'

'You do realise this is entirely illegal,' Lucy pointed out. 'If it comes out, it would definitely mean your career was finished.'

'The people who come here to train to be agents of the Special Operations Executive are prepared to sacrifice everything they have for their country, including their lives, Flight Officer,' Llewellyn replied with a reasonable appearance of injured dignity. 'My career, even my freedom, would be a small price to pay compared to that. I would have given everything to ensure Krystina was able to achieve her objective. Why would I kill her? After all, I was the one who raised doubts about the cause of death.'

'It would not be the first time someone at the centre of a case painted themselves the hero to cover their involvement in a crime,' Kalisz pointed out. 'The cause of death would have been revealed by the post-mortem. If you had not "raised doubts", as you say, you would have been branded incompetent or a fool, which no doctor would tolerate.' Llewellyn glared at him, but stayed silent. 'These drugs…' Kalisz resumed. 'It's clear they affect the consumer's ability to achieve certain objectives. Is it possible they also affect their behaviour in other ways?'

'There are a few minor side effects,' Llewellyn admitted. 'Such as having trouble sleeping, which is why Krystina came to me for sleeping pills – headaches and the like – but nothing that would suggest an increased predilection towards violence, if that's what you're suggesting.'

'Nevertheless, I'm going to need a list of everyone you supplied with black market drugs over the last two months.'

Llewellyn went very still. 'I'm afraid that would breach doctor–patient confidentiality, Major.'

'Confidentiality?' A snort of anger escaped Kalisz. 'Two people are dead and their murderers still walk free. Do you think I will allow your false notions of honour to stand in the way of my investigation? As Flight Officer Devereux has pointed out, your dealings with the black market have been entirely illegal. I will give you a simple choice, Major Llewellyn. You will provide me with the names of these patients, and tomorrow you can still be sitting at this desk with your previous misdemeanours entirely between you and your conscience. Alternatively, you and Sergeant Connors will be on the first train from Fort William in handcuffs, facing charges of misuse of military supplies, prescribing illegal drugs and dealing on the black market.'

'I'm afraid a long custodial sentence would be inevitable,' Lucy said.

Llewellyn's florid features twisted into a grimace not unlike pain. His hand automatically reached for the whisky bottle, hesitated, then withdrew. Eventually, he took a deep breath and stood up. A battered metal filing cabinet stood in the corner of the office, and he had to crouch to reach into the deepest recesses of the bottom drawer and retrieve a slim, unmarked folder. 'The last two months, you say?'

'That will suffice,' Kalisz assured him. The medical officer took a single sheet from the file and handed it over. 'Thank you, Major.'

A short list, and on the face of it, the names, each with a brand of drug adjacent, told him very little: Krystina Kowolska, of course: one Witold Grabski – presumably the Pole from Borrodale House; two that might be Czech; a John Smith; and one surprise. 'This drug you provided for Major Dempsey... It was for his arm injury?'

'No, it wasn't, as a matter of fact.'

'Then what?'

'The drug in question is experimental. I was at first reluctant to prescribe it, but Dempsey was most persistent. It's what is known as a sexual suppressant.' He graced Lucy with a tight smile. 'Designed to subdue the... er, libido. The word is familiar to you, Major?'

'Of course,' Kalisz said. 'You will correct me if I'm wrong, Major Llewellyn, but this would appear to suggest Major Dempsey was ruled by his passions to such an extent that he sought medical help.' He paused, but Llewellyn declined the opportunity to intervene. 'Is it possible, then, that this passion could have been driven by the undoubted charms of Krystina Kowolska?'

Llewellyn laughed. 'It seems you're not quite the great detective our Mr Churchill has been led to believe, Major Zamoyski. If you were, you'd have noticed that Dempsey is probably the last person around here likely to be attracted by Krystina's charms.'

CHAPTER 29

Eleven a.m.

Kalisz sat in the battered Austin while Lucy arranged their transport to the two training houses that could only be reached by boat. It would take most of the afternoon. He doubted whoever was in charge of the vessel would be happy to be called out on New Year's Day, but the occupants of Glaschoille and Inverie, isolated on a nearby peninsula, would continue to be suspects until he was able to rule them out. Unlikely suspects, it was true, being so distant, but he'd taken time to inspect the foreshore at Arisaig before breakfast. The stony beach, and the makeshift jetty in the little bay nearby, might make an enticing landfall for someone expert in watercraft.

Lucy appeared at the passenger side and slipped inside the car. 'The skipper of the boat will be at Mallaig harbour at one o'clock. That should give us time to take a look at the firing range at Glasnacardoch Lodge, which is on our way. There's something else, Jan.'

'Yes?' He could tell it wasn't something good.

'I had a call from London. They've turned down my request to check the files. Just a flat "no". Maybe it's because they're busy on some big project, or perhaps I don't have quite the level of authority I thought I had. The best I could do was to ask for the request to be considered at a higher level.'

Kalisz considered for a moment. It was a disappointment, but not a disaster. 'Then there is nothing else to be done. We will see what they have to say at the weapons facility about the bullet that killed Lieutenant Fontaine.' He studied her. The aristocratic profile reminded him of a very beautiful woman in a medieval painting he'd once seen, but he couldn't remember where. 'Did you know?'

She turned to him with a look of mild amusement. 'About Dempsey? Does it matter?'

'I'm a detective. I don't like to miss things, especially things that are in front of my nose.'

'If it makes you feel better, it wasn't that obvious.'

'Then how?' He set the car into motion.

'Most men look at me in a certain way.' Lucy stared straight ahead as they started up the driveway. 'At first you take it as a compliment, but you get to an age when you know better than to give them any encouragement. Dempsey didn't look at me at all, Investigator. In fact, he seemed much more interested in you.'

Kalisz choked back a laugh and shook his head. Their route took them through the village, where Kalisz noticed small family groups of locals making their way purposefully between the houses. Sometimes two groups would meet, and the elders swapped handshakes and shared drinks from bottles whisked from inner pockets or shopping bags.

'Isn't it a little early for this?' Kalisz frowned.

'In Scotland on New Year's Day it's never too early.' Lucy smiled. 'They call it first-footing. The tradition of visiting friends and neighbours to bring in the new year with a gift of coal and *uisge beatha*, the water of life, as they call it here. They'll be at it all day.'

'I want to stop for a second or two at the police station. I have a couple of questions for Constable MacDonald.'

'Do you want me to come with you?'

'There's no need, I won't be long. Just stay in the car.'

When he returned, Lucy asked him if he'd discovered anything of interest.

'In fact, I did. It appears there is more to this Sergeant Connors than meets the eye.'

Outside Arisaig, a rutted single-track road alternately hugged the shore and wound its way in a series of precipitous climbs and swooping drops through dunes and patches of woodland. A few miles later, the road crossed the foaming waters of the river Morar by an ancient bridge in the shadow of an arched railway viaduct, then through the village and up the hill by the cemetery. At one point a steam train raced past them along the tracks to their right. Lucy studied her map.

'Glasnacardoch shouldn't be far now.'

They turned a sharp bend, and a substantial white house became visible among the trees to the right of the road. Kalisz pulled into the short driveway and cut the engine, to be greeted by the distant sound of firing from the hills behind the house. Pistol shots by the sound of it, occasionally punctuated by the chatter of some kind of automatic weapon.

'Can I help you?' A sandy-haired officer, wearing a crude sheepskin jacket over his uniform blouse and a kilt with a red check pattern, appeared from around the side of the house as they got out of the Austin. The man had a boyish, unlined face apparently untouched by war, until you looked into the grey eyes and saw something buried deep in there – emptiness, or perhaps a shadow of memory – that suggested otherwise.

'We're looking for Major Maxwell,' Lucy replied.

'Well, you've found him.' The lack of welcome in his voice left no doubt as to his feelings. 'So you'd better come inside, I suppose. You're here about the casualties up at Arisaig? The colonel told me you might be coming by.'

'Why do you call them "casualties", Major?' Kalisz asked. 'It's an unusual term for two people who were murdered.'

'Because everybody who dies around here is a victim of the war – ' Maxwell craned his head to study Kalisz's insignia – 'Major. Doesn't matter whether they die in an accident or from their own careless bullet, they're all casualties to me.'

They followed him round the house and through a back door into an area that appeared to double as an office and a kitchen. Racks lined the walls, holding rifles and machine guns of various types, including a German MG34 Kalisz remembered less than fondly from the Polish retreat of 1939. Maxwell waved them to two chairs on the other side of the table and took his own seat opposite. When they were settled, Kalisz withdrew the cardboard box Llewellyn had given him from his briefcase and removed the lid. 'Well, this is the not so careless bullet that killed Lieutenant Fontaine, Major.' He placed the box on the table. 'I'd be interested in what you can tell us about it, but first I have to ask where you were on the night of Christmas Eve?'

'That's simple enough,' Maxwell said. 'I was on leave at my parents' place near Dumfries. I didn't get back here until Boxing Day.'

'And the bullet?'

Maxwell pulled the cotton wool nest from the box and laid it on the table to study the bullet. 'Certainly a 7.65mm pistol round, which makes it unusual in its own right. Probably of German or possibly Czech manufacture.'

'Why unusual?' Lucy asked.

'Because not many mass-produced pistols are chambered for 7.65 ammunition.' The weapons expert shrugged. 'The MAB Model D, a French pistol – we have one in the armoury – and the Model 27, which was made by the Czechs until they came under new management in 1939.'

'Is it possible that a student might be in possession of any of these weapons?'

Maxwell's eyes narrowed at the question.

'There's no need to be coy, Major,' Lucy assured the instructor. 'Major Zamoyski is investigating this case at the direct instigation of the prime minister, and has his complete trust.' She waved an elegant hand towards a phone on the table. 'All you have to do to check our security credentials is to phone the colonel at Arisaig House.'

Maxwell shook his head. 'That won't be necessary. I have orders to provide you with complete co-operation. It's just that one becomes so used to secrecy around here, it becomes a habit. In answer to your question, Major, it is perfectly possible there are examples of the MAB and the Model 27 in the various training schools. Most of our current batch of students have, shall we say *experience*, of working in France, where it would be simple enough to lay hands on a MAB. Our particular weapon was still in its place when I checked the armoury this morning.'

'Who are the people we can hear firing in the hills?'

'That's some chaps from the French section who marched over from Rhubana Lodge last night. They're on the range with my sergeant.'

'Would that be Sergeant Connors? I was told he would be here today.' Kalisz ignored Lucy's puzzled frown.

'No, the sergeant is over at Traigh, putting some of our other students through their paces.'

'Another time, then.' Kalisz nodded. 'As it happens, Rhubana Lodge is on our list for later today. Would it be possible to have a word with them?'

'I don't see why not.' Maxwell looked at his watch. 'Their transport isn't due for another couple of hours. I can take you myself, if you don't mind a short trek through the heather.'

—

'A short trek' turned out to be a lung-bursting half-mile ascent through damp, clinging foliage and stinking black bog that sucked at their boots and soaked them to the knees. At first, Kalisz thought Maxwell's pace – a high-kneed, long-striding gallop that propelled him up the slope at astonishing speed – was designed to punish the interlopers. But gradually it became clear this was his natural hillman's gait, and the Pole and Lucy huffed and puffed to keep up, helping each other over streams and across granite crags. At last, they reached the summit and looked down into a valley between the hill where they stood and another a quarter of a mile away. A small lake twinkled in the distance, a pool of glittering obsidian surrounded by the dull brown of the winter heath, bathed for a moment in a patch of sun that escaped from the blanket of cloud above. In the gully between the hills, a firing range had been set up, with butts and targets and a wooden hut nearby to provide shelter from the biting wind that cut through Kalisz's tunic like an icy razor. By now the shooting had ceased and they could see a small group of men huddled in the lee of the hut.

Thankfully, Maxwell chose this moment to pause, seemingly mesmerised by the mountain panorama that stretched before them, but, when he spoke, it was on the subject of his work.

'In the past at Glasnacardoch, we taught people to shoot. Pistols, mostly, and the Sten. Now, the only weapons we teach are those manufactured by the Germans and their Axis allies. Guns like that MG you saw in the armoury, and our own heavies, like the Bren and the three-inch mortar, which are increasingly being dropped to Resistance outfits in Europe. These days the emphasis is mainly on teaching people to teach other people how to shoot, and how to maintain their weapons. The aim of every circuit command group that passes through here is to turn the limited fledgling Resistance operations which already exist into small armies, capable of surviving brief contacts with the enemy. Hopefully, we provide them with the skills to do that.'

He set off down the hill with Kalisz and Lucy in his wake. By now, four of the soldiers below were lined up fifty paces in front of the targets with squares of white visible in front of them. Kalisz puzzled over the squares until he was close enough to see the disassembled weapons that lay on the white cloths. An army sergeant approached each of the men in turn to tie a strip of dark cotton over their eyes. 'This seems to be a feature of the training here,' Kalisz remarked.

'There are no street lights in the forest, Major, so there is no point in sending anyone into occupied Europe without giving them the wherewithal to operate without hesitation in the pitch dark. Likewise, if you have the Gestapo kicking in the door, the last thing you're going to do is switch the bloody lamp on so you can cock your Sten.'

Kalisz accepted the rebuke in silence as the sergeant completed his task and took up a position to the rear of the centre of the line.

'May I have your attention, gentlemen.' His parade ground roar echoed from the surrounding hills, though his listeners were less than six feet away. 'Lying at each of your feet is a disassembled weapon with which you are all familiar – in this case, a *Maschinenpistole* 40, with the annoying and rather pointless metal stock removed. At the word of command, you will assemble the said MP40 by touch only, insert the magazine, remove your blindfold and fire a three-second burst at the target in front of you. I don't have to tell experienced soldiers like you the consequences of firing early and blindly. With a rate of fire of five hundred rounds a minute, your three-second burst will send the bulk of the thirty-two 9mm Parabellum bullets in the magazine into your poor benighted oppo next door, with undoubtedly fatal consequences. The good news is that the first three to fire will get a nice hot cup of tea and a lift home in a warm three-tonner. The bad news is that the last man will be returning to his base by Shanks's pony.'

While he gave his instructions, the sergeant returned to the hut and emerged with a machine pistol of his own.

'Always expect the unexpected,' Lucy murmured.

'On the command,' the sergeant called. 'Begin.'

Without hesitation, the men crouched over the stripped-down guns and their hands began to fly among the parts with incredible speed. A rasping burst from the sergeant's MP40 cut the silence with astonishing violence, but not a hand wavered, and the bursts continued until the man on the right had assembled his weapon. With one final snap of the wrist he forced home the magazine, ripped off his blindfold and lined the gun's sight up with the target.

Click.

CHAPTER 30

OPERATION BISHOP

Rue Thomassin, Lyons

Click.

Krystina was out of the bed in a single bound, with the Browning pistol that had been under her pillow gripped firmly in her right hand.

The bedroom door was partly open and she crouched beside it, willing her heart to slow and with the questions racing through her head. How many were they? Gestapo or Milice? How had they found her?

'Marie?'

She felt a liquid surge of relief at the familiar voice, but she knew she couldn't lower her guard. 'Are you alone?'

'Of course.'

'Then come to the door and keep your hands where I can see them.'

'Marie, it's Guy. You have nothing to fear from me.'

'That's for me to decide. Show yourself, but if you're not alone, the first bullet is for you.'

Guy Moreau stepped into the gap, where Krystina could confirm he was on his own and unarmed. She moved past him into the room, covering the outer door with the pistol. Nothing. She let out a long breath.

'You shouldn't be here, Guy. How did you get in?'

'If I'd known you were this nervous I would have knocked.' The cheese-maker shrugged. 'Freddie gave me the key in case I ever needed somewhere to lie up for a day or two. There's something I need to tell you and something you need to see.'

'Not Raoul?'

'This is about Raoul.'

'All right,' she said. Guy Moreau didn't scare easily, but she could tell he was frightened, and not just because she'd threatened to kill him. 'Tell me.'

'One of my drivers was up in the Monts du Lyonnais this morning, doing his normal collections. He found the area crawling with Gestapo and security police. The…' He choked on the next word and had to try again. 'The Maquis du Mont is gone, Marie.'

'Gone?' she demanded. 'Be specific, Guy. Gone into the hills or—?'

'Dead, then,' he rasped. 'All dead, or on the way to Montluc, which is as good as dead. Henri and his family were burned alive in their farmhouse.'

Krystina said a silent prayer for that brave, stolid, foolish man, his shrewish wife and their two sons – bright, laughing boys of seven and nine, who'd fought for the privilege of carrying her suitcase. 'He knows this for certain?'

'He was told,' Guy said. 'But he did see for himself Lucienne and six others hanging from a balcony. Thirty dead and twenty taken was the rumour. How many knew?'

'About me? Perhaps four or five, but they only knew me as Odile. What about the Polish *reseau* at Saint-Pierre?'

'Nothing, as far as I know. Franco said he is taking his people into the hills. He will not have anything more to do with Lyons until he has spoken to Max.'

They'd had a run of bad luck or bad timing after the railway sabotage mission, with operations against enemy transport links and infrastructure aborted because of false alarms, mechanical failures or the proximity of German units. Just recently, however, things had changed, and after a few more successes Raoul had come up with an ambitious plan to attack a railway marshalling yard in the city and blow up a vital turntable. But the size of the operation was such that the loss of the maquis and the Poles would deal a fatal blow to his hopes.

It was, by any scale, a disaster, but they had been taught that these things happened to a circuit, and that the only thing to do was regroup and start again. A question occurred to her. 'Who is this Max I keep hearing about?'

'Max is the work name for the person charged with unifying all the Resistance movements in the south of the country. It's rumoured that he is based not far from Lyons.'

'You seem to be well informed for a man who only became active in the Resistance a matter of weeks ago, Guy.' Krystina kept her tone perfectly neutral, but she could tell the words had hit home.

'Do you truly think so little of me, Marie?' Guy snorted his contempt, and she was surprised how much it hurt. 'You asked me to gather intelligence and that is what I do. My men talk to the people in the town and in the mountains, and then they talk to me. That's how I heard the rumour about Max. There is also another rumour. Apparently the British have dispatched a deadly female assassin to the city to kill the head of the Gestapo.' He met her gaze and held it. 'I'm sure that if this lady believed I was an informant, she would not hesitate to put a bullet in me, as you suggested earlier.'

'I'm sorry, Guy. I shouldn't have doubted you. But this news… What was it you wanted me to see?'

'Maybe it would be better if I just walked away.'

'Please,' she said.

–

Guy led her through the streets to the Place Bellecour. It was approaching nine o'clock, and they walked quickly, as if they were a couple hurrying to get home before the ten o'clock curfew. He stopped opposite a corner bar and drew her into a nearby alleyway, where she could see into the lit interior through a gap in the blackout curtains.

'You know what this is?'

She nodded, too furious to speak.

'What will you do?'

'What needs to be done. It would be better if you go home now, Guy.'

'D'accord.' He walked away, his narrow shoulders hunched as if he were carrying an enormous weight, leaving her alone with her anger.

The bar was called Le Moulin à Vent, and was a notorious haunt of the city's Gestapo agents. Through the gap in the curtains, Krystina had a view of three men sitting, drinking and laughing together: Raoul, Freddie and Émile.

She waited, knowing they'd have to leave soon because of the curfew. Freddie and Émile went first, Freddie with an affectionate arm draped over the Frenchman's shoulder. Raoul appeared a few moments later and set off in the opposite direction. She waited to make sure he wasn't being followed by anyone else, then set off after him. A week earlier, he'd walked out of the apartment where they were staying with a lame excuse that he needed some time alone. She knew where and she knew why, though she wasn't supposed to be aware of either. He would take a circuitous route, because he wasn't entirely a fool, which meant she could reach the address before him.

She waited in the shadows at the entrance to another alleyway – the shadows seemed more her natural element than the light these days – until she heard him approach, humming a familiar French song. As he passed by, she called his name. He turned with a look of bewilderment and fear, but before he could react she dragged him off the street.

'What in God's name do you think you were doing tonight?' She kept her voice low, but there was no doubting the venom in her tone.

'I might ask you the same.' Raoul glared at her. 'This is hardly standard operating procedure.'

'It was you who put me in charge of security,' she hit back. 'Tonight I saw the security of the entire circuit placed in jeopardy. Just be thankful I don't put a pistol in your face while I'm asking the questions. I want to know why three key members of Bishop were rubbing shoulders with the Gestapo in a bar, while our entire operation is being torn apart.'

She saw the look of utter consternation on his face. 'What do you mean? All I did was take Freddie out for a birthday drink. Christ, I invited you to come along.'

'And I said no, because I thought it was a stupid idea. You didn't tell me you were taking him to the Moulin à Vent. What in God's name were you thinking, Raoul?'

He shook his head. 'It was Freddie's idea, or maybe Émile's.' Something in his voice made her wonder about that, but she let it go for now. 'He said it would be fun to tweak the tiger's tail. There were only two other customers and never a hint of danger. We stayed for one drink. Toasted the barman and then left. It was all a bit of a lark.'

'"A lark"?' She couldn't believe what she'd just heard. 'You placed the lives of every single person you are responsible for in danger. While you were sipping pastis with the Gestapo, twenty of our people were being strapped to tables in the basements of Montluc Prison to wait for their torturers.'

'That can't be…' The implications of what she was saying slowly dawned on him. 'Are you saying the entire network is blown?'

'We don't know enough to be certain yet.' She told him what she'd been told about the destruction of the Maquis du Mont, and the Polish *reseau* in Saint-Pierre taking to the mountains.

'They must have made a mistake.'

'Maybe it was us who made the mistake. Franco certainly seems to think so.'

He leaned back against the brick wall. 'I can't believe this is happening.'

'Well, it is, and you have to deal with it. As your security officer, my first piece of advice is to stop sleeping with a married French woman whose husband is in a prisoner-of-war camp. Half of Lyons knows about it.'

He flinched as if she'd slapped him. 'Christ, you're a cold bitch, Marie.'

'Yes, I am. So, will you?'

'Elise said you would try to break us up. She said you're jealous.'

'Jealous?' She actually laughed. 'You of all people should know better than that, Raoul. It means nothing to me. Just an itch that needs an occasional scratch. So, will you?'

'I'll think about it.'

'And while you're thinking about it, have a think about Freddie and Émile?'

'What do you mean?'

'Open your eyes. They're too close.'

'Of course they're close. Émile told Freddie he'd been a WT operator in a fort on the French frontier. Freddie wants to train him up as his replacement. It could save us weeks if anything happened to him.'

Krystina went cold inside. It was so much worse than she had thought. But if Raoul couldn't see it, she would never convince him. It was all part of their world – a man's world. They needed the camaraderie and the bravado and the make-believe brotherhoods to survive.

'Tomorrow, I'm due to disburse the funds from the last drop to Guy and the cell leaders in the south of the city.' She struggled to keep her voice even. 'Once I've done that, I'm going up to Saint-Pierre, using my French-Polish identity, to try to re-establish contact with Franco. Once things have quietened down, I'll be able to travel into the Monts du Lyonnais to see if there are any survivors, and start an inquiry into what happened to Henri and the others. Do you agree?'

He nodded, and she turned and walked away.

'Will you report this, Marie?'

'I'm a cold bitch. What do you think?'

She didn't look back.

The next evening, Krystina returned to the apartment after a trying day reassuring those who'd heard about the destruction of the maquis that they were safe. It had left her worn out and sick to death of being confined to the stone canyons of the city, however beautiful they were. She needed to get out into the wide open spaces and clean air of the mountains.

She used the master key she'd been given to open the apartment door. The instant she stepped inside, her whole world went black.

CHAPTER 31

Glasnacardoch, Arisaig

'Oh, shit.'

A moment of shocked paralysis before the soldier's fingers tore at the jammed weapon. As he struggled to find the fault, one after the other, his comrades completed their task and fired off a burst at the targets.

'Make your weapons safe,' the sergeant instructor ordered. 'That means you're dead, Lieutenant,' he said without rancour. 'No point in being quickest if you're left standing there with a soft cock in your hands while some Hun blows your fucking head off. That's something to think about on the long walk back to Rhubana.'

The officer in charge of the men – a saturnine, whip-thin captain with a low voice and an easy authority – called them together.

'Not what I'd have chosen you to see.' Major Maxwell shook his head. 'But better to learn the lesson here than out in the field. A word, please, David,' he called.

The captain dismissed his men, jogged towards them, halted and saluted. 'My apologies for that, sir. Lieutenant Butler had a jam. In too much of a hurry to position the recoil spring properly. An easy mistake to make, and one I can assure you he won't repeat.'

'That's why you chaps are here, Captain – to learn from your mistakes. But that's not why I called you over. Major...?'

'Zamoyski,' Kalisz introduced himself with a tight smile.

'Yes, Major Zamoyski and Flight Officer Devereux. This is Captain Malpas. You'll have heard about the casualties down at Arisaig House, David? The major is investigating their deaths.'

'What's it got to do with us, if you don't mind me asking?' The captain didn't hide his irritation, and Kalisz noticed he wasn't deemed worthy of a 'sir'. 'We have a job to do here, and not much time to get it done. With respect, we don't have time to worry about some unstable woman who managed to get herself killed by her boyfriend.'

Kalisz heard Lucy's intake of breath at his side, and he stepped in before she could say anything. 'Nevertheless, I also have a job to do, Captain, and that job is to ask questions. Firstly, I wonder how you appear to know so much about the murder and the victims, when each of the training schools is meant to be isolated from all the others? You describe Krystina Kowolska as "unstable". How could you be in a position to know that?'

'Word gets round.' Malpas had a square chin that jutted so aggressively, Kalisz had to resist the urge to discourage it with a straight left. 'We meet on the ranges and on exercise. It's natural everybody sizes one another up. It was common knowledge Krystina – if that's what her name was – was burned out. If her mission had gone ahead, she would have been a danger to everyone she worked with. Maybe...'

'Maybe what, Captain?' Kalisz placed the emphasis on the final word.

'Nothing... sir.' Malpas straightened. 'Is there anything else?'

'Only that her *boyfriend* did not kill her, but I intend to find out who did. And may I ask how you and your men spent Christmas Eve?'

'Sergeant Mercier?' the captain called to one of the men, who were now helping the instructor to clean the machine pistols. Another of the same type: lean, hard and self-assured. 'The major here wants to know how we spent Christmas Eve.'

'You had us in our bunks by twenty-two hundred hours, sir, and not a drop of festive cheer touched our lips.' Mercier spoke with a faint accent and a hint of self-mockery. 'You said there'd be plenty more Christmases, and in the meantime we'd a war to win.'

'You were together for the entire night, Sergeant?' Kalisz said. 'This is important.'

All the humour vanished from Mercier and his eyes hardened. 'I spent twenty nights in a row going from one cold bed to another across Brittany to stay one step ahead of the Gestapo, sir. I learned to sleep lightly, and I can tell you no one left Rhubana Lodge on Christmas Eve.'

'Thank you, Sergeant.' Kalisz nodded. 'Captain.'

'We won't need that truck, sir,' Malpas said to the major. 'If Lieutenant Butler is going to walk back to Rhubana, we're all walking back.'

'Carry on, David.' Maxwell turned to Kalisz. 'You mustn't mind Captain Malpas. This will be his third trip over the water, and he has the scars to prove it. The decision to accompany Butler is typical of him. He's determined to mould his team into the most efficient circuit in this theatre of war. I'll let you see yourselves back to HQ while I help the chaps clear up, if that's all right with you?'

Kalisz and Lucy headed back up the slope. 'I'm sorry for dragging you up a mountain for no purpose,' he said.

'I can understand why they don't want us here.' Lucy glanced back to where the soldiers had stopped working to watch them leave. 'But don't you think that captain's reaction to a perfectly sensible question was just a bit too furious? Yes, you'd be annoyed, but that unnecessary blackening of Krystina's reputation and his lack of any human response to her death didn't seem real to me. I was watching the others when you asked where they'd been that night, and if looks could kill, you'd be as dead as Jean-Marc Fontaine.'

'You make a good point.' Kalisz turned to watch the men tidying away their equipment. 'But that would implicate all four of them in the killings. Is that likely? True, it would have meant that suspending Krystina's body would have been much simpler and quicker.' He nodded to himself. 'I think perhaps we will return to Captain Malpas and his men at a later date. Maybe we can get permission to interview them one at a time? In the meantime, we have other fish to fry. Isn't that what you say?'

It only took them a few minutes to drive from Glasnacardoch Lodge to the port of Mallaig, where a small cargo boat waited for them by the quayside. A group of sailors were loading sacks and boxes onto the vessel across a precarious-looking ramp that rose and fell alarmingly with the considerable swell. They worked under the supervision of a young naval officer who looked as if he was just out of school.

'If you'll wait here, sir, ma'am,' the officer suggested politely. 'We're taking the opportunity to get some supplies across to Glaschoille. The old girl has had engine problems since Christmas and they're getting a little light on the basics.'

'What exactly do they do at Glaschoille and Inverie?' Kalisz frowned as he noticed the choppy, white-capped sea beyond the harbour mouth.

The young man's smile froze until Lucy reached into her pocket and showed him her security pass. He shrugged. 'They train for small boat operations. Canoes and kayaks, mostly. Paddle power. Covert beach landings, that sort of thing.'

'No larger vessels?'

'There's an ancient tramp steamer they use to practise disembarking their collapsible boats in all weathers, but I've never seen it move in the six months I've been here.'

'Lieutenant…'

'I'm just a midshipman for now, sir.' The youngster grinned. 'My lieutenant's exam isn't for another six weeks.'

'Midshipman…' Kalisz returned his smile. 'You obviously know these waters well. Is it possible someone from either of the training schools on Knoydart could have canoed as far as Arisaig House on Christmas Eve?'

'Lord, no, sir.' The sailor puffed out his cheeks. 'Twelve or fourteen miles in one of those cockleshells, in what was probably the worst storm we've had this winter? I doubt even the instructors would have made it out of Loch Nevis with the wind in their teeth and six-foot waves in their faces. No, sir, I'd say it was impossible.'

Kalisz nodded. 'Then we won't waste any more of your precious time. Thank you, Midshipman.'

'A pity,' Lucy said as they walked back to the car. 'I was looking forward to a boat trip.'

'I wasn't.'

'But no point wasting an afternoon when there was no chance of the people on Knoydart being anywhere near the murder scene.'

'I should have thought of it earlier.' Kalisz shook his head. 'We'll use the time to interview the people at Camusdarach, Garramor and Traigh House on the way home.'

'When we get back to Arisaig, I'll ask the colonel to radio Glaschoille and Inverie and have their COs confirm the whereabouts of their students.'

'Even better.'

'You still look more troubled than you should, now that we've eliminated almost fifty per cent of our potential suspects.'

'That's the problem, Lucy. I'm not really certain we've eliminated them at all.' Kalisz waved a hand at the hills and islands around them, and the waves pounding on the shore. 'Look at it. It's all too vast. Who knows what's hidden out there? Churchill said this was a place of secrets.

What if there's a secret we don't know about, that holds the key to all this? Maybe it would be better if your military police had become involved.'

Lucy waited until he'd released all the frustration that had been building over the past few days. 'All right,' she said. 'If that's what you want, I'll ask the prime minister. Maybe it is too much to ask of one man.'

Kalisz took a deep breath and released a burst of bitter laughter. 'And confirm his opinion of his pet Polish policeman? No, we'll keep going until we find what we're looking for or run out of road. Anyway, I'm not just one man, Lucy Devereux. We're a team, now.'

On the way home they recrossed the river Morar, now a raging, foam-flecked torrent. Downstream of the bridge, a platoon of soldiers had strung a rope across the river and were negotiating it one by one. Each man balanced on the narrow strand of hemp on their stomachs and pulled themselves along with their arms, while their comrades shouted encouragement from the banks. Weighed down by packs, and with rifles slung over their shoulders, the rope bowed so they hung a few feet above tumbling waters that streamed over the jagged rocks.

Kalisz stopped the car to watch. 'Better you than me, my friends,' he said quietly. 'Are they some of our students, do you think?'

'I can hardly bear to watch.' Lucy grimaced. 'But their green berets would suggest they're Commandos— Oh, God.'

Without warning, the man on the rope lost his balance and toppled down to hang by one hand, booted feet trailing in the rushing waters. Seconds later he lost his grip and plunged into the stream, disappeared, then surfaced again in a tumble of arms and legs. For a moment the soldier seemed certain to be swept to his death, but somehow he managed to reach up and grasp a low-hanging branch. As he clung to the slim lifeline, his comrades swiftly created a human chain and, with a superhuman effort, managed to drag him to the shore.

'Brave men, and tough.' Kalisz sighed. 'But with training like this, it's a wonder any of them ever reach the battlefield.'

'I suppose it all has to be as realistic as possible,' Lucy said. 'Hence so many accidents. The Commandos are the elite. They're trained to think independently, never to take a step back, and to sacrifice themselves for their friends without a second thought.'

'Then I think you will win this war after all,' Kalisz said.

'Why say "you", Jan? Poland is our ally. If we win, you win also.'

'One of your politicians said a few years ago that he was reluctant to anger Hitler because of a quarrel in a faraway country between people of whom he knew nothing,' Kalisz replied with a wry smile. 'When the war is over, I rather fear Poland will be the faraway country and the quarrel will be with the Russians.'

They'd decided to visit the training houses closest to Arisaig on the way back. Camusdarach Lodge – more of a farmstead, really, that lay between the road and shore – proved frustrating when the officer in charge refused point-blank to wake his men, who were sleeping after a night exercise. The next house, Garramor, was empty, but with signs of recent occupation. ·

When they pulled up at Traigh House, the final training school before they reached Arisaig village, Lucy turned to Kalisz. 'Perhaps now would be a good time to tell me about Connors?'

'Yes, Lucy.' Kalisz smiled. 'I must apologise for that. You will have realised by now that I prefer to concentrate on one mystery at a time. Constable MacDonald has many things "on his plate", as you say here, but, in my experience, he is a very good policeman. It occurred to me that if Connors had been suggested as a suspect, even one with what looks like a solid alibi, the least the constable would have done is check his background. So it transpired. Connors is not just running drugs for Major Llewellyn – I did not mention this to the constable, of course – but he also has a lucrative sideline selling poached game directly to hotels in Glasgow. A sideline which requires the collaboration of several other members of the Arisaig staff.'

'If he's part of a gang and he did kill Krystina –' she frowned – 'he didn't need Llewellyn to help him string her up.'

'Exactly. There is the additional factor that the sergeant is not just any old gangster. According to MacDonald, he was suspected of being a gangland enforcer, which means he is not unacquainted with violence and blackmail. Apparently, Colonel Baldwin and the other people running the schools do not believe this is an impediment to his employment.'

Lucy gave a little whistle. 'Well, that does put a different complexion on things. Do you have your pistol with you?'

'Oh, I have seen you at work, Flight Officer.' Kalisz grinned. 'I'm sure we can handle a mere mobster between us.'

The British captain in charge of the facility showed the irritation with which Kalisz was becoming all too familiar, but he reluctantly summoned his trainees from where they were practising close combat by the beach. They gathered, stony-faced, while he explained that his men spoke no English – a lie, judging by the smirks his words prompted – and assured Kalisz that none of them had left the farm on Christmas Eve. Kalisz accepted the untruth with equanimity – he'd expected little more – but his eyes were on the man standing in a vest and trousers in the freezing cold, watching the events with close attention.

'That may be the case,' he said. 'But I'm sure Sergeant Connors here is perfectly fluent in English.'

'Not so you'd notice.' The captain laughed. 'He's from Glasgow. Sergeant,' he called, 'this gentleman would like a word.'

Connors trotted over and came to attention in front of Kalisz and Lucy. 'Sah,' he barked.

The man who studied Kalisz with deep-set, hard little eyes wore the slightest trace of a smile on what might be termed a 'lived-in' face – the map of his days etched in every crease, wrinkle and scar. He had the build of a honed middleweight boxer, all shoulders and muscled arms, and a wild look in his eyes sent out an unmistakeable challenge. In that instant, Kalisz decided Connors was, without doubt, as dangerous a man as his reputation suggested. He smiled back and resisted the urge to throw an exploratory punch.

'I'm told that Colonel Baldwin interviewed you about the death of Warrant Officer Kowolska, Sergeant. However, the investigation is now my responsibility, so I would like to go over the details again, if you are willing?'

'Willing and able, sah.' Connors had a thick accent and a rapid-fire delivery that tested Kalisz's grasp of the words. 'If the captain can spare me?'

The captain nodded and shepherded his men away.

Kalisz beckoned the sergeant into the shelter of the house and out of the biting wind. 'You must have been surprised to become a murder suspect?'

'No, sir.'

'No?'

'No.' Connors shook his head. 'If you're here, it's because you've been hearing whispers about the old me.'

'The old you?'

'That's right, sir. So you know I'm no stranger to a bit of blood and snotters, if you see what I mean.' Kalisz wasn't certain he did, but when he looked to Lucy for a translation, she was staring with a look of fascinated horror. 'In my opinion,' Connors continued, 'there's been a simple misunderstanding.'

'So you deny threatening to kill Warrant Officer Kowolska?'

'Not at all, sir.' Connors grinned. 'When she threw me in front of the lads and laughed about it, she annoyed the fuck out of me.'

'So?'

'So, where I come from, "If you do that again, ah'l fuckin' kill ye" is almost a term of endearment. It was said in anger, but I meant no harm by it.' Connors brought his face close enough to Kalisz's that the Pole could smell the bitter-sweet scent of whisky on the other man's breath. 'And in any case, I have an alibi, right?'

'Yes,' Kalisz conceded. 'But a man with your reputation, given your... business dealings... with Major Llewellyn, would not be beyond *manufacturing* such an alibi.'

'So he told you about that.' Connors laughed. 'The doc's not a bad lad, but he can be a wee bitty naive. Look, copper...' His voice became serious. 'I'm no fuckin' angel, but the fact is that I liked the lassie, and I couldn't have killed her the way they say they did, because she was better than me. Now, you can waste your time trying to put me in the frame, or you can go out and catch the real killers, and good luck to you. Because that's the God's honest truth.' He straightened and made an extravagant salute – 'Sah' – before executing a perfect about-turn and marching away.

Lucy let out a long breath as she watched him go. 'Well, that was interesting. What do you think?'

Kalisz gave her a wry look. 'I think Sergeant Connors is shrewd, dangerous and about as crooked as they come, but that there was a certain amount of truth in what he said. He doesn't give a damn what we think of him. He had motive, his background makes his alibi insubstantial at best, and his business associates provide the possibility that he had opportunity. In short, he is still a suspect.'

'But not at the top of the list?' she suggested.

'No.'

'So where do we go from here?'

'Back to Arisaig House,' Kalisz said. 'What did you say about the Commandos? Never take a step back. Maybe we learned nothing today, or maybe, somewhere along the way, we planted a seed. I need to write down my notes and check over everything we've discovered over the last few days.'

'And me?'

'I still believe that what we're looking for is a link.'

'I'll call again when we get back.'

The road from Traigh hugged the shoreline, small sandy bays linked by ancient rock formations, white-capped, blue-grey waves lashing the mud-brown beaches, driven by the strengthening wind. They turned a corner and, to their right, Lucy noticed a small group of figures on the beach. 'Jan?'

'Yes.'

'It's those children again.'

'So?'

'I don't believe that's a rock they're climbing on.'

Kalisz slowed and looked towards the shoreline, where five or six evacuee children were taking it in turns to caper about on a large, dark cylindrical object that didn't look a natural part of the beach.

'No. I think it's a mine.'

CHAPTER 32

1:30 p.m.

They left the car beside the road and approached until they were about a hundred paces from the dark object, which Kalisz now recognised as some sort of large parachute mine: a two-metre metal cylinder filled with explosives and dropped from the air to block busy seaways. Now that he considered it, maybe a hundred paces wasn't nearly enough? He remembered the enormous gaps torn in Warsaw's streets early in the war by parachute mines very similar to this one. If it went off, it would likely turn the beach into a bay. 'Get away from there,' he roared into the wind.

The four boys and two girls turned at the unexpected interruption, but showed no alarm. They were from the same group who had tied cans to the Austin's bumper. Aged between about ten and fourteen, the boys all had close-cropped heads and wore shorts and oft-patched woollen jumpers, while the girls, long hair streaming in the gale, were dressed in what looked like some kind of identical school dresses under thick serge coats. Their feet were encased in rubber wellingtons, apart from the eldest boy, who wore scuffed work boots that might once have been brown or black, or possibly somewhere in between.

It was the eldest boy, a mocking half-grin on his freckled, bony features, who shouted a reply. Kalisz realised with a pang that the lad was probably around the same age as his son, Stefan, who was at this very moment possibly putting his life on the line as a Resistance courier in Warsaw.

'Whit's it goat tae dae wi' youse?' the boy shouted.

Kalisz frowned at the incomprehensible words and turned to Lucy for aid. 'I'm not entirely certain,' she said, 'but I think he's telling you to mind your own business.'

'Shit.' Kalisz felt an upswelling of anger growing inside. 'I didn't fly all the way across Europe to get myself killed by a bunch of juvenile idiots playing tag with four hundred kilos of explosives on a Scottish beach.' Nevertheless, he started walking towards the little group on the sands. After a few moments he realised Lucy was keeping pace with him. 'What do you think you're doing?'

'Mr Churchill said I was never to leave your side.'

Kalisz snorted. 'Maybe under the circumstances he would prefer it if you walk in front and shield me from the blast, yes?'

She laughed nervously. The children watched them approach, but two of them continued their game. 'What are you going to do?'

'I'm going to ask them politely to leave the beach before they get blown into very small pieces. What else can I do?'

'Please get away from that thing,' he called as they came closer. The mine was half-buried in the damp sand, but he could see dials and panels on the casing. 'It's not a toy. It's a parachute mine, and if you trigger it, the blast will leave so little trace of you that your mothers and fathers won't know which of you they're burying.'

'I've no' goat a da',' one of the younger boys said.

'Shut up, Kev,' snarled the oldest boy. 'Whit do you ken anyways, grandad? It canny go aff. It's a magnetic mine. Ma bruthuh telt me aboot them, afore he was killed. It'll no' explode unless a ship sails o'er the tap o' it.'

Kalisz went closer and realised the boy was correct. The mine was of a type designed to sit on the sea bed, and would be triggered by the pulse caused by the earth's magnetic field when a large metal object – a ship – passed over it. There was no external way to trigger it.

'But what if it's booby-trapped?'

'Eh?'

'The Nazis are tricky characters, believe me. Sometimes they will set a device to ensure the mine can't be tampered with. If you'd put pressure in the wrong place it would have exploded.'

The children frowned and moved carefully in a tight group away towards the road. 'Aye, ye're no' as clever as ye think, Billy.'

'Shut up, Kev.'

'I hadn't thought of that,' Lucy said, as they considered the mine.

'Well, you should. The Nazis are devious and ruthless, and they revel in terror. They'd blow a bunch of British children to pieces without blinking an eye.'

'Get away from that bloody mine.' A loud roar echoed across the beach.

'Is that who I think it is?' Lucy frowned.

'Our friend Major Gunn,' Kalisz confirmed, as he watched Gunn limp across the sands from a lorry marked BOMB DISPOSAL, with the help of his stick. 'It's a mine of the magnetic variety,' he called. 'And, according to our experts, unlikely to explode unless we drive your truck over it.'

'You haven't touched it?' Gunn crouched beside the cylinder.

'No, but they did.'

'Christ.' Two other soldiers were unloading equipment from the lorry and he called to them to bring it to him. 'It's one of the new buggers, so it might have a light-sensitive trigger inside the fuse compartment.'

'So you are a bomb disposal expert as well as a Royal Marine Commando? You are a courageous man, Major Gunn.'

'It's all just technical, really, knowing which wire is which.' Gunn became a different man as he inspected the mine casing in minute detail. He almost seemed to be enjoying himself. 'And if you make a mistake you won't feel a thing. Before I joined the Commandos I was a Royal Engineer, so it's all pretty routine. Everyone else around here will be over there risking their necks before long. It just made sense to do my bit. Now, you'd better fuck off before I cut the wrong wire and solve all our problems in a flash.'

'A brave man, perhaps –' Kalisz hunched his shoulders against the chill wind as they walked across the open beach back to the car – 'but not the most pleasant.'

When they reached the car, he opened the driver's door and stepped back as several pounds of sand and shell poured out.

'Little ba—'

'Don't be too hard on them, Jan.' Lucy laughed as he scooped sand from the car with his hands. 'Look at it from their point of view. Plucked from their families and their homes at the start of the war, labelled and put on a train with no idea of their destination. They would have been terrified. And where did they end up? In a village barely worth the name, hemmed in by mountains and the sea. Some of them had probably never seen a field before they set off. These Highland communities can be intensely insular and, for all their New Year revels, families keep themselves to themselves. The children live with people who have taken them in as a matter of duty, not choice. Some of them will be kind enough, but others will be anything but. This is a predominantly Roman Catholic area, and there will be boys and girls here who've been brought up to hate Catholics without ever having met one, or even a basic understanding of what the word means. They're always hungry, but more to the point, they're bored.'

'You make it sound like Hell.'

She shook her head. 'Hell is where they came from. Tenement buildings riddled with dry rot, bare floorboards, damp bed linen and four families sharing a single toilet on a landing. Playing at being sailors with a tin can for a yacht in a puddle that's probably been created by leaking sewage. Do you have places like that in Warsaw? I only ever saw the best of it.'

'We do.' Kalisz remembered a crumbling apartment block in Praga that evoked similar images. 'Places where you wouldn't enter a building without your baton drawn and a dozen men as a backup. Communities like that create hard, unyielding men who are often hard on their families, through shame that they can't give them anything better, more often than not. You're right – there's no point being angry with them.'

He cleared the last of the sand and put the car into motion with a crunch of gears, and she gave him an affectionate smile. 'The ironic thing is that, though they probably hate the place now, they'll grow up thinking of it as a paradise where they had the best time of their lives.'

'No one will believe them if they say they danced on an unexploded mine and lived to tell the tale. Paradise.' He switched on the tiny – near ineffectual – windscreen wipers as a token gesture against the sleet that now battered against the windows.

The road into Arisaig village ran past an old church with a square tower, a fine building, flanked by the ruins of a second, much more ancient chapel, surrounded by moss-covered gravestones. As they approached, Kalisz saw a tall figure in uniform stoop to walk through the church porch, removing his side-cap as he entered. He brought the car to a halt.

'I'll just be a minute,' he told Lucy. Nevertheless, she made to join him. 'Please,' he said. 'It's a small thing, and of little consequence, I believe.'

He reappeared with seconds of his minute to spare.

'What was that about?' she demanded, still not quite pleased at having been sidelined.

'The man we saw entering the church was Private Greaves, the soldier who discovered Krystina's body. He seemed a very decent person, and the fact that he came here to worship on his own appeared to me to confirm that impression. I wanted to ask him a question.'

'What question?'

'Whether he was the person who wiped the camouflage paint from Krystina's face.' He saw Lucy blink. 'His answer was yes. He didn't try to hide it, would take any punishment that came his way. It seemed to him wrong that such beautiful features should be concealed behind a warlike mask, even in death. Llewellyn left him to lay the bodies out in the makeshift mortuary, and he used his handkerchief to clean her face.'

'It's a court martial offence to interfere with a military crime scene.'

'I'm sure it is, but what good would it do our investigation to punish him? Men like Private Greaves are currently in short supply in this violent world of ours. The more of them who are alive to grace it when the Nazis are defeated, the better.'

Kalisz drove on. As they passed the police station in the village, he eyed MacDonald's motorcycle and considered paying him another visit, but decided that would wait. For now.

CHAPTER 33

Warsaw

1–2 January 1944

On New Year's morning of 1944, *Kriminalkommissar* Wolfgang Fischer of the Warsaw Gestapo looked down at the body lying on the frosty grass beside the Kanał Piaseczyński. A fool, and now a dead fool. It made him quite angry to think of all the potential wasted in that lifeless corpse. He had an urge to give the prone form a kick, but it wouldn't do in front of the waiting soldiers and policemen. This was a busy area, even at this time of the year, where people came to walk and fishermen sat by their poles attempting to lure the few tiny inhabitants from the inky depths. Fischer had no doubt he'd been meant to find the body of his informant sooner, rather than later. A message, then.

Until his demise, the young man had been well placed to open the door to one of Warsaw's largest black market operations, and thus deliver Fischer the greatest coup of his career. Not just because it would have given him the organisation's leaders and their corrupt suppliers. The information squeezed from them in the cellars of Aleja Szucha would almost certainly have led him to the very heart of the Polish terrorist structure in Warsaw. Fischer had been providing the dead man with information and support that had assisted his rise through the ranks of one of the smaller operations of what the detective sensed was a vast web of strictly compartmentalised organisations. And just when he was on the brink of breaking through to the next level, what did he do? He sold the location of a family of fugitive Jews he'd stumbled upon during his black market duties to the *Ordnungspolizei* for a few hundred lousy zloty.

'He's remarkably untouched, considering,' the SS medical officer supervising the removal of the corpse observed. 'No signs of torture or defensive wounds. All I could find was some bruising on the back of his neck where they'd held him under.'

Fischer nodded. The condition of the body had surprised him. In these circumstances, he would have expected to see signs of violent and prolonged interrogation. After all, the man had been exposed as a traitor. Yet there was something almost paternal about the manner of his passing, as if the death had been a matter of some regret. It bore thinking about. He had a vision of his enemy as a cunning, ruthless brute, but this did not fit that image. It would not do to underestimate his adversary.

–

Back in his office at Aleja Szucha, Fischer scattered the case files across his desk and studied the contents. Sometimes the disorganisation, confusion and lack of structure helped the conscious mind unearth some gem of information or link that had been hitherto buried in the unconscious. He'd been on the trail of the shadowy figure he knew only as 'The Bulgarian' for almost six months. Not that his quarry had been known by that name at the beginning. It had started the way it always started: an arrest; an interrogation. A once-defiant prisoner broken in body and spirit. And that was just the start of their agony. Eventually, a suggestion, barely even a hint, that only Fischer had found of interest, of a possible guiding hand behind many of Warsaw's criminal enterprises. Fischer's informant had promised a way in, but that door was now closed. When one door closed, one looked for another. He put in a call to the head of administration.

The first time the name 'The Bulgarian' had been mentioned in a report was from the interrogation of a Jewish courier captured following the liquidation of the ghetto. Under torture, the woman confessed to hearing that the supply of guns to the Jewish Combat Organisation had involved someone known as 'The Bulgarian', but had been unable to add anything useful before she died. Then there had been a hint in a notebook owned by a murdered Gestapo officer that a person of the same name might be part of a conspiracy to defraud the state. When the case was closed and the killing attributed to Jewish bandits, it was decided that mention of The Bulgarian had been part of some complex deception.

Fischer was still puzzling over the lack of any links when an assistant appeared in the doorway an hour later. 'You asked for the clerks to check again for Warsaw files containing a mention of anything or anyone who might be associated with Bulgaria? This had been overlooked during the earlier search.' He handed Fischer a piece of thin paper. 'It was tucked away in a police custody book from before the war. The entry mentions the arrest of a man called Dimitar Petrov on a charge of smuggling. It records his nationality as Polish, but the name is certainly of Bulgarian, or possibly Russian, origin.'

Fischer studied the piece of paper. 'Thank you, Graf. I see this mentions a Warsaw police file reference number. Arrange for it to be collected and brought here.'

'I've already made the application, sir, but according to the clerks at police headquarters, no such file exists. They suggested it might have been destroyed in the raids of 1939. I also asked them to cross-reference the name against their other criminal files, but either this person doesn't exist or he's whiter than snow.'

'Interesting. Remind me about the Kripo detective who put in a request for information about "The Bulgarian" in regard to the Weiss murder investigation. What was his name again?'

'*Kriminalassistent* Hofle, I believe.'

'Then I shall want to speak to him.' Fischer frowned.

'That won't be possible, sir. I'm told *Kriminalassistent* Hofle is dead. Killed in the line of duty.'

'By God, Graf, you can be irritatingly competent.'

'Thank you, sir. It has often been said that my memory is my greatest asset.'

'It wasn't a compliment. Where did he make the application from?'

'Department V on Nowy Sjazd, sir.'

Fischer picked up the paper he'd been studying earlier. 'Curiouser and curiouser. Our custody book also originated in Nowy Sjazd.' He considered the files on the desk. No, something wasn't right here. Wolfgang Fischer had learned long ago not to believe in coincidences. 'Find out precisely how Hofle died, and I'll need a list of all the Polish police personnel of Nowy Sjazd 1 who were on duty the day this custody report was filed. The clerk who made the entry may know something about this Petrov, or the missing file.'

Graf sighed. 'I'm afraid that may take some time, Herr *Kriminalkom-missar.*'

Fischer smiled and slipped on his jacket. 'Don't worry, Graf. First thing tomorrow morning will do.'

–

The Gestapo agent was back in the office before nine the next morning, and Graf made his report within the hour. 'It appears that *Krimin-alassistent* Hofle died of a surfeit of enthusiasm during the liquidation of the ghetto, sir. He volunteered to serve under General Stroop as an auxiliary trooper with the Twenty-Second SS Police, and was shot by a Jewish sniper during the clearing of Gęsia Street at the beginning of May. This is the list of people from police headquarters at Nowy Sjazd you asked for.' He handed over a sheet of paper. 'I'm afraid all of the clerks were released from their positions when it was taken over by the *Kriminalpolizei*. It would take some time to track them down for questioning.'

Fischer glanced at the paper with a shrug of disappointment. 'It was a long shot in any case.' A name on the list caught his eye, and he called out as Graf was leaving the office. 'Wait. Let's test your prodigious memory again. What were the names of the Kripo detectives who worked on the Weiss case?'

'That would be Gersten and Kalisz, sir. You'll no doubt remember Gersten was badly injured in the ambush when we lost the suspected *Armia Krajowa* liaison officer.'

Curiouser and curiouser indeed. Fischer picked up the phone and spoke into the receiver. 'Get me Department V, Warsaw Kripo.' He waited until the connection was made. 'Hello, *Kriminalkommissar* Fischer, Gestapo, here. I'd like to speak to Investigator Kalisz, please.' Graf waited while his superior listened to a quite lengthy explanation before putting the phone down.

'You have that look, sir,' he suggested.

'It turns out that our Investigator Kalisz is on sick leave, suffering from a disease he contracted while he was a prisoner of the Jews during the liquidation of the ghetto.'

'Now that is a coincidence, Herr *Kriminalkommissar.*'

'Get me the Kalisz file.'

CHAPTER 34

Arisaig

6:30 p.m.

'Major Zamoyski, may I have a word?'

Colonel Baldwin was waiting by the door of Arisaig House's dining room with one-handed Major Dempsey and Llewellyn, the medical officer. The expressions on their faces told Kalisz this wasn't good news, and for a moment he wondered if he was about to be pulled off the case. Before he could make up his mind how he'd react, Baldwin drew him close.

'We've lost one of our chaps.'

'Lost? You mean dead?'

'No, Major, I mean lost. He had breakfast in his mess this morning, but didn't appear for a pretty vital class on a new type of portable radio receiver this afternoon. The instructor thought he might have been taken ill, but he wasn't in his billet. According to the lieutenant it was like the *Mary Celeste*. Everything squared away perfectly, as if for an inspection. He hasn't been seen since—'

'Excuse me, sir,' Kalisz interrupted. 'But may I ask who we are talking about?'

'One of our French students at Borrodale. A sergeant WT operator and armourer named Pierre Renan.'

Kalisz froze. 'Jean-Marc Fontaine's room-mate?'

'That's correct. But it was my understanding that you had ruled him out as a potential suspect.'

'I've ruled no one out at this point, Colonel. We have no suspects, so that makes everyone a suspect.' He met Llewellyn's eyes and the medical officer looked away.

'Well, we have parties searching the foreshore, and my security people are asking discreet questions in the village and at the station. I've also informed the authorities at Fort William to check incoming and outgoing trains. If he's alive, we will find him—'

'We have to remember,' Major Dempsey cut in, 'that Sergeant Renan has extensive experience of undercover work. He is no virgin in this line. He would be quite capable of providing himself with a set of false documents – a new identity, even, especially if he had time to prepare in advance.'

'I will need to see his rooms immediately.'

'Of course, Major,' Dempsey said. 'I'll accompany you. I have the key here.'

'And will someone please ask Flight Officer Devereux to meet us there?'

–

The lounge at Borrodale House was empty when they arrived, and Dempsey assured them the rest of the house had been thoroughly searched. There was no sign of the Poles. Kalisz insisted on waiting until Lucy arrived, looking flushed and breathless and probably just out of the bath. He explained the situation to her.

'So he either knew something he wasn't telling us and he's been killed to keep him quiet,' she said, 'or he's run away to stop that happening?'

'Unless we were wrong and he was one of the killers in the first place,' Kalisz pointed out. 'I want to search his room, but it only needs one of us. Major Dempsey can provide any assistance I need. I'd like you to talk to Yvette. Find out if Renan has been acting strangely lately, or anything that might be of interest.'

Lucy nodded, but she stood her ground. 'Remember you asked about the tree?'

Kalisz frowned. It took him a moment before he remembered. *Of course, the tree.* 'Yes?'

'Apparently it's what is known as a red maple. The original owners of Arisaig House were avid collectors of exotic species and must have planted it sixty or seventy years ago. Interestingly enough, it's a native of Canada, like our victim, Lieutenant Fontaine. An odd coincidence, don't you think, Jan?'

'There are no coincidences in a murder inquiry,' Kalisz said thoughtfully. 'At least until they have been fully considered and dismissed. I ask myself, what if the killer is sending us a message? If that is the case, it is a remarkably subtle one. And why send a message if the original intent was to disguise the murder of Krystina Kowolska as suicide? Of course –' his frown deepened – 'there is also the possibility that the choice of tree is designed to muddy the waters in the event of the original ruse being discovered. We will discuss it more fully later, I think.'

He turned to Dempsey. 'The colonel mentioned that the instructor looked for Sergeant Renan in his room. Do you know if he disturbed much?'

'Not for certain,' Dempsey said. 'He was looking for the man, nothing else. I doubt he rummaged through his underwear drawer, if that's what you mean.'

Kalisz studied the major for a moment, seeking any sign of mockery or suggestion of the proclivities Llewellyn had hinted at, but found none.

'When we enter the room, you will stand by the door, please, while I carry out my inspection. Only move if I ask you for assistance.'

'Is that all, old boy?' Dempsey guffawed. 'If I'd known, I'd have ordered up one of the mess waiters. Still, one aims to serve. Very happy to oblige.'

Kalisz led the way upstairs and used the key Dempsey handed him to enter the room. He paused in the doorway long enough to take in the detail of a room which had been left in soldierly perfection: blankets squared off, surfaces dusted, floor cleaned. When he was satisfied he had everything fixed in his mind, Kalisz went over the room with the same methodical precision that he'd used in his search of Krystina Kowolska's quarters. Yet if he'd expected the same results, he was destined to be disappointed. No loose floorboards or skirtings with little caches of treasure. No coded notes. In fact, not a hint of evidence, nor of the personality of the man who had lived here.

'Are we done?' Dempsey drawled.

'Yes.' Kalisz crouched to have a last look at the base of the lockers. 'He's been very thorough.'

'Long gone, I suspect. These chaps know how to disappear.' Kalisz nodded distractedly and then joined him at the door. 'Is there a reason you think the woman – Yvette, isn't it – would have an idea where he might be?'

'No reason. They're both French and they share a mess. It seemed a good idea to ask the question.'

'Of course.' Dempsey frowned. 'Should have thought of that myself. Well, I'll let you know if our chaps come up with anything.'

Kalisz said goodbye at the door and walked down through the woods in the darkness towards where the bodies of Krystina and Jean-Marc had been discovered. The wind whipped through the trees, and the rustle of the branches dulled every other sound. He'd gone perhaps thirty paces when the smell of cigarette smoke alerted him to another presence, and he slowed. A circle of glowing red moved languidly from behind a tree at head height. Gradually Kalisz's eyes made out the tall figure of Jerzy behind the lit cigarette.

'You're out late tonight, Major Cop,' the Pole said. 'You need to be careful, the woods can be dangerous at night.'

Kalisz tensed, fists bunched and ready to react. He remembered the deadly Commando knife with which the Pole had been so familiar. Where was it now? But when he spoke, he managed to sound more unruffled than he felt. 'I just wondered if you'd seen anything of Pierre Renan today?'

'You knew we were here?' The new voice came from behind him: Jerzy's comrade, Witold.

'Of course. They told me up at the big house,' Kalisz lied, instantly feeling a little more secure now the Poles believed he hadn't just stumbled into them.

'We heard him.' The tension had gone from Jerzy's tone, and Kalisz visualised the bored shrug that accompanied the words. 'The usual morning sounds. But we didn't see him.'

'Had he been acting strangely?'

'He's a Jew.' The Pole snorted. 'They're all strange. Maybe he killed the woman. I hear she didn't like the Jews too much.'

'Yes?' A little warning bell pinged in Kalisz's head. 'Where did you hear that?'

'Around.'

'Sure. Around.' Kalisz grunted. 'For what it's worth, I don't think Pierre Renan killed Krystina Kowolska, but maybe he knows who did.'

'Then it's probably just as well for him he's done a runner.'

'You don't think he could be dead?'

'Not Pierre. He was a slippery one.'

'Then he'd better hope I get to him before the killer does.'

'That's the truth,' Jerzy agreed.

'Goodnight.' Kalisz slipped past the shadowy figure towards the parkland and Gardener's Cottage.

'Goodnight, Major Cop.' Now there was a hint of a smile in Jerzy's voice, but it wasn't a pleasant one. 'Stay safe.'

Kalisz felt more secure once he was out of the loom of the trees. The encounter with the Poles had disturbed him, but it had also left him with the question of precisely where they fitted into his investigation. Links… it was all about links. He looked at his watch. He could spare half an hour, and with luck, half an hour was all it would take. He angled back towards the big house.

A few minutes later, having picked up what he needed from his room, Kalisz slipped along the side of the house until he reached the ground-level window he'd noticed from inside the file room. There was no time for finesse, and he jemmied the window with the Fairbairn–Sykes fighting knife that Sykes had given him as a souvenir. The gap was narrow, but Kalisz was naturally slim and made more so by the Warsaw occupation diet. He slipped through with ease, tentatively using the wooden filing shelves fixed to the walls as a precarious ladder to reach the floor.

Once inside, he switched on the torch he'd brought. Each shelf was labelled with a letter of the alphabet. *Where to start?* He riffled through the Gs, looking for Grabski, but there was no sign of one, Witold or otherwise. MacDonald had given him chapter and verse on Connors, and Llewellyn was an open book. *Think.* Eventually Kalisz found the files of two people who might be central to the case. One was Pierre Renan's, and it provided him with one tiny nugget of interest. The other concerned David Malpas.

–

It was almost eleven when Kalisz knocked at the door of Yvette's cottage. He could tell the moment Lucy opened it that she'd discovered something significant.

In the light of an oil lamp he could see Yvette sitting at the small kitchen table, but what was different was the suitcase, apparently packed and ready and surrounded by bags, that stood in one corner of the room.

'I have been seconded to another mission,' the Frenchwoman said. 'I must be ready to move as soon as you have màde your report about Krystina. I'm to be a replacement, with a circuit in the north.'

Her voice was lifeless, and her eyes dull, as if she hadn't slept for days. Kalisz knew the import of what she said was tantamount to a death sentence. The circuit had lost its radio operator, likely to Gestapo *Funkabwehr* operators, whose listeners scanned the airwaves of every occupied territory seeking out clandestine transmissions. The Germans would be waiting patiently for the replacement to begin transmitting in their area.

'Pierre left Yvette a note,' Lucy said.

'Pierre is not a coward,' Yvette whispered. 'He is not running away. He will join the Free French forces.'

'Of course,' Kalisz assured her. 'May I see the note? Is it in English?'

'No, French.'

'Then perhaps you could read it to me. In English.'

'He says he—'

'Just as it reads, please, Yvette.'

'*Pardon.*' Yvette frowned. 'My dear Yvette, I must go away or they will kill me. I can feel them watching me all the time. Tell the Polish policeman I think I saw a Commando officer walking across the park from the point on the night Kowolska and Jean-Marc were killed. This is not goodbye, *ma chérie*, we will meet again when it is over.'

'You said you were together in the cave all night.'

Yvette shrugged. 'He went pee-pee at one point. He was only gone for a moment. This is the first I have heard of any Commando.'

'Did he ever give an indication of who this "they" he talks of might be?'

'No.'

'The Poles who share his house, perhaps?'

Yvette shook her head, but after a moment's hesitation she frowned. 'There is one thing. I know I should have told you, but it doesn't matter now he's gone. Pierre did threaten to kill Krystina at one point.'

'To her face?'

'No. Only to me. He said he'd been told she was a traitor, and that if he didn't kill her she would kill him.'

'But he didn't say who told him?'

'No.' She clutched the note to her breast like a talisman.

'I think I will have to keep the letter, Yvette,' Kalisz said gently.

'Of course.' She handed over the sheet of paper.

'But perhaps I could give you this in return. I think she would have wanted you to have it.' He reached into his pocket and placed Krystina Kowolska's gold Patek Philippe watch on the table. 'I doubt it would ever have reached her step-parents in Poland, if they're even still alive.'

When they left, Yvette was holding the watch in her hands and studying it, with tears running down her cheeks.

'So the Commando officer must be Gunn?' Lucy said as they returned along the path to the main house.

'Not necessarily,' Kalisz corrected her. 'There are probably two or three score Commando officers within about a ten-kilometre radius. Besides, Gunn's orderly said he was on exercise with his men all night. That would be a very difficult alibi to break, especially when the only person who claimed to see him has disappeared. I know he's arrogant, and that he treats women as objects to be used, but we mustn't allow our prejudices to interfere with the investigation.'

'But it could have been him,' Lucy persisted.

'So we won't discard him entirely. But I'm going to need more before we concentrate all our efforts on Major Gunn.' They were just approaching the house, and Kalisz reached into the breast pocket of his jacket and pulled out a small notebook. 'I fear this may be of greater significance.' He handed Lucy the notebook, open at the page where he'd written what he'd discovered in the file room. She was just able to read what it said in the light from the window of the officers' mess. 'We were looking for links. Now it looks as if we may have one.'

CHAPTER 35

2 January 1944

Kalisz brought his paperwork up to date after breakfast and it was late morning before they took the road east towards Fort William in the battered Austin. For once, there was no hurry because they knew precisely where their next subject would be for most of the day. Kalisz could tell Lucy was annoyed and her first words confirmed it.

'I suppose it's too much to ask where you got the information?'

'Would it make any difference?' It weighed on his conscience that he'd gone behind her back, but the investigation came first, and the reality was that the investigation had taken a significant step forward. 'Facts are facts, and if he denies it, we just have to go through official channels.'

'But you don't think he'll deny it?'

'Not with what we also have from Krystina's diary. By the way, where are we going?'

'The exercise they're carrying out is at the Glenfinnan railway viaduct.' Lucy studied the map on her lap. 'You would have passed it on the way to Arisaig. You can't miss it.'

'It was dark.' The snow fell in swirling gusts driven by the wind, and Kalisz could feel the tyres struggling for grip on the narrow road. 'A viaduct is a bridge, yes?'

'Technically, yes, but I suspect there must be some difference, otherwise they would just call it a bridge, wouldn't they?'

'You didn't train as an engineer?'

Lucy turned to him with narrowed eyes. 'I know how to blow things up, if that helps.'

He concentrated on the winding road for a while.

'You said your mother was Polish?' he said, to break the silence.

'Yes,' Lucy nodded. 'We used to visit my grandparents in Warsaw for holidays. They had a rather grand apartment on Ujazdowskie. What is it like there now?'

Kalisz wished she'd left the question unasked, but he decided he couldn't avoid an honest answer. 'You would weep if you saw it now, Flight Officer Devereux. Only Nazis now live on Ujazdowskie. It is part of the German-only zone around Gestapo headquarters. And Warsaw? Warsaw is a city without a heart. I don't mean psychologically – for all their suffering, there is plenty of fight in the Poles yet – but physically. One of the first thing our conquerors did was move every Jew in Warsaw into a few thousand houses in the very centre of the city. Then they surrounded it with walls to create what is called a ghetto. Imagine four hundred thousand people forced to live in a walled enclave of just a couple of square kilometres? The Nazis planned to starve them to death, but the Jews did not die quickly enough for them. That was when they decided to "resettle" them in the east, "resettlement" being just another euphemism for killing. Day after day, week after week, the trains left the *Umschlagplatz* until only fugitives who had vowed to resist remained, along with those privileged few who'd been accorded the right to be worked to death. In the end, a few hundred young men and women, armed only with pistols, rifles and grenades, fought off thousands of SS backed by machine guns, flamethrowers and artillery for an entire month.' Kalisz felt his voice falter at a memory that was all too clear. His mind filled with faces that had to be thrust away before he could regain his composure. 'The SS had to burn and gas them out of their bunkers. Then they demolished the entire ghetto, building by building and street by street. Imagine your City of London as a field of rubble without one brick standing on another. That is what Warsaw is like now.'

Another mile passed in silence before a faint rattle in the engine compartment caught Kalisz's attention. He had no idea how long it had been there, but it became markedly worse with every bump in the road surface.

'Don't you think you should take a look at that?' Lucy suggested.

Kalisz shrugged. 'I'm not too sure how much good it will do. Like you, I've been taught how to sabotage a car, but I wouldn't know where to start to fix it.' Nevertheless, he slowed and drew into the next passing place. She handed him his greatcoat from the rear seats, and he got out of the Austin into the biting wind.

It took him three attempts to open the car bonnet, but eventually he managed to raise it and prop it in the upright position, where it shook with every snow-laden gust. What was he expecting to see? An engine, yes. He could see an engine. When the snow blew in, the flakes hissed as they touched the hot pipes. Kalisz pulled out a handkerchief and carefully began to test the more readily familiar parts for movement. Some of them were hot enough to burn his fingers if he hadn't protected them; some were oily, but in his experience all engines were oily.

'What can you see?' Lucy called.

Kalisz only grunted. Maybe the rattle came from down the side. He looked into the gap over the wheel arch. And froze.

He held his breath as he stepped back from the car, and walked gingerly to the passenger door. 'I think you should get out of the car, Lucy, but try not to make too much movement.'

'What is it?'

'I think it's a bomb.'

She opened the car door but, instead of walking away, she rummaged in her satchel and withdrew the small torch he'd last seen in the temporary mortuary. As he watched, she ducked her head beneath the bonnet and shone the light into the interior.

'You're right, Investigator, it's a bomb.'

'Don't touch…'

But Lucy was already tugging at something with her right hand. 'Enough plastic explosives to blow us and the car into the middle of next week, and this…' She held up what looked like a thin metal tube. 'A time-pencil detonator. Do you know how they work?'

'Vaguely.' Kalisz moved a little closer, feeling that his previous caution might be seen as somewhat excessive, given the lack of alarm, or even concern, in her voice. 'Should you be waving it about?'

'It's harmless. If it was intended to work, this area –' she pointed to a copper-coloured band on the tube – 'would have been crushed to break the glass capsule inside and release a copper chloride solution. The chloride then begins to corrode a length of iron wire. The wire snaps to release a spring, which strikes a percussion cap, which detonates a length of Cordtex.'

'Bang.'

'Indeed,' she said. 'This is a ten–minute time-pencil,' she handed the object to him. 'You can tell by the narrow black band at the top, but you can get them to go off after anything from ten minutes to twenty-four hours, depending on how far away you want to be when it explodes.'

Kalisz studied the little cylinder. 'How readily available would equipment like this be in the training schools?'

'Very. Every student will practise with explosives and detonators several times during their training. It would be simple to mislay a time-pencil and hoard away a few ounces of explosives.'

'That's what I thought. But it appears this was just a warning?'

She nodded. 'What do you want to do with it?'

'Hold on to it,' he handed the time-pencil back, 'and the plastique. Well apart, naturally.' Lucy laughed. 'I'd prefer it if we kept this to ourselves,' Kalisz continued. 'If Baldwin hears, it would give him the perfect excuse to send me back to London.'

'We just act as if nothing has happened?'

'Nothing *has* happened. We had a little car trouble, that's all.'

'All right,' she agreed, but he could tell she wasn't happy. 'Who do you think might want to frighten us off the case?'

'Oh, I can think of a few. Sergeant Connors might find it amusing. Major Gunn knows his way around explosives. The two Poles would consider it as an interesting training exercise. It could even have been sanctioned by Colonel Baldwin, who I doubt is the bumbling bureaucrat he appears, and who would very much like to see the back of us for the good of the station.'

'Interesting that the man we're going to see is currently trying to blow up a bridge.'

'Isn't it. Then again, everybody around here seems to be planning to blow up something.'

A little later they passed a church and a couple of houses that might have constituted some kind of small hamlet. The road wound down the hillside to the head of a bay, where the waves of a sea loch lapped against a small beach close to a giant pillar that looked like some kind of primitive lighthouse. The vast expanse of riffling, sleet-pocked grey water seemed to stretch forever, flanked by precipitous, tree-cloaked slopes. It was the kind of vista that warranted a moment's reflection, but Lucy instructed Kalisz to turn left, in the opposite direction, where a farm track led up the valley.

Driving carefully to avoid the potholes, Kalisz followed a narrow river, little more than what the locals called a burn, and he wondered that anyone would bother coming all this way to attack whatever comparable structure crossed it. It was only as they rounded a bend in the valley that he became aware of the true scale of the challenge these men had set themselves. Bit by bit, a massive man-made edifice appeared: a chain of soaring, water-stained grey columns, supporting enormous semi-circular arches that filled the valley in a long, elegant curve. He slowed to a halt about six hundred metres short of the structure, on a piece of flat ground where an army truck was already parked. He estimated the viaduct must be five or six hundred paces in length and thirty metres high in the centre. It had been built to carry the railway line across the valley, but he could make out no sign of the line itself from this angle.

'Twenty-one arches,' Lucy said, before he'd finished counting.

They could see uniformed figures scurrying about near the centre of the bridge, with one pair actually hanging on ropes metres below the parapet, working to attach large packages to the two central pillars.

The eastern end of the viaduct looked more or less inaccessible because of the angle of the slope and the thick scrub. That meant they had to cross the stream, and it took them several minutes before they could find a suitable fording place. Eventually, they were able to start the long hike up to the level of the railway line. The hill was steep and the heather clad slope treacherous and Kalisz was sweating by the time they were halfway to their destination. When they did reach the level of the single railway track, they discovered that the only way to reach the soldiers was to follow the railway line.

'Is this safe?' Lucy asked as she stepped tentatively from wooden railway sleeper to sleeper.

'That depends on when the train's due.' Kalisz grimaced. 'Hopefully our saboteurs have a timetable. If they start running, so do we.'

'Halt and identify yourselves.' The shouted order came from a soldier in a camouflage smock who had emerged from a bush on the hillside above. He had his rifle to his shoulder, and Kalisz hoped the man was as professional as he looked, because the muzzle was trained on his chest.

'Major Zamoyski,' he replied, 'to see Captain Malpas.'

'Sir.' The soldier came to attention. 'I'm afraid he's a bit busy at the mo.'

'Nevertheless, I...'

'That'll be all, Busby.' Malpas, his face streaked with camouflage paint, appeared from the direction of the viaduct. 'I'll see to this. You get back to the chaps and remind them we have only thirty minutes or less before the next train arrives.'

'I hope you don't believe the Germans will make it as easy as this for you, Captain.' Kalisz surveyed the operation ahead of him. 'In my experience, they don't believe in leaving bridges unguarded.'

'If there's a garrison, either we blow it by night...' Malpas sounded supremely confident. 'Or the Resistance chaps will keep the Nazis busy while we place our explosives. We don't underestimate the difficulties facing us, I assure you, Major. A brace of anti-tank mines under the rails and a few hundredweight of dynamite for each centre pillar should do the job.'

'Will you be using time-pencils, by any chance?'

Malpas frowned and shook his head. 'Much too risky,' he said. 'No, someone will be close by with a detonator, ready to blow it when the time is right. Now, what can I do for you?'

'I think you know that perfectly well, Captain Malpas... or would you prefer that I call you "Raoul". That was your work name when you were in charge of the BISHOP circuit, wasn't it?'

'I see...' Malpas said carefully.

'Good. Then perhaps you can explain why you didn't mention you were Krystina's circuit commander on her last mission to France?'

'I'd prefer not to.'

'In that case, Captain,' Kalisz said, 'I'm arresting you on suspicion of the murder, or involvement in the conspiracy to murder, of Krystina Kowolska. The handcuffs, if you please, Flight Officer?'

'No, please.' Malpas put his hands up in a gesture of capitulation. 'You must believe me – I had nothing to do with Krystina's death. Ask your questions. I have no reason to hide anything.'

Kalisz drew him away from the tracks into the shelter of a fold in the hill, which provided at least a little protection against the freezing, gusty wind. He dropped his head so he could speak directly into Malpas's ear. 'Krystina Kowolska came to you a week before she was killed, seeking your help and support. Instead, you betrayed her trust.'

'How do you…?' Malpas took a step back. 'No, I didn't betray her. She wasn't looking for help, she made crazy accusations. I told you, she was burned out. I made my feelings known to Colonel Baldwin, but he told me to mind my own business. He said the only mission that matters is the next one.'

Kalisz sensed this, at least, was true, but that was no reason to ease the pressure. 'No, that won't do. Maybe you did tell him she was burned out, but your report into BISHOP describes her as an exemplary agent who showed enormous courage, even under terrible torture. You even said you wouldn't hesitate to work with her again. So what changed?'

'Nothing…' Malpas shook his head. 'Everything. When I was exfiltrated back to London after BISHOP fell apart, they weren't interested in the truth. They told me what to write and I signed it.'

'What is the truth?' Lucy raised her voice to be heard against the still rising wind.

'That she was too weak to withstand interrogation. She started talking at the first sight of a whip.'

CHAPTER 36

OPERATION BISHOP

Montluc Prison, Lyons

As she swam out of the darkness back into the blinding light, Krystina couldn't make up her mind which pain to focus on first. Her head throbbed like an over-inflated football and felt as if it was filled with wet cotton wool, but the fire in her shoulders and the strain on her wrists shrieked at her to do something about it. It was only as her mind became aware of her true physical situation that the real terror set in. The instant she realised she was hanging by the arms, her head darted to the left, and her teeth closed on the seam at the corner of her blouse collar where her only salvation lay.

'Is this what you are looking for?'

Krystina opened her eyes to see a blond-haired man in riding breeches and shirtsleeves standing in front of her. He had bland, indeterminate features, but ice-cold, soulless blue eyes, and a uniform jacket with the rank insignia of an *SS-Obersturmführer* hung from a chair behind him. In his right hand he held a small capsule.

'Unfortunately, this avenue is closed to you, but there are others.' He had a soft seductive voice entirely at odds with his demeanour, which emanated menace the way a glowing fire emanated heat. 'You can save me a great deal of effort, and yourself a great deal of pain, by providing me with everything you know about Operation Bishop – the names of all your associates, your safe houses, your ciphers, the location of your communications equipment and arms caches. Do not concern yourself with concealing anything. Most of this information is already in my hands. Well?'

Krystina let her head drop. She was suspended by chains from the ceiling of a small, windowless cell, with her feet inches from the concrete floor. To her right, a man in SS uniform sat at a portable desk, with a pen poised over a pad of paper. More significantly, on a table in front of her lay the instruments of torture her interrogator intended her to see, and to fear. And fear them she did – a deep-seated terror at her very core. Not fear of pain, or even death, but fear that she wouldn't have the courage or fortitude to stay silent. Whatever they did to her, she must buy Raoul time.

'No?' Her captor's dead eyes seemed to glow with anticipation. 'What else could I have expected from the famous Raven?' Krystina's heart stopped at the mention of a work name that should have been known to only two people in Lyons. If he knew this, what more did he know? 'There is a railway security detachment who would very much like to meet you, to discuss the murder of two of their comrades. But my ornithologist friends tell me it is possible to teach a raven to talk, and, believe me, I am an expert in such matters.' He picked up a multi-stranded whip from where it had been soaking in a bucket of water. 'Let us begin.'

—

'Has she talked yet?'

'No, she is terribly brave. For some of them, the very act of suffering gives them strength. They embrace it with an almost religious fervour. But it is just a matter of time. You say Raoul is still determined to attack the marshalling yard?'

'So it seems.'

'Then he must be stopped.'

'Yes.' The informer gave himself time to choose his words. SS-Obersturmführer Klaus Barbie was a man to be treated with care. 'But it is more difficult now. Since the destruction of the Maquis du Mont and the arrest of the woman, Raoul has been much more secretive. He trusts no one. He has dispersed the people who Raven had contact with, all the old safe houses have been closed down, the radios moved to different locations and the codes changed. If I do get word of the attack, it will be at the very last minute.'

'Then what the woman can tell us has no value. Her usefulness is at an end. I cannot allow the attack on the marshalling yard to succeed.

Perhaps it is time the leadership of the Bishop circuit went the way of the Maquis du Mont?'

'If that happens. *my* usefulness will also be at an end,' the man pointed out. 'Fingers are already being pointed. If you arrest Raoul and the others, suspicion will undoubtedly fall on me, and everything we have done will be for nothing. If the slightest shadow of suspicion hangs over me, I will never get close to Max.'

Barbie considered for a moment. The informer was undoubtedly correct.

Max.

Max was the key to everything, and he was so close Barbie could almost smell him. Once he had Max in his hands, he was confident he could extract the information that would allow him to roll up every Resistance organisation in the south of France. No, it would not do. But... perhaps there was a way.

Klaus Barbie shook his head in admiration of his own genius. 'What if I told you that by the time I destroy Bishop, far from being under suspicion, you will be a French hero, and the only man in a position to rebuild the *reseau* in Lyons. You will not have to go looking for Max. He will come to you.'

–

Krystina lay on the concrete floor praying for death, every fibre of her being a pulsating microcosm of agony, each with its own separate, maddening pitch. It had been twenty-four hours now since her last interrogation. After she'd tried to chew through the artery in her wrist they'd chained her to the wall, so she was lying in her own filth and she could barely move her hands or feet. She would have wept, but, like prayers, she'd run out of tears a long time ago.

Bile rose in her throat at the thought he'd defeated her. She'd done everything they'd trained her to do to keep her secrets buried deep, through the beatings, the pliers, the glowing cigar tips, and the suffocating awfulness of the *baignoire*, where they held your head under water until you were shaking hands with death, only to pull you away again. But the electrical machine had finished her. The next time she saw the wires and the cattle prod, she knew the words would spill from her like the waters from a burst dam.

It was over. What came next didn't matter.

Time meant nothing. Only the ominous click, click, click of the approaching jackboots along the corridor. And here, as if she'd summoned them with her own fear, they came. She bit her lip to stop herself from crying out.

The cell door swung open to reveal a single guard, who fumbled at the chains with his keys to release her arms and feet.

'Can you stand, Marie?'

Krystina looked up into his face, her mind a whirl of confusion. 'You?'

He dragged her to her feet. 'It has all been arranged, but we don't have much time. We must get you to the laundry.'

CHAPTER 37

Arisaig

'I would never have sanctioned it. It was too risky. Émile did it all on his own initiative, against my express orders, using the cell he'd recruited personally. When they got her out of Montluc I had no option but to get involved. We smuggled her north and she was flown back to England in a Lysander.'

'How did you know Krystina had talked?' Kalisz demanded.

'We heard later from a contact inside the jail.' Malpas was belligerent now. 'One of Émile's people who'd helped with the escape. Look, she was caught because she made a mistake. Because she didn't take enough care. I should have sent her home long before it happened.'

Kalisz and Lucy exchanged a glance. 'Perhaps it wasn't Krystina who was careless,' he said. 'Your first name is David?'

'That's correct.'

'"Why doesn't D understand?"' Lucy quoted from Krystina's journal. '"I tried to tell him, but it's as if he's not listening. His carelessness could have killed us all." You don't deny she came to see you at Rhubana?'

'No,' Malpas said. 'But I wouldn't let her through the door. It wouldn't have been right. We talked by the shore in the rain.'

'So what does she mean? "His carelessness could have killed us all"?'

'I told you,' he snapped. 'She was making wild accusations.'

'But she did say it?' Lucy persisted.

'She was talking about something that happened in May of last year, not long before she was taken. We were close to exhaustion – all of us were. It was our WT operator's birthday, and I felt we needed a little time to relax. I arranged a private room in a hotel owned by a trusted résistant, and I treated him and one of our French contacts to dinner. Krystina thought it was a bad idea and stayed at home. We all got a little drunk, and someone suggested we go to a bar to finish off the night. She was furious when she discovered where we'd been.'

'Why?' Kalisz asked. 'She knew you were going out. Why would that make her angry?'

Malpas opened his mouth to reply, but a soldier ran up and saluted. 'Train, sir.'

'Clear the track, Corporal.'

A few moments later they heard the sound of a steam train approaching and a sharp whistle. The train appeared from a cleft in the hills beyond the viaduct and made its way across at a sedate pace.

'Wait for it,' Malpas muttered.

When the engine reached the centre of the bridge, Kalisz blinked as two sharp cracks rang out, clear even at fifty paces. A cheer went up from the train and a grinning overalled figure appeared at the cab window, waving a cap.

'Fog warning charges on the rails,' Malpas explained as the train rushed past. 'It gives the lads a boost and the train crews think it's a great lark.'

Kalisz had to bite his tongue. It was as if this was all a game to the British. They seemed to have no idea of what the Germans were capable of, a fact Malpas appeared to confirm with his next words.

'The bar was a known haunt of Gestapo agents.' He saw Kalisz's look. 'You don't understand. Being in the field is nine tenths waiting, boredom and tedium. It builds up in your head. Sometimes you need a safety valve.'

To Kalisz, Malpas's explanation for his actions sounded panicky and defensive, and he wondered who really was close to burnout. 'But Krystina didn't think so?'

'She threatened to report the incident to headquarters.' Malpas shook his head. 'It rather strained our relationship.'

'You were her lover,' Lucy said, as if the thought had just occurred to her.

'What? What makes you think that.'

She turned to another page in her notebook. '"D thinks he can take up where he left off, but it can never be." She came to you for help and you tried to take advantage of her. What happened when she turned you down?'

'It wasn't like that.'

'No?'

'We were in love.'

Lucy struggled to hide her disdain, but it was Kalisz who spoke. 'Perhaps *you* were, but I doubt if Krystina ever truly loved anyone. Was there anything else?'

'She kept asking if I was the one who was undermining her at Arisaig House.'

'And were you?'

'No.'

'And yet at our first meeting you told us Krystina was burned out. Was that your own interpretation, or did someone else plant the seed?'

Malpas stiffened. 'I would say it was the general opinion at HQ.'

'So Colonel Baldwin—'

'Among others.'

'Major Dempsey, or the affable Major Sykes?'

'No, not Sykes. I would say he was supportive of her. But I think he was wrong. After seeing her for myself, I think Baldwin was right, but he felt he didn't have the rank to do anything about it.'

Kalisz nodded thoughtfully. 'What happened to BISHOP after Krystina was extracted from France?'

They were interrupted by another soldier in camouflage face paint. 'That's everything tidied away, sir.'

'Thank you, Sergeant Mercier. Join the lads in the three-tonner and I'll be with you in a moment.' Malpas reached into his top pocket and took out a packet of Player's cigarettes. 'Let them have a fag.' He tossed the packet to the other soldier. When Mercier had gone, Malpas stood, blinking and looking very tired.

'You were going to tell us what happened after Krystina left,' Kalisz reminded him.

'We kept on the move, of course. Never slept in the same house two nights in succession. Even then the Huns were never more than half a step behind. We'd sometimes see the ring of troops closing on the house we'd just left. It wasn't too bad for those of us who could travel light, but the WT operators had it tough. That was when they got Freddie.'

'Freddie?'

'Our wireless operator. First-class chap. Everyone liked Freddie, even though he was what you might call "a bit different" and didn't care who knew. We were to rendezvous at a remote house north of Vaugneray, one we hadn't used before. I was watching the place, ready to make contact, when I realised there were Germans in the trees around me. So I went to ground, which is where I witnessed what happened next.'

'Yes?'

Malpas's face seemed to have frozen. Only the lips were free of the paralysis and his voice had become a flat monotone. 'Freddie must have got wind of them closing in, because smoke started billowing from the chimney. It's what we're taught, you see. Even if it's the last thing you do, the code books and the one-time pads must be destroyed. That was just like Freddie. He knew he was trapped, but he did the right thing. Still, they took their time, and it must have been another ten minutes before they kicked the door in and dragged Freddie out. Normally, he would have been taken to Montluc for interrogation, but the security detachment was commanded by a man called Klaus Barbie, an *SS-Obersturmführer* and a notorious sadist. Barbie must have sensed Freddie's peculiar tastes, or perhaps he knew about them from Krystina or some other source. He thought it would be amusing to place a stick of dynamite down the back of Freddie's trousers and light the fuse. I could hear them laughing as he danced about, trying to dislodge the dynamite, and I saw the moment he knew he was going to die. He threw himself towards Barbie, but before he could reach him the charge went off and blew Freddie to pieces.'

Kalisz waited for more as the silence lengthened, but Malpas seemed to have run out of words.

'Barbie definitely made no attempt to question Freddie?' Lucy demanded.

The captain shook his head.

'But don't you see?' She turned to Kalisz. 'This means Krystina didn't betray anyone. You would have changed all your codes after she was taken?' She addressed the question to Malpas, who appeared bewildered, but nodded. 'It's standard SOE procedure in these circumstances,' she explained. 'Likewise, the members of the BISHOP circuit would have accessed a new list of safe houses. A wireless operator, with all his knowledge of the network, its personnel and procedures, would be an enormous prize for the Gestapo. The only reason this Barbie could have had for not taking him in, was that he was already in possession of the information Freddie had. That was why the Nazi security services were always just one step behind. Someone was informing them where you were. Not Krystina, because she'd left France weeks earlier. It was also why this Barbie felt he could murder poor Freddie without questioning him. They must already have had access to the codes.'

'I don't understand.'

'Flight Officer Devereux is suggesting you were being betrayed by someone in your organisation, Captain,' Kalisz said. 'But it was not Krystina Kowolska. Perhaps it is time you returned to your men,' he said gently.

They accompanied Malpas back down the slope.

'Oh, just one question more,' Kalisz said. 'What happened at the end of your conversation?'

'Krystina was angrier than I've ever seen her before. She said she wouldn't let me kill any more heroes. For some reason, she held me responsible for the loss of one of our *reseaux* in the mountains, but I swear it was none of my doing. Then she stole one of our canoes and set off up the loch.'

'That would be Loch Morar?'

'Yes. It was the last time I saw her alive.'

CHAPTER 38

'You're very quiet, Jan?'

'I was contemplating the mystery of lochs and lakes.' Kalisz smiled. 'But I doubt I'll ever understand it.'

The truth was that he felt more at peace standing here in the shadow of the tall pillar he'd noticed earlier, than at any time in the past four years. From his position on the narrow beach at the head of the sea loch, a long bay stretched away in front of him between the arms of the tree covered mountains, rippling waters a chill grey beneath the low, sleet-laden clouds. Despite the icy wind that stung his ears beneath the uniform cap, there was a tranquillity to be had here, a balm to the soul, he'd seldom experienced before. Was it some quality in the air? Or the fact that the vastness of the sky and the agelessness of loch and mountain made humanity seem so insignificant and transient? Perhaps it was the sense of being an integral component of some glorious other-worldly masterpiece?

Kalisz let out a long breath, exalting in the past two hours of freedom from the burdens imposed on him by the war, and, more recently, Prime Minister Winston Churchill. An unlikely escape engineered by Flight Officer Lucy Devereux who, in a moment of genius, had announced that, since they'd always been going to miss lunch, she'd brought along a picnic of spam sandwiches and a thermos flask of actual coffee. They'd eaten in the car, talking about anything but the case and the war. Shared memories of places she'd been in Warsaw; mostly museums, galleries and concert halls, but also the great gardens and fine houses and palaces. He'd discovered that her mother was a cellist and her father a historian, from whom she'd inherited his passion for the past. She'd revealed that the soaring stone pillar before them had been built to commemorate the Highlanders who'd fought and died in the abortive Jacobite Rebellion of 1745. In fact, if Lucy was to be believed, Charles Edward Stuart, the 'King Over The Water' had raised his standard at this very spot. Bonnie Prince Charlie, it turned out, had a surfeit of charisma and charm that made men follow him, but was no military strategist. Like Hitler in Russia, he'd made the elementary mistake of believing that capturing territory would win him a kingdom, when the reality was that it meant nothing if you didn't destroy your enemy's army. Charlie had crossed the border and marched south, before the English woke up and chased his ragtag army of clansmen to a place called Culloden and annihilated them. The statue of a kilted warrior topped the towering pedestal, silhouetted against the setting sun. Kalisz looked up at the solitary figure and wondered at the fate of the man who'd inspired the image.

'Time we were on our way,' he said reluctantly.

Back on the road, as the light faded, his mind turned to his earlier conversation with Malpas beside the railway line. 'I believe our interview with the captain raised some interesting questions.'

'Yes.' Lucy's lips pursed in distaste. 'Poor Krystina. She suffered so much and was prepared to sacrifice even more, yet just about every man at Arisaig treated her like an outcast. In all the time we've been here, only Doctor Llewellyn and Sykes have shown even the slightest sympathy. She went to Malpas looking for some sort of help or understanding, and he more or less accused her of being a traitor. I felt a bit sorry for him, but in his own way, he's as bad as Gunn.'

'I was thinking more in terms of how their conversation ended.' Kalisz frowned. 'She must have had some kind of transport to get from Arisaig to Rhubana. Why would she steal a canoe and paddle up Loch Morar on a night when, according to Captain Malpas, the weather was foul?'

'I suppose she might have just wanted to be alone,' Lucy suggested.

'This is what women do when they're upset?'

'Of course.' She gave him an odd look. 'How long have you been married?'

'Our jobs often keep us apart,' Kalisz muttered defensively. 'But to get back to my point... I don't believe Krystina Kowolska did anything at random. She visited Malpas because she was searching for answers. We will perhaps never know her motivation for going out on the night she was killed, but I am certain she had one. When she took that canoe and headed up the loch, she had a reason.'

'What reason?'

'I don't know yet,' he admitted.

'What's that?'

They'd reached a point where the waves almost lapped the road. Kalisz could see the outline of a truck, and torches waving on the pebble beach. He was tempted to keep going, but he recognised Constable MacDonald's police car parked in front of the lorry. He drew up behind the two vehicles.

'Another mine?' Lucy suggested.

They got out of the car and made their way tentatively towards the light of the torches, across rocks made slick by a coating of thick seaweed and studded by whelks and limpets. Kalisz could see the silhouettes of two figures crouched over something lying on the shingle beach, while four soldiers stood nearby. As they approached, one of the men rose and Kalisz recognised Doctor Llewellyn's florid features in the torchlight.

'Ah, Major Zamoyski,' the medical officer said. 'Just in time. These fellows were out looking for our French chap from Arisaig, but they stumbled on something entirely different. Come and have a look.'

'I'll stay here,' Lucy said. 'I've no problem with dead people, but bodies that have been in the water for a long time give me the shivers.'

'We know he's been in the sea for just over a week, because he was lost on a night-landing exercise on Christmas Eve,' Llewellyn informed Kalisz as he approached the corpse. The gulls had taken his eyes and most of his tongue, but he must have spent days face down in the surf; the motion of sand and waves had removed most of his features, giving the swollen face an anonymous, Buddha-like quality. Internal gases had bloated his body, so the buttons of his uniform tunic were strained to breaking point, and he still wore his heavy army boots.

'Who is he?'

'One of Major Gunn's men.' MacDonald looked up from where he'd been searching the body. 'A Commando sergeant.'

'And he was lost on the twenty-fourth of December?' Kalisz remembered Gunn telling him he and his men had been on exercise that night, but he hadn't mentioned where.

'They were doing mock landings between *Eilean Gobhlach* and *Rubha Aird Ghamhsgail*.'

Kalisz frowned at the incomprehensible Gaelic names.

'I believe he means that island out there –' Llewellyn pointed towards a dark mound just visible in the dying light – 'and Borrodale Point.'

A lightning bolt of comprehension flashed through Kalisz's mind. 'Borrodale House is less than two hundred metres from where the body of Krystina Kowolska was found.'

MacDonald grunted and rose to his feet. 'I mentioned that to Major Gunn when he came in to report his missing man, but he said his Commandos were together at all times. He supervised the search himself.'

'With the greatest respect, Constable...' Kalisz tried to contain his frustration. 'A night search along two kilometres of rocky coastline would suggest the very opposite of togetherness.'

'Well,' MacDonald said stiffly, 'I believe you'll have to take that up with the major yourself.'

Kalisz returned to Lucy and explained what he'd just heard.

'That means he was in a position to kill Krystina and Lieutenant Fontaine, despite all his denials,' she said. 'He's been lying to us. We should bring him in for questioning.'

'But we suspected that already, from what Yvette told us about Pierre Renan,' Kalisz pointed out as they returned to the car. 'It does not change the fact that he would have needed the help of at least one other person to suspend Krystina's body. That means two or more men were absent from the search for a considerable amount of time, which would certainly have been noticed by the others on the exercise. Given that the murders are now common knowledge, it seems unlikely to me that this would not have been reported in some way. At least I now understand why Krystina's killers didn't just put her body in the sea. They would have seen the beams of the searchers' torches.'

'Even so...'

'We cannot allow our distaste for the major to cloud our judgement.'

'You mean *my* distaste?'

'No, I do not. But in any case, I think we can agree that the major is not going anywhere for the moment. His commitment to his soldiers is one of his few redeeming qualities. I think there are other priorities we need to investigate before we question Major Gunn again.'

'What do you mean?' Lucy demanded.

'In the journal, Krystina talked about a "Tenth House". By my calculation, we have encountered nine so far. The first name that was mentioned was Meoble Lodge, which I would guess from your map is STS 23. Arisaig House is, of course, STS 21. The two schools on Knoydart, I believe we can discount entirely.'

'Inverie and Glaschoille.'

'We have Traigh, Camusdarach and Garramor, the houses closest to Arisaig, Glasnacardoch, the weapons training facility, and Rhubana, where Captain Malpas and his team are quartered. Colonel Baldwin talked about STS 23 and "another house", but I have never heard the name of that house mentioned.'

'He also said it was empty,' Lucy pointed out.

'But what if it wasn't?'

'Let me have a look at the map.' She retrieved a map case and her torch from her satchel.

'Remember MacDonald and his talk of the students who raided a lodge house?' Kalisz hurried on. 'The ones who led to Colonel Baldwin's ignominious arrest. He talked about tracing them to "the house up the loch". Yet a training facility on Loch Morar has never been mentioned. Someone is concealing something from us.'

Lucy studied the map in the glow of the torch, and the list in her hand.

'I think this must be it,' she said.

Kalisz slowed enough to be able to glance at the map. STS 23b. Swordland.

CHAPTER 39

3 January 1944

'Baldwin is away, and Major Dempsey says he doesn't have the authority to allow us to visit STS 23b without his permission.' Lucy's face mirrored Kalisz's disappointment as she emerged from Dempsey's office into the hallway of Arisaig House after breakfast.

'Do we need his permission?' Kalisz asked. 'If it's empty, what difference does it make whether we go there or not?'

'It amounts to an order, Jan. Yes, you're here on an investigation sanctioned by Winston Churchill, but Baldwin is in charge. If it's a stand-off between you and the commanding officer of Arisaig over something that's more or less conjecture, there will only be one winner.'

'When will Baldwin be back?'

'Not till tomorrow afternoon at the earliest.'

Kalisz chewed his lip and considered for a moment. 'All right, but I'm not giving up on this. We'll see Baldwin tomorrow. In the meantime, I have a report to write up, and I'm sure you'll also have work to do. It won't do any harm to take a step back from the investigation for a day. Sometimes it helps you see things more clearly.'

They parted, and Kalisz spent the morning in his room, pulling together all the details of the investigation. As he worked, he experienced a growing sense of frustration that he couldn't see any discernible pattern. Gunn had a motive and possibly the opportunity, but he couldn't have acted alone – and was he the type of man who would have cold-bloodedly executed the unfortunate Lieutenant Fontaine? Kalisz searched his mind until he conjured up a picture of the pistol Gunn carried at his belt: some kind of revolver, probably a Webley, which the British favoured. A big gun that fired a big bullet, and certainly not the one that had killed Fontaine. Who else? Llewellyn and his crooked Sergeant Connors? Kalisz knew better than most that killers came in all shapes and sizes, but nothing about the medical officer said 'cold-blooded murderer'. Even though it was possible that Connors had pressurised Llewellyn into providing him with an alibi, Kalisz's instinct suggested both of them were in the clear. He'd no doubt the Poles, Jerzy and Witold, were capable of cold-blooded murder, but the training log confirmed they'd been on exercise twenty miles away. The only other person 'in the frame', as the Americans would say, was the Frenchman, Pierre Renan. Yvette had said he was only gone for a moment, but that could mean anything. He undoubtedly hated Krystina, as she had hated him, but it would mean she'd been killed on impulse. How, then, had Renan suspended the body on his own? Perhaps Kalisz was wrong, and it was possible for one man to achieve what appeared impossible. The only other scenario he could think of was that Renan had sought help from his room-mate, Fontaine: somehow persuaded him – at gunpoint? – to help hang the woman he yearned for. No, that was just fantasy. *Enough.*

A bell announced lunch in the mess and Kalisz descended the stairs, stopping for a moment to speak to the clerk at the front desk. Inside, he saw no sign of Lucy, which was reassuring. Sykes was there at his usual table, presumably between classes, studiously ignoring Dempsey at the opposite end of the room. Kalisz ate without appetite, but he knew he would need all the sustenance he could get, so he consumed the stodgy pie and watery potatoes automatically, followed by some kind of cloyingly sweet pudding.

Back in his room, he began his preparations. He filled a backpack with a felt-covered water bottle, four Hershey Bars and three surplus bread rolls from the dining room, adding a pair of binoculars, a torch and a compass he'd requisitioned from stores. He folded his greatcoat into a tight roll and tied it with string someone had been foolish enough to leave lying around. Then he waited, lying on the bed until a clock struck two. He checked his watch to be certain and then rose, hitching the backpack over one shoulder and with the greatcoat under his left arm.

Kalisz stood by the door for a moment, listening for the telltale sound of footsteps on the polished wooden floorboards, but heard nothing. He slipped out, and quickly made his way down the stairs and through the hall. Did he imagine it, or could he sense eyes watching him as he walked up the hill to the main road, where the car he'd requested was waiting? But there was nothing he could do about that.

–

An hour later, Kalisz was negotiating the narrow, winding, poor excuse for a track that flanked the north shore of Loch Morar, on a squat, underpowered BSA motorcycle. Constable MacDonald had been almost fawningly eager to co-operate after showing his irritation on the beach the previous night, and had demonstrated how to start the machine and warned Kalisz against its tendency to yaw to the right. Just as well, because to the right lay the chill, dark waters of the mile-wide loch, only a jutting tree root and a twitch of the steering away from disaster. Forest and scrub covered the steep slope on his left, overhanging the track and leaving much of it in shadow. MacDonald had reckoned on a journey of nine or ten miles to the house. The first four along the familiar road from Arisaig to Morar had been simple enough. When Kalisz crossed the river he turned east and followed the shore, as he'd been instructed. After about a mile, the track abandoned the loch and took to the hills. The policeman had called the weather 'dreich', if Kalisz had caught the word correctly, and it captured to perfection the all-encompassing mist and the ominously low cloud that shrouded the surrounding mountains. Here and there he passed heaps of moss-covered stone and earthen field boundaries, suggesting this eerie, desolate landscape had not always been as empty as it was now. But, as he continued, the condition of the track worsened and the journey became a stop-start battle between man and machine that required all Kalisz's concentration, interspersed with howled complaints from the racing engine.

After a further hour, he began to wish he'd listened to MacDonald's suggestion that he might be better to hire a boat from one of the men who fished the loch. But that would have meant tying up at the jetty below Swordland Lodge, and Kalisz didn't intend to announce his presence if he could help it. He ran the police constable's directions through his mind. Soon the track would begin to hug the shore again, and this time it would stay there, hemmed in by the mountains plunging almost vertically into the loch. The going became more treacherous with every twist and rise in the trail, until he feared he would have to abandon the bike long before he'd planned. It was only when he reached a small sandy bay and the track turned away from the loch once more that he realised he'd reached his destination. The lodge should be in the wood he could see some three hundred metres ahead, and hopefully out of earshot. He switched off the BSA's engine and ran it off the road into the trees. A cursory check of his surroundings and a longer wait, lying unblinking amid scrubby bushes, until he could be certain his arrival hadn't been noticed. Only then did he huddle into his greatcoat with his back against the engine to make the most of the dying warmth, and close his eyes to wait for dusk.

A fading silvery light allowed Kalisz to make his way with confidence along the shore towards the woods, and Swordland. Mist lay over the water and moorhens chirred to one another among the reed beds. There was something about the damp pine scent of the place that reminded him of fishing trips to the Masurian Lakes with his father and his brother Henryk. A time of tranquillity, when peace was taken for granted and war unthinkable. His father was dead now, heart and spirit broken by the brutal Nazi occupation, and Henryk hadn't been heard from since he'd been captured during the Red Army's advance into Poland in 1939. Kalisz still lived in hope, but he knew the most likely explanation was that his brother lay among his comrades in the sandy soil of the Katyn Forest, with an NKVD bullet in the back of his neck.

Halfway to the house, a whiff of woodsmoke provided a solution to one of the questions he'd come here to answer. Swordland was certainly occupied by someone. He reached a wooden landing stage, where an ancient cabin cruiser floated beside the makeshift jetty, and turned inland. A worn path led through a stand of stunted birch trees until he had the house in view about thirty paces away.

Swordland Lodge was a much larger house than Kalisz had expected in this remote wilderness: not as grand as Arisaig, but certainly on a scale similar to Borrodale. The lodge was constructed of pale grey stone and with the same dark slate roof, studded with at least ten chimneys. A covered porch stretched most of the length of the frontage and, as he watched, a light appeared, flickering in a downstairs window until it settled into a soft yellow glow.

Kalisz ducked low at the sound of a door opening. Feet crunched on a gravel path and a voice called out from the house, '*Verwenden sie nicht das ganze papier, Gunther.*'

It took a moment before Kalisz's dulled mind worked out that the caller was speaking German. He risked a look at the person who was walking down a path to the lodge's outhouses, and his whole body seemed to freeze. For a moment he struggled for breath.

The man was wearing the uniform of the Waffen-SS.

CHAPTER 40

Warsaw

3 January 1944

Maria Kalisz lay back in her favourite chair, exhausted after a long shift at the hospital, her first since Jan's disappearance. She was glad Stefan wasn't at home, because it meant they didn't have to pretend everything was fine when in reality each day was an eternity of anticipation, filled with fear and anxiety at the lack of any news. More than a week now, and not a word. Why couldn't they tell her something – anything? Even a lie would give her something to hold on to.

The soft tap at the door sent a shiver of anticipation through her. Was this the answer to her prayers? She felt no fear or sense of threat as she rose to answer the knock. If the Nazis had come for her at last, they would have kicked the door in.

She had a moment of confusion at the sight of a well-dressed stranger in a dark overcoat. A tall young man in his late twenties or early thirties, with handsome, regular features and dark hair parted on the left side. It was only when she looked into the washed-out blue eyes that reality dawned, and the word hit her like a hammer blow: Gestapo.

'Mrs Kalisz? I am here to speak to your husband. *Kriminalkommissar* Wolfgang Fischer, Gestapo.' He didn't wait to be invited in, but brushed past Maria into the hallway. She hesitated for a moment as a second, older man appeared at the top of the stairs. He was carrying a large briefcase. He gave her a cold look and followed Fischer into the apartment.

Heart pounding, Maria followed them through to the lounge. The two men studied their surroundings with more than normal interest before the older of the pair placed the briefcase on the floor. A pile of Stefan's books lay on top of a sideboard, and the man picked them up one by one and studied them before casting them aside. Had she left anything incriminating lying around? What about Stefan's room? God only knew what was up there.

'I am afraid Jan isn't available, Herr *Kriminalkommissar*,' she said in a halting German that she hoped would hide her nervousness. 'He is a detective with the Warsaw *Kriminalpolizei*—'

'We are aware of his background, Mrs Kalisz,' Fischer said. 'You won't mind if *Kriminalsekretar* Lindauer inspects the rest of the house? Nothing sinister, I assure you.' A smile flickered on the thin lips that suggested the opposite. 'Merely part of our operational procedure.'

'Please.' She nodded her compliance to the older man, but he was already making for the kitchen. 'Yes, my husband was recently taken ill as a result of his duties, and is being treated at a specialist facility in Gdynia—'

'You mean Gotenhafen?'

'Yes, of course – Gotenhafen.' The Nazis had renamed the city soon after the Occupation, but to Poles it would always be Gdynia. 'He has a virulent skin problem which the doctors fear may be contagious. It means he has to be kept in isolation and completely shielded from direct light.'

Fischer nodded. 'That confirms what I have been told by *Hauptsturmführer* Hoth at Department V, and also that I have your attention and co-operation.'

Lindauer appeared from the hallway. 'The house is empty, sir.'

'Very well, you may leave us.'

When his partner was gone, Fischer settled himself in the chair where Maria had been sitting a few minutes earlier, retrieved a file from the briefcase and opened it in his lap.

'You will note that you are standing while I sit. Do you know why that is?'

'No, I don't, Herr *Kriminalkommissar*.'

'It is so you fully understand your position, Mrs Kalisz. Outside this room you may be the respected wife of a Warsaw policeman and a valued nurse, but within these four walls, you are entirely within my control. Your husband is *Volksdeutsche* and has certain rights. You, on the other hand, are a Pole and have none. Am I making myself clear?'

'I think so.'

'No.' The Gestapo agent shook his head. 'That was a little too meek. The other thing you must understand is that you cannot deceive me. I have been in this position many times, and I have seen and heard every form of deception.' The pale eyes studied Maria in a way that made her shiver, and Fischer's voice was all the more chilling for the entire lack of emotion. 'The fact that you are an attractive woman means nothing to me, but I could order you to remove your clothing and you would have no choice but to comply. I could probe your most intimate places searching for hidden messages, and I would be perfectly within my rights. If you resisted, it would be my duty to restrain you and transport you to Szucha Avenue, where you would be subject to a much more rigorous form of examination. There is nothing whatsoever your husband could do to save you.' Maria had to choke back the bile that rose in her throat. 'Now, this is the Gestapo file for Jan Kalisz –' he tapped the document case on his lap – 'who is a person of interest in an investigation I am conducting. There are suggestions…' He lifted up a piece of paper and studied it. '…that he may have links to the primary subject of my investigation, a man we know only as "The Bulgarian".' Maria felt as if her legs would collapse beneath her, and she had to clench her fists to stop them shaking. 'Of course, it's possible that these connections may be of a professional nature, and therefore entirely legitimate. Only your husband can tell us that. But what is not in doubt is that, if they exist, he will be able to confirm the identity of a dangerous criminal whose name, and the locations of his various enterprises, are currently unknown to us.' Fischer removed a second, much larger file from the briefcase and pulled a grainy picture from among the pages. 'Have you ever seen this person?'

It was a photograph of a man's head and shoulders taken from behind and from an oblique angle, and almost certainly from a distance, judging by how out of focus it appeared.

'No,' Maria lied. 'I've never seen this man in my life.'

He stared at her for a long time. 'Perhaps I'll have better luck with your husband when I speak to him tomorrow night.'

'I told you, my husband is in hospital. He cannot talk to anyone.'

Fischer produced a bark of laughter. 'My dear lady, you would be astonished how many people who believe they have nothing to say find their tongues when they are confronted by the Gestapo. There is one more thing.' He reached into the pocket of his overcoat and drew out a card. 'When your husband returns to duty, you will call this number once every day and report his activities of the previous twenty-four hours. I want to know Jan Kalisz's every movement.'

Maria stared at him. 'I'm sorry.' She shook her head. 'This is impossible. I cannot spy on my husband, whatever you threaten to do to me.'

'You Poles.' Fischer rose to his feet and Maria took a step back from his threatening presence. 'Will you never learn?' He picked up a photograph from the sideboard: a picture of the family together in a Warsaw park, in the days when the sun shone and no one lived in fear. 'You have a son, aged what? Fourteen? A handsome boy, isn't he. A pity if anything should happen to him.' The Nazi's voice hardened. 'If you do not do as I say, he will be arrested and placed in a concentration camp. It does not matter on what charge – we will find something. When he reaches the camp, I will personally ensure he shares a barrack with the pink triangles. You understand what this means?'

Maria had to bite her lip to stop it quivering. She nodded.

'And not just any pink triangles. These will be the rough boys from Berlin, men with exotic tastes and large appetites. He will be very popular among his new friends. Now, do we understand each other?' He handed her the card and she held it between her trembling fingers.

'Yes, Herr *Kriminalkommissar*, we understand each other perfectly.'

When the Gestapo agent left, he gave her a look. She wasn't certain what it meant, but it left Maria feeling as soiled as if he'd put his hands on her. She felt something trickle down her chin, and when she reached up to touch it her fingers came away slick with warm blood from where she'd bitten through her lip.

Maria struggled to control the emotions churning inside her – nausea, fear and disgust all bubbling together – but the principal sensation was an all-consuming hatred. *That pig.* She went to the bedroom and took Jan's police-issue pistol from the drawer. A Walther 9mm, and that was about all she knew. But one thing was clear in her head: she wouldn't be taken, and she wouldn't allow them to take Stefan. Back in the living room, she sat for a moment with the gun in her lap, willing her heart to slow and her mind to settle.

Who could she turn to? Roziki? Yes, he would help her, but there was a risk she might lead the Gestapo to him, and by extension, the family he was sheltering. Of course, there was another possibility: the people who'd placed Jan in danger in the first place. She dialled a number she'd been told to memorise when she was sent to Gdynia.

'I would like to speak to Katya, please.'

A clipped voice answered, sharp and disapproving – 'There is no one here of that name' – and put the telephone down.

Maria sucked in a breath, replaced the receiver and dialled a new number. Her last chance.

'May I speak to Mr Marconi?'

The familiar rumbling tones echoed in her ear, and she almost collapsed with relief. She explained in short, cryptic sentences what had happened.

'A file, you say?'

'Yes. He was carrying it in his briefcase.'

'And he said he was going to see Jan tomorrow night?'

'Yes.'

'I'll be in touch.'

Maria replaced the phone, and picked up the Walther as the door opened and a tall figure walked into the room.

'Stefan, can you show me how to work this damned thing?'

The boy's eyes widened in astonishment. She knew it wasn't because his mother was pointing a pistol at him, but because he'd never heard her swear.

'Of course, Mama.'

CHAPTER 41

Arisaig

The last time Kalisz had been this close to the grey-green jacket with its black collar and twin silver lightning flashes had been in a Warsaw park a month earlier. On a bright winter afternoon, a cheerful *SS-Unterscharführer* had almost tenderly positioned nooses around the necks of a terrified young couple on a makeshift gallows. He'd still been smiling when he kicked away the plank on which they stood, to leave them dangling in the air as they choked their lives away.

Now Krystina's references to 'the Tenth House' began to make some sense. Clearly, she had come here and seen what Kalisz had just seen. How would she have reacted? And what were the consequences of that reaction? Could this have anything to do with her death? Certainly, those who wore that uniform were capable of killing, and doing so without thought or any semblance of conscience. But the question that Kalisz needed to answer first was precisely who these men were.

As the light faded, two more soldiers, wearing mottled camouflage smocks and uniform trousers tucked into jackboots, left the house and headed directly towards him. He edged back into the bushes as they followed a path down to the jetty, carrying bulging rucksacks and coils of rope. They passed within feet of him, and he could hear their muttered complaints in German about tomorrow's early start and going without breakfast. He guessed they were loading the boat he'd seen, and it was confirmed when they returned for a second consignment of equipment.

When they'd been back in the house for several minutes, Kalisz slipped away through the trees and returned to where he'd hidden the motorcycle. He'd originally intended to discover if the house was occupied, and, if that was the case, return to Arisaig and demand to be allowed to question the residents. But the bizarre nature of what he'd seen here required further investigation. Yes, he'd been told students at the training schools worked with enemy weapons, but why wear Nazi uniforms – and those of the hated and feared SS, at that?

The complaints he'd overheard represented an opportunity to discover more. It was a gamble – there was no guarantee all the occupants of Swordland would be taking part in the early morning exercise they'd talked about – but what did he have to lose? A grumble in his stomach reminded him he'd consumed only a dry bread roll since lunch, and he took a swig of musty water from the water bottle as he bit into a second roll to stave off hunger. A bundle of damp moss, leaves and heather would do as a mattress, and he wrapped himself up in his greatcoat with his backpack for a pillow. He had a momentary pang of conscience that he hadn't left a note for Lucy. She'd wonder where he was when he didn't appear for breakfast. Hopefully, he'd finish what he had to do here and get back before she became too concerned – or worse, reported his absence.

Kalisz closed his eyes, but sleep proved impossible. It didn't take long to discover he'd badly underestimated the cold, and overestimated the insulating quality of his greatcoat. The chill from the ground below seemed to eat into his bones and, as the air temperature dropped, icy knives cut through the thick cloth of the coat and his hands and feet quickly became numb.

–

4 January 1944

He must have dozed, because the rasping thud as someone started up the engine of the cabin cruiser jolted him from a half-dream. Above him, the skeletal branches of an ash tree etched the first faint pink dusting of the coming dawn.

The sound of the boat rose as it accelerated from the jetty, then gradually faded, but still Kalisz didn't move. It wasn't just the cold; a kind of terror had gripped his heart and immobilised him. For a split second he had to fight to remember *who* he was. It struck him that he hadn't even thought about his home or his family since New Year's Day, three days earlier. Warsaw, with its constant threat of death and atmosphere of all-consuming dread, seemed an entirely different world. He'd become spellbound by the puzzle of solving the mystery of Krystina Kowolska's death, and, if he was being honest with himself, intoxicated by the power Churchill had invested in him. This new Kalisz/Zamoyski, with his tailored uniform and major's insignia on the shoulder, had dazzled him to the point where he had begun to lose sight of what really mattered.

Where were Maria and Stefan now? Were they even still alive? Both were involved with the Resistance, Maria as a nurse and Stefan as a courier, and they regularly took risks that terrified him. She'd still be in bed, he was sure. With coal in such short supply, they'd taken to lying beneath the covers together until the last possible moment, with every coat in the house on top of them. Eventually, Maria would leave Stefan in bed, splash water on her face, and dress in as many layers of clothing as she could comfortably wear. Then she'd prepare a meagre breakfast from what she'd gleaned from their ration cards the previous day: a thin slice of bread with the consistency of sawdust, a scraping of what passed for margarine, and perhaps a shrivelled pickle or two. A tear ran down Kalisz's cheek as the image formed in his head. The contrast between the privations of Warsaw and the plenty of the Arisaig mess, with its piles of bacon and eggs, mountains of toast and urns of hot, coal-black tea, eaten by a roaring fire in an atmosphere of serenity, seemed impossible. How could both represent reality?

Now Kalisz understood the cold fingers that had gripped his heart on waking. It was not fear he would never see his wife and son again, but the real and genuine fear of returning to the corrosion of the soul that was the daily tightrope walk of his deadly double life. He wasn't even sure if he could ever force his legs to carry him the length of Nowy Sjazd and up the stairs of Department V again.

–

8:30 a.m.

Gradually, the gloom faded; his surroundings took on definition and he could make out the clump of trees that marked the lodge. He rubbed his hands together to get the circulation back, grimacing at the pins and needles that accompanied the act. His eyes searched the skyline for the chimney smoke that would signal occupation, but there was no sign of life. He retrieved a slim leather pouch from the pocket of his greatcoat, before reluctantly abandoning the coat, and set out cautiously towards the house. A different route this time, avoiding the shore in case the cruiser made an unexpected return. As he climbed through the stunted pines to approach Swordland from the north, he was puzzled by what might have been pagan symbols suspended from the branches. The sight added another element to the puzzle and gave him pause for a moment, but that would have to wait until he had time to give it more thought. Thankfully, the rear of the lodge was a featureless wall of cold grey stone, and he slipped round the corner of the building and moved down towards the loch. The first ground-floor window he reached was quite small and appeared to belong to a kitchen. It was unlit, and he could see little in the gloom of the interior. Ducking beneath the sill, he continued until he came to a larger window. This time there was just enough light to see inside. Some kind of dining hall, occupied by a table surrounded by six or seven chairs.

Satisfied that the house was uninhabited, Kalisz walked quickly to the front of the building and into the shadow of the porch. A heavy double door guarded the main entrance, and when he tried the handle, it was locked. An irritation, but reassuring in its own way, because it was another sign of an empty house. Kalisz studied the old-fashioned mortise lock, a type that appeared encouragingly familiar. He unwrapped the leather pouch and studied the contents: a set of wire picks of varying lengths and bent at the end to make a right angle, and four steel tension tools of different sizes. The tools had been the gift of a Mokotów burglar who'd made the decision to go straight. In the past, they'd been helpful to Kalisz in situations where the Warsaw policeman's traditional approach of a solid shoulder or a well-placed boot wouldn't have been appropriate.

The tension tool was basically just a four-inch steel rod with a rough key shape at one end, and bars attached to the other to allow it to be turned with minimum effort. He inserted the key end into the keyhole and turned it slightly until he felt resistance. Holding the tool firm, he took one of the picks and worked it in beside the tension tool. Once it was inside, he twisted it carefully using his fingers and feeling for the moment the levers – there were three of them – lifted. It was a process that demanded patience and a light touch, and he was out of practice, so it took longer than was comfortable. At last the final lever lifted and the pressure of the tension tool drew the deadbolt back. When he withdrew the pick and the tool, he realised he hadn't breathed for more than a minute.

The hinges creaked horribly as Kalisz opened the door, and the sound grated on his already overstretched nerves. If the house was occupied they were certainly aware of his presence now. He waited for another few moments, just to be sure, then slipped inside.

In front of him lay a broad hall, with doors to left and right and a stairway directly ahead. He ignored those to the left. He'd already seen the kitchen and dining room from outside. The first door on the right opened into a sitting room with a view out over the loch. A worn tartan rug partly covered a warped dark wood floor, and the musty scent of decay and damp hung in the air. One wall held a dartboard at the centre of a pockmarked circle that said nothing for the players' marksmanship. Ashes, cold to the touch, in the fireplace, and on the mantelpiece, a single ornament that froze him in position for a moment. He turned abruptly and went back to the outer door. Yes, he'd missed it when he entered, but now everything began to make some sense.

He searched upstairs, where it appeared only three of the six bedrooms were being used, each showing evidence of at least two occupants. That puzzled him for a moment, but it made sense once you understood this was an environment designed to encourage comradeship and mutual support – a brotherhood, even. Each of the beds had been squared away in a precise, military fashion, and neatly folded shirts and underwear filled the drawers. When Kalisz cautiously checked the labels he discovered every piece of clothing was of German manufacture. He found no documents or any other form of identification.

Back in the hallway, he studied his surroundings with increased focus. Why hadn't he seen it earlier? The floorboards in the gap on the far side of the stairs were noticeably scarred by the hobnails and heel irons with which the Germans shod their jackboots. On the face of it, the only place it led was into the shadows beneath the stairway. So why did that area appear so well used?

He ducked beneath the stairs and there, cut into the flock wallpaper, was a barely visible door. The handle was little more than a depression in the face, but when he pulled it, nothing happened. As his eyes adjusted to the gloom he noticed the dark eye of a small keyhole just below the handle. This time he had to select his smallest tension tool and pick, but it took only a few moments before he heard the distinctive click of the bolt sliding back.

Pitch dark inside, naturally. He shrugged off his backpack and fumbled for the torch he'd packed. When he flicked the switch on the side, the faint light from the bulb illuminated a wooden stairway that led down into some kind of substantial basement or cellar. An oil lamp hung on a hook to one side of the stairs, and he laid the torch aside and pulled a small matchbook from his pocket. The first match didn't strike, but when he tried a second the wick flared to light up his surroundings. It took a moment for his eyes to acclimatise to the brighter light, and even when they focused he had trouble taking in what confronted him.

Against the bare stone wall to his right stood a rack of six vaguely familiar – but certainly unusual – machine pistols. They had long barrels and odd, curved magazines, several of which lay on a table in the centre of the room, where someone had been interrupted while loading them from boxes of short, stubby bullets. Perhaps more significant, and more familiar by far, were the pair of Luger automatic pistols that sat on the other side of the scarred wooden tabletop. The Luger P08 was a standard weapon throughout the German military, a 9mm pistol valued for its reliability. One of the weapons had been stripped down to its component parts for cleaning, but the other was still complete. What made it most interesting was the cylindrical noise suppressor, or silencer, attached to the muzzle. Scattered among the weaponry lay Waffen-SS drill and arms manuals, photographs of SS soldiers marching in formation, in combat somewhere Kalisz guessed must be in Russia, and at leisure in cafes and spas.

His attention was drawn to the large map pinned to a wooden frame that dominated the far wall. When Kalisz studied it, he noted that the map covered a wide area from southern Germany and Austria to eastern France. A red line led from Germany to Strasbourg and then on to France, ending somewhere around Reims in the Champagne region. On closer inspection, the line followed the route of a railway. To the side of the map were diagrams and photographs, including one picture of a large train in a siding. Kalisz's eyes flicked from the map to the photograph, and the accompanying diagrams, and it all came together. The audacity of it took his breath away.

Or would have, but for the little circle of cold steel that pressed into the back of his neck and sent a shudder down his spine.

'It won't do either of us any good if you kill me,' he said in German.

'Oh, I don't know.' He almost collapsed with relief at the sound of Lucy Devereux's cultured tones. 'It may make me feel better about being discarded like an old dishcloth.'

'You can remove the pistol now, Lucy.'

'Yes...' The barrel stayed in place for a few seconds longer than necessary. 'I suppose I can.'

When Kalisz turned, Lucy was slipping the pistol into the pocket of the voluminous parachutist's smock she wore over her uniform.

'Perhaps I should apologise?'

'Perhaps,' she said. 'But I'd prefer it if you explained why this –' she swept a hand over the display on the wall – 'has any relevance to Krystina Kowolska's murder. Is there a reason we shouldn't just walk out of here and forget what we've seen?' She peered at the map. 'What are we seeing, anyway?'

'I think Mr Churchill is planning to assassinate Adolf Hitler.'

CHAPTER 42

'What?' Lucy demanded.

'The photograph is the big clue,' Kalisz explained. 'That train you can see in the picture is the *Führersonderzug Brandenburg*, and is Hitler's mobile headquarters. It is pulled by two of the most powerful locomotives in the Third Reich, and has a personal carriage where the Führer can spend time alone, a sleeping car, bathing car, dining cars, signals unit, and accommodation for the men of the *SS-Begleitkommando* who make up his close bodyguard.'

Lucy frowned. 'You seem to know an awful lot about this train, Jan.'

'Hitler travelled in the *Führersonderzug* when he visited Warsaw in 1939. It had a different name then, but let us say it became an object of interest to certain people. Hitler is known to be incredibly conscious of his security. I doubt even Churchill could access the precise floor plan, but I'd guess that somewhere in this room is a layout of the train in its entirety and at least an approximation of the interiors of the individual carriages. The second clue is that red line on the map, which originates at Berchtesgaden in the Bavarian Alps and follows the main railway line through Alsace to north-eastern France. Berchtesgaden is where Hitler likes to relax between invasions.'

'I wouldn't have thought that fact was in wide circulation either – certainly not in Poland.'

'You'd be surprised.' He met her gaze. 'The Warsaw Gestapo and the SD talk about little else. With the Russians over the Dnieper and advancing further west every day, a posting to southern Germany becomes ever more attractive.'

'But I still don't understand how you think this is enough evidence to come to your rather colourful conclusion? A picture of a train. A couple of silenced pistols and a rack of rather odd-looking machine guns.'

'I'll get to the machine guns,' he said. 'But first, take a look at the uniform jacket on the chair in front of you. Don't move it, or the chair. Just look.' He waited while she crouched beside the jacket and saw her eyes widen as she noticed the SS collar flash. 'The men here speak German, and only German, because I believe they are Germans. They wear Waffen-SS uniforms and study SS training manuals. The jacket has a black ribbon on the cuff with the name of Adolf Hitler embroidered in silver on it. That ribbon is the insignia of the *Liebstandarte* Adolf Hitler. The *Liebstandarte* was formed as Hitler's personal guard, and they still supply the men of the *Begleitkommando* who provide his close protection. Your odd-looking machine gun in the rack is what is known as an MP43. There's no reason why you would recognise it because it only began being issued about six months ago. It's a very efficient weapon, but in short supply, which is why the Waffen-SS have exclusive use of it. These guns were probably captured at Kursk, or in some other Red Army advance that overran an SS supply depot, and sent to the British for evaluation. What makes them significant for us is that the first weapons of this type were issued to the men of Hitler's *SS-Begleitkommando*. Do you still think I'm mad?'

'I didn't say you were mad,' Lucy said. 'It's just that it sounds like an awfully big leap to make. I'm still not entirely convinced, but I have a feeling you're not finished yet.'

'And you would be correct.' Kalisz turned to the map. 'Assume for a moment that Hitler is in Berchtesgaden when Churchill launches his long-awaited Second Front. British and American forces will cross the channel to create a bridgehead...'

'And Polish.'

'Yes,' he agreed. 'Poles, Canadians such as our unfortunate Lieutenant Fontaine, Free French patriots like Yvette and Pierre Renan. And they will land where? The shortest route is between Dover and Calais, but it could be anywhere from Brittany to the Scheldt estuary. For me, the further west the better.'

'Why do you say that?' Lucy asked.

'Because if you strike inland from, say, between Calais and Dunkirk, where the beaches are so welcoming, you will inevitably find yourself fighting on both flanks, and under massive pressure from east and west. Also, it's perfect tank country, as the Nazis proved in 1940. Better to land in Brittany or Normandy and move forward on a broad front, with the coast guarding your flank and the Panzers struggling in the rugged terrain.' He shrugged. 'But it does not matter to us precisely where. What matters is that someone calculates that when he hears the news of a landing, Adolf Hitler will move his headquarters closer to the front line, using his personal train. If I'm correct, they plan to derail the *Brandenburg* at some point during its journey. Captain Malpas is preparing for just such a mission. In the chaos that follows, the men from Swordland will somehow find a way to board the *Führersonderzug*, either trick or fight their way to Hitler's quarters – the silenced pistols would be very effective in such a scenario – and kill him.'

Lucy studied the photographs on the table. 'You make it sound almost plausible.'

'On the contrary,' Kalisz said, 'it is both insane and impossible. This is Adolf Hitler's train. In Poland, if an important cargo is being carried on the railway, the Nazis take hostages at every station and every village along the route – men, women and children – and line them up beside the tracks. If there is the slightest hint of sabotage on that section, they are machine-gunned where they stand. That is what they will do when the *Brandenburg* moves into France, and the hostages will be the families of the railwaymen who maintain the line. Men who know every metre of the ground, and who will be ordered to walk the track before the train passes. If, by some miracle, our friends manage to place their explosives and derail the train, the chances of the agents posing as SS guards gaining access to the carriages are minimal. Firstly, because the main instinct of Hitler's entourage will be to defend him. Some will undoubtedly survive the crash and their weapons will be ranged outwards. The appearance of a small group of unknown SS men might cause some initial surprise, but they are more likely to be arrested or shot than welcomed. Secondly, as is his habit, Hitler will be accompanied by a second train carrying at least a battalion of Waffen-SS soldiers. They would reach the scene within minutes, surround the crash site and sweep the surrounding area, arresting anyone they find – military or civilian.'

'You're saying this is a suicide mission?'

'I think that's a fair description, whether it fails, or even in the highly unlikely event that it succeeds.'

'All the more reason we should get out of here, Jan, and forget everything we've seen. This was a mistake. It has nothing to do with Krystina Kowolska.'

Lucy turned to leave, but Kalisz stood his ground. 'It has everything to do with Krystina. Did you notice the small decoration on the door-post when you entered the house?'

'No.' She looked bewildered. 'I had other things on my mind.'

'Just a small pewter plaque, but there are more of them fixed to the bedroom doors upstairs. It's what's known as a mezuzah. There's also a distinctive ornament in the main room, which may be more familiar to you. A menorah.'

'Oh...' She drew in a breath.

'Yes, Lucy, the men who live here are not just Germans. They are German Jews. And this is a secret worth killing for.'

CHAPTER 43

Eleven a.m.

One thing with which Kalisz had no argument was that they'd outstayed their welcome in Swordland. He hastily checked that everything was exactly as it had been when he entered the room.

'Do you really believe one of these pistols killed Lieutenant Fontaine, Jan?'

'I don't know.' He opened the door to allow her onto the stairs, before following and closing it behind them. 'But there's something odd about them, even apart from the silencer. I need to have a closer look, possibly with Maxwell. One thing is certain – everyone in this house is a trained killer. That's why we'll be coming back here tomorrow.'

'Tomorrow?'

'We either get Colonel Baldwin's permission to interview these men and inspect their weapons, or you'll phone Churchill. If that doesn't work, I'll call Prime Minister Mikołajczyk myself and get the Polish government-in-exile involved. I won't give this up, Lucy. I owe it to Krystina to follow up every lead.'

'You really don't care how many enemies you make, do you, Jan?'

'Would you do any less if Krystina was one of yours?' He didn't hide his exasperation.

Lucy froze at the sound of a snapping twig from somewhere in the gardens. 'What was that?'

Kalisz moved past her and listened. She offered him her pistol, but he shook his head. They couldn't confront the occupants of Swordland with a weapon. That would be asking for a bullet in the brain. Was it even loaded? In God's name, he hoped not, remembering the feeling of the cold steel against his neck. Their only chance was to persuade whoever was out there that this visit was a legitimate part of the investigation. Another crash among the bushes. He edged the door open a few centimetres and risked a look outside, and was rewarded by a flash of movement among the trees. They weren't even bothering to hide their presence. He took a deep breath and stepped out into the morning light.

'Who's there?' Lucy demanded.

'It's safe to come out now,' Kalisz said. She joined him on the porch and he pointed to their left, where three red deer does were nosing through the leaf mulch beneath a few skeletal apple trees, seeking out the rotting remains of last year's windfalls.

Kalisz set off towards where he'd hidden the motorcycle, then realised he had no idea how Lucy had arrived at Swordland. 'I came by boat.' She pre-empted his question. 'A small motor boat kindly loaned to me by Captain Malpas, who feels he is in debt to us. I'd offer you a lift, but that motorcycle of Constable MacDonald's would probably sink her.'

'Take care, Lucy.' Kalisz smiled.

'I'll meet you back at the police station.' She didn't return his smile. 'Then we have some hard talking to do.'

–

As it turned out, she was waiting for him in the Austin when he crossed the bridge over the river Morar around mid-afternoon. Lucy pulled in behind him as he headed south towards Arisaig to return the borrowed motorcycle. When they were approaching the village, Kalisz was greeted by the familiar sight of the evacuee children playing some kind of war game among the dunes, armed with sticks for rifles and stones for grenades. One of them – a girl – ran across the road in front of him, so close he had to swerve to avoid her. He roared at her to be careful, and she rewarded him with a 'V for victory' two-fingered salute, which he found quite touching in the circumstances. As he swept onwards, he became aware of the Austin closing up on him. A horn sounded and he looked over his shoulder to see Lucy waving a hand to signal him to slow down.

They both rolled to a halt and Kalisz dismounted from the bike and walked back to the car.

'What is it?'

'We've got to go back,' she insisted. 'He had a gun.'

'They all had guns.' Kalisz laughed. 'Guns made of driftwood.'

'No, Jan, you don't understand. One of the boys from the beach was waving a pistol about. I'm certain it was the real thing.'

Kalisz waited until Lucy managed to turn the Austin in the narrow road and followed her back to where the children were playing. They stopped a short distance away, allowing the evacuees to become used to their presence. The children eventually tired of the game and sat in a circle, sharing something from a paper bag produced by the oldest boy.

Lucy got out of the car and gave Kalisz a look that told him she would take the lead. They walked towards the little group on the dune, with Kalisz slightly behind her right shoulder. As they approached, several pairs of eyes watched them before dropping to concentrate on what they'd been doing.

'Is it not cold to be sitting out here in the open?' Lucy accompanied the words with a smile. 'Surely you've somewhere warmer to be?'

The eldest boy looked up. Kalisz tried to recall his name. *Billy. Yes, that was it – Billy.* 'Like where?' He snorted. 'Naeb'dy wants us aroon. Onywise –' he looked up at the cloud-filled sky – 'it's no tha' cauld. Cauld's when yiv goat ice on the inside o' yir windaes.'

'What's that you're enjoying?'

'Sugar,' a pigtailed girl in a coat two sizes too large said brightly, prompting a grunt of irritation from Billy.

'What a treat,' Lucy said. 'Sugar's so hard to come by these days. Funnily enough, when I was in the village this morning I heard that Mrs Ramsay at the shop had mislaid a bag.'

'So?' Billy glared his defiance. 'Ur ye gonnae grass us up?'

'You mean inform on you? No.' Lucy shook her head. 'We're not informants, Billy, though we are looking for information. It's our job to find the truth. And to find the truth we need something called evidence...'

'D'ye mean this, miss?' Billy grinned and held up the empty paper bag and shook it. 'Nae evidence here.'

The children all laughed. 'No,' Lucy said, 'although I'd advise getting rid of the bag before you go back to the village, or Constable MacDonald might have something to say about it.' She let her eyes drift across the circle of children until they locked on a slight figure trying not to be noticed. 'I was thinking more of the item... Kev, isn't it?... is hiding under his jacket. Can we see it, Kev?'

235

'It's mine. Ah foun' it.'

'Ah told ye ye should hae gi'en it tae me.' Billy sniffed.

'You alwiz get everythin', Billy. It's mine.'

Kalisz noticed the girl had picked up the paper bag and was licking the last grains of sugar from its depths. 'Wait here a moment,' he said. He ran to the motorcycle and retrieved his backpack before returning to the group. He opened the pack and pulled out a partly consumed Hershey Bar. Lucy immediately saw what he intended and took it from him.

'What if we trade for a look?' The question was aimed at Kev, but she had half an eye on Billy's reaction. The older boy licked his lips. 'Kev is being a bit shy about where he found his treasure, Jan. But he's a good lad and I think he wants to help us.' She broke off a piece of the chocolate and offered it to Kev, who eyed it hungrily. 'One square, just to let us see it.'

A moment's hesitation before the boy reached beneath his jacket and held up a gleaming pistol in both hands. Kalisz's heart thundered as he recognised that the Luger was identical to the weapons he'd seen on the table at Swordland, right down to the screw fixing for the silencer. He reached for it without thinking, but Kev drew it away.

Lucy shot Kalisz a look. 'Don't worry, Kev,' she reassured the boy. 'Here, have two squares and tell us how you found it.' Kev put the pistol on his knees and accepted the chocolate, but it was Billy who replied.

'We were up at the cave by the big house where the spies do their swiving—'

'Billy!' the girl interjected.

'We sometimes listen frae outside.' Billy shrugged. 'It doesnae do any harm.'

'How do you know they're spies?'

'Oh, c'mon.' Billy puffed out his cheeks and the others laughed. 'Everybody roun' here knows. Kev was feeling brave, so he sneaked in. That's where he found it.' He glared at the younger boy. 'Only he didnae tell anybody for ages.'

Kalisz pulled the three unopened Hershey Bars from his pack and the children gasped. He handed them to Lucy.

'I'm sorry, Kev,' Lucy said. 'That weapon is government property that may have been used in a crime. We need to have it tested to know for certain. We won't take it, unless we have to, but I'd prefer to buy it from you.' She offered the three bars to the boy. Kev's eyes widened, but he maintained a firm grip on the Luger.

Kalisz had expected some argument from Billy, but it was the girl who spoke.

'Let them have it, Kev.'

Kev passed the Luger to Lucy in exchange for the Hershey Bars, which he handed to Billy to share out. Lucy studied the pistol and Kalisz saw her go pale.

She shook her head. 'There's a round in the chamber and it's ready to fire.'

CHAPTER 44

'Did you tell him?' Lucy asked, as Kalisz got into the car after returning the motorcycle to the police station at Arisaig.

'Constable MacDonald was out. I put the keys through the letterbox.'

'But you would have told him we've found the murder weapon?'

'There are certain questions we still need to answer.' Kalisz kept his eyes on the road ahead.

'What questions?' she demanded. 'We agreed it's the same type and calibre as the weapons we saw on the table at Swordland. It even has the serial numbers removed, just like them. Surely we need to have it tested by ballistics as quickly as possible?'

'The whole point of having the murder weapon – and yes, you're right, I am certain this is the pistol used to kill Jean-Marc Fontaine – is as a means of discovering who fired it. Our friend Kev discovered the weapon in the cave below Arisaig House, which immediately points the finger of accusation at Pierre Renan. Yet we are sure Pierre could not have killed Krystina. If Yvette is telling the truth, he didn't have the time or the opportunity. It means the real killers planted the Luger in a crude attempt to implicate Pierre, and that may be their first mistake.'

'So what do we do now?'

Kalisz considered for a moment. 'First, I think we must speak to Yvette.' He saw Lucy's puzzlement. 'Pierre may not be the killer, but he is a weapons expert. It's possible this pistol passed through his hands *on the way* to the killer, and she may have seen it in his possession. After that, I will speak to Colonel Baldwin and insist we are given access to the men at Swordland. With this evidence in our possession, he cannot say no.'

Twenty minutes later they knocked on the door of Yvette's cottage, but there was no answer. Lucy looked through a window into the kitchen area. 'The last time we were here she had all her belongings packed, ready to go. Now they're gone.'

Kalisz cursed under his breath. 'So much for waiting for my report.'

As they made their way back up the path to Arisaig House, Kalisz heard shouting and noticed a small group of men practising unarmed combat on the parkland in front of the formal gardens. He recognised them as the Czechs from Traigh Lodge, but the instructor was the man who interested him most.

Lucy had the Luger P08 – now with an empty chamber and magazine – in her bag. 'Can you let me have the pistol and wait for me up at the big house?' he said.

'After what happened, I shouldn't let you out of my sight,' she said. But she handed over the pistol. Kalisz made his way down through the wood and across to the grass. The instructor gave no sign of having noticed his approach, but Kalisz knew he'd been identified before he left the trees.

'I wonder if I may have a word, Major Sykes?'

Sykes turned to meet him with his oddly challenging, benevolent smile. 'Made some progress have you, Zamoyski? Very glad to hear it. The colonel thinks your presence is gumming up the works, and I'm not sure I disagree with him. Carry on killing each other, you chaps.'

They walked a little way before Kalisz drew the Luger from his greatcoat pocket.

'I wondered if you recognised this weapon?'

'Why should I?' Sykes shrugged.

'Because you are Major "Two shots to the heart" Sykes, the... What is that expression I remember from the old cowboy movies? Yes, I think I have it... the *Deadeye Dick* of STS 21. Anyone from the schools who is going to fire a pistol in anger will have been taught by you at some point. You also specialise in silent killing, and, coincidentally, as I suspect you have already noticed, this pistol has a fitting for a silencer.'

Sykes sniffed, but he took the gun from Kalisz's hand and pretended to study it. 'This is a Luger P08 pistol, barrel length four inches, with a thumb safety catch, which at the moment is in the down position. It has what is known as a toggle-lock mechanism, and the position of the *Geladen* indicator tells me it is not currently loaded. What makes it different from other Lugers is that it is chambered for a 7.65mm Parabellum round used in early versions of the weapon, whereas this is obviously of recent manufacture. Possibly sourced from Switzerland, where the army still uses this calibre of the weapon. The standard Luger Po8 takes a 9mm bullet. As you say, the barrel has been modified with a screw thread, which is probably designed to fit a custom-made noise-suppressor. Is there anything else?'

'You are not curious about the weapon?'

'The fact that it is in your possession would suggest you believe it is the weapon that killed Lieutenant Fontaine. Since it's of the same calibre and modified for silent assassination, I would concur, subject to ballistic confirmation. I congratulate you, Major.'

Kalisz graced him with a wintry smile. 'Of course, possession of the pistol means nothing if you do not know who pulled the trigger.'

For the first time, Sykes's voice registered emotion. 'You think I killed Fontaine?'

'You told me yourself that your only defence is that you are too expert a killer to have carried out such an amateurish double murder. If you are that good, is it not possible that you choreographed the entire event to make it appear so? There are identical pistols to this at Swordland Lodge, and I couldn't help noticing the targets scattered through the gardens and woods, each with the distinctive double bullet strike in the chest area you teach so effectively.'

Sykes drew in a long breath and his eyes drifted up to the house overlooking them. 'Look, Major, what can I do that will convince you that I am not your enemy and I did not kill Lieutenant Fontaine? I want to see Krystina Kowolska's killers brought to justice as much as you do. Of all my pupils, she was the most complete, and, if you can believe it, I was fond of her.'

'Very well,' Kalisz agreed. 'Tell me what you know of Swordland.'

Sykes considered for a moment. 'I can't talk about the mission.'

'No, there is no need.'

'However, the mission parameters are such that it requires highly specialised weaponry and training. The men at Swordland are the best of the best. Trained to a razor's edge of competence and utterly dedicated to their mission. Without their unique attributes, there would be no mission. Each of them is a volunteer from X Troop, Number 10 Commando, a unit which has a top secret designation because it is entirely manned by German-speaking Jews. Not just German-speaking, but native Germans, refugees who came here when the Nazis began their campaign of persecution and murder. I trained the students at Swordland in the usual methods of silent killing, and made them familiar with the properties of the silenced Luger Po8, which could be vital to the completion of their assignment.'

'You are aware of Krystina Kowolska's antipathy towards the Jews?'

'I am.'

'And if she antagonised them in some way that might endanger their mission?'

'No.' Sykes shook his head. 'I see where you are going with this, but it couldn't be. Whatever Krystina might have said to them would never have angered them to the point where they killed her. I said they are dedicated. They are also disciplined. To kill her and be discovered in that act would guarantee the mission would be scrapped. They would never risk that. Even if she did threaten to blow the mission, a single phone call from Maxwell to the colonel would have seen her in a cell for the rest of the war. However important her mission, it would always be subordinate to that of the men at Swordland.'

It took time to register, but eventually Kalisz realised what he'd just heard. 'Maxwell? Major Maxwell?'

'The very one. As well as being in charge at Glasnacardoch, he's also the conducting officer for Swordland. I hope this has been helpful, and put you at ease regarding my involvement.'

'Yes.' Kalisz gave him a distracted look. 'You've given me much to consider, but I truly believe we are closing in on Krystina's killers.'

'If that's the case, I'd advise you to be extra careful, my friend.' Sykes clasped his shoulder in a way that would have been almost tender, but for the grip of iron. 'If there's one thing I've learned in my long, eventful life, it's that an animal is always at its most dangerous when it's cornered. And there is no more dangerous animal than a man.'

CHAPTER 45

Warsaw

4 January 1944

'This weapon is a Mark Two Sten gun.' Stefan hovered close with a frown of concentration as Dimitar Petrov's big hands assembled the machine pistol with surprising dexterity. It was a cheap, utilitarian-looking weapon, made from pressed components of spray-painted steel. 'In 1941 the British needed a machine gun with the firepower of the American Thompson, and they needed it quickly. This was the result. Don't be fooled by its looks. It is a very effective weapon.' He completed the assembly and inserted a narrow box magazine into a socket on the side of the gun. 'The Sten fires at a rate of five hundred rounds per minute, and that means you have to be gentle on the trigger. On fully automatic, this 32-round magazine will last about four seconds. But you have to get close. Accuracy is not its strong point.' He pulled back the cocking handle, locked it into the non-firing position and handed the gun to Stefan. 'What do you think?'

'We've stripped them down, but I've never fired one.' The boy frowned as he weighed the weapon in his hands. 'Where did this come from?'

'The RAF parachuted a batch of weapons into the Kampinos Forest for the Resistance, but the SS got to it before the *Armia Krajowa*. They were destined to be destroyed. Fortunately, one of the quartermasters saw them as an opportunity to make a profit. We've had dealings with him in the past and we came to a price, so here we are. Hopefully you won't need to fire it. Tonight you and your mother will be acting as lookouts. This is only for your protection if we get into trouble.'

Eight of them were huddled around a table in the dining room of the Bulgarian's estate house on the northern outskirts of Warsaw. Maria fiddled with the torch she'd been given, switching it on and off to make sure the batteries were still working, aware she was annoying the others but unable to help herself. Four of Petrov's anonymous, hard-eyed associates packed weapons, equipment and hand grenades into hessian bags, or filled pistol and machine gun magazines from boxes on a scarred tabletop. Antoni Roziki stood to one side of Stefan, with a cigarette in his mouth and a Luger pistol dangling from his right hand.

'Wouldn't it be better to wait until we hear back from your Underground contact?' the mechanic asked Maria.

'It would be too late.' It was Petrov who answered. 'I've dealt with these people and I know how they work. Even if she wanted to help, she would have to run it past her superiors and they would have to pull a team together. By the time they were ready, Fischer would already be in Gdynia and Jan Kalisz would be on a wanted list. No, if it's to be done, we have to do it ourselves. The question is, are we prepared to deal with the consequences?'

That brought a pause. Everyone in the room knew that in revenge for the killing of a senior Gestapo officer, the Nazis would unleash an orgy of bloodshed that would consume the lives of many of their fellow Poles.

'Every time we strike a blow at the Germans, there is a price to pay.' The raw maturity in Stefan's voice sent a glow of pride through Maria. He looked at his mother and she nodded for him to continue. 'This is my father's life we are talking about, but even if it was not, I believe we would be right to go ahead. Hundreds are dying every day in Pawiak Prison and the camps at the whim of the Occupiers. What we do tonight will mean the deaths of many more, but at least they will have died for a reason. The subterfuge that the Resistance have put in place in Gdynia to protect my father's mission is an indication of its value to Poland's and to the Allies' cause. If we do not stop this Gestapo agent, it will all have been for nothing. I say we go.'

Petrov looked to Roziki for any sign of dissent. There was none. 'Then we are agreed?' The mechanic nodded. 'In that case, I suggest we get some rest.'

'How will we know when to leave?' Maria asked.

'The Gestapo are not the only ones who have spies. Fischer will have to sign out a car and a driver if he is to travel to Gdynia overnight. We will be told, and our position gives us an hour's head start to the ambush site. After he leaves Warsaw, there is only one likely route he can take. Bogdan, who I trust entirely in these matters, has already scouted a suitable position.'

–

Maria laid her head on the table and she must have slept, because when the phone rang it exploded in her head like the clanging of a church bell. By the time she'd opened her eyes, Petrov had already picked up the receiver. He listened for a few seconds without making any reply before replacing the phone. A jerk of the head sent his men on the way to the waiting truck with their sacks of weapons and equipment. Stefan followed them, carrying the Sten awkwardly with both hands. Roziki was sitting at the table with his eyes closed, and Maria had a feeling he might be whispering a prayer, but to whom, she didn't feel entitled to ask. Eventually, he rose, picked up his pistol and walked out after the others with a wry smile of resignation on his puckish face.

'He seems nervous,' she said, almost to herself.

'If anyone tells you they are not nervous when embarking on an enterprise of this nature, they are lying, Mrs Kalisz,' the Bulgarian rumbled. '*Kriminalkommissar* Fischer signed out a Daimler-Benz Type 320 four-door sedan staff car from the transport section at Szucha Avenue a few minutes ago. He will be escorted by a motorcycle combination, and will likely be accompanied by at least two others in the vehicle. Are you ready?' Maria nodded, tension restricting her ability to speak. 'Then we should go.' Petrov reached under the table and picked up what turned out to be an enormous machine gun, which he slung over his shoulder as easily as if it were a walking stick. He noticed her look of surprise. 'A *Machinen Gewehr* Model 42,' he explained. 'Probably the finest machine gun in the world. If one cannot provide the manpower, Mrs Kalisz, one must rely on firepower.'

–

Maria squeezed into the cab of the truck beside Petrov while Roziki drove northwards across rutted and cratered back roads and trackways. Thankfully, the black market overlord had left his machine gun in the rear, where, if she was any judge, Stefan and two of the Bulgarian's associates would be rattling around like dried peas in a can. Roziki's muttered curses punctuated the journey as he struggled to keep the dimmed rear lights of Bogdan's motor car in sight.

'When Himmler ordered that Warsaw should be sealed off from the rest of the country to stop farmers selling their supplies in the city, we were forced to seek alternative routes for our goods,' Petrov explained. 'If we had taken the main road tonight, we would undoubtedly have had to try to talk or bribe our way past a barrier at some point, with all the perils that entails. Bogdan knows these less travelled routes and how to avoid Nazi checkpoints better than any man,' he assured Maria. 'We will get there on time.'

Maria found the big man's presence oddly comforting at a point when her head was a whirling maelstrom of doubt and dread and fear. She – and only she – had brought them to this point. She told herself she had had no alternative after Fischer's approach threatened Jan's exposure and death. But, in doing so, had she needed to involve Stefan? Perhaps there'd been an element of selfishness in her craving for his support and approval. Yes, he would have resented being left at home when his father's fate hung in the balance. But surely a proper mother would have placed her son's life ahead of her own, and even her husband's? The sight of the boy with a sub-machine gun in his hands had sent a shudder through her. She'd known all along that his membership of the Grey Ranks might lead to this, but witnessing it was very different. What if Petrov was wrong, and Stefan was placed in a situation where he was forced to fire the gun? She would be responsible for turning her son into a killer. For a moment, the blizzard of emotions threatened to overwhelm her and she had to fight for control, her fingers hooking like claws into the truck's worn leather bench seat. Gradually, she managed to calm her pounding heart. The decision had been made and there was no turning back now.

–

Forty minutes later they reached a crossroads. Bogdan parked the car at the side of the road and Roziki pulled in behind him. Bogdan's narrow features appeared out of the darkness at the lowered window.

'This is the place, boss, pretty much as you specified. Those trees back there will hide the truck from anyone coming down the road.'

'Good work,' Petrov said. 'Get the men together.'

He helped Maria out of the truck and went to the rear, where Stefan and the others were unloading the weapons and equipment. When Roziki had joined them they formed a huddle round the Bulgarian, who shone a torch on a patch of bare ground and produced a large knife from beneath his overcoat to scratch a crude diagram of the crossroads in the dirt. 'This is how it will be.' He spoke with a calm authority as he used the knife to emphasise his words. 'Bogdan and Ryszard will take out the motorcycle escort here, a little to the north, and immediately block the road ahead with the car. You, Mr Roziki, will wait here until the Daimler passes, then drive the lorry into the road to cut off the Nazis' escape route. In the meantime, Jerzy and I will be pouring fire into the Gestapo car and its occupants from both sides of the road. You may join in at your leisure. Are we clear?'

The men nodded. Bogdan needed no command. He picked up a coil of wire rope and an MP40 machine gun and set off, with a nod to a similarly armed Ryszard to accompany him.

'What about us?' Maria asked.

'We need to know when Fischer's arrival is imminent. You will note that the road climbs from here to a ridge half a kilometre to the south. From the top of that ridge you will be able to see the lights of any approaching vehicles. One of you will watch the road at all times, and the other will be ready to make the signal. Our quarry will be quite distinctive – a single headlight in the lead and a pair of headlights behind. When you see that configuration, use a single long flash of the torch to alert us they're on their way—'

'Define "long".'

Maria wished she could unsay the words as soon as they left her mouth, but Petrov laughed. 'The count of three would suffice.'

'And if the car is in front?' Stefan asked.

'Then we improvise. If that's the case, use three short flashes. We will do the rest. Now, you'd best be on your way. We should have thirty minutes or so.'

Maria and Stefan followed the road to the top of the rise and positioned themselves by a gate in a stone wall that would have given them a clear view north and south, were they not in pitch darkness. Stefan took the watch, eyes to the south and hands gripped on the body of the Sten, periodically lifting the weapon to the firing position as if imagining a scenario where he might have to use it.

'Mama?'

'Yes, Stefan.'

'I'm cold and I'm frightened, but I'm glad you brought me. For the first time, I feel as if I'm part of the fight.'

'You've always been part of the fight, Stefan.' Maria managed a smile. 'And we're all frightened – even, I believe, Mr Bulgarian. I'm glad I brought you, too. I wasn't sure whether it was the right thing to do, but now that I'm here, I wonder if I would have had the courage to do this on my own.'

She felt the warmth of his hand on hers. 'You're the bravest person I've ever known.' She heard the smile in his voice. 'And Dada, of course. I wonder where he is?'

'I wonder that, too.'

Thirty minutes turned into an hour, and Maria was beginning to fear the Gestapo agent had taken a different route when they heard the distant hum of an engine.

'Mama?'

'Yes, I hear it.'

'There!' Stefan's young eyes caught the glint of an approaching light on the line of the road long before she did, but it was too soon to make out the configuration. Maria had to fight the urge to test out the torch to make sure the battery was still working. They followed the light as it approached and the sound of engines grew clearer. Maria felt a thrill of concern as it disappeared for a moment, but the vehicles must have been hidden among trees, because when they emerged the leading light was much closer. 'One headlight in front and two behind,' Stefan announced confidently.

'You're certain, Stefan?'

'Of course.'

How could she doubt him? She stood up and pointed the torch in the direction of the ambush site. One prolonged flash as she counted to three. Those moments in the shocking glare of the light made her feel terribly vulnerable, but she knew she was shielded from the approaching cars by the bulk of the wall.

Now it was up to Petrov. All they could do was wait.

They crouched low as the motorcycle roared over the brow of the hill with the Gestapo Daimler following fifty metres behind. In the light from the car's headlamps, Maria saw that the soldier in the sidecar was sitting behind a machine gun, the exact duplicate of the one the Bulgarian had carried, and for a moment she wondered about his confidence in the ambushers' firepower.

Seconds passed, each feeling like an eternity. From her vantage point Maria could see the rear lights of the Daimler as it approached the crossroads. A resounding crash and a shriek of metal in the distance as Bogdan's bow-taut wire did its work. She saw the motorcycle's headlight twisting and tumbling in a bizarre trajectory that ended with a second crash as the bike hit some solid object. The squeal of tyres. Roaring engines. A stab of light and the rasp of a machine gun being fired in short bursts, accompanied by the curious sound of a stick being dragged across an iron fence as the high-velocity bullets tore into the car's metal body. Sharp cracks that Maria recognised as pistol fire were quickly silenced as the staccato clatter of a sub-machine gun joined the cacophony. She could imagine the Daimler and its occupants being shredded by Petrov's bullets, and she felt a moment of pure exultation that Fischer was no longer in a position to hurt her family. Then the finale. A sudden flash lit the night sky, followed by the crunch of an explosion and the almost simultaneous *whump* and billow of flame as the car's petrol tank exploded.

All the breath seemed to be drawn from Maria, and her legs gave way beneath her.

Stefan loomed over her. 'Mama, are you hurt?'

'No, Stefan, I just feel a little light-headed. Give me a moment.'

There'd been no discussion about what happened afterwards, but Maria knew the Bulgarian would want to leave the ambush scene as swiftly as possible. She pushed herself to her knees and allowed Stefan to help her to her feet. They made their way cautiously downhill through the bushes by the side of the road towards the flickering glow of the burning car.

Halfway to the truck, the sharp snap of a twig froze them in place. Maria still held the torch in her left hand, and her finger automatically went to the switch. She gasped at the grotesque, bloodied face illuminated in the startling light of the beam: Fischer, his suit torn and spattered with gore, one hand to his eyes and the other holding a pistol. Stefan hauled up his Sten gun, but when he pulled the trigger the only sound was a click. As the boy pounded at the sub-machine gun's safety lock, Fischer's battered features twisted into a grim smile. He lifted the pistol and almost casually lined up the sights on Stefan's face.

The first bullet from Jan Kalisz's police-issue Walther took the Gestapo agent square in the chest. Fischer was probably dead by the time he hit the ground, but Maria found that she couldn't stop squeezing the trigger. Round after round jerked the prone body until the magazine was empty. The firing pin was still snapping in the empty chamber when her son gently removed the weapon from her hand.

He held her close in the shocked silence that followed.

'You will never say anything of this night to your father.' She choked out the words. 'Do you understand, Stefan?'

Stefan's eyes narrowed and, for the first time, she saw open defiance there. But she held her son's gaze and eventually he nodded. When he turned to walk away Maria felt a moment of self-disgust. Who was she to dictate to him what he could tell about what would be the most remarkable night of his life? But she would not take back her words. Could not.

If she was to live with the weight of Fischer's murder on her conscience, she would bear it alone.

CHAPTER 46

Arisaig

'I'm afraid Colonel Baldwin isn't available, sir.' The CO's clerk dashed Kalisz's hopes of an early meeting. 'He was supposed to be back today, but we've been told tomorrow at the earliest.'

'Is there a problem, Major Zamoyski?' Dempsey appeared from his office across the landing.

'I had hoped to arrange an interview with the colonel at the earliest possible moment. Perhaps I could impose on you to make the arrangements when he returns?'

'I'd be delighted, of course,' the one-handed major said. 'But I should warn you that the commanding officer is becoming somewhat impatient at your lack of progress. He's even been overheard wondering why our gallant Polish allies are being allowed to hinder the progress of the war.'

'Nevertheless...'

Dempsey smiled. 'It might help if I knew the reason for such an urgent interview.'

'It concerns the students at Swordland Lodge. We have reason to believe that a weapon linked to the lodge may have been used in the murder of Lieutenant Fontaine.'

'Goodness me.' The major tutted. 'That is worrying. May one ask how you came by this information?'

Kalisz hesitated. 'I would require your complete confidentiality.'

'Of course,' Dempsey said. 'Come into my office.'

When the door closed behind them, Kalisz placed the Luger on Dempsey's desk. 'This weapon was found in a cave in the woods between the house and the jetty. It fires ammunition of the same calibre as the pistol which killed the lieutenant. It also, as you can see, has a screw fitting for a silencer or noise-suppressor, which would account for the fact that no one heard a shot on the night in question.'

'Progress indeed, Major Zamoyski.' Dempsey gave a rueful shake of the head. 'But I don't remotely understand how this is connected to Swordland Lodge.'

'Major Sykes has confirmed to me that the students at Swordland have been trained in the use of this rather unique weapon.' Kalisz noticed a slight tightening around Dempsey's eyes that suggested he wasn't impressed by Sykes's candour, but Sykes could look after himself. 'I do not say categorically that one of them killed Krystina Kowolska, but I believe this is sufficient evidence to justify giving me access to interview the occupants of Swordland Lodge. That is the case I wish to make to Colonel Baldwin, and if necessary, I will make it to a higher authority.'

'Your tenacity is admirable, Major.' Dempsey's tone said the opposite. 'But I should warn you, Colonel Baldwin is unlikely to respond well to threats. I'd keep the higher authority to yourself when you meet him, if I were you.'

'So you will arrange a meeting?'

'First thing in the morning. I'll send you a note when I have a definite time. Does that satisfy?'

Kalisz nodded. It meant he could be kicking his heels at Arisaig until lunchtime when he had better things to do, but there was no helping it. 'Thank y—' He was cut off by a thunderous knock at the door and a burly sergeant entered without ceremony.

'Pardon the intrusion, sir,' the man said. 'But I thought you'd want to know right away. They've found a body in the hills between here and Inverailort. Not sure whether it's one of ours or the other lot.'

'Christ.' Dempsey marched to the door and retrieved his greatcoat from where it hung on a metal hook. 'Just what we need with the colonel away. Sergeant, gather a section of the odds and sods, a dozen should do it, and organise a three-tonner. Make sure they're all properly equipped, it'll be bloody freezing on those hills in this weather. I'll lead the way in the Humber. Major Zamoyski, I dare say you should come along as well. Another silly accident, no doubt, but best to be certain. Would you do me a favour, and ask the doctor to meet us at my car with his equipment? Now, Sergeant, just exactly where are we going?'

Kalisz ran to the medical officer's office and passed on Dempsey's instructions, before dashing up to his room to retrieve his greatcoat and backpack. Lucy appeared just as he was completing his preparations.

'What's all the commotion about?'

He told her what was happening. 'I don't think—'

'No, I trust you to keep me in the picture this time, Jan, and the prospect of a ride in the back of a three-tonner frankly doesn't appeal. Do we have any idea who it might be?'

Her words carried a certain emphasis, but he wouldn't be drawn. 'It could be anyone. I don't see any point in speculating until we find out more.'

'How very policemanlike.' Her tone was amiable enough, but he found that the words stung. 'Do let me know when you *find out more.*' She turned away and left him with a mind in turmoil.

–

Kalisz sat hunched in the cramped rear seat of the Humber, next to a large metal box. It was secured by a pair of clips and appeared to have some sort of stencilled writing on the top. The contents only became clear when the major hit a pothole, and the clips sprang open to reveal an untidy pile of what appeared to be harmless cardboard cylinders.

'I wouldn't tamper with that, Major.' Dempsey flashed a smile over his shoulder from the driver's seat. He'd fixed a contraption over his stump that allowed him to guide the Humber in conjunction with a modified steering wheel. 'You might get a bit of a fright from the old flash-bangs. Nothing like it for chivvying up the more tardy students.'

'Are you mad, Dempsey?' Llewellyn, who occupied the passenger seat, barked. 'If we go off the road, we could all be blown to kingdom come.'

Dempsey laughed, but the track deteriorated with every few hundred yards, and as the car lurched and bumped over the ruts and boulders Kalisz eyed the ammunition box with increasing apprehension. It was a relief when they were eventually waved to a halt by a pair of Commandos and directed to a patch of level ground, where a three-ton lorry and a jeep were already parked.

The first person Kalisz saw when he got out of the car was the sergeant who'd been the subject of Lucy Devereux's unarmed combat lesson. He realised they must be close to the quarry where Gunn had carried out his blindfolded exercise in trust, and wondered, for a moment, whether that was a coincidence.

'Sergeant,' he called. 'Is Major Gunn around?'

The soldier approached at the double and gave a smart salute. 'I'm afraid the major is indisposed, sir. You'll just have to put up with me. Sergeant Perkins.'

'Very well, Sergeant.' Kalisz looked back at the car, where Llewellyn was preparing his equipment. 'Have you identified the body yet?'

'The body, sir?' Perkins frowned. 'We don't have a body as such. Just a few bits and pieces. Not only do we not know *who* it is, we're still working out *what* it is, which is why I'm glad to see the doctor. We wouldn't even be here if Private Harris hadn't got lost and slipped on what he later identified as part of someone's lower digestive system. Harris was part of the rearguard at Dunkirk, sir, where Herr Hitler's artillery provided him with an intimate knowledge of the inner workings of the human body.'

Llewellyn appeared and the sergeant repeated his salute. 'Sarn't,' the medical officer acknowledged the salute. 'Major Dempsey suggests that when our chaps come up, you should create a perimeter around the scene.'

'I'm afraid the scene, as you call it, sir, is rather widespread and, so to say, indeterminate. It appears that the deceased person was in close proximity to a piece of high-explosive ordnance at the time of their demise. If I could suggest that the lads from Arisaig might be more fruitfully employed joining my chaps in the search for body fragments?'

Llewellyn blinked. 'Yes,' he said. 'I can see why that might be more useful. Just run it past Dempsey first. The three-tonner from Arisaig should be up in a few minutes. In the meantime, I suppose I should have a look at what you *do* have.'

'We've set up a tent out of the wind over there, sir —' Perkins pointed in the direction of the quarry — 'and laid out the fruits of our labours on a groundsheet. Not that there's much.'

—

Kalisz alternated between helping the searchers and sheltering from the wind in a second tent erected by the Arisaig contingent, who'd fired up a portable stove and were handing out cups of scalding milky tea to revive the freezing men. A dark patch of ground with a small crater at the centre appeared to indicate where the explosion had occurred, but only an ordnance officer would be able to tell them what had caused it. The search was hampered by the rough, heathery ground and deep snow in the gullies, which made the body fragments – none so far could be graced with the term 'part' – difficult firstly to detect, and then to recover. After about two hours, Kalisz went to the tent where Llewellyn was investigating the remains.

'Any progress?' he asked the medical officer.

'So far, all I can tell you is that the cause of death will be recorded as "explosion causing the disintegration of the person". Apart from that, the deceased was wearing what appears to be British army uniform –' he used a pair of tweezers to pick up a charred piece of khaki-coloured cloth that lay next to what might be part of someone's lung – 'and –' he used the point of the tweezers to indicate a pile of tiny objects – 'wearing a watch.'

Kalisz studied the watch fragments, fearing he'd find evidence of the Patek Philippe he'd presented to Yvette – no one could tell him when she'd been posted or who had authorised it – but the tiny golden cogwheels told him nothing.

'I dare say we'll recover something a bit more substantial if we stick to it. Boots always seem to survive with the feet intact inside in these circumstances, and oddly enough—'

'Sir.' Sergeant Perkins' head appeared through the tent flap. 'Major Dempsey thinks you should see this in situ where we found it.'

Even though it was barely mid-afternoon, the gloom made it feel like evening and the temperature was dropping rapidly. Kalisz rammed his officer's uniform cap as far as he could onto his skull and pushed his hands deep into his greatcoat pockets, envying the Commandos in their ear-warming woollen cap comforters. Perkins led the way down the hill for what seemed like an inordinate distance until they reached a gully, where two men with torches waited beside Major Dempsey.

'Astonishing that it flew this far, really.' Dempsey took a torch from one of the men and shone it on the decapitated head that lay cushioned in a patch of snow.

Kalisz looked down at the face of Pierre Renan, his features twisted in a mask of sheer terror.

'It's often not easy to read the faces of the dead.' Llewellyn might have been making a diagnosis of indigestion. 'But I'd say this chap knew he was about to be blown up.'

CHAPTER 47

5 January 1944

Lucy was waiting for Kalisz at the bottom of the stairs when he went down to breakfast. The investigation team had stayed on the hill until Kalisz was certain they only had one body on their hands, adding a booted foot, half an arm, and a score and more of other anonymous pieces of flesh to the remains tent. Perkins had suggested he stay on the site with his men to ensure no animals interfered with the scene, and they would resume the search when the light was better next morning.

'You didn't wake me,' Lucy said.

'There was no point in disturbing you. It wouldn't have changed anything.' Kalisz brushed a hand over his eyes. His restless night had been filled with images of the dead man's face, in life and in death. 'Better that you had a decent night's sleep.'

'It can't have been easy up there.'

'No. The effect of high explosives on a human being rather dents one's faith in a higher power.' Kalisz realised he was missing something. 'So someone told you?'

'Major Dempsey. I met him earlier. What do you think Pierre Renan was doing on the hill, Jan?'

'I don't know,' Kalisz admitted. 'Dempsey thought he might have been trying to make his way to the station at Glenfinnan without being identified. Apparently he knew the mountains well enough.'

'But you don't believe that.'

'From what little we found, it seemed clear Pierre hadn't equipped himself for a trek in the hills. He would have known it was suicide to go out without an overcoat at this time of the year, and especially in these conditions. Of course, suicide is another theory Dempsey suggested. A man at the end of his tether, perhaps implicated in the murders of

256

Krystina Kowolska and Lieutenant Fontaine. He could have taken a stick of dynamite and gone up there to end it all.'

Lucy frowned. 'But that would go against everything he said in his note to Yvette. "This is not goodbye, *ma chérie*, we will meet again when it is over.'''

'Precisely. On the other hand, it seems to be a basic element of the human condition to seek sanctuary in high places in times of threat or danger.'

'You think he was being hunted?'

'I believe it's possible, yes, but I doubt we will ever know. By the time we reached the crime scene – if it is one – it had been trampled by dozens of Commandos, so any original footprints would have been obscured. It was also impossible to tell one set of tyre tracks from the other in the slush.'

'So we leave Pierre Renan to the Special Investigation Branch?'

'That would probably be best,' Kalisz agreed. 'Did Dempsey say anything else?'

'Apparently Colonel Baldwin has given us permission to visit Swordland and interview the occupants, providing the conducting officer of STS 23b agrees.'

'Our friend Major Maxwell.'

'That's right. He lives in a cottage on the loch, not far from the lodge.'

'Then we are wasting our time.' Kalisz turned for the stairs. 'Wait here until I get my things together.'

'Aren't you going to have breakfast, Jan?'

'You sound like my wife, Lucy.' Kalisz smiled. 'But I seem to have lost my appetite. Do you think Captain Malpas will let us use his boat?'

–

Maxwell must have been watching their approach from the remote cottage by the loch shore, because his kilted figure was waiting to help them moor their motor boat when they reached the rickety wooden jetty.

'I suppose you'd better come in,' was his only greeting.

He led the way to the house – a squat, low, single-storey building with small shuttered windows and a moss-covered shingle roof that had seen better days. The interior matched the exterior: one room to sleep in – a camp bed with rumpled blankets was visible through the doorway – and the other to cater for all other needs. An iron kitchen range for cooking, a sink, but no sign of any water supply, and a table and four sturdy chairs that Kalisz guessed had been liberated from Swordland Lodge, a mile up the loch. Paint flaked from plastered walls patterned with damp and mould, to litter the bare flagstone floor. A spartan, joyless place, much like its occupant.

Maxwell lit an ancient oil lamp that hung from the low ceiling and motioned them to the table.

'From your lack of reaction, I would guess you were expecting us, Major?' Lucy ventured.

'I had word from Arisaig that you might be popping by,' Maxwell acknowledged. 'But after your last visit I'd have been surprised if you hadn't come back either officially –' the grey eyes flickered to Kalisz – 'or otherwise.'

'You knew about that?'

Maxwell shrugged. 'A couple of us watched you from the hill. My fellows would have been tempted to intervene if I hadn't been there to stop them. They're good chaps, but they are very protective of their mission, as I'm sure you can understand from the time you spent in the cellar.'

'And yet,' Kalisz said, 'a little bird at Arisaig told me your "students" would never resort to violence, because to do so would doubly jeopardise their mission.'

'Ah.' Maxwell nodded. 'Major Sykes. And you were talking about Raven.'

It took Kalisz a moment before he remembered the file he'd read in the cellar of Arisaig House. Code name Raven: Krystina Kowolska. 'So she did come here?'

'Oh, yes. She appeared one evening out of the mist and started throwing stones at the house. She must have been here before, because she clearly knew who my lads were. When the students gathered to see what the commotion was about, she shrieked at them that they belonged in the fires with the rest of their filthy families, and countless other obscenities. She was entirely deranged, you see. Vermin and baby killers, she called them. "The Nazis will turn you to soap and I will wash my arse with you," if you can believe it. Such a refined, beautiful human being possessed by so many demons. There are limits to anyone's patience, even soldiers as disciplined as these. Eventually one of the chaps, Manfred, snapped and went for her. Threw her to the ground and laid into her with his boots. He might have done her some real damage if I hadn't appeared on the scene. I'd certainly have been tempted if I was in his position.' His gaze locked on Kalisz. 'You've seen what they are, and this young lady is certainly aware, so I can be quite frank with you. A clever young lad, forced to flee Germany or Austria, his family slaughtered or imprisoned, travels to Britain, determined to fight the Nazis. And what welcome did he get?' Maxwell snorted through his long nose. 'His saviours labelled him an "enemy alien". They packed him off on some hell ship to the Canadian prairie or the Australian outback, where he'd have been left to rot if it hadn't occurred to our rulers that even "aliens" could wield a spade in the Pioneer Corps. Fortunately, someone with influence saw their potential, and decided to make use of their intelligence, fitness and hatred of the Nazis. They were forced to give up everything that linked them to their previous lives, even their names, but they found comradeship and a new home in the Commandos. They are the elite of the elite – X Troop. When I think of what they've done, it rather embarrasses me to call myself a soldier. They shed blood during that fiasco at Dieppe, and on the shores of Sicily and in countless small raids. Would cheerfully give their lives for a crack at Herr Hitler. Then along comes this crazy woman to remind them of everything they've lost and jeopardise their best chance to make a real difference.' He hesitated for a moment at some memory. 'The odd thing is that she made no attempt to defend herself. Almost as if she wanted to be hurt.'

'What happened then?' Lucy asked.

'I put her back in her canoe and pushed her out into the loch.'

'You weren't concerned that she might be badly injured in some way?'

'I really didn't care if she lived or died, Flight Officer.' Maxwell seemed surprised she needed to be told. 'She was an impediment to my ability to do my job, and therefore to the war effort. As much an enemy as the Nazis, if you like. There's a radio transmitter up at the lodge.' He saw Kalisz's look of surprise. 'Yes, Major, you didn't search the place quite as thoroughly as you thought. I called Arisaig House and told them they should get rid of her, the sooner the better. They said they'd have her watched, and if she breathed a word about Swordland she'd be out. To be perfectly honest, when I heard she'd been found hanged, I thought someone had taken my advice.'

Lucy flinched as if she'd been slapped, and Kalisz laid a hand on her arm. He reached beneath the table for his backpack, retrieved the Luger pistol they'd taken from Kev and laid it on the table. Maxwell's expression hardened when he recognised it.

'It would appear that one of your "chaps" mislaid his personal weapon, Major,' Kalisz said. 'I'm surprised you didn't mention the Luger when we were talking about weapons with a 7.65mm calibre. Major Sykes tells me there are many still in circulation.'

'It must have slipped my mind.' Maxwell picked up the weapon and studied it. 'Where did you get it?'

'This was found in a cave not far from where Krystina Kowolska and the unfortunate Lieutenant Fontaine met their end. I believe it is the weapon used to kill the lieutenant. That is why I must insist on interviewing your students about the pistol and their whereabouts on the night of the murders. Obviously,' he said more placatingly, 'it would help if you were to accompany us.'

Maxwell rose from the table. For a moment his presence seemed to fill the room with menace, but he turned away and went to a cupboard beneath the sink, where he retrieved a bottle and three chipped army-issue mugs. 'Whisky?' He showed them the bottle. 'Not bad stuff.' Without ceremony, he placed two of the mugs in front of Kalisz and Lucy and poured each of them a generous measure before doing the same for himself.

'Normally, I'd like nothing better than to accompany you to Swordland, Major Zamoyski, and you could interview my protégés to your heart's content. However, I'm afraid that won't be possible – don't get up, there's really no point – because they're not here. They left on the first stage of their mission late yesterday afternoon. Under the circumstances, I think the best thing to do would be to raise a glass to them, because none of the poor buggers is going to be coming back. To Oper— No, that won't do. Let's keep it simple. To success.' He raised his mug and drank the contents in a single swallow.

For a moment Kalisz felt a wave of anger grow inside him, but he closed his eyes and waited for it to subside. Eventually he managed a bleak smile. 'What is it that the French used to call you people? "Perfidious Albion", wasn't it?'

'That was in reference to England,' Maxwell corrected him. 'But we Scots have been called much worse.'

'Very well.' Kalisz raised his mug. What else was there to do, but be magnanimous in defeat? This wasn't Maxwell's doing. He would have had his orders. 'To success, and to the end of this obscenity of a war.' He drank, but his attempt to emulate Maxwell ended in a choking cough. Lucy moved to help him, but he waved her away. 'Very good,' he croaked to her. 'You should try it.'

'I'm genuinely sorry you had to come all this way for nothing, Major.' Maxwell led them to the door and out into the light.

'You understand that I will have to complain to Colonel Baldwin about this... this subterfuge.'

'Then I wish you the very best of luck.' A wintry smile accompanied the words. 'Our Colonel Baldwin is a mere figurehead. An administrator, rather a good one, but what we call a pen-pusher. Operationally, and this is strictly between us, the man who really runs the show is Major Dempsey, and it is to him, if anyone, you should complain.'

'Thank you for your hospitality,' Kalisz said. In her disappointment and anger, Lucy seemed to have trouble with the niceties of the moment. Maxwell accompanied them down to the boat.

'What is that?' Lucy suddenly came alive at a swirl of water by the boat and the sight of a sleek head that appeared – or half-appeared – on the surface of the loch before ducking down again, only to reappear once more, chewing on a small fish.

'Why, that is an otter, Flight Officer,' Maxwell said. 'The most delightful of all God's creatures. I shall miss this place, you know.' His eyes drifted out over the loch to the cloud-enshrouded mountains beyond. 'It looks desolate now, but you should see it when spring brings the place alive, and the air is filled with the scent of wild flowers and your ears with the soft buzz of countless bees. When you can experience the true enormousness of the sky, the extraordinary purity of light, the sharpness of the hills and the clarity of the water.' They stared at him. This was an entirely different Maxwell from the austere soldier of a few moments before. 'Come here in the summer, and savour the speckled trout that forage among the margins only a short cast away from providing you with your supper. Watch the otters frolic in the shallows with their kits. We have brought the war here, with our guns and our bullets and our bombs, and our death and destruction, but I do believe that when all that is gone, this is one of the closest places to paradise on this earth.' He paused, and looked embarrassed. 'You must excuse me my enthusiasms, but sometimes they are the only things that keep one sane.'

'You say that you will miss it –' Kalisz didn't hide his puzzlement – 'but it is surely now, with the Second Front mere months away, that these schools, and the people they train, will come into their own? Your students will light a fire at the heart of Europe that will consume Hitler and all his Nazi underlings. You and your like have never been more necessary or important.'

'In this moment, that is probably true, Major Zamoyski, but you must consider Arisaig, and all who serve here, as a shooting star. We appear, we create a moment of wonder, and we are gone forever. Once the Allies have a foothold in Europe, this war will be a battle of giants, as it already is in the East. Their millions against our millions. Tanks by the thousand. Enormous armadas of aircraft. There will be no need of pinpricks. And that, let us face it, is all SOE provides in the grand scheme of things – pinpricks. The little armies the likes of Captain Malpas form from those who have refused to be cowed will be crushed or brushed aside by the Panzers, because their very existence is predicated on clandestine warfare, not outright battle. They have neither the firepower nor numbers to even hold their own. Oh, I'm sure there are people planning for a next stage. What else are we all good for? Your Poles have already set up their own shop down in the south-east because they understand that when France is taken, this type of warfare will have had its day in the West, but it may be their only recourse against what is to come in your homeland.' His gaze became almost pleading. 'D'you see?'

'Oh, yes, Major, I see most clearly.'

–

'What was all that about?' Lucy asked, as they made their way down the loch towards Rhubana.

'Major Maxwell has given me much to consider, and I believe he knows it. When we return to Arisaig, I must ask you to impose upon your friends in London again. Find out all you can about Witold – I believe his second name is Grabski – and Jerzy, the two Bosnian Poles who are billeted at Borrodale. If the Poles have their own "shop" in the south-east, where they are training our people in clandestine warfare, I wonder what reason two Polish patriots have for being at STS 21?'

CHAPTER 48

Kalisz blamed himself. He'd given Dempsey all the warning he needed to move the Germans away from Swordland and far beyond his reach. It had never occurred to him that the major might be the ultimate authority in charge of the mission to kill Hitler. Would Kalisz have done anything different if he'd believed some foreign interloper might jeopardise an undertaking of such magnitude? One which might truly achieve that most sought-after objective, of changing the entire course of the war. The answer was probably not.

That left the question of whether Kalisz should take the matter further. It irked him that Dempsey, sitting in his accustomed place on the far side of the mess room, might be inwardly gloating about his triumph over the annoying little Polish detective. On balance, however, he thought not. There was an old Polish saying his father used to use that seemed appropriate in this situation: 'Don't call the wolf from the forest.' Swordland was one of those secrets about which Churchill had warned him to 'close your ears and deny temptation'. Kalisz doubted Dempsey had even mentioned the matter to his nominal superior, Baldwin. Maxwell had no reason to. Best, for everybody, that it had never happened at all.

He said as much to Lucy when she came down to lunch, and she seemed relieved he'd come to the decision. They were just discussing their next move when a clerk appeared at their table.

'Major Zamoyski? Telephone call, sir.'

'Excuse me,' he said to Lucy.

Outside in the hall, he picked up the phone from the clerk's desk. 'Zamoyski?'

'How goes the hunt for Krystina's killer?' a quiet voice asked. It took a moment before Kalisz identified it as belonging to Major Richard Gunn.

'You know I can't tell you that, Major, especially given that you may still be a suspect. Why didn't you tell me you were just over the next headland the night she died? I even had a statement suggesting you might have been on the meadow below this house.'

'So the little Frog Jew told you, did he? Not that it'll do you much good now, if what my sergeant tells me is correct.'

'Yes... Interesting that he met his rather spectacular end on what might be called your "patch".'

'Christ, you've got some impudence, Zamoyski,' Gunn exploded. 'Trying to implicate me in another murder I didn't commit.'

'I do nothing of the sort, Major Gunn,' Kalisz assured him. 'All I am suggesting is that it might be of value to both of us if you were to come to Arisaig House for interview. It would be purely voluntary, of course, and should you decide to be represented by a lawyer, military or civilian, I would not object, and nor, I am sure, would Flight Officer Devereux.'

'No, Major, I have a better idea. I have something for you – proper hard evidence, not like your deluded fantasies about me. I want you to meet me alone, tonight, at Polnish Church. You know it?'

'The white church on the hill between Arisaig and Inverailort?'

'That's right. Be there at nine, and I will give you information that will allow you to blow this case wide open. Come alone.'

'But—'

'Alone,' Gunn rasped. 'If I see any sign of that nosy secretary of yours or anybody else, the deal's off. Do you understand?'

'I understand.'

'And come unarmed,' Gunn said, almost as an afterthought.

'Of course,' Kalisz said, but the other man had already hung up.

'What was that about?' Lucy asked when he returned to the mess, looking thoughtful.

'Just Constable MacDonald, thanking me for returning his motor-cycle.'

–

Snow began to fall in thick, damp flakes that quickly carpeted the road as Kalisz drove from Arisaig to the little church he'd noticed on the way to Glenfinnan. By the time he reached Polnish, the snow covered the track up to the chapel and he decided to leave the Austin by the roadside. He waited until the luminous hands of his watch indicated five to nine before getting out into the snow. A bright three-quarter moon glowed a faint orange and turned the surrounding landscape into a fairytale wonder of silver and gold as he walked up the track, hands driven deep into his greatcoat pockets against the cold. He kept his head down, and he noticed the faint tracks of a vehicle beneath the most recent covering, which at least seemed to indicate his journey hadn't been wasted.

Had he been right to come alone? Only time would tell the truth of it. Lucy, of course, would resent being excluded, and rightly. Another small sin to be expunged, assuming the opportunity arose. Gunn's voice on the telephone had contained the brittle quality of a man living on the edge. Kalisz realised now that he'd handled the Commando officer poorly. Much more might have been achieved if he'd used flattery instead of threat. He'd driven Gunn into a corner, where he believed he was the main suspect. Now Gunn thought he needed to bargain with a piece of evidence that might have been given freely, and more promptly, if the circumstances had been different.

The big question was: what evidence did he have?

A sign appeared in the moonlight, and for a heartbeat Kalisz wondered if he was in the correct place. He was searching for Polnish Church, but the flaking paint announced that he was approaching Our Lady of the Braes Chapel. The church itself loomed out of the swirling flakes of snow: a sturdy building, made more so by staunch buttresses, pure white apart from the darkened windows and a single black door. To reach it he had to pick his way across the railway line, and when he approached he could see a motor car parked behind the building, but he couldn't make out the type. There was no one in sight, so thankfully the meeting would take place inside.

No words of welcome from Gunn at the arched doorway, but Kalisz didn't blame him for staying out of the cold. The door had a large keyhole and a simple latch, and it opened silently when he pushed it. He walked inside, glad to be out of the wind, and gently closed the door behind him. Inside the church a patchwork of light and dark greeted him. Pools of moonlight from the stained-glass windows illuminated rows of ancient wooden benches that faced the altar, but it was from the shadows on his right that Gunn emerged to push a pistol barrel into his ribs.

'I…'

'Shut up.' Gunn held the weapon against him as he searched his greatcoat and tunic for any hidden weapons. 'Am I going to have to knock you down to search the rest of you?'

'There's a fighting knife taped to my left calf.'

Gunn took a step back. 'Take it off – very carefully – and put it on that pew across there.' Kalisz did as he was ordered. He didn't recognise the word 'pew', but Gunn seemed satisfied when he placed the knife on the nearest wooden bench. 'What did you think you were going to do with that?'

Kalisz shrugged. 'It didn't seem very sensible to come here completely unarmed.'

'Well, much good it will do you now.' The pistol was back, but this time the barrel was screwed painfully into Kalisz's neck. 'You've caused me no end of trouble with my superiors. Give me one reason why I shouldn't kill you?'

'Because you have evidence for me that might solve my case, Major Gunn. Your vanity may require this little charade to belittle and perhaps frighten me, but I believe you would also wish to see that happen.'

Kalisz ignored the gun at his neck and walked towards the front of the church, studying the main window, which was brilliantly backlit by the moonlight.

'Stand still, or I'll shoot you.'

'You're not going to kill me, Major.' Kalisz ignored the order. 'All it would do is implicate you in all the other deaths.'

'You've already done that.' Gunn's words emerged as a frustrated snarl.

'It is true that there is enough circumstantial evidence that I could probably persuade Prime Minister Churchill to have you arrested, but I would much prefer to see the real killer brought to justice. Wouldn't you? Perhaps the evidence you claim to have will exonerate you.'

'Or you might use it to incriminate me.'

'We'll only know if you tell me.' Kalisz turned to face him. 'So it *was* you who was in the grounds that night? Pierre Renan didn't recognise the individual, by the way. He only described you as a Commando officer.'

'Bastard.'

'So I ask myself… why were you there, if not to hunt down and kill the woman who destroyed your military career?'

He'd expected an outburst from Gunn, or at least a denial. Instead, the major suddenly lost all his fire. 'That's the thing, you see. She did destroy my career, but she also saved my life. Every man who was on the course with me in 1941 was either killed or captured a year later at a place called Dieppe. If it hadn't been for my gammy leg, I'd have died with them in one of the most pointless slaughters of the war. I'm not even sure why I left the chaps that night and went to Arisaig House. I remember watching the windows of the cottage until the lights went out, trying to get up the courage to knock on the door. I think I just wanted her to know. To understand. To tell her that I wasn't the man she thought I was – or, at least, not *only* him.' He shook his head as if he was trying to clear it of some dark vision. 'I've not been myself. Maybe that had something to do with it. Lack of sleep. Nightmares. I'd been dreaming about Dunkirk. There was this bridge that I'd been ordered to blow. We waited and waited until all our people were across. The sounds of the tank engines got closer and closer. But the refugees just wouldn't stop coming – hundreds of them with their prams and carts. Mothers with babies. Children leading a dog, herding a cow, or carrying a goat. No command or threat was enough to keep them off the bridge. I delayed until an army officer put a pistol to my head and ordered me to do my duty. Then I pushed the plunger. The bridge seemed to rise ever so slowly into the air, and all those men, women, children and babies rose with it. As they rose, they began to disintegrate, arms, legs and heads separating from torsos, and then it rained body parts for what seemed like an awfully long time. I was watching them when I did it, you see, and I remember their faces so full of relief that they were going to reach safety. And then I pushed the plunger, and they were just bits and pieces of human beings.'

Kalisz sympathised – he truly did. He'd seen enough innocents die himself. But that was war. He needed to get Gunn back on the subject. 'So the lights went out. What then?'

'Then I left.'

'Just left? Surely you must have seen something?'

'It was pitch dark,' Gunn protested.

'Not so dark that Pierre Renan didn't see you. Or that someone was unable to hunt down Krystina Kowolska and snap her neck. Put a bullet in Lieutenant Fontaine's skull.'

'I didn't see anything.'

Kalisz felt the faint puff of a cold draught on his cheek and struggled to concentrate. Yes, there had been a certain inflection to the word 'see'. 'So you didn't *see* anything, but you *heard* something?'

'Turn around.'

'No.'

'Turn around or I will shoot you, Major.'

'I need to know,' Kalisz pleaded.

'Turn around and I'll tell you.'

Kalisz turned his back.

'It's neater this way, you see, Zamoyski. Certainly neater for me.'

So this was it. Kalisz sensed his adversary moving closer. Tensed for the moment the gun butt would smash into the back of his head. Then it would be over a cliff and into the sea for Churchill's detective. 'Tell me.'

'I heard a whispered conversation that night in which a word was repeated several times. That word was *"zdrajca".*'

Kalisz heard a soft thud, followed by the sound of someone slumping to the floor.

'I was listening for you, but I thought you hadn't come.' Kalisz turned round on legs that would barely hold him upright.

'I paid this place a visit earlier,' Major 'Bill' Sykes said. 'A little oil on the door hinges was all the edge I needed.'

'Is he dead?'

' 'Course not.' Sykes chuckled. 'We did this all the time in Shanghai. A little tap behind the ear with one of these.' He showed Kalisz the small leather-covered cosh in his right hand. 'It's as good as a lullaby. I doubt that he really intended to carry out his threat, but I couldn't take any chances. He'll be out for about two hours. What do you want me to do with him?'

Kalisz considered for a moment. By rights, he should have Gunn arrested. He certainly deserved it. But there was a war on, and Major Richard Gunn was a highly efficient part of the British military machine. The only people to whom he was a danger were himself and

Jan Kalisz; with the information Kalisz now had, he didn't doubt he'd be gone from Arisaig by the end of the week.

'Throw him in the ice house for the night,' he said. 'Let him out after Doctor Llewellyn has had a look at him. Maybe he can give him a pill for those nightmares.'

'All right.' Sykes picked up the limp body and lugged it over his shoulder. 'By the way, that word he said he heard… What did it mean?'

'He said "*zdrajca*", and he pronounced it surprisingly well. It's a Polish word and it means "traitor".'

CHAPTER 49

Dempsey's office light was still on when Kalisz returned to Arisaig, close to midnight, and he pondered for a moment before finally knocking on the wood-panelled door.

'Enter,' came the familiar aristocratic drawl.

The one-handed major was sitting at his desk, hunched over a pile of paperwork. He showed no surprise at seeing Kalisz at such a late hour. 'Reports and more reports.' He nodded at the papers with a wry smile. 'Every student is assessed in every subject at every stage of the process. I sometimes suspect we generate enough bumf to bomb the enemy into submission without bothering with the Second Front.'

Kalisz had no idea what 'bumf' was, but he understood the sentiment. One thing interested him, though. 'And how did Krystina Kowolska fare under this intense scrutiny?'

'Ah,' Dempsey said. 'Warrant Officer Kowolska was different, you see. Special. Sometimes she deigned to attend an assessment meeting and sometimes she did not. Sometimes her assessments were satisfactory, very occasionally one might describe them as "glowing". Mostly, they were not. But she had what we call "friends in high places". Colonel Baldwin was called on to return her to her unit several times by members of staff, but knew it was pointless unless he had the most damning and incontrovertible evidence of her inability to do her job.'

'Which was not forthcoming?'

'No.'

'I wonder if I can ask you something, Major? It might be called a presumption, because I sense you are not a man prone to speculation, but I would value your opinion on a matter of some importance.'

'How intriguing.' Dempsey smiled. 'Ask away, old boy.'

'As you know, my investigation focuses primarily on the violent deaths of Warrant Officer Kowolska and Lieutenant Fontaine, but there was one other important – perhaps vital is a better word – aspect that Prime Minister Churchill wished me to consider. One which has been keeping me awake at night, because I now realise I am in no way equipped to come up with an answer.'

'And that is?' Dempsey didn't hide his interest.

'Does Warrant Officer Kowolska's death in any way suggest that her particular operation has been compromised? The prime minister was most insistent that the answer to this question could affect the course of the Second Front, if not the entire war.'

'I see.' Dempsey bowed his head and contemplated the papers on his desk, but it was clear the question had stirred something in him. 'If you'll bear with me for a few moments, Major Zamoyski… I believe the subject merits a certain level of consideration, not just because of the original source of the question, but because, in a way, it impinges upon the fate of every man and woman who has trained here, past and present.'

Kalisz studied his surroundings as the minutes passed. On the surface, the office of a typical military administrator: everything in its place, even the pencils laid out in a neat row on his desk. Pen ready to hand by the ink bottle. It must have been a fine – even luxurious – room before the army took over the house. Now it had a rather battered and unloved air and had been partitioned into sections, of which this was one. A row of wooden filing cabinets stood to attention along one wall, as if waiting for inspection.

Dempsey coughed, and Kalisz gave him his full concentration once more.

'Firstly,' the major said, 'I would suggest to you that, unless you have evidence to the contrary, Krystina Kowolska's death was precipitated by her own actions. I, certainly, have no reason to believe otherwise.' He looked at Kalisz for some confirmation of his view, but received only a look of continued inquiry. 'Arisaig is a place where everything is secret. Yet, in a way, what we do here is anything but secret, certainly not to anyone who walks through the door of this clandestine world. We prepare soldiers – volunteers – for perilous missions behind enemy lines, to do as much damage as is possible using the few resources that will be at their disposal in such an environment. Whatever Mr Churchill says, at Arisaig, no mission – or agent – is more important than any other. It has been my experience that the people who pass through our hands are almost uniquely courageous.' He looked up, ready for any challenge to a statement that some would have described as ridiculous, after four years of a war that had inspired acts of courage, seen and unseen, that could sometimes be described as beyond human comprehension. 'Each of them knows they may die doing their duty, possibly in the most dreadful of circumstances, and faces up to that possibility in their own fashion. We are a brotherhood here, Major, despite some of the things you may have experienced and witnessed. I would stake my own life that not one of my students, even those unable to complete their training, would do *anything* to jeopardise their own mission, or that of any other. Therefore, my answer to Mr Churchill's question would be no. I do not believe Krystina's mission has been compromised. My only proviso would be that, God forbid, you have not discovered anything to suggest this station has been infiltrated by our common enemy?'

'I have not,' Kalisz assured him. 'And I thank you for your candour and transparent honesty. The prime minister will be relieved.'

'Then if that's all...?'

'It is not, Major. I'm afraid I must ask you for permission to re-interview the two Polish soldiers who shared accommodation at Borrodale House with Pierre Renan and Jean-Marc Fontaine.'

'Isn't that something you should take up with Colonel Baldwin?'

'Perhaps, but I have found that the colonel tends to resent my intrusions, and he generally delegates such responsibilities to his most able subordinate. In this case, I thought it best to "cut out the middleman", as I believe you English say.'

Dempsey rewarded his flattery with a doubtful half-smile. 'May I ask why you feel you must speak to these men again?'

'It is the detective's task to follow the many strands in an investigation to wherever they may lead, and then, in some way, weave them into a tapestry that provides a moment of insight and clarity, and, *tutaj jest*, we have the whole picture set out before us. In the case of Krystina Kowolska and Jean-Marc Fontaine, the tapestry is still not complete. I believe the two Poles may be able to fill in some of the gaps. Would one o'clock suit, do you think? I have a meeting with Constable MacDonald at Arisaig in the morning.'

'Of course.' Dempsey rose and ushered him to the door. 'I'll make sure they are waiting for you at the house.'

Kalisz murmured his thanks.

'Oh, I should have asked earlier. Was your visit to STS 23b productive?'

'Alas.' Kalisz shook his head. 'Due to some administrative error, the birds had flown. But it does not matter too much. If the pistol proves a match for the weapon that killed Lieutenant Fontaine, I'm sure I can use Mr Churchill's authority to track them down.'

CHAPTER 50

6 January 1944

Six a.m.

Kalisz tapped lightly on Lucy's door, waited, then tapped a little louder.

After a few moments he heard the sounds of movement, and the door opened a few inches to reveal a tousle-haired waif in striped pyjamas, who glared at him from bleary eyes. 'Don't you know what time it is?' she hissed. 'It's still bloody dark.'

'Meet me at the car in five minutes,' he said.

'Five minutes?' Lucy sounded incredulous. 'Don't you know anything about women, Major? I'll be there in ten.' The door closed with a click and an emphasis that was the quiet equivalent of having it slammed in his face.

It had snowed more heavily overnight, and they had to clear two inches from the front and rear windows of the Austin before they could move. The inside of the car was like an icebox, and Lucy shivered inside her WAAF greatcoat.

'So you've arranged a meeting with Jerzy and Witold at one o'clock in the afternoon, but we're going to knock on their door at six in the morning. Why?'

Kalisz strained at the wheel as if will alone would get the Austin up the slope to the main road. 'Call it a hunch.'

It was only a short drive to Borrodale. As he approached the turn-off onto the short track that led down to the house he cut the lights and then the engine.

'These are not the type of men who are going to appreciate a surprise, Jan,' Lucy warned.

'And that is precisely why we are going to surprise them. Ready?'

They got out of the car and walked through the snow towards the house. Kalisz could see a faint light in one of the windows, but it was the sound of voices from the far side of the building that attracted him. In the pink glow of the tail lights of some kind of motor car, Jerzy was visible, loading a pair of large kitbags and a clothing trunk into the boot. Witold was working on a front tyre with some kind of handpump. Kalisz waited until Jerzy had completed his task and closed the boot before he stepped out of the shadows and into the light.

'Careful, Jan,' Lucy whispered.

'*Gdybym mógł zamienić słowo...*'

Jerzy looked up, startled, but it was Witold who reacted the quicker. He rose and turned, and Kalisz's senses shrieked a warning as he saw the long-barrelled pistol in the Pole's hand. In the same instant he registered a soft *phut*, and threw himself to one side as something plucked at his coat.

The crack of two shots split the snow-deadened silence, and Witold was hurled back against the car, to spin and fall face down in the snow. Kalisz looked up from where he'd dived in time to see Lucy swivel with her Browning automatic to cover Jerzy.

'You brought a gun?'

'Call it a hunch,' she said. 'Stop!' But Jerzy paid her no heed as he ran towards the barn behind the main house.

'Let him go,' Kalisz said. 'He won't get far.' He pushed himself to his feet and went to where Witold lay. He turned the Pole over and winced at the amount of blood that already stained the snow. One look was enough to tell him the man was dead. Both bullets had gone straight through his heart. 'Good shooting.' He picked up the pistol the Pole had fired, another of the silenced Lugers that had been supplied to the men at Swordland. 'I wonder why he—'

The sound of an engine interrupted him, and a motorcycle erupted from behind the barn and sped up towards the road. Kalisz opened the car door and saw the key in the ignition. He pushed Witold's body aside and climbed in, throwing the Austin keys to Lucy.

'Get back to Arisaig, and have Colonel Baldwin radio the staff at Inverailort House to set up a roadblock on the Fort William road. Then he should get a search party together and follow my tracks.' He slammed the door shut to stifle any possible argument and rammed the car into gear, cursing as the wheels spun in the snow. Gradually he regained control and made his way with more propriety up to the road.

The one benefit of the inches-thick carpet of white was that it deadened the effect of the potholes, but it also meant it was almost impossible to tell where road ended and the verge began. Kalisz was forced to hunch over the steering wheel and stare into the subdued glow of the headlights to follow the line of the pocked tarmac surface. A metallic bang against the side of the car told him the handpump was still attached to the front tyre, but that was the least of his concerns. Fortunately, Jerzy's progress had left a single wheel track in the snow, and once Kalisz had found the narrow furrow he was able to make better progress. He drove carefully, but sometimes not carefully enough. There were times when the rear wheels lost their purchase, and the unfamiliar vehicle ended up side-slipping towards trees – or, on one occasion, what he felt certain was the dark, empty void of a cliff edge. Any incline brought the threat of spinning tyres and an early end to his pursuit, but somehow he always managed to harmonise gears and throttle in a way that ensured he made some progress. He found he was sweating, despite the cold, and the metronomic sweep of the struggling single windscreen wiper had a hypnotic quality that might have proved troublesome had he not been in such a high state of alert.

Jerzy must have been having many of the same difficulties, because Kalisz began to get glimpses of a faint red light in the distance when he topped the swooping rises in the twisting, undulating, barely visible highway. With a bit of good fortune, he would catch up with the Bosnian Pole before they reached the roadblock at Lochailort. If his situation had been different, Kalisz would have closed his eyes and sent a prayer to the competent Sergeant Perkins. In any case, he had no intention of overhauling Jerzy. Sykes was certainly correct that an animal is always at its most dangerous when it's cornered. Kalisz had a feeling Jerzy could be very dangerous indeed.

Witold's violent response to his polite request to 'have a word' puzzled him. Of course, he'd chosen the early hour to surprise them, and to thwart Dempsey's almost certain attempt to repeat the trick he'd performed at Swordland. They were involved in some way with the deaths of Krystina Kowolska and Jean-Marc Fontaine; he was certain of that now, and in truth they'd never been far from his mind. But any evidence he had against them was circumstantial, to say the least, and balanced by the entire lack of a motive. He doubted the interview would have changed anything. All they'd needed was to hold their nerve, and Dempsey would soon have contrived to send them off on some suicide mission where they could be cheerfully shot to pieces, taking as many Nazis with them as possible.

Dempsey.

Kalisz's consciousness had focused on the urbane major through a long, sleepless night. A dozen fragments of conversations he'd had over the past week whirled through his head, teasing and tempting until they'd finally coalesced into certainty. Dempsey had either killed Krystina Kowolska, or the Poles had killed her on his orders. Jean-Marc Fontaine had merely been in the wrong place at the wrong time, driven by his obsession with Krystina. Kalisz's problem was that the evidence against Major Dempsey was thinner by far than that against the Poles. So thin, in fact, it was barely worthy of the term 'evidence' at all. His only chance of bringing the major to justice lay with the man on the motorcycle, now a hundred and fifty paces ahead. Witold's reaction had been a tacit admission of guilt. The silenced Luger tied both men to the killing of Fontaine, and the killing of Fontaine implicated them unequivocally in the murder of Krystina Kowolska. Kalisz had no doubt he could put a case together solid enough to place Jerzy on the gallows. But where was the justice in that if the prime mover in the whole affair walked free? To get Dempsey, he needed Jerzy to talk. Only the Pole could provide the testimony that would put Dempsey in the dock, where he belonged.

It was still full dark, and the big flakes of snow slapped against the windscreen, but dawn could not be far away. With dawn there would be nowhere for Jerzy to run. Even if he managed to slip through the net at Lochailort, the police at Fort William would be waiting for him. *Too close.* Jerzy must have slowed, because now Kalisz was less than a hundred paces behind the tail light of the motorcycle. It was only then he noticed the glow of headlamps beyond the fugitive Pole, but the lights weren't on the road – they were angled towards the trees. Kalisz's heart stuttered as he realised what he was seeing. A lorry must have skidded on the bend, and now it was blocking the roadway. Jerzy was trapped. If he tried to manoeuvre his way past the crash, he must know Kalisz would be on him within seconds.

Jerzy was almost at the lorry when the terrain made his decision for him. The tail light swung left and he gunned the bike towards the hills. It took a moment before Kalisz realised what was happening; then he saw the lights of the motorcycle fishtailing up the slope and understood. This was where the track turned off towards the quarry where they'd found what was left of Pierre Renan, and where the Commandos did their mountain training.

Common sense dictated that Kalisz should stop here and wait for the search party, which couldn't be far behind him, but he didn't hesitate. When he reached the turn-off, he spun the wheel left and crashed the lever into the lowest possible gear. This was where he needed traction rather than speed. Jerzy wasn't going anywhere. The bike was infinitely more agile than the car, but the narrow tyres wouldn't have the same grip. All Kalisz had to do was keep moving and he'd eventually hunt the Pole down. On the other hand, he knew that the moment he stopped, he'd never get the car into motion again.

The tyre marks stood out clearly in the headlamps now, even though the red glow of the rear light was lost in the constant snow flurries that whipped across the hillside, driven by the gale. As the track grew steeper, the snow deepened. Kalisz gentled the throttle to keep the wheels from spinning, but that meant losing speed, and every time he lost momentum he knew there was no chance of getting it back. His heart quickened as the angular shape of the motorcycle appeared in the centre of the track, abandoned and lying on its side. No chance of driving round it, so he braked to a halt and cut the engine, leaving the headlights lit to illuminate the scene.

It had been cold in the car, but the first bite of the freezing wind made him gasp, and the big snowflakes landed like slaps against the exposed flesh of his face. He pulled up the collar of his greatcoat and hunched his shoulders as he made his way up the hill, boots crunching in the new-fallen snow. Jerzy's footprints led away from the motorcycle in a direct line northwards. They were clear and sharp for the moment, but Kalisz knew that couldn't last. The blizzard would soon fill in the tracks and his opportunity to hunt down the fleeing suspect would be lost.

He drew Witold's pistol from his pocket, where he'd placed it almost unthinkingly after the shooting. By now there was just about enough natural light to make out Jerzy's prints. After about a hundred metres the trail left the relative flat of the road and veered right on to the fractured ground of the mountainside, where the going became much more difficult. Here earth and sky seemed to merge into a single disorientating white blanket. Kalisz tried desperately to picture the terrain as it had been on the day he'd visited Gunn's exercise, but he couldn't be sure precisely where he was. He guessed that Jerzy was trying to make his way through the hills to Lochailort, where he could steal some kind of transport.

A gaping void appeared without warning to his right, and Kalisz thanked God he'd been following directly in Jerzy's tracks. In this blizzard, the slightest deviation would have taken him over the quarry edge and onto the rocks below. Soon after the quarry, the trail led him through a narrow gully. He'd only gone a few paces when it felt as if a sandbag had hit him on the shoulders. The pistol flew from his hand and he found himself face down, eating snow. When he tried to lift his head, he felt the prick of a knife point against his jugular vein and he froze.

'Don't move,' Jerzy said in Polish. 'You stupid fucking cop. Don't you know when to give up?'

'It appears not,' Kalisz said in the same language. 'What happens now?'

'Now I kill you.' Jerzy sounded as if the thought amused him.

'What I don't understand is why you decided to run, and why Witold tried to shoot me?' Kalisz wasn't certain whether the threat was genuine, but he knew the best way of delaying a fatal outcome was to keep Jerzy talking. 'We had nothing tangible to link you to the murders. All you had to do was keep your mouths shut.'

'He said you would put a noose around our necks, and even suggested we kill you before we took off. I had the key to the cookhouse door and he told me which room you were in. Witold's gone a little crazy lately and he would have done it, but I said we didn't need any more blood on our hands.'

'Then why kill me now?' Kalisz didn't have to ask who Jerzy's 'he' was. 'You know you won't get away with it, because there are only so many places you can run and by now they'll all have been alerted.'

'Because I can feel that noose tightening round my neck.'

'What if I told you I could save your life?'

'How would you do that, copper?'

'You'd have to stand up in court and testify against him. But first I need to know why you killed Krystina Kowolska. Fontaine, I can understand, but Krystina was just another student.'

Jerzy laughed. 'You know the funniest thing about all this?' Kalisz breathed again as the pressure of the knife eased. 'We didn't kill anybody. All we did was agree to get rid of the body. He said she was a traitor who would have cost a lot of people their lives if she'd lived. But it needed to look like an accident. If it hadn't been for the Commandos down by the shore, she'd have been in the sea and that would have been that, but we had to come up with something different. We didn't even know the Canadian was dead until the next morning. Then, later, after you arrived, he asked Witold to plant a pistol where Frenchie went with his woman.'

'Krystina Kowolska was no traitor.' Kalisz dared to lift his head. Jerzy sat with his back against the gully wall. The knife was gone, but he held a Browning pistol in his right hand and it was pointed at Kalisz's heart. 'She suffered the torments of Hell in a Gestapo cellar to buy her circuit time. They'd changed all their radio codes and had a new set of safe houses by the time they broke her out of Montluc Prison. The information had to come from someone else who had inside knowledge of the organisation *after* she flew back to England.' Jerzy grunted as if he'd been punched. 'If you didn't kill anyone,' Kalisz continued, 'that's all the more reason to testify against him. He set you up to take the fall for the murders.'

Jerzy shook his head regretfully. 'Not going to happen, copper. Remember that camp I told you about. Jasenovac, upriver from Gradiška? Well, Witold and me made one mistake too many, and that's where we ended up. At Jasenovac they don't like to waste bullets, so they use a knife – a *srbosjek*. It means "Serb cutter", and they're very creative with it. The guards like to make it last. Eyes, nose, lips… everything gone before they finally get the business done. That's what was going to happen to us. I still wake up sweating when I dream about Jasenovac. But the major – captain, he was then – somehow got us out of there. You understand? We *owed* him. A debt so great it could never be repaid. So Jerzy won't be testifying.' He got to his feet, the pistol still covering Kalisz. 'Don't even think of following me, or I'll put a bullet in your gut.' Then he was gone, out into the snow. The last words Kalisz heard were, 'You can thank me for doing you a favour.'

He was still puzzling over them when the sound of a single shot cut through the whistle of the wind.

CHAPTER 51

By the time Kalisz located Jerzy's body, three British army lorries had fought their way up the snowbound track to the little plateau beside the quarry. Their occupants stood beside them, being briefed for a search they'd now be relieved to discover would be unnecessary. Major Dempsey was the man giving the briefing, and Kalisz noticed with surprise that Gunn was one of the officers standing beside him, along with Major Sykes. A little to one side, Captain Malpas stood talking to Lucy in the shelter of one of the trucks. As soon as she noticed Kalisz, Lucy broke off the conversation and ran towards him.

'Jan,' she cried. 'You're all right. When I saw the car I thought...'

'You'll be glad of this by the look of you, sir.' Sergeant Perkins appeared with a thick woollen army blanket.

Kalisz thanked him and shrugged the blanket over his shoulders. 'You can tell the major there's no need for a search party. And let the medical officer know he has a body to look at, about two hundred metres beyond the quarry.'

'Ah, so it's like that?' Perkins looked thoughtful. 'Two hundred yards beyond the quarry, you say?'

'Of course, Sergeant. Yes, two hundred yards.'

'Then we'd best get to him before this snow covers him up. Ma'am.' Perkins saluted and marched off towards the trucks.

'So Jerzy's dead?' Lucy said. 'You were crazy to go after him alone, Jan. He might have killed you. Why risk it when he was always going to be caught anyway?'

'I hoped to persuade him to testify against the man who gave them their orders, but it turned out that was never possible. Our Jerzy was full of surprises, not least his old-fashioned concept of honour.'

Lucy opened her mouth to ask a question, but she was cut off by the approach of a smiling Dempsey. 'If you could excuse us, Flight Officer, I'd very much like a word with Major Zamoyski. A private word.'

Lucy looked to Jan and he nodded. 'Very well,' she said. 'I'll tell Captain Malpas what's happening.' She frowned. 'If I can find him.'

'I believe congratulations are in order, Major,' Dempsey said heartily. 'The sergeant tells me you got your man.'

'In that case, I must have expressed myself poorly.' Kalisz didn't return the major's smile. 'The reality is that one of the suspects I wished to question shot himself.'

'And thereby incriminated himself,' Dempsey persisted. 'If that other fellow's violent reaction to your arrival at Borrodale House hadn't done so already.'

'Perhaps,' Kalisz agreed. 'But their actions also open themselves up to other interpretations. For instance, would it surprise you if I said that I suspected a guiding hand lay behind the murders?'

Dempsey went very still. 'One would have thought that a fantastic theory.'

'Not at all. At first I struggled with the lack of a motive for Krystina's killing. Then I kept hearing the word "traitor" being mentioned in connection with her, despite Warrant Officer Kowolska's record making her the most unlikely turncoat one could imagine. That, as it was meant to do, put me on the trail of the comrades she'd served with, including the very brave Captain Malpas, and even those such as Yvette, who were about to serve with her. But, like most murders, the real motive was much more simple. Revenge.'

Kalisz thought he heard a rustle in the small stand of trees sheltering them from the wind, but Dempsey appeared not to notice.

'Please enlighten me further.'

'The key to this entire affair is, of course, Sergeant Frederick Burns, who was the radio operator for the BISHOP circuit. He trained here at Arisaig, and I believe you formed an attachment to him. Is that correct?'

'Oh, much more than an attachment, *old boy*.' Dempsey seemed happy to talk now. 'Freddie made me complete in a way you would never understand. He lit up every room he entered, and enlivened the existences of all who were fortunate enough to know him. He was as brave as a lion, too, which is ironic, because at heart he was a frightened, rather insecure little boy, whose entire life had been dedicated to proving he was as good, if not better, than the "normal" people. But you were wrong, you know. She was a traitor – that Kowolska woman. She betrayed Freddie and the BISHOP circuit, and she would have betrayed many more if she hadn't been broken out of prison. It may sound callous, but the Poles did SOE a favour by killing her, and, after all, this is war.'

'No, Major Dempsey. It is you who are wrong.' Kalisz struggled to keep his temper. 'The timings and the treatment of your poor friend Freddie make it most unlikely that he was betrayed by Krystina Kowolska – "that woman", as you so disrespectfully describe her. But it is the manner of her escape from Montluc Prison that always perplexed me. It was much too simple. In my experience, the Nazis would never leave their prisoners so poorly guarded. And so it turned out. Flight Officer Devereux received a signal yesterday which confirmed that Émile, the "hero" who freed Krystina, was, in fact, a Gestapo double agent. We know this, because he eventually betrayed the wrong man, a senior Resistance leader called Max, a very courageous Frenchman whose real name was Jean Moulin. Max's comrades quickly concluded the deed could only have been carried out by one man. Émile escaped their vengeance, but he is now serving with a French SS unit on the Eastern Front.' He waited for some reaction, but Dempsey's expression didn't alter from the habitual disparaging smile that now made Kalisz's fist itch to wipe it from his face. 'And the Poles didn't kill Krystina Kowolska – you did. Major Sykes told me that something about the technique used to break Krystina's neck troubled him. The hold itself was the standard one taught here, but the manner didn't quite fit –' he dropped his gaze to focus on Dempsey's empty cuff – 'almost as if there was something physically different about the perpetrator. You then convinced the Poles to help you make Krystina's death look like suicide, only for the infatuated Jean-Marc Fontaine to stumble on the scene. Naturally, he could not be allowed to live. So you shot him using one of the silenced pistols destined for your German students at Swordland Lodge. I don't hear any denials, Major?'

'Why should I waste my breath denying such an obviously deluded fantasy, Zamoyski?' Dempsey didn't hide his contempt. 'They do say you Poles are prone to being overwrought, but I have to say, this takes the biscuit.'

Kalisz studied him, seeking the single shred of contrition that would mark any normal human being, but found none. 'I might actually have had some sympathy for you if you truly believed that in the terrible act of killing Krystina, you were ridding Arisaig of a traitor who had caused the loss of your lover. But Pierre Renan's death would have put an end to that.'

'Oh, there's more?' Dempsey snorted.

'You lost your hand in Yugoslavia, Major Dempsey. Is that where you also lost your mind? Because the manner of Pierre Renan's death was the work of a psychopath. At first I couldn't even understand why he had to die. All he wanted was to escape, to rejoin the fight for his country. I inspected the armoury records last night, before I spoke to you, and discovered that Pierre Renan was covering for the armourer at Glasnacardoch on the day the batch of Luger Po8s destined for Swordland were delivered. Pierre signed for ten pistols, but by the time they reached their destination, Major Maxwell and the Germans were annoyed to find that the package only contained eight. It is my belief that Pierre knew you were the only man who could have interfered with the consignment after it left Glasnacardoch. So Pierre had to die, but it is entirely beyond my imagination to fathom why you would make the manner of his passing replicate that of the tragic Frederick Burns.'

Dempsey actually laughed. 'You do understand that, even in the unlikely event of my being involved in the manner you so vividly describe, the evidence against me is entirely circumstantial. You think, you believe, you make assumptions and interpretations, but you can prove precisely nothing. Any lawyer would laugh you out of court, Major Zamoyski, and your face tells me you know it. If you present this case to Colonel Baldwin, he will think you mad. No, you have your murderers, Major. You have your Poles. I'm sure they will entirely satisfy Mr Churchill.' He leaned forward so he was speaking directly into Kalisz's ear. 'My sacrificial lambs, as it were,' he whispered. 'Accept your defeat with dignity, and be very careful while you're still in Arisaig.'

Kalisz watched him walk away through the snow, with a seething ball of anger and despair burning in his heart. He'd failed. Failed Krystina, failed Fontaine and failed Pierre Renan, brave soldiers who'd been prepared to die for their country, but who instead had become the victims of a sordid desire for retribution. Worse, he'd failed his country.

Dempsey was right. Without Jerzy's testimony, he didn't have a case worth the name. Just a few strands of what the major had called assumptions and interpretation. Oh, he could tell Churchill he was certain in his own mind that Dempsey was behind the killings, but he rather thought the British prime minister would prefer the much more tangible – and opportunely dead – villains, Jerzy and Witold, to take the rap. In any case, blackening Dempsey's name wasn't justice. Of course, Kalisz wouldn't give up. Of course, he'd strive to find that vital piece of the jigsaw in his last few hours at Arisaig, but the chances of success were minimal – and he knew it.

'You don't look like a man who's just wrapped up an important murder case, Jan.' He looked up as Lucy approached. 'Especially one that's going to earn you the gratitude of both our governments.'

'You would be surprised how little satisfaction there is in solving a murder, Flight Officer, because there is almost always a tawdry, wretched, unsavoury motive like revenge, greed or jealousy at the heart of it.'

'So what was the motive in this case?'

'We can discuss that later.' He managed a tight smile. 'In the meantime, may I ask you to request a ride back to Arisaig with Captain Malpas or Major Sykes? I am a little shaken by events, and I need some time by myself to think.'

He saw the look of dismay on her face in response to the abrupt dismissal. Clearly there were things she wanted to say to him.

'Very well… sir.' She saluted and did an about-turn. He was surprised that her patent distress caused him more pain than Jerzy's entire weight landing on his back. He watched Perkins and another soldier carry Jerzy's body on a stretcher to one of the three-tonners. The other man was Sergeant Connors, and as he went by he gave Kalisz a wink.

When the trucks had left, Kalisz stood for a while in the churned-up snow, eyes streaming in the chill wind. Why had he stayed when it would have been so much easier, and less hurtful, just to take Lucy back to the house? The answer lay in his vow to Krystina Kowolska: *I will find your killer if it is humanly possible, so help me God.* Well, he had found her killer, but there was also the promise – unspoken, it was true – that he would bring them to justice. Justice. He needed to think about justice, and to do that he needed to be alone. He'd had very fixed ideas about justice as a young policeman. Then, justice was indelibly linked to the rule of law and the police code of conduct. That meant even the guilty had rights, and force must be used only when all other options had been exhausted. Some of his older colleagues had laughed at his naivety, but, by and large, he'd stuck to his principles. Occupation, subjugation and the Nazis had forced him to reconsider. It quickly became clear that the Nazis would never face conventional justice for the crimes they committed on a daily basis.

On a hot day in June 1940, in Room 320 of the Europejski Hotel in Warsaw, Jan Kalisz had dispensed summary justice to an SS officer and serial killer called Hans Wolff, also known as The Artist.

Wolff had deserved to die.

Major Frank Dempsey deserved to hang for the murders of Krystina Kowolska, Jean-Marc Fontaine and Pierre Renan, but he never would.

Kalisz took a deep breath of icy air and slipped the silenced Luger from his pocket. He checked the magazine. Seven bullets.

He only needed one.

Someone had turned the car for him and the keys were in the ignition. It only took him a few minutes to get back to the road. He took his time on the way back to Arisaig House. No one planning to commit murder should be in a hurry.

It was easy to kill a man if you had a pistol and he wasn't expecting it. The trick was to do it and get away with it. Kalisz didn't plan to spend the rest of the war in a British prison, or worse.

It was all quite clear in his mind. He would lure Dempsey to some remote spot. Shoot him in the head without warning from close range. Place the pistol in his remaining hand and walk away. If Dempsey's body was found, verdict: suicide. With a little luck, Kalisz would be back in Poland by then, and no one was going to come after him there.

Kalisz parked the Austin in the driveway beside one of the three-tonners and walked down to the house. Dempsey's Humber was in the courtyard, but there was no sign of the major. As he reached the front door, a sergeant he'd never seen before stepped in front of him.

'What's going on, Sergeant?' he demanded.

'I'm sorry, sir. Colonel Baldwin's orders. You're not allowed entry until he's spoken to you.'

'Ah, Major Zamoyski.' Baldwin appeared in the doorway. 'I'm glad I caught you. Dempsey tells me that you have found your murderers, which means that your investigations at STS 21 are concluded. In the circumstances, and given the delays your presence has already caused to our programme, I have decided it is in the best interests of the war effort that you leave for Fort William immediately.' He handed Kalisz a brown paper envelope. 'Your travel documents. You have my thanks for all your efforts.'

Kalisz spluttered. 'I must protest, sir. My belongings...?'

'Have been packed and are waiting in the truck. Do I need to call for a party to escort you to your transport?'

Kalisz took a deep breath. 'That will not be necessary, sir. I hope I will be given time to say my farewells to Flight Officer Devereux and Major Sykes.'

'Of course.'

Kalisz looked round as Dempsey left the house and went to his car, where he had a conversation with Sykes before getting into the big Humber. The Pole watched, helpless, as the man he knew was a triple murderer turned the car and drove away to continue with the rest of his life. Justice? What had he been thinking? Of course Dempsey would make certain Kalisz was off the base before he could cause any further trouble. He'd been outmanoeuvred again.

'Jan?' He saw Lucy Devereux marching across the courtyard towards him.

'Lucy, I must apologise...'

But he saw she was too angry to be interested in his apologies.

'This just arrived from London.' She handed him a thin sheet of official paper – what the British called a 'flimsy'. Kalisz read the message, which confirmed that Major Francis Dempsey, MC had served in Yugoslavia with the Bosnian Poles now calling themselves Jerzy and Witold, and had sponsored their return to Britain. 'Why didn't you arrest him?'

'Arrest him for what?' Kalisz said wearily. 'There isn't a man in this theatre of war who wouldn't look at the evidence we have and conclude that the renegade Poles, Jerzy and Witold, killed Krystina and Jean-Marc. We cannot place Dempsey at the scene of the crime. We cannot link him to the weapon that was used. Our presumed motive is nothing but a theory. The two Poles are the only thing that connects him to the murders in any way, and they're both dead.' He lowered his voice as Sykes came to join them. 'It is finished, Flight Officer. Over.'

'Congratulations, Major Zamoyski,' Sykes said cheerfully. 'Case closed – isn't that what they say?'

'May one ask what you talked about to Major Dempsey?'

'And yet –' the good humour in the unarmed combat instructor's voice remained undiminished by Kalisz's cold inquiry – 'you continue to ask questions. As it happens, I was asking the good major how he wanted to handle the deaths of our two Polish friends. We can't have it known, outside official circles, at least, that two murderers penetrated the very heart of Allied secret operations. He settled on one suicide and one unfortunate accident, though how –' he smiled at Lucy – 'Witold Grabski managed to accidentally shoot himself twice in the heart will be quite the puzzle for Major Llewellyn.' For a moment, something in the northern sky seemed to attract Sykes's attention, but Kalisz could see nothing but whirling snow. 'You must be pleased to have been able to provide some justice for your compatriot, Major?'

'I don't thi—'

Kalisz's reply was cut short by a sudden flash of light in the dawn gloom, followed by the soft *crump* of a distant explosion, then a series of even brighter flashes interspersed with loud bangs. Finally, a pulsating ball of smoke and flame rose from the road above the house, to be lost in the snow-heavy clouds.

'Christ,' the sergeant who'd stopped Kalisz exclaimed in horror. Colonel Baldwin was still standing beside him, and while all around reacted with shock, the colonel barely appeared to register the explosion before turning away and disappearing into the house.

'I dare say that will have been the petrol tank,' Sykes said, in the tone of a man discussing last week's grocery list. 'I told him time and time again he was asking for trouble, carrying those damn fireworks. An accident waiting to happen. Well, I suppose I'd better go and see what's left. Would you like to accompany me, Major?'

Kalisz shook his head, as much in an attempt to clear his whirling mind as to decline Sykes's offer. 'I think perhaps that in this instance, the incident might be best left to your Special Investigation Branch.'

'A prudent decision, I believe. In that case, if you'll excuse me. Flight Officer.' Sykes nodded amiably to Lucy and walked away.

It took what seemed like an age for Lucy to find her voice. 'Did I just dream that?'

'No.' Kalisz watched as Sykes organised a dozen men and led them up the driveway towards the billowing smoke. 'I do believe that justice has been done and our murderer, Major Dempsey, has just gone to meet his maker. Most fortuitous, don't you think?'

'But Sykes...?'

'Major Sykes never bothered to conceal his dislike of Dempsey, but if he was the major's nemesis, I doubt we could ever prove it. In any case, it doesn't have to be Sykes. I'm fairly certain someone was listening on the hill while Dempsey was telling me what an idiot I'd been. Why not our friend, Captain Malpas, Krystina's lover and an explosives expert? Or Gunn, the bomb disposal specialist whose career might have been destroyed by all this? Given the colonel's distinct lack of reaction, one might even suspect this is simply an example of the Special Operations Executive cleaning up its own mess. And, of course...' Kalisz allowed himself a smile. 'There is another possibility. May I ask if you still have the plastique we found in the car?'

Lucy's eyes narrowed. 'I asked one of the sergeants to keep it in the brick explosives store below the house.'

'That was my very poor Polish idea of a joke, Lucy,' Kalisz assured her. 'But it may not be a coincidence that the store is within a hundred paces of the ice house where Major Gunn spent last night. No, as Colonel Baldwin said on my first day here, accidents happen at STS 21 and people die. I firmly believe Major Dempsey's death will be dismissed as just another tragic Arisaig accident.'

'Perhaps that's for the best?'

'Perhaps it is.'

A shudder ran through Lucy. 'We should get back into the house.'

'What will you tell Mr Churchill?'

She considered for a moment. 'That you got your man. As Major Sykes said, the case is closed.'

'And no secrets?'

'No secrets.'

'So I can go home?'

She nodded.

'Yes, Jan. You can go home.'

EPILOGUE

'The old man wanted you to have this.'

The 'old man' was Winston Churchill, and Kalisz's benefactor was his aide, the man the Pole knew only as 'Jock'. Kalisz warily accepted a silver hip flask. The SOE dispatchers had been very careful to ensure he carried nothing that would link him to England, and he studied it for any identifying marks.

'Don't worry,' Jock assured him cheerfully. 'The flask is Polish-made, but the contents are from an area with which you've become rather familiar over the past few weeks. To keep out the cold, he says.'

'Please thank him for me.' Kalisz struggled to stow the flask in the voluminous zip-fronted parachutist's overalls he wore over his civilian clothing. The specially designed outfit was equipped with numerous pockets, but most of them were already filled: a pistol, a knife, a small entrenching spade. A money belt they'd strapped around his waist held an inordinate amount of gold coins and weighed him down, making every movement awkward. They were walking across the boggy grass from a farmhouse that had been incorporated into the airfield, towards a large barn. Away to his right, almost lost in the fading light, the enormous shape of a converted Halifax bomber stood silently waiting. During his briefing he'd been told the flight to Poland could take seven or eight hours, so it made sense that the pilot wouldn't start his engines until the last possible moment to save precious fuel.

'You should probably know you have Lucy Devereux to thank for your ticket home.' Jock spoke with the exaggerated drawl Kalisz had come to associate with the English patrician class. 'The prime minister – and I, I have to admit – were rather disposed to making use of your undoubted talents here in Britain, at least until after the Second Front is launched. Secrets, you see.' His lips twitched into a tight smile. 'A little bird told us you might have been privy to a few too many during your investigations at STS 21.'

'It was very kind of her to speak for me,' Kalisz said. 'But the prime minister had nothing to fear. A straightforward case of jealousy and revenge, and I was much too busy to take an interest in what was going on around me.' The lie came surprisingly easily. He doubted Jock was convinced, but they wouldn't turn him back now. 'In any case, I have the little pill they gave me at the house and I do not intend to be captured.'

They entered the barn, where a young female dispatcher with 'Poland' embroidered on the shoulder patch of her WAAF tunic waited for them at a long table that held a single parachute. Kalisz picked up the bundle of canvas and webbing and weighed it dubiously in his hands.

'Your first time, sir?' the dispatcher said in Polish. 'Let me help you.' She ducked under the table and helped Kalisz into the shoulder straps, with the pack firmly against his back.

'I was told you'd done a course?' Jock frowned.

'They ran me through the basics.' Kalisz shrugged. 'So I know the "drill", as you say. A kindly sergeant pushed me off a tower with my eyes closed, but there was no time for a proper practice jump.'

'Excuse me, sir.' The girl bent low to draw the bottom straps between Kalisz's legs and pulled them tight. 'The straps are all attached to this quick-release mechanism here.' She tapped a circular box on his chest. 'But don't be in too much of a hurry to use it, yes? Best to wait till you're on the ground.' She grinned, and Kalisz had to resist the urge to hug her.

Jock handed him his cloth jump helmet and led him to the door. 'The other chaps will be pleased to see you,' he said. 'They must have been waiting for an hour or more.'

'Other chaps?' It was the first Kalisz had heard of it. 'I'm not going in alone?'

'Lord, no.' The other man laughed at his naivety. 'These flights can only take place during the ideal combination of bright moonlight and suitable flying weather. This is the first time this month the weather Gods have been kind. You're fortunate we managed to tag you on to another mission. A four-man team and nine containers of weapons and ammunition. I wouldn't bother trying to get to know them, they tend to be a dour lot.'

'I doubt they've had much to smile about for a long time.' Kalisz felt bound to defend his countrymen. He held out his hand and Jock shook it.

They reached the entrance hatch towards the rear of the giant aircraft. 'I suppose all there is to say is good luck,' Jock said. Kalisz nodded and turned towards the hatch. 'Oh, there is one more thing. Should you ever be in contact with the higher echelons of the *Armia Krajowa*, the prime minister would be grateful if you would tell them that he urges caution.'

Kalisz stopped in the entrance. 'Caution? Caution about what?'

'They'll know what he means.'

'Does he really believe they would listen to me?'

'Perhaps, perhaps not,' Jock said. 'But he never misses an opportunity to make his point.'

Churchill's aide turned and disappeared into the darkness, and Kalisz hauled himself into the cramped, ill-lit interior of the Halifax fuselage. A hand took his arm to help him to his feet. 'This way, sir.' An airman, bulky in sheepskin-lined flying gear. Another Pole. Likely the whole crew were Polish. The airman guided him to a metal bucket seat situated towards the front of the plane. 'If you need to go, there's a chemical toilet behind the curtain opposite the entrance hatch.'

Kalisz thanked him and tried to make himself comfortable in the seat with the lump of the parachute at his back. It was only then he was able to take notice of his companions: four men, seated on the opposite side of the narrow metal tube, all dressed in the same camouflaged parachute overall he wore. Dark, intense eyes studied him with no sign of welcome, or even acknowledgement, which wasn't too surprising if he'd kept them waiting for an hour. Dangerous men, and very effective at what they did, if he was any judge. The Polish operatives of the Special Operations Executive were known as the *cichociemni*, the 'dark and silent ones'. Their mission would be to organise and train some fledgling Resistance movement in the homeland. At last, the Halifax's four Merlin engines coughed into action and settled down to a dull roar, and the men relaxed back into their seats. But not before Kalisz realised he recognised one of them.

It took him a moment before he could place the blunt nose and narrow, piercing eyes. Yes... It had been at a staff briefing for intelligence officers in Warsaw almost five years earlier, just before the outbreak of the war. The man would have been a lieutenant colonel then, so God only knew what elevated rank he held now. Kalisz wondered what had brought him here, and he guessed the other man was thinking the same. He'd certainly been recognised in turn. A genius, they'd said back then, but stubborn. If you disagreed with him, you'd better be right.

The converted bomber lurched into motion and Kalisz held on to his seat as the plane bounced across the grass towards the concrete runway. After a moment or two the pilot turned the aircraft to the left. A short pause as he gunned the engines. They began to move again, slowly at first, but picking up speed with every second. Kalisz closed his eyes and gripped the metal seat even more tightly. The entire plane vibrated as they thundered along a runway that seemed to go on forever. He could almost feel the pilot straining at the controls, willing the enormous fuel-heavy metal beast into the air. Then the rubber tyres lost their grip on the earth, the juddering disappeared, and they were rising. Kalisz opened his eyes to find the man opposite staring at him with what might have been a hint of a smile on the thin lips. He closed them again and settled back to endure the flight.

By the third hour, Kalisz wanted to kill whoever had designed the bucket seat. Whichever parts of him didn't hurt had long since gone numb, and repositioning himself only changed the order of things. His multiple layers of clothing did nothing to keep out an all-pervasive cold that seemed to eat into his very bones. At times he had to clench his teeth to avoid crying out his frustration.

He tried to occupy his mind by imagining the route they were flying. Not direct, obviously, which would have taken them over Amsterdam, Hanover and Berlin, where the night fighters swarmed and anti-aircraft guns by the thousand waited to fill the skies with red-hot metal. Jock had said their course would take them out over the North Sea to Denmark, which must be pretty much where they were now, then on into the Baltic, and finally south to enter Polish airspace over some quiet part of the coastline. The opposite man's eyes opened again. Kalisz rummaged in his overalls to retrieve the hip flask, and offered it to him, only to be answered by a regretful shake of the head. Too bad. Kalisz shrugged and worked at the screw cap with shaking fingers. He took a long pull of the contents and revelled in the peaty, liquid fire that seemed to permeate his entire body. God bless Winston Churchill. The whisky made him sleepy, and he dozed for a while until he felt a hand on his shoulder.

The officer loomed above him, and behind him Kalisz could see his compatriots hooking up their static lines in the glow of a red light in a panel on the plane's side.

'*Powodzenia.*' The word was lost in the roar of the engines, but his meaning was clear: Good luck.

'*Do ciebie również.*' Kalisz replied: To you also. The soldier nodded and moved away to take second place in the line of men.

The dispatcher bent low to open a hatch in the bomber's belly, and Kalisz winced at the whiplash of freezing wind that filled the fuselage. The first *cichociemni* took his place on the edge of what the RAF crews called the 'Joe Hole'. 'Canisters gone,' the dispatcher roared. In the same instant the light changed from red to green. The first soldier vanished and the second, third and fourth followed him into the void in an unbroken line.

'Ten minutes.' The dispatcher showed Kalisz both hands with fingers extended.

Ten minutes? Kalisz was still going over everything he'd been taught when the man returned, motioning him to get to his feet. 'The pilot has seen the signal,' he shouted into Kalisz's ear. A red glow filled the fuselage. The dispatcher helped him hook his static line to the wire above the Joe Hole, and, as instructed, Kalisz took his seat on the edge. He grimaced as the slipstream tore at his legs, and his mind screamed that this was madness. Would he even have the nerve to jump?

But suddenly the light was green and he was falling out into the darkness. An almost instantaneous tug, and he experienced a violent pain in his crotch as the parachute snapped open to slow his descent. Engines fading into the distance and a moment of silence before the ground came up to smack him on the soles of his feet. He pitched forward on to his face in a non-regulation landing that would have made his instructor wince. Kalisz lay for a moment with his nose in the wet grass, revelling in the sweet scent of it, before he realised the parachute was tugging at his shoulders.

He pushed himself to his feet and punched the release box, hauling at the straps to pull in the billowing silk. A soft glow away to his left must be the signal fire.

'Wolf.' Someone called from the darkness.

Kalisz dropped the chute and drew his pistol, his reeling mind searching for the codename he'd been issued. 'Iron,' he remembered eventually. 'Iron.'

The shadowy figure of a young man appeared.

'Kazimierz sent me.'

Kalisz felt something in his throat.

He was home.

AUTHOR'S NOTE

The genesis of the book that became *Blood Vengeance* occurred long before Jan Kalisz was a twinkle in his creator's eye. Early in my writing career, I disappeared down one of those research rabbit holes on the internet with which every author will be familiar. While scrolling through an archive, I came across a single paragraph from a 1940s local newspaper recording the discovery of the body of an unnamed Polish servicewoman in unexplained circumstances on the foreshore at Arisaig. Being aware of the area's links to the Special Operations Executive (SOE), my first thought was that the victim must have had some sort of relationship with the organisation. Who was she? Could she have been an agent? How had she died? My further investigations came to nothing. I closed the file with the vague thought that there was a book in this somewhere. Later, I made the same search many times, but I was never able to find the story again. Yet the information must have stuck in my mind, because when I decided that this Polish detective I'd created needed some time away from the constant oppression of Occupied Warsaw, the seed was already planted.

In many ways, Arisaig and the surrounding area during this period is the perfect environment for a crime novel. For most of the war, this wild landscape of storm-lashed beaches and jagged mountains was populated largely by trained killers. The elite soldiers of the Commando special service brigades exercised across the mountains around their base at Achnacarry, and the men and women agents of the SOE learned their craft in the hunting lodges scattered around Special Training School 21 at Arisaig House. When Churchill describes the area in the novel as 'probably the most dangerous place in Britain', he is not exaggerating. A list of service deaths at Arisaig and Achnacarry during World War Two contains more than fifty entries and makes sober reading. Death by gunshot or drowning was commonplace. Men fell from mountains in climbing accidents, were blown up by their own mortars or explosives, and succumbed to injuries suffered in car and motorcycle crashes. More than a few died of heart failure from their own exertions. The casualty list includes soldiers from Britain, America, Poland, Czechoslovakia, Norway and New Zealand.

Just occasionally, when you are researching a book you come across a nugget of information that seems to validate all the effort you put into the project. With *Blood Vengeance*, this happened when I stumbled across the log of Arisaig Police Station, from the Fort William Archives. In it, the local constable, PC Logan, records every crime he had to investigate and duty carried out from the beginning to the end of the war. It's a wonderful document that details the minutiae of Highland life during the period – the issue of firearms certificates, tracing straying sheep, investigating car accidents and minor assaults – but also the stresses and strains of life in the West Highlands Protected Area. One entry describes a burglary at a country house that was traced to four 'students' at one of the SOE training schools, and culminates in the caution and charging of 'Colonel Baldin at Arisaig House' for refusing to reveal the culprits' names. A particular puzzle was the number of thefts and break-ins involving teenage boys and girls, until it dawned on me that these were evacuee children from Glasgow who'd been relocated from the city to the 'safety' of Arisaig.

The majority of the characters who populate *Blood Vengeance* are entirely fictional. Krystina Kowolska is a composite of several female SOE agents, all of whom can be characterised by their immense courage, strength of will and spirit of self-sacrifice. Few were flawless, but there's no suggestion that any of them harboured the anti-Semitism attributed to Krystina in this book. It was a privilege to spend time immersed in the stories of these incredibly brave women, many of whom left Arisaig to go to their deaths in Nazi concentration camps. The circuits Krystina joins in the book – ATHLETE and BISHOP – are also fictional, but similar missions took place all over France with varying degrees of spectacular success or tragic failure, and the operational details are as accurate as I could make them.

Krystina's friendship with General Sikorski's daughter Zofia provides the *raison d'être* for bringing Kalisz to Britain, and it is true that the mysterious plane crash off Gibraltar in which Sikorski, Zofia and nine others died caused great strain to the Alliance at a crucial time.

German Jews from X Troop of 10 Commando Brigade did prepare in the west of Scotland for Operation Foxley, an audacious and probably suicidal plan to assassinate Hitler, which was later abandoned. They were brave men who fled their homeland to escape persecution and take the fight to the Nazis, but most received a chilly welcome in their new sanctuary. Many were interned as enemy aliens and sent abroad, and it was only as the war progressed that the powers that be recognised that their knowledge and language skills might be useful. They fought in North Africa and across the European theatre, and many gave their lives in the cause of freedom.

Two of the book's non-fictional characters are Major Gavin Maxwell and Major Eric 'Bill' Sykes. Gavin Maxwell was a Scottish naturalist and author of the acclaimed memoir of West Highland life *Ring of Bright Water*, who served as a weapons instructor at Arisaig between 1941 and 1944. 'Bill' Sykes was a bona fide SOE legend who, along with his colleague William Fairbairn, taught silent killing at Arisaig House. Together, they were the inventors of the deadly Fairbairn–Sykes fighting knife.

These days, what was the Arisaig training area is a place of peace and tranquillity. The stunning, rugged beauty of the mountains, lochs and beaches cannot be exaggerated, and, most fortunately, the roads are much improved. Should you happen to visit, you'll always be assured of a welcome at the Land, Sea and Islands Centre on the village foreshore, which features a permanent exhibition highlighting the area's links to the Special Operations Executive. And be sure to pay a visit to the nearby memorial to the Czech and Slovak agents who trained at Arisaig, and met their fate fighting for the freedom of their homeland.

Special thanks for their help with this book must go to SOE historian David M. Harrison, who kindly sent me his incredibly detailed booklet on SOE training at Arisaig, and Seb Barrow, a railway enthusiast who guided Jan Kalisz on his journey from London to Arisaig with spellbinding accuracy. Among the many books that gave me an insight into the workings of SOE and its operations were *Secret Agent: The true story of the Special Operations Executive* (David Stafford), *Secret War Heroes* (Marcus Binney), *Violette Szabo: The life that I have* (Susan Ottaway), and *Odette* (Jerrard Tickell). The story of the Jewish Commandos of *X Troop* (Leah Garrett) is quite astonishing, and the wonderful *War Diaries 1939–1945* of Field Marshal Lord Alanbrooke shed light on the wartime life of

Winston Churchill. Martin Gilbert's magisterial *The Second World War* helped provide a background and the essential chronology of the times. As always, I'm indebted to my editor Craig, copy-editor Steve, and all at Canelo who have helped make this book what it is, and hugely grateful for the support of my agent and my wonderful family.